A MIRROR ABOVE THE ABYSS

OLEG LURYE

Some characters in this novel are real, and appear here under their true names, while the names and distinguishing features of some others were changed. Still other characters are fictitious, and any resemblance is purely coincidental.

Most events described in this novel really happened. Certain details are a result of many years of the author's research, but some characters, as well as connections between them, were either invented by the author or represent his own version of events.

Oleg Lurye,
2021

He found in the mirror a face, which
itself in a sense
is a mirror.

(Joseph Brodsky)

CONTENTS

Chapter 1
FIRST DANGER. PARIS, 2018.. 1

Chapter 2
THE BEGINNING—WASHINGTON, D.C. TWO WEEKS EARLIER 5

Chapter 3
THE MARSHALL ARCHIVE. PHOTOS AND COINCIDENCES................... 18

Chapter 4
FAREWELL, PRESIDENT KENNEDY. DALLAS. NOVEMBER 22, 1963 ...38

Chapter 5
THE CONTROLLER APPEARS. PARIS AGAIN...........................60

Chapter 6
JIA 70

Chapter 7
HIS HOLINESS SURVIVED. VATICAN, MAY 13, 1981 92

Chapter 8
FIRST NAMES. PARIS ONCE AGAIN...................................... 115

Chapter 9
MR. LEVINE AND NEW NAMES. FOR THE CONTROLLER. LONDON ... 134

Chapter 10
THE LOST BILLIONS AND A BANKER'S DEATH. MONACO, 1999 ... 167

Chapter 11
THE TRIAD IN SEARCH OF PAUL MOREL. LONDON.......................... 189

Chapter 12
FAREWELL, JIA 210

Chapter 13
HIERONYMUS BOSCH AS A LURE. DON DOMENICO. ROME 223

Chapter 14
FAILED SALE OF A NON-EXISTENT BOSCH 246

Chapter 15
WHEN SKYSCRAPERS FALL. NEW YORK. SEPTEMBER 11, 2001 265

Chapter 16
SERGIO. FIRST ENCOUNTER. SOMEWHERE IN THE INDIAN OCEAN. 292

Chapter 17
SERGIO. A HOUSE ON THE ISLAND 310

Chapter 18
SERGIO. DAY TWO 323

Chapter 19
SERGIO. REVELATIONS IN THE EVENING 342

Chapter 20
THE BOOK ITALY. ISCHIA 353

Chapter 21
THE DEVIL'S ADVOCATE. ITALY. ISCHIA 369

Chapter 22
THREE MONTHS LATER. NEW YORK 378

Chapter 23
SERGIO. LAST ENCOUNTER. NEW YORK 388

Chapter 24
TEN DAYS LATER. YACHT PAOLA. INDIAN OCEAN 402

1

First Danger
Paris, 2018

The midday din of Paris spilled through the open window and into the hotel room. Max Malin, lying on a huge bed, heard the incessant babble of idle tourists as though it were inside the room. The chatter was occasionally blotted out by the even louder howl of police sirens, which came at strictly measured one-minute intervals, now quite close, now farther off. The sticky June heat, too, made its way uninvited into the room, on a stultifying breeze that barely ruffled the light curtain. Malin was aware that he should close the window and turn on the air conditioning, but the idea of artificial silence accompanied by equally artificial coolness struck him as even more insufferable than this heat. Perhaps some television? No, to hell with it – he already knew everything they would say. Whisky? Too early. A walk, then, and a coffee? Better, better.

He got up and headed for the door, glancing in the large mirror on his way. Looking back at him was the kind of dark-haired thirty-five-year-old man beloved of young female James Bond fans – trim, above average height, dressed in blue jeans and a blue T-shirt under which could be discerned a honed, sinewy figure. Deep-set dark eyes, light stubble, and a sprinkling of grey that

1

had started to fleck his generous head of hair dating back to his difficult days in the army. All in all, Malin, who was fastidious about his appearance, was satisfied with his reflection. He ran his hand through his hair and left the hotel room.

At the entrance to his hotel—the Hotel Lotti on Rue de Castiglione—Malin looked around, sidestepped a milling group of Japanese tourists festooned with cameras, and headed for the nearest café on the other side of Rue Saint-Honoré. He was halfway across the pedestrian crossing when he heard the sound of a car engine, vibrating unnaturally, loud enough to smother the din of the traffic and the tourists . A silver Peugeot jumped the red light and, with a slight change to its trajectory, came hurtling straight at Malin.

The whole thing took no more than a few seconds, seconds which hung in space. The car was less than a meter away when Malin's training kicked in: his body, acting without conscious intervention, performed an almost impossible jump backwards, escaping the imminent impact and knocking down the small Japanese man standing behind him.

Without slowing, the car took the corner onto Place Vendôme and disappeared.

Malin straightened up and helped the terrified man, who was more shaken than hurt. The rest of his group came running over, agitated, and speaking rapidly in Japanese while they gathered up the man's camera and tablet, which had gone flying. Then one of them—the one Malin had knocked over—switched to English.

'Are you okay? It must have been a drunk, or a drug addict. We need the police. Do you remember the number?'

'I'm absolutely fine.' Malin let out a long breath. 'I'm sorry I sent you flying. No choice, I'm afraid… I didn't get his number, so there's no point calling the police.'

A couple of minutes later, after a large dose of sympathy from the Japanese tourists, Malin took his leave of them and returned to the hotel. He was somewhat shaken, but managed to squeeze out a smile and, falling easily into his journalistic habit, offered an internal commentary on what had happened. *So, someone tried to run you down? What's the big deal? Why does it set your heart thumping like that? You've obviously forgotten how to live on the edge these last few years.*

The Peugeot had scared him even more than the bullets he'd encountered in the days when he'd worn a green beret. His new line of work had made him go soft...though evidently his reflexes had not deserted him. That, at least, was good news.

In a small brasserie across from the Lotti, Malin settled himself at a corner table under the bright red awning. *Coffee, please.* And after that damn Peugeot, a double cognac to go with it. His third sip was just burning its way down his throat when his tablet beeped, signaling the arrival of a message.

Someone had remembered his existence.

It was Richard, head of the *Washington Post* investigation department and Malin's immediate boss.

The message came from an anonymous IP address and was signed 'X'. Malin, following the link indicated in the letter, got into the cloud storage, entered a password known only to him and Richard, and opened the letter. This was their private code, which they used only in extreme situations.

> *Problems. Charles has had an accident. I'm leaving. They're looking for you. Disappear. The Big Boss has decided you no longer work for us because you 'tried to publish false information'.*
>
> *They've already talked with the Big Boss. Find me the usual way. Yours ever. X.*

3

It had begun. Richard had warned him.
No. It had all started much earlier. In the spring.

2

The Beginning—Washington, D.C.
Two weeks earlier

Malin was thinking back over his career, in light of his huge break, and not his only one at that. Not for the first time, he thought about arriving in Washington from St. Petersburg with his Russian parents, at the age of six. He'd gone on to graduate from Harvard, done a spell in the marines, and then by the age of thirty-five become one of the *Post*'s leading journalists.

His colleagues saw most of his sensational investigative journalism as the product of happy coincidence. Malin, they said, was simply always in the right place at the right time. Few understood that every 'bombshell' was the result of painstaking and sometimes fruitless work, as if he were a prospector, washing and re-washing tons of river sand, who only at the bottom of the hundredth or even thousandth pan saw the glint of a few grains of long-awaited metal. And after all that, the work of developing the gold vein was still yet to begin. His was careful work, and slow, every small detail double-checked, and connections made between things that at first sight looked as if they did not belong together.

The only person who knew everything—or almost everything—about Malin's work was his boss, Richard Berwick, a veteran newspaperman who had worked at the Post since Watergate.[1] Despite their age difference, the two had become friends, and Malin, the only bachelor on the whole team, often found himself invited to Sunday lunch with the Berwick family at their modest town house in Glover Park.

Now, it was early morning on a warm April day. The sun blazed in through the windows, closed tight to keep in the cool drone of the air conditioning. Malin was thinking not about work but about a cup of coffee and the day's first cigarette when the phone in the editorial office gave out a shrill bleep. A man with an eastern accent introduced himself as Charles and said he had in his possession unique documents that he was ready to show in person.

'I will talk only to Max Malin. Is that you? Is it?'

'Yes, it's really me,' Malin replied with a smile, 'And I'm listening to you carefully.'

'I have a copy of an archive for which everybody is looking,' the man said slowly. 'I cannot say more over the phone because they listen to everybody, especially to you journalists. Do not begrudge half an hour to meet with me. I am sure you will like what you see.'

By 2.45 p.m., Malin was sitting in a café near Capitol Hill and pondering the ways of fate. He was a popular journalist, and thus often besieged by all sorts of madmen with stories of aliens, or of secret Russian super-weapons implanted in the brain of every American.

---

1. The Watergate Scandal (1972-1974) was a major political scandal in the USA that led to the resignation of President Richard Nixon. The Washington Post journalists were able to prove illegal activities of a number of persons who made attempts to install bugging devices in the Democratic National Committee headquarters at the Washington, D.C., Watergate Office Building during the 1972 presidential election campaign. This is the only case in the history of the United States when a President had to relinquish his duties prior to the expiration of his term of office.

Such activity tended to peak with the onset of spring fever. Not everything was a dead loss, though. Sometimes they actually brought along documents, videos, and information so unique and valuable as to cause chills to settle at the pit of one's stomach. Malin's intuition told him that this was such a time. At any rate, he very much hoped so. The paper had not published a sensational investigation in two months.

At exactly three o'clock, a small, dark-haired man of about fifty approached the table. He was in a formal suit, which clearly annoyed him, and it seems that he was dressed only to blend in with a huge number of clerks eating their lunch at neighboring tables

'Malin, good afternoon. I recognized you immediately, although you look a little older in the photograph. I am Charles.'

'Hi. Have a seat. Coffee? Water?'

'Thank you. Coffee, perhaps. The coffee here is the best in town.'

The waiter brought their order, and they sat in silence for a few minutes, savoring the truly magnificent coffee unique to this establishment. Then Charles started suddenly, as if he had remembered something, and began to speak quickly:

'Nobody sent me to you, and I represent no one but myself. A complete copy of an archive that has long been of interest to journalists has come into my possession. Take a look at a few pages.'

He proffered some formatted sheets of paper covered in closely written text. A light breeze immediately tried to pull the paper out of his hands, and the two men caught each other's eye and smiled. A fragile beam of contact between them.

Malin read slowly, his eyebrows curving upwards in surprise.

From my study of the tragedy of 11 September 2001, I, Air Force Captain Philip Marshall, conclude that the attack in which the buildings of the World Trade Center in New York were destroyed was not organized by Al-Qaeda or any other organization acting under orders. The crime was organized by a third-party entity run by an English-speaking man, probably on behalf of the US intelligence services or their individual representatives acting as inter-mediaries. The other participants, including Arab terrorists, merely assisted in carrying out the plan (some were mercenaries, while the 'kamikazes' were ideologues). I have proved the existence of this organization and its involvement in the organization of the bombings. My confidence in my conclusions is affirmed by an audio recording of a telephone conversation made two hours before the planes crashed (for some reason, this conversation was not included in any of the reports of any commission of inquiry), along with certain other evidence and my own logical conclusions.

Malin looked up and spoke slowly, carefully enunciating each word.

'If I am not mistaken, you are offering me the missing archive of the late Philip Marshall?'[2]

'Correct. You are not mistaken.'

'I will repeat my question once more, very slowly.

---

2. **Philip Marshall** (1959–2013) was an ex-pilot and author of several books investigating the events of 9/11. In March 2013 he was found shot dead inside his house. The police also found the bodies of his two children and his dog. The circumstances of the carnage contradict the official explanation that Marshall first murdered his children and then committed suicide. He died a few days before the release of his new book dedicated to 9/11, which the writer himself called 'a bombshell'. He announced that the book would contain key information related to the secrets of the World Trade Center destruction. Marshall's archive disappeared.

And perhaps I can offer some more detail. Are you in possession of Marshall's archive? Philip Marshall, who was found murdered along with his two children, and whose death we are being asked to believe was suicide? The same Marshall who carried out his own investigations into the 9/11 attacks and concluded that they were ordered by high-ranking Americans? The same Marshall who has already published several books on the subject, and before he died declared that he was in possession of information of a sensational nature? Do I understand you correctly, Charles?'

'Yes, yes, and once again, yes. The copy I have of the archive is in digital form. Will that suit you?'

'How did you come by it and what do you want for it?' Malin felt a small shiver deep inside. He had not been expecting such a break. This was his next bombshell.

'As to your first question, I can only tell you this,' said Charles, in a low voice. 'Let's just say I happened to stick around when that tragedy befell that man and his children. I had a chance to copy the information from his computer's hard drive. Which did not "disappear", by the way; it was removed by the FBI in the course of their investigation. I cannot say more than this. As to the second part of your question – I want fifty thousand dollars. And I want you to forget, right here and now, that I exist. Agreed?'

'Agreed.' Malin felt a great release of adrenaline, like a hunter who had caught up with an animal he was tracking. The only thing left was to take one good, un-spoiled shot. 'I need some time to resolve the money matter. How can I find you tomorrow?'

'That's a bit tricky, but let's try this. Give me your number and I'll call you around the same time of day. Oh, another thing – can you guarantee that the NSA, the FBI, and the police will not be expecting my call tomorrow? Can you guarantee that I will not experience the same fate as Marshall? If anything started to go wrong tomorrow, I would be able to figure it out immediately and beat it for good. You would never see me again, not me and not Marshall's archive. As you may have realized by now, I'm a pro. The archive will then fall into other hands, and it will no longer be journalists or even Americans.'

'Charles, I care very much about my work. My aim is to make headlines – big ones! But first I have to discuss your offer with my boss and with the editor-in-chief. They're the ones who will decide if they want to buy your material.'

Charles nodded without saying anything.

A minute later they left the café. They were plunged right away into the throng of Washington's government clerks, rushing about on apparently urgent business. Malin soon lost sight of his guest, who disappeared among all the busy people talking at one another a mile a minute or eating as they trotted along. The man was indeed a pro. One who suddenly, urgently, needed money.

As Malin walked towards his newspaper office, he got to mulling things over. A strange feeling started bothering him, one he had felt before. Sure, he knew that this was, once again, a lucky break. But there was a deeper feeling as if some dark matter started pulsing inside his chest, behind his ribs. It bothered him more with every passing minute. He felt real pressure deep inside, some lingering, hidden doubt, such that he could not really relish his new success.

Malin went straight up to the third floor. He wanted to see his boss, Richard, right away. He found him enjoying a donut and a cup of coffee as usual.

'Can you imagine that Malin?' Richard said with a little laugh. 'I just don't have the guts to abstain from this crap. I know I shouldn't eat donuts. I know the number on the scale is almost the same as my height, but I like 'em, you know how it is...'

'You've been trying to kick it for years now, right?' Malin interjected. 'But you never win. Why not give up? If you can't win, you'd be much better off if you just relax and enjoy.'

'No, no, my young friend, giving up is a terrible idea. Didn't they teach you that at Fort Davence? Well, I've gotten so good at not giving up that now I can pass this donut on to you. It's the last one, anyway...'

Almost instantly, the jokey donut aficionado once more became Iron Berwick, a man known to everyone in the field – *everyone*. Every single investigative journalist, going back a couple of generations.

'Fine. Let's get down to business. You have something really great for me?'

'You better sit down, Richard,' Malin said, placing several pages on the table in front of his boss. 'You see, this guy, Charles – he's offering us a copy of the Philip Marshall archive that had supposedly disappeared. He showed me some of Marshall's judgments. Marshall maintained that an American organized 9/11, someone taking orders from certain D.C. big shots. Also, that all those Arabs, the pilots, were just clueless minions who had no idea what they were being used for. There are some authentic leads in the archive. You know, of course, that Marshall had been digging for twelve years looking for proof to support his version of events. He kept looking for the real instigators of that act of terrorism, and for the real perpetrators. He had published some evidence before, but every time he did, the authorities said the claims were coincidental or far-fetched.'

'Are you sure it's sound?'

'Yes, Richard. My gut feeling is that Philip discov-

11

ered something big. So big he wound up dead. And his kids too.'

'Oh yeah, and his dog...' Berwick nodded. 'The official version of his death was that he went crazy, shot his children and then killed himself. Don't snort you cynic you! I know well enough that when the stakes are so high, any idiotic explanation the government offers becomes the only one for the investigators. There is a shitload of inconsistencies in the official version of Marshall's death, plus the fact that his archive somehow mysteriously disappeared. Okay, so what does this Charles guy want?'

'Well, I have no doubt that he's as much a "Charles" as I am Hillary Clinton. I'm one hundred per cent sure that this guy is or was with some secret service. And that he might be directly related to the extermination of the Marshalls. He could have copied the archive during the confusion right after the event, but whoever the killers were, they must have eventually taken it with them. What Charles wants is obvious, I guess. He needs money, so he's ready to give us a copy of the archive for the sum of fifty thousand.'

Richard grew pensive as he tipped back against his chair, which grumbled and squeaked under his more than two hundred pounds. He started speculating out loud:

'We do have a special fund, of course, which is used for buying this type of material, but I can't make a decision because it's a pretty large sum. I'll have to go and talk to the Big Boss. Also, if we use this material, we'll most definitely clash with the State Department, the NSA, and the FBI. This is extremely sensitive information, so who knows what the Big Boss will do when he learns about this offer.'

There was a short pause.

'Oh, wait, wait!' Berwick said. 'Here's what we could

do – we could present it as a journalistic version of events, just our own deductions, you know. Then we can proudly submit all documents to the official Investigative Commission, let them check and recheck the evidence. Of course, they'll study it for a long time and then bury it. But we would still be able to publish it from that angle. Okay, stay here. I'll go and ask for the money.'

Malin paced Berwick's large office for at least an hour while he waited for Berwick to return. His bad habit of striding back and forth when he was excited was an annoyance to all his friends, but it was the only way he could relax a bit and direct his thoughts to what was on his mind.

This time, though, he couldn't concentrate on the matters at hand – these documents, 9/11, his sensational new break. But why? When his gaze fell by chance on the calendar on Berwick's desk, he realized immediately what was the matter. Lord, how could he have forgotten? It was the 26th. His father's birthday. He would have been…how old? God, seventy-two. All at once, Malin was overwhelmed by a flood of memories, a mosaic of past events, with certain images sharper than others, emerging from the snow of time.

Here he was at eight, riding in a cab with his parents through the bitter cold of Leningrad. They were taking their leave of the city. At the time, they had felt it was for good. His mother was crying almost inaudibly, and for a long time his father stared out the window, gritting his teeth without uttering a word. Then, holding his son's hand, he spoke in a bitter, unfamiliar voice:

'Maxy, I love this city so much that it almost hurts. But we're leaving for God knows where across the ocean. Into the unknown. We need to leave this socialist gloom behind. It's so you can grow up in a different world, one that seems freer. And so, I can do my work

13

out there, in the US. But one thing is really bothering me, Max: what if your mom and I are making a grave mistake? What if things change here? Will you eventually blame us for leaving?'

Maksim could only smile in response to his words, as children do when they think that something in the future might bring some fun, even if nothing is clearly defined. He nodded while his father was speaking, and then pressed his cheek to his hand. Max Malin's memory of that moment was of a black-and-white Leningrad rolling by outside the cab windows, the Neva covered in snow, and the sharp, needle-thin steeple of the Peter-and-Paul Cathedral pricking the grey morning sky. That was back in 1986.

Twenty-eight years had passed since then. His father, a renowned mathematician who became a professor at George Washington University, had died of a stroke in 1998. He had never again seen his favorite city, his Leningrad, now St. Petersburg again. Malin's mother had died a year later, after a road accident. Maksim Malinin, who had become Max Malin in the United States, graduated from Harvard, and spent a couple years freelancing for some D.C. newspapers. Eventually, however, he gave it all up, and decided to try something else. Something much more serious, or so he thought at the time. So, he joined the army.

He successfully passed the Army Physical Fitness Test[3] and, as his instructors were impressed with his physical fitness and proficiency in Kyokushin martial arts, he was enlisted in the Special Forces of the US Army. When Malin became a Green Beret, he got a full year's training in the art of war at Fort Bragg and Fort

---

3. The US Army Physical Fitness Test, or APFT, was designed to test the muscular strength, endurance, and cardiovascular respiratory fitness of soldiers in the United States Army.

Davence.[4] Later, he was sent to defend his country's interests with the 10th Special Forces Group, which was based in Stuttgart, Germany. He killed terrorists and took part in what were called peacekeeping and humanitarian operations. All this meant a tough time for him, with many deaths and a lot of blood. His own blood, and others' deaths.

In the winter of 1998, Malin had returned to the cold and silent city of Washington, D.C., a conceited place that proudly wore the senseless grandeur of a capital.

He took over his parents' house, rearranging everything inside it to create a contemporary bachelor pad, with minimalist interior design. Then he got back into journalism, finding an internship with *The Washington Post's* investigative unit. Only a year later, his first investigation had rocked the media: a report on corrupt links between Pentagon officials and military electronics manufacturers. As a result, four high-level officials had lost their positions at the Defense Department. Two of them went to prison. Further sensational investigations followed. Malin found reliable contacts all over the place, from White House officials to real mobsters. Malin's life had become linked to hundreds of people, many eager to befriend him, some positioning themselves as his nemeses. Of course, both types wore the same obsequious smiles in his presence. He got his first Pulitzer in 2007, then was sent to Afghanistan, then to Iraq, and on and on it went.

Blood and more blood. And pain, of course, lots of it... There was no way he would ever forget 2008, when he saw the Afghan boy of barely twelve with a gunshot

---

4. These are military installations of the United States Army. Fort Bragg is the home of the Army's XVIII Airborne Corps and is the headquarters of the United States Army Special Operations Command.

wound in his abdomen, entrails spilling out. The boy had screamed so loudly with pain, and at such a high pitch, that Malin, who happened to be close by, could stand it no longer. He knew the boy was a goner, so he did the only thing he could do for the boy, striking him with a yohon nukite,[5] short and powerful enough to stop his suffering for good.

Too many memories rushed through his brain, flickering past. They stopped abruptly when Berwick hurried back into the room, filling the space right away with his boisterous manner, elated at his success.

'All right, my man! Your Charles guy gets his dough, and we'll have the scoop of the decade. Well, a bit stripped down, but still. In a nutshell, our Big Boss was torn between his yearning for the material you would get us and his fear that he might get spanked by at least the State Department and the FBI, if not others. But I kept pushing, so he took some time for closer reflection. I had to wait twenty minutes in his parlor! Can you imagine that? Me, Iron Berwick, sitting around on a tiny chair like a schoolboy! Then he called me into his office and told me it was okay as far as he was concerned. But there are some conditions. He wants to personally peruse all the materials when you get them. And when you write your report for the newspaper, he will be the only one with final say on the wording. Also, your report should treat the whole thing as a hypothetical version of events, and there have to be tons of question marks – he stressed that point, tons and tons of question marks, nothing definite anywhere, no outright claims! You get the idea?'

---

5. The yohon nukite, or spearhand strike, is used in karate as a means of attacking an opponent's soft tissues. The impact is made with the tips of four fingers pressed together and slightly bent at the joints. The strike is designed to cause permanent debilitating injuries, but, with training, can become lethal.

'I do, Richard. Same old thing: how to get a scoop without the spanking. What about the money?'

'You can have your fifty grand tomorrow morning. Then you'll meet Charles, get the stuff from him, and make three copies of it right away. One copy you'll pass to the Big Boss in person. Got it? Go ahead!'

'Who gets the second copy?'

'Your new success seems to have taken its toll on your mental abilities, my dear friend. The second copy is for me, of course, and you keep the third. That's that. Give me a call when you're done, please.'

3

The Marshall Archive
Photos and Coincidences

Evening fell. It was that sad hour when the sun's last, weary rays finally dissolved in the vague twilight. Max Malin sat on a low, sagging couch in his office, which took up most of the ground floor of his rather small house. A fat snifter sat on the coffee table by the sofa, next to his laptop, but the cognac inside had stayed untouched for over an hour.

He had gotten the money from the newspaper office that morning and met Charles a short time after he called. They did the exchange quickly, unnoticed by anyone, as far as Malin could tell. He'd handed over five stacks of bills for a small memory stick containing, supposedly, "The Marshall Archives". Now he was at home trying to make sense of the hundreds of files saved on it. There were even secret materials related to the National Commission on Terrorist Attacks Upon the United States, a body that had been specially created to investigate the 9/11 terrorist attack.

It was a mystery, of course, how Marshall could have gotten hold of all these materials. The bulk of this invaluable information was made up of documents that hadn't been made public in the Commission's final report. There was no explanation for this. As it turned out, the executive director of the Commission, Philip D. Zelikow,[1] an official during the Bush administration, had given directions to a team code-named A1 "to prepare a thorough report on the most successful Al-Qaeda operation: the 9/11 attacks." After that, all investigations had been meticulously adjusted to align with this directive. Among the documents, Malin also found a letter from twenty-five ex-officials of the US government, dated September 13, 2004,[2] which stated:

The routine omission of information has become a major flaw in the Commission report. For some reason, the Commission disregarded very important data on many topics of which the undersigned have first-hand knowledge, and which were brought to the attention of the Commission. The Commission was also provided with information regarding serious problems and shortcomings of the operations inside government agencies, but these issues were not reflected in the report at all. The Commission report simply does not highlight key issues that exist in the operations of any of our agencies related to intelligence, aviation security, and law enforcement. Omitting such major, topical issues leaves the report flawed and misleading, thus discrediting it in a major way and casting serious doubts on its validity.

The first of the twelve files in the addenda to this let-

---

1. **Philip David Zelikow** (born 1954) was the executive director of the National Commission on Terrorist Attacks Upon the United States from 2002 to 2004. He also served on the President's Foreign Intelligence Advisory Board (*PFIAB*).

2. Former high-level officials of the FBI and CIA sent a letter to the US Congress in which they expressed their doubts regarding the findings of the 9/11 Commission as well as its recommendations. The letter was signed by 25 persons who previously worked at the CIA, FBI, US Customs Service, Department of Homeland Security, Federal Aviation Administration, and the US Army.

ter left Malin completely convinced that his newspaper had not been scammed out of their fifty thousand dollars. It contained the transcript of a recording of a phone conversation between two men, one who went by the name James and another who remained unnamed. The only reason given for having recorded this phone call was the fact that James was speaking with his anonymous counterpart from an undisclosed location in the FBI office, at 26 Federal Plaza in New York.

Malin reread the transcript and listened to the audio again and again. James's voice was bland, even devoid of character, providing no clues as to his age. The other, unnamed man spoke with the pleasant, somewhat muted baritone of someone over fifty. He had domineering, willful overtones in his voice that he made no attempt to conceal. Malin was taken aback to find that this conversation, which had occurred just one hour and fifty-four minutes before the first plane struck the WTC tower, was not mentioned in any of the official commission reports dealing with 9/11. Malin started the recording one more time:

> **James:** *Hello! Is that you, my friend?*
>
> **Unknown:** *Yes… Were you expecting someone else to answer? And why are you calling me now? It's five minutes earlier than scheduled.*
>
> **James:** *There are changes to the plan. Boss just made a new decision. Suddenly. But his decision is not up for discussion.*
>
> **Unknown:** *What new decision? With less than two hours left before the event… The birdies can't be stopped anymore.*
>
> **James:** *Let all three birdies fly on. They are needed and eagerly expected. The decision was made, however, not to destroy the two big nests complete-*

ly. Whatever the birdies can do is fine. It'll be good enough. But as for the third, the smaller one... Let it fall after the birdies arrive.

Unknown: *Are you crazy? That's impossible! The system runs on its own, so the two nests will collapse on their own. Probably within an hour after the arrival. And the third will do the same, a little later. So, nothing can be changed at this point. Nothing! Everything is already set up and there's no way anyone can change anything. Millions were shelled out to set it up. Besides, no one who rigged the system is around anymore. Only they might have been able to do something this late in terms of introducing changes, but, as I said, they are not around anymore...*

James: *What do you mean?*

Unknown: *They aren't around anymore. They were expendable...*

James: *Listen! I don't give a flying fuck about those people. All I know is that the destruction of the first two nests must be avoided. I mean, the two large nests. There should be no complete destruction! The third one may disappear... This is what the Boss decided. All other agreements are still in force. No money should be paid back. Let the birdies strike, but that should be it!*

Unknown: *This is what I can tell you. We can do a lot. But I'm not God, and I can't stop the mechanism that's already started working. All three birdies will arrive in about two hours, and all three nests will fall down. First the first two, then the third a little later. And that's that! Of course, no one would mention anything about money in the end. And no one would pay anything back anyway. What don't you get? All of the job's details were discussed in advance. You paid, and I got the job done. And now you're telling me that the final stage, something we've*

21

been working on for two months, should be called off. And that only at the last minute when, technically speaking, nothing can be done. Nothing!

James: Hey now, let's not put it like that. Let us... listen, the only thing that has to be called off is the complete demolition of the two big nests. For the simple reason that their total demolition would be the only point we won't be able to explain away. Because they're too big and too stable. The Boss may have some other reasons, too. You have, after all, received everything you've asked for, so you may disappear, no problem. All you have to do is...

Unknown: James, why don't you and your moron of a boss go and fuck yourselves? Why can't you grasp the simple fact that the bomb is falling, and can't be stopped midair? It is not, I repeat, NOT possible, since it was already dropped... In short, everything will happen the way it was agreed on earlier. With all due respect, I do not think that you and I will ever hear of each other again. And I don't even exist for you anymore...

James: Hold on, my friend! Hold on... (The call is dropped.)

By the time he realized how late it was getting, the darkness filled Malin's room. Dark objects dissolved completely, and lighter ones became obscure silhouettes. In the reflection of the mirror, the dull gleam of the laptop screen turned into dancing flares of light. He felt as if time had slowed to a halt. It had stopped in September 2001. Eighteen years had not passed between that date and the present. Not eighteen years of pain, tears, lies, nice words and nonsensical results presented as established, indisputable truth.

He remained still, sitting in the dark wanting to prolong this feeling of lost, wasted time. He felt like staying there, eighteen years ago, so he could start everything anew. So, everything would be different. So that all these commissions wouldn't tell their lies anymore. So that everyone would know for sure how the most awful crime of the new millennium had happened. And for what. And who had really done it.

He kept rereading the experts' conclusions, which stated that under no circumstances could those gigantic buildings have collapsed just from airplane impact: they were constructed, after all, around a formidable frame of concrete and steel. There were statements that both skyscrapers were blown up from inside, according to some plan, and that the strikes of the "birdies" were only an official cover-up for the merciless destruction of the thousands of people within. He read claims that explosions were done using Thermate,[3] a patented version of Thermite, a powdered mixture used in incendiary bombs. Thermate has sulfur and potassium permanganate additives to the usual mix of powdered aluminum and metal oxide, making it powerful enough to cut through tank armor or fortified bunkers, for example. Researchers did find sulfur in the remains of the collapsed buildings, even though sulfur was never present in any part of the airplanes or buildings. The FBI immediately classified these findings as secret and arranged for the evidence to be destroyed. Even the remaining parts of the steel frame were removed since they could serve as clear indicators of internal explosions perpetrated using Thermate.

_____

3. Thermate is variation of Thermite, a mixture of powdered aluminum (or, more rarely, magnesium) with various metal oxides (usually iron oxides). When ignited it produces great amounts of intense heat. Its usual burn temperature is around 2300-2700 degrees Centigrade, but much higher temperatures can be achieved if more powerful oxidizers are used (such as nickel oxide, chromium oxide or tungsten oxide).

Malin looked over the photographs that had also made it into the Marshall Archive. In the debris, one could immediately see what was left of the beams, molten by enormous heat that could only have resulted from a Thermate explosion. A normal fire originating from the explosion of an airplane filled with aviation fuel, which is kerosene-based, would never have produced such a high temperature. There were hundreds of photographs, with flying debris, fountains of dust, and running people…

Oh, so many people. Malin's eyes were glued to what the photos had captured: all those people, their frantic movements, their facial expressions. They looked as though the last days of Pompeii had been transported into the 21st Century. He saw photographs not only from the explosion sites, but from the neighboring streets. In them, people were standing still, some were raising their heads, trying to shield themselves with their hands, briefcases, or handbags. Others were running in all directions, running into each other…

Here was a photograph, for example, taken half an hour after the impact of the second plane. In it, two women were running past a shop window on Washington Street. At the same time, a young man with a baby in his arms was walking in the opposite direction. Huge clouds of dust were reflected in the glass. A tall man of sixty or so stood at the left side of the frame, his posture relaxed. He was looking up, his beautiful dark-haired head tossed back. In fact, he was looking with apparent interest at the scene behind the photographer. That is, where the WTC skyscrapers used to be. The man was completely impassive. His face betrayed neither fear nor bewilderment. He seemed only to be studying the scene. Suddenly, Malin froze. He felt as if he were suddenly falling into a deep abyss. He had seen this man somewhere else; he was sure of it. In a completely different setting, under completely different circumstances.

Malin had always had a unique knack for remembering faces. Any faces. Of any age and from any situation. With even a short glimpse of a person he would be able to recognize them, even years later, regardless of any age-related changes. He instinctively retained the person's features, manner, and gaze; these details were stored forever in his memory.

Now, he got that same familiar feeling of recognition. The longer Malin looked at the photograph of this middle-aged man who was standing on Washington Street on September 11, 2001, the more certain he was that this was someone he had seen before. Malin studied his face, scrutinizing his high brows, his straight nose, strongly pronounced cheekbones and thin, tightly closed lips. The man's large eyes were especially distinctive: his gaze was calm and hard, yet somehow also sad. Ah, at last, he had it! He knew it now. Eureka! It was him! But how could it be?

One day, way back in the summer of 2000, Malin had received a phone call from an old acquaintance, a colleague, the Russian investigative reporter Oleg Artayev. In the mid-90s, they had written several reports together about corruption in the Kremlin, which they published in the U.S. News & World Report.

Oleg, very agitated, had told Malin that he was investigating the disappearance of over four billion dollars, which had been part of a loan to Russia guaranteed by the International Monetary Fund. This was a sensational piece of news, of course. It had happened in August of 1998. Following a very complex sequence of facts, first-hand accounts, and documents, Artayev had been able to pinpoint almost all participants in this skullduggery, yet something was still missing from the full picture...

'You see, Malin!' Artayev had spoken very quickly. 'There's some kind of a logical dead end. Complete mystery. In July of 1998, the IMF allowed a credit of 4.7 billion dollars to Russia, right before the default. But that money never reached its destination. These billions coming from Edmond Safra's[4] Republic National Bank of New York were dispersed to various accounts in accordance with the directions of Mr. Assianov, then Russia's Deputy Finance Minister. Needless to say, that money disappeared and could never be traced.

'When Safra had realized that what was stolen was not just a part of the full sum, as had been agreed upon, but rather all of the money, he had gotten so scared that he declared his willingness to testify to the FBI. This office had apparently been interested in the matter of the loan, at least for a time.

'Right after that, Safra got a visit,' Artayev had told Malin, fidgeting nervously with his thin-rimmed spectacles. 'Boris Berezovsky,[5] the Russian billionaire, and someone else came to see him in the south of France. They talked with him for hours, and, following that

---

4. **Edmond Jacob Safra** (1932–1999) was a billionaire, a banker of Lebanese origin. In 1966 he founded the Republic National Bank of New York, one of the most successful financial organizations in the USA. Safra was suspected of having links to the Mafia. He died under strange circumstances on December 3, 1999 when his bodyguard and nurse started a fire in his Monaco home.

5. **Boris Abramovich Berezovsky** (1946–2013) was a Russian billionaire, a business oligarch with close ties to President Yeltsin's "Family". Beginning in 2001, he was under investigation in Russia because of major fraud and embezzlement charges. After 2003 he lived in Great Britain. On March 23, 2013 he was found dead in the bathroom in his house in Berkshire. His death was officially recognized as suicide. However, this is considered doubtful by those who knew Berezovsky personally.

conversation, Safra panicked so much that he moved permanently to his quarters in Monaco, which had very sophisticated security systems, including a well-fortified nuclear bunker. This did not save his life, though. He died in December of 1999 in his bathroom when a strange fire occurred. He had not yet revealed anything about the transfer of stolen billions through his bank.'

'I heard about this, of course,' Malin had replied, 'but I don't know any details. But having said that, I'd be happy to help, if I can.'

'Thank you, Malin! I would guess that you can. Here comes the juicy part of the story,' Artayev had continued. 'Way before that tragedy, a big Russian delegation headed by Assianov went to conduct talks at the IMF. That was in the summer of 1998, and that delegation included many Russian officials and bankers. There are photographs of the event, of course. They were all quite well-known people, so I was able to figure out who was there – all except for one gentleman, who appears in some photos right next to those top Russian officials. I couldn't place him, and I have no idea who he might be. I sent you the photos with a circle around him. He's tall, he's got dark hair, with a tinge of grey. He might be over fifty, perhaps older. There is nothing on him anywhere, and no one knows who he is.

'Well, I wouldn't be so keen on finding him, you know, but there's this one surprising fact,' Artayev had continued. 'That man was with Berezovsky during that visit to Safra, the last meeting with the banker before his death. Those who witnessed Berezovsky's visit were able to recognize the second visitor. That man accompanied him into the building where Safra had agreed to meet them, in the south of France. And it was after that man's visit that Safra got scared and rushed to his fortified bunker, only to die in a fire. Yet no one, not

even the Swiss investigators tracing the money laundering schemes related to the Russian billions that disappeared, no one was able to identify the man who came
to visit Safra, even though they had his photo. The only
unusual thing they noted was that even Berezovsky acted respectful to this guy. He actually looked pretty anx-
ious, which was definitely not his usual mode of behavior. But anyway, this wasn't, you know, established fact,
so to speak, just a personal opinion of the investigators
who got to see the video recording of the visit…'

'This is all very interesting, of course,' Malin had
said, already fired up – as he always got when he heard
a mysterious story. 'But, well, I'm not sure there's any
way I can help this time. I'm sorry…'

'I wish you could. Please try something, at least. Try
rattling your connections in the States. Maybe you'll be
able to find out who this man is. Or at least where he
came from? How was it possible for him to join the official Russian delegation? Why and how did he emerge
from nowhere that time in France when they met Safra?
I'll send you his photos. Oh, something else. And the
most interesting part, as far as I'm concerned. Security
cameras caught sight of this mysterious person in Monaco one day before Safra's death. He was staying for two
days at Hotel de Paris, a very luxurious place. He registered as a Russian businessman under the name Igor Larionov. He left the hotel one day after the banker's death.'

When Malin had received the images, he'd tried his
best to fulfill his Russian colleague's request, but to no
avail. Even his most dependable contacts at the FBI and
CIA hadn't been of any help. No one had known anything
about a 'Larionov'. That, or they were pretending they
didn't know. A month later, Malin had told Artayev about
his fruitless efforts. The photographs, however, remained
in his laptop memory labeled 'Unknown Russian'.

28

And now Malin began searching feverishly through his old files, trying to find something about this 'Unknown Russian', who somehow, just maybe, was turning out to be an 'Unknown American' as well. When he finally located the photos, he opened them up on the screen, next to the photo from 9/11. Bingo! It was the same person – the one who had presented himself as 'Larionov'. The only difference was that he looked a bit older in the image from New York. More salt and pepper in his hair. And probably certain, yet almost imperceptible changes to his face. Was it that he dyed his hair or got a bit of a face-lift? Or was it just the passing of time? The photos were taken three years apart, after all.

What is it? Malin mused. This can't be coincidence, right? But, hell, why not? What would prevent "Larionov" from moving to the US in those three years? And then he could have been around the WTC, purely by accident, on the day of the tragedy in New York. Not possible? Why? Shit, why am I wasting my time on him at all now that I've just received this sensational information about the twin towers disaster? Do I need him for that, too? Why am I stressing over him? My task is clear. I have to write up a piece claiming that the monstrous affair could have been arranged from here – from inside the US. How else could I interpret a conversation in which someone in the FBI building, on behalf of some mysterious 'Boss', demands that the buildings not be blown up, only hit by the planes – and basically at the last moment, too… Meanwhile his interlocutor, obviously someone directing the attack, refuses to fulfill this demand, claiming that the progress of the operation, once started, could not be stopped, as there was no one around who could do it – that was a real killer! Watergate pales in comparison to this. What matters most right now is that I keep my head on straight, at least until the article is published. Shit! It's morning already. I'd better snooze for a couple of hours.

He'd just drifted off when the first rays of the morning sun reflected off the windows across the street, and then his phone rang persistently, shrilly, and loudly. Malin, disoriented, jumped up immediately and grabbed his phone. It was Richard – and he was calling from a number he used only for emergencies – that is, only when there was a real danger of someone listening in to his calls. They both knew quite well that this was still a vulnerable option, and they used this rather primitive trick rarely, and only for really short exchanges, not longer than twenty or thirty seconds.

'Hi, boss,' Malin muttered.

'Listen carefully. You're smart enough to understand. Everything has changed. Because of the archive. You gave me and the Big Boss everything you got, the whole archive, right? Right?'

'Sure,' Malin lied, thinking of the full copy he had secretly made. 'I went straight to you after my meeting with the source. I copied the archive for the editor-in-chief, and I left the original with you. Now I'm waiting for your decision on how we can use it. I'm dying to see what's in there.'

'Come to my office in an hour. And bring your entire old archive on 9/11. Have you got it? Move your ass! I'll be waiting for you here.'

When Malin heard Richard say, 'move your ass!', he knew right away that something really serious was going on. A well-mannered intellectual, Richard was rather picky about his parlance, so they had agreed some time ago that this phrase was their code for conveying that some big issue had come up. Well, who would have expected anything less? Even after his quick perusal of the Marshall Archive, Malin had realized quite quickly that it would be a miracle if they allowed him to publicize all of its materials. Even Snowden's revelations felt like a Sunday-school picnic compared to what he had in his hands.[6] Publishing this material now would be a political death sentence for certain persons in the higher echelons of power, current and former alike.

Malin first copied all files from his laptop to a mini flash drive another source had given him. Then he did what had worked for him many times before when he wanted to hide something important: he put it in plain sight. So, he simply dropped the drive into the pocket of his jeans. Then he deleted some personal mail from his laptop, including pictures of several girls he'd been seeing, including some from a recent trip to a Sri Lanka resort. He put the laptop into a case. He knew, of course, that those who might be processing Berwick now would have the means to recover any deleted files, so this was just for show. Pretending for their benefit that he was deleting anything at all that might be sensitive or personal.

Minutes later his silver Corvette, his dream car (a dream that had only come true a year ago), was rolling smoothly over the asphalt of Wisconsin Avenue, wet after a light morning rain. The car's powerful engine purred gently.

At this hour, the newspaper office was still in that state of early morning silence that Malin liked most of all. This silence had a degree of tension, like the tension that engulfs a track athlete the moment before

---

6. **Edward Joseph Snowden** (born 1983) is a former CIA official who leaked classified information from the National Security Agency (NSA) in 2013 to The Guardian and to The Washington Post. His disclosure confirmed the fact that the NSA was routinely monitoring communications between citizens of many states around the globe.

they dart forward, cheered on from the stands, towards their victory. Hundreds of newspaper employees would soon start running from cubicle to cubicle, as dozens of phones rang simultaneously, and chugging printers spouted countless pages. Right now, though, as Malin walked down the corridor, he could hear only the echoing of his own steps. The few colleagues who had been on night duty, prepping the morning issue, greeted him with silent nods.

Malin was almost knocked off his feet by an attractive young woman who came hurtling around the corner. It was Jane Thompson, tanned, svelte, looking like a miniature statuette. Malin had liked her a lot for some time, but he had never done anything to strike up something more intimate. The 25-year-old journalist had been married, then she had gone through a messy divorce.

'Hi, Malin. Sorry about that. Well, I was about to call you anyway.' Jane talked fast, grabbing Malin by the arm. 'Listen, JFK's birthday is coming up in May, so I'm preparing a big piece about him.[7] I have stories from people who witnessed the shooting in Dallas. I found so much related material! And I've been trying to figure out who's who in these thousands of photos. And there's video, too, of course... But there are several people I couldn't place at all. I need your help. And I need it really badly.'

'My friend, I'm on my way to Richard, who wants to see me very urgently. The old man has been waiting on me long enough that he might organize a little auto-da-fé for me. How about you shoot your questions to my email, and I'll look at them later today and help out if I can. Okay? Sorry, dear.'

---

7. JFK is short for John Fitzgerald Kennedy, 35th President of the USA, who was assassinated in Dallas, TX on November 22, 1963.

'Okay, I'll send you everything. Good luck!'

He gave her a light kiss on the cheek and entered Richard's office. It was clear that he was expected there.

Malin was surprised when he walked into the office to see a grey-haired, gaunt, middle-aged man in an expensive grey suit sporting a chic Don Quixote goatee sitting in Richard's chair. Malin thought that the man who so unceremoniously occupied the chair had most probably never heard of the old hidalgo, so he would not be aware of his likeness to Cervantes's noble character, to someone who bravely attempted to fight windmills. Richard greeted Malin curtly, beating a path back and forth through the narrow, long space in his office.

'Hello, Malin. Meet Mr. Valevich of the FBI.'

After this introduction, the roar of thunder crashed, a deep and booming voice most incongruent to the appearance of the FBI Don Quixote. One might have thought he was speaking through a booming trumpet.

'Pleased to meet you, Mr. Malin. I regularly read your reports, you could say I'm a fan of yours. But let's get down to business. You have recently received some fakes from a middleman, someone who is known to us. He appears to have bamboozled you, so to speak, pretending that you were getting from him an archive of documents collected by the estimable and, alas, late Mr. Marshall. He was successful in getting a large sum of money from you for some worthless files, which either he or some of his accomplices created. I am sorry you fell prey to those top-class swindlers.'

Malin understood what Don Quixote was trying to achieve and saw Richard's face, who diligently but unsuccessfully demonstrated his disinterest in this matter. Malin couldn't stand it.

'Hey, what's this all about, Mr. Velevich? That goes for you too, Richard – how could the FBI find out about our office's internal affairs? And more to the point: about *my* new project? Who told you, Mr. Velevich, of my sources? According to this country's laws, the news-paper can only reveal them after a court ruling! Even I haven't seen any of the files yet, I left both copies with Richard…but judging from your response, I'm starting to suspect there must be something really big in there. Or am I wrong?'

'Malin, Malin!' Don Quixote boomed again. 'Sorry to call you by your first name, but, well, I am twice your age… First of all, my name is Valevich, not Velevich. Secondly, to be honest, I'm glad to hear you have yet to familiarize yourself with those fakes. Did I hear you say that you have not, I repeat, NOT,' his voice suddenly took on a vaguely threatening tone, 'seen the contents of the flash stick which that shark sold your newspaper? Is that true?'

Malin, who remembered well what Richard had said to him over the phone, decided to follow this line of conversation, in the interest of avoiding open conflict. But surely such a reaction from the FBI was only confir-mation that the documents were telling the truth, and that they dealt with dangerous issues.

'I am sorry, Mr. Valevich. I did not misname you on purpose. And I must have overreacted, of course. But imagine this: here is a journalist who found sensational materials and his newspaper agreed to finance the in-vestigation. Next morning, he is – that is, I am – roused out of bed at daybreak, told to come to the office in a jiffy, and here I see you telling me that everything we got is just a big sham, a hoax, a swindle.

'So how am I supposed to feel?' Malin went on with his show. 'All I could do yesterday was look here and there as I copied files for the editor-in-chief. I saw some-thing about explosions at the WTC, some transcripts of phone calls. And a ton of photos…but I was planning to get into all the details today, so that I could actually start my investigation. Well, looks like I was wrong… In short, Mr. Valevich, I don't want any problems, of course.'

'Look, Malin,' Richard spoke in an unnaturally cajoling voice, 'why don't we do it this way: give over your laptop to Mr. Valevich so that they can check it out for a while. That might convince them that you're not involved in any of this… No offence meant, but this is the Big Boss's decision.'

'No problem, sir. But I'd like to check my laptop again. In case there's something I left there which is necessary for me. Can I do that if it's here in your presence, Mr. Valevich?'

'Sure, sure, that's fine,' Don Quixote droned.

Richard caught his breath, wiped his forehead with a large handkerchief and then spoke again:

'Something else, Malin. You've been asking for an excuse to go to Paris, right? There's a topic for you there now. You've heard about that Bettencourt lady, the owner of L'Oréal, and her illegal financing of Sarkozy's presidential campaign.[8] Mr. Valevich told me his sources in Paris indicated that the Bettencourt affair seems to be coming up again. Why don't you go there, dig around, talk to the right people, and then we'll print your piece on the matter around mid-May. Anyway, move your ass, boy. It's your favorite topic anyway.'

The Don Quixote of the FBI nodded solemnly. Malin could not care less about Sarkozy, or all other French politicians put together, but he got Richard's signal right away. He knew he had to disappear from US territory.

---

8. French authorities suspected that ex-president Nicholas Sarkozy was receiving, in violation of the law, large financial donations from L. Bettencourt, owner of L'Oreal, during his 2007 presidential campaign.

Well, France was not the worst option. Plus, he already had experience staying away from his home country: two years ago, when Malin had been able to get proof of financial fraud at the Pentagon, Richard had told him to go into hiding in Jordan. The publication of the article had created such a big uproar that several top officials at the defense ministry had lost their jobs, and Malin had been able to return to Washington only some time later.

The next morning, Malin was ready to leave for Paris. Richard, who came to see him off at Washington's Dulles Airport, told him:

'Don't be mad at me, Malin! I have nothing to do with this. Well, you know I wouldn't, of course. When the Big Boss got to see some of the files in Marshall's archive, he almost had a heart attack... Two hours later this Valevich guy was already in my office, sitting around like that, telling me his lies about fake files, shams, and hoaxes. And you know what? I don't even think it was our Big Boss who notified the FBI. It seems that they already knew about the leak and were just probing into who would end up with the materials. So of course, they pinpointed us. The Big Boss just happened to agree with the FBI's point of view. Or maybe only pretended he did. Anyway, he wanted to avoid trouble, so he gave away his copy to them. And he also told them about you and me. He had to...'

'That bitch!'

'Calm down, Malin! First, don't fret! Someone is certainly watching us right now. So, all we should be doing is a bit of talking, laughing, and saying our goodbyes. We're old friends, aren't we? Second, you're going to have to stay away from the US for a while now. You get some rest. I don't need any of that Sarkozy bull, of course. None at all, even for free. Our French colleagues have already done their best to make the matter crystal clear, and we're not interested in rewriting their stuff. Have fun until the dust settles and things get forgotten. Meanwhile we'll pretend we believe the archive is a fake.'

'Richard, is there any chance, even a very small one, that we'll be able to make it public? At a later point, of course. Much later…'

'To be honest with you, Malin, no, I don't see any chance for that, none at all. Forget about it. Unless your goal in life is to be known as 'recently deceased Max Malin' – and to take me with you, for that matter. I hope things will calm down soon. You must understand this, Malin: this is not about exposing an embezzler at Pentagon or a corruption case at the State Department. This is much, much bigger! And much more gruesome! So, let's not look at this as our lucky chance for fame. Better to write it off as a simple blunder. Shit happens, you know how it is. Well, that's it, then! Good luck to you! Elizabeth says "hi".'

'Thank you! Give her my regards.'

A large group of school kids was already milling around at the gate. They were leaving for a tour of historical castles in the Loire Valley. Parents, educators, and teen tourists created a constant din, interrupted at times by the exclamations of emotional mothers. As Richard pressed Malin's hand goodbye, he said in a low voice:

'Communication as usual. Through the same channels. Extreme circumstances to be defined as before. Good luck…'

4

Farewell, President Kennedy
Dallas. November 22, 1963

The grey roofs of Dallas were slick with rain from the cold drizzle that fell all morning. The wind, which had no rest during the night was chasing low, fractious clouds across the sky. The cutting draft from the north made the doors of café entrances clap again and again and knocked down newspaper and flower stands showering people raindrops. But on that day, no one in Dallas was paying much attention to nature's helter-skelter. Everybody was anticipating the Big Event.

A tall, dark-haired man in his thirties registered at a hotel on Lemmon Avenue while on the opposite side of the street Tom Walker walked quickly towards a phone booth, turning up the collar of his long, expensive coat. A passerby would only be able to get a clearer view of him by coming right up to the booth and wiping rain off the glass.

Walker was an exquisitely beautiful man, but his was a callous beauty: black hair combed back, aquiline nose, and finely delineated, thin lips. But his eyes... His eyes were mesmerizing: cold depths contrasted with flashes of soft, yellowish light that seemed to surface quite suddenly. The strange quality of his eyes inspired a curious mixture of attraction and fear in onlookers. He had a gaze that felt like an abyss that drew people in for just one more look…

Walker dropped a coin into the slot, dialed a number and, upon hearing a hasty "hello!", said in a somewhat unnatural, jerky manner:

'It's me, Kiddo. What about the airport?'

'Everything's fine. Air Force One is about to land in a few minutes. There are droves of us journalists here. Easily a hundred or so. Plus, gawkers, about the same number. I guess I'm the only one hanging around this phone booth here… Listen! There are wonders happening with the weather. The clouds and rain are gone now. The sun is shining. Looks like he might ride in a car with an open top. Where you are, the weather may get better, too…'

'What about security?'

'Lots of them. Even in New York, there was nothing on this level. They're checking everybody. There are snipers on the rooftops. Oh, here! Here it comes! Call this number in about ten minutes.'

After hanging up, the man lit a cigarette, still standing inside the phone booth. His back to the street, he was thinking that today was probably the most important day in his life, and that he was already thirty-three years old. Life had been rather stormy, mind. What was going to happen today was the climax of his activities of the last several months, during which he had analyzed every detail of the upcoming event. Hundreds of people were involved, though most of them hadn't a clue as to the scope of the operation in which they had agreed to participate. They were unaware of their actual roles, their minds only on the good money they'd make. In fact, only Walker knew the whole picture. Oh, he was standing tall today. Only the weeping sky was higher.

He had been preparing this event in Dallas for almost a year, fine-tuning the precise conditions. Right now, however, standing inside the fogged-up phone booth, he suddenly felt a strange fear rising from deep within him, a clammy feeling that rose slowly, spreading all over his body. It started at the roots of his hair and then dropped all the way down, down to the toes. A wave of fear...and another wave... But it wasn't related to a feeling of danger, or to any realization of the horrifying consequences of the upcoming event. Not at all. It was simply a fear that something might not go precisely according to plan. Only that. Walker shook his head, driving away the phantasm: no, he had taken into account any and all possible options, and impossible ones, too. No mistakes would be made. He had calculated each and every aspect correctly, thought about every possible detail, down to the most minute, and he had paid what was due to all involved. Today was his day and his hour.

Walker dialed the same number again.

'How now?' he asked in a low voice.

'He's off! They're off! A minute ago. With the top down. He's in the back seat, with Jackie next to him. Governor Connally and his wife are seated in front of them. Next comes a car with security guards, and Vice President Johnson is in the third car...all according to protocol.'

'Thank you! All clear. Signing off.'

The person on the other end of the line had been right. Leaving the booth, Walker readied himself for a gust of cold wind but found that the weather had changed drastically in those few minutes. The rain had stopped, leaving behind only a sweet morning freshness in the air, dark asphalt, and a few last drops slowly descending the glass of the store showcases. The wind had died down, too, and the first rays of the faint November sun were shooting through the clouds, which were pushed apart. It was as if the sun wished to bid farewell to the man who was meant to go within the next twenty minutes.

Walker crossed Inwood Road, directing his steps towards Elm Street. He had to get through vast crowds of spectators who stood on both sides of the president's route. It was difficult to appear calm, to move without haste. There was, however, a frantic thought rushing about in his brain: would he be able to make it to the next phone booth within the next two minutes? Walker had rehearsed many times before, counting how many steps it would take him to cover the distance, timing how long he would need, even considering the possible difficulty of moving through a crowd. But despite his best calculations, he had not foreseen that so many locals would show up today at Lemmon Avenue and Main Street.

Tens of thousands of Dallas residents filled the streets. They were there with their children, parents, friends, and girlfriends. Whole crowds of journalists were out too, equipped with cameras, camera stands, and microphones. Today was their day as well. All these people had been expecting this Event, and now it was happening. The motorcade carrying John Fitzgerald Kennedy, the 35th President of the USA, was slowly moving onwards through Dallas, greeted by the crowd's loud acclamations.

Tom Walker finally made it to the next phone booth. But when he reached it, something inside him snapped – the booth was occupied. A huge policeman was inside, happily chatting on the phone. The expression on his face meant that he was most probably talking to his wife or girlfriend. It didn't look as though he was reporting to his superior regarding his special mission to ensure the President's protection...

Walker could not wait even seconds. Something sparked in his brain like an electric shock. He tapped on the glass window with a coin and when the policeman turned around, looking very surprised, Walker pointed in the direction from where the motorcade was about to appear, shouting quite loudly:

'I'm very sorry, sir! But the President is coming up any moment now. I'm from the *Daily Mail* and I must urgently send a report to my newspaper.'

A beat later he added:

'I know that your call is also very important, but I'll be very quick. Please, sir! This visit is such a big thing for our city!'

The policeman, all smiles, stammered something into the receiver and stepped out of the phone booth. He was obviously a bit embarrassed that this journalist had overheard him using the phone for a personal call while on duty. Walker thanked him guardedly and started dialing his number. A moment later a male voice answered his call.

'It's me,' said Walker in a low voice. 'Option one. Everything according to plan. Mary and the baby are already onsite.'

'Got it. Thank you. All clear.'

That was all. Walker, exhaling with relief, left the booth and started walking through the crowds towards the railway overpass on Elm Street. He had some twenty minutes left now.

He looked around at the people in the crowds with great interest. Thousands were standing along the curving street that disappeared under the bridge. People were calling to one another. Many were smoking or chewing something. They held their children high so that they too would see the oncoming motorcade. There was a festive feeling in the air, especially because of the sudden appearance of the sun in the November sky. These people were mostly ordinary folks, and this was their day, their celebration of a president of whom they were very proud... It didn't matter that they didn't really know where this pride came from. Just as they didn't know that Kennedy was not so different from any of his predecessors or, for that matter, from those who would come after him. To bolster his career, he had used whatever methods were at his disposal in order to defeat his political competitors. He even had some contacts with the mob, and he most certainly provided any possible assistance to those business circles that were close to him. He was just like the rest of them all...only more likable. And it didn't hurt that Jackie was such a cutie!

Tom Walker suddenly felt as if these people had come here today not to cheer on their president, but rather to be present during his own plan's implementation. A plan he himself had conceived and put into operation. He, whose name today was still Tom Walker. All these people had come to watch how President Kennedy would die. They came to express their grief, to run through the streets, to weep as if they were professional extras he had hired for the show. What a strange sensation it was!

Time crawled at such a slow pace that it seemed as if it were bumping into every little tree in the street, clinging to the lawns, to the police cars. As Walker came closer to the grey building of the schoolbook depository, which stuck up absurdly beyond the intersection of Houston and Elm, he felt as if the minutes grew longer with his every step.

Walker stopped at the place he had selected several days before as his preferred observation point. It was at a large white concrete structure, a pergola in the middle of the park lawn, just before the entrance under the triple overpass. This was a better location for surveying the neighborhood of the approximate point where the Event was conceived to happen.

Walker kept an eye on the windows of the sixth floor of the depository, switching his attention to the hedge on the grassy knoll to the right of Elm Street. Suddenly he felt someone moving up and standing next to him. It was a rather plump, bald man with an amateur film camera, coming to occupy a spot nearby.

'Great location here,' gasped Walker's newly appeared companion. 'I'll film from here if you don't mind. Name's Zapruder.[1] Yes, it's Za-proo-der. I manufacture clothing, but I shoot films as a hobby. I'd like to capture Kennedy's visit to Dallas.'

'Richard Abrahamson,' Walker said, by way of introduction. 'I'm here to watch the event. I hope I won't be in your way.'

The fat film enthusiast burst out laughing. He didn't answer Walker's polite remark, pointing at a young lady standing next to him:

'This is my assistant – oh, they're coming, I guess. Let's start filming!'

Walker looked discreetly once again at the windows of the depository, then at the hedge on the knoll, after which he drew himself to his full height, looking at the road in expectation of the motorcade's arrival at any minute. The din of the cheering crowd grew louder as the cars containing the president and his entourage drew nearer. It almost sounded like an avalanche com-

---

1. **Abraham Zapruder** (1905–1970) was a businessman from Dallas, co-owner of Jennifer Juniors, Inc., a clothing manufacturing enterprise, and an amateur film maker. He shot a 26-second-long film on November 22, 1963, which turned out to be the most detailed documentation of Kennedy's assassination.

ing down the slope of a mountain. Thousands of tumultuous cries echoed around the concrete buildings. Rays of the still-present sun reflected from shop windows, creating intricate patterns on the backs of the onlookers standing along the road.

The first to emerge from around the curve of the street was a group of motorcyclists. The first car followed them slowly, moving smoothly. It was long and looked almost like a predator. President Kennedy was sitting in the third row of seats, looking a bit tired. Nevertheless, he kept smiling and waving to the crowds with his right hand, at times resting it on the massive door. Just as the car passed a large information board obscuring Walker's view, the loud report of a shot was heard. It was so different from the din of the crowd that it was clearly audible. Kennedy clutched his hand to his throat. Jackie bent to him, perhaps to ask something.

Time stopped for Tom Walker. There was only loud countdown hammering inside his head: "One, two, three, four… It's now, girl! Do it!"

Two shots rang out simultaneously during the fifth and the longest second. They were executed synchronously, creating a single, stinging, deadly sound. The bullet from the sixth floor of the book depository went straight up into the sky, as planned. The second bullet shot out of a sniper rifle, held confidently in the arms of a woman behind the hedge, on the grassy knoll. It was her bullet that struck the head of the 35th US president, John Fitzgerald Kennedy.

The woman walked quickly down the grassy knoll. Stepping only about five meters away, she put her rifle into a baby pram waiting there, with a real six-month-old baby boy whimpering inside it. She put on thick glasses and started walking away, exhibiting no haste. Only thirty seconds after the second shot, the woman was gone, nowhere to be seen…

After the second or, rather, the third shot, the one from the knoll, President Kennedy's head was tossed back. Jackie somehow managed to crawl onto the back hood of the car. A security agent from the escort car had already reached them. The motorcade picked up speed and disappeared under the overpass. Zapruder's camera kept whirring for some seconds. He must have filmed the whole operation – that is, the assassination of an acting US president. But now he simply stood there without saying a word, completely dumbfounded. He was still staring at the underpass through which the last car of the motorcade had passed less than a minute ago.

Tom Walker turned his back to the roadway, walking quietly towards another lane. He knew a great panic would very soon ensue. He could make it a couple of hundred yards before police and security agents ran up towards whoever was still standing there at the curb, throwing people onto the ground, waving their guns, yelling something into their walkie-talkies. No one understood yet what was happening. What had just happened.

Walker walked farther and farther from the place where the Event had occurred. Something he had successfully engineered, down to the last detail. A cold wind came up all of a sudden, got up the flaps of his long coat, even under his suit jacket. Shivering, he wrapped himself tighter into his coat, lifted the collar again, and started walking faster. Two blocks later, Walker got into another phone booth, dialed a number, and almost immediately heard a rather raspy female voice say:

'Hello?'

'It's me. Tell me what's up.'

'Mary called. The toy is already swimming in the Trinity River. She gave the baby back to his father. She will meet Morgan in an hour at the agreed spot.'

'What's the news?'

'They called the priests for the last rites. Is that enough?'

'Yes, quite.'

There was intense silence for a while. Walker realized the woman on the other end of the line was hesitant about asking something important.

'Now, baby, what's up? Tell me. Spill.'

'Hey, listen. I think I've got a clue about what will happen to Mary…but…what about me? Something similar?'

'You silly goose,' Walker muttered, through clenched teeth. 'You'll be all right. The money's already in your account. You must leave town, of course. Not right away, but in a couple of days. Go south, way south, to the land of eternal summer, where no one will ask any questions. Of course, you'll have to forget everything and just have fun out there. Live for the hell of it, and don't worry! You have nothing to do with what's happened, so you're not to be blamed for anything. And I have never been a part of your life. Nothing happened between you and me over the last couple of months. Live on. Enjoy!'

'Thank you. Still, I did love being with you… Good luck, and farewell.'

Walker crossed the street and walked away. There were two more things to deal with, and then the project would be in perfect shape.

A heavy, invisible cloud was slowly descending on the city. Its enormous dimensions engulfed Dallas's every nook and cranny, exerting pressure on everyone. People were slowly coming to terms with the extent of what had just happened. Suddenly policemen were everywhere. They wandered aimlessly from one intersection to the next, scrutinizing the faces of the passersby and talking loudly over their walkie-talkies. Large crowds of locals milled around cafés where TV sets were kept at full volume. Walker caught bits of phrases. "The President is still alive… Oh, they already called the priest… Governor Connally also got hit by a bullet, but it was a ricochet and he's all right… Kennedy's dead… Why? And why here in Dallas?"

One could get the impression that the locals felt as if they were to blame for the fact that this assassination had happened in their city. As if they were guilty of not keeping him safe. As if they were indeed asking that question: why here? Why in our city? Why not in New York or Chicago? It would have been so much easier for them to endure. They would have watched it on TV, read in their newspapers. They would have certainly been sad for a minute or so…but that would have been it! Now, however, they felt like accomplices to the crime.

Soon Walker reached an old, nondescript Toyota parked on Swiss Avenue. About an hour later, he drove up to Sam Houston Park. Leaving his car in the parking lot, he started walking down a trail that led deeper into the woods.

Autumn was already almost done with its work: the trees were bare, their wet bark glistening dimly. Yellowish leaves, slowly turning brown, rustled softly under Walker's feet. No one else was around. No one ventured into this large park today. Well, not quite no one: in the distance, there was a pair of people, perhaps two lovebirds, now quite cold, who appeared for a moment in a small clearing between the trees. They certainly did not notice Walker as he sauntered down the trail.

Several minutes later, Walker saw what he'd been expecting to see. A woman was sitting on a bench, her head bent low, touching her knees. Her grey coat was certainly too large for her, and its wide collar was almost hiding her head. Disheveled strains of dark hair hung down loosely, almost touching the ground. Walker sat down next to her. He looked at her for a while, then touched her neck. She was dead. A small syringe at her feet still contained a bit of clear liquid, with some blood in it as well.

Walker knew that sometime later that day the police would discover this woman in the park. Mary Ashley, a drug addict, a widow who had died of an overdose. Morgan had done an excellent job. As usual.

He walked away about a hundred yards, then turned around and looked at the woman once again. For the last time.

He had always liked Mary, a lot. A former athlete of around thirty, she had been extremely skilled in the use of all types of weapons, especially sniper rifles. She had previously fulfilled a couple of other sensitive contracts for Walker, in Europe and in Asia. Her husband, Michael, had died in April 1961 during the failed operation in the Bay of Pigs. Since that day, Mary had only two wishes. One was to revenge herself upon President Kennedy for her husband's demise – she felt that he was personally to blame for it. The second was to save up twenty thousand dollars so she could get out of 'this blasted USA' and settle somewhere on an island in the southern seas. She wanted to meet a real friend there, have a child with him, and live under the palms at the ocean beach.

'*I am so sorry, dear,*' Walker said to her in his thoughts, '*that I could make only your first wish come true. After all, it was you who killed Kennedy. You alone, not that brainless schizo Oswald. Your first and only shot went through the head of America's president – the head you hated so much. But, well, there was no way an island in the middle of an ocean could have become a reality for you, dear. This was too serious a matter, so the conditions were that no trace should be left behind, no leads, zero…even if you were going to end up on an island in the middle of nowhere. I'm truly sorry…'*

Walker waved his hand and started walking fast towards his car. The sky hovered low, as if aiming to touch the park trees with the shreds of darkened clouds driven by a sudden strong wind from the city. There were new clouds moving in, getting darker and darker, filling the horizon, and leaving no streak of light anywhere in the sky. Raindrops, large and heavy, started thumping against the hood of the car.

The air inside the car was very humid. Walker switched on the heat and fiddled with the knob of the radio.

The announcer was reading, in a somewhat muffled voice, a report about Kennedy's death, which had been confirmed an hour earlier, and about the arrest of Lee Harvey Oswald,[2] who was suspected of killing the president. Oswald had also shot and killed a policeman later on. This happened on a local street, quite close to where Oswald lived. Then he'd gone to a movie theater but was arrested there.

'What an idiot!' Walker chuckled. 'Some bunny gone bonkers… It was the right choice, after all, to leave him unaware of what's been happening. He was clueless, thank God, until today, and now he's gone completely loony… But I wonder how it was possible that he hit the president with his first shot. Why the hell did he aim at Kennedy at all? He was told to shoot off the mark! I don't get it. And why in God's name did he kill

---

2. **Lee Harvey Oswald** (1939–1963) was the only official suspect in the killing of John Kennedy. He was said to have shot him from the sixth floor of the book depository in Dallas. He, however, denied his responsibility for the killing stating that he was a 'patsy'. Oswald was killed by nightclub owner Jack Ruby under very strange circumstances, only two days after Kennedy's death, during his transfer from the city jail to the county jail.

that policeman? What a nut! Well, at this point none of it matters anymore. In the end, everything went according to plan.'

The car was moving slowly away from the park and to the highway, heading towards the city. Walker mused in time with the movement:

Okay, fine, all that Oswald was there for was to shoot twice to distract attention away from Mary's shot. His first shot would have been towards the president's car – well, towards the motorcade in general – and the second one had to be for the sound of it. Harvey was told that his role was to imitate an attempt on the president's life in order to intimidate him. That was supposed to make him "more favorably disposed" to certain ideas, "more manageable". Oswald did not know, of course, about Mary hiding behind the hedge on the grass knoll. Nor did he know that her task was to hit the president's head at the same time he made his second shot so that, later on, they would identify Lee Harvey Oswald as the one who killed Kennedy.

That was my ideal plan. At its core, the intended course of events was not changed, even if Oswald did disrupt it at first by aiming at the president. What was that about? Some unknown personal grudge, perhaps. But Kennedy's dead now. There were no links between Walker and the officially recognized killer, Oswald. Well, not that Walker was the one dealing with him, anyway.

Of course, no one will trust Oswald when he tells investigators that he had been offered the incredible opportunity to only mimic an attempt on the president's life in exchange for remuneration that would resolve his dire financial situation. And he'll go down in history books, that's for sure… The situation appears so logical that any other version would appear to be pure nonsense. Only one finishing touch was needed to close the story. One final action will cut short any possibility of an investigation and leave only question marks in the whole affair of the assassination – that will be Oswald's public murder by a sudden, unexpected avenger.

That part wasn't obligatory, of course. Yet Walker felt he may have omitted some details when coming up with his plan. That he may not have noticed certain subtleties. Even his mind had its boundaries. That was why the death of Lee Harvey Oswald was to become the final stage of the most high-profile murder of the twentieth century. Only after that would his contract be completed.

He finally made it to the highway, one of many cars in the huge flow of traffic. Walker felt that the locals were already starting to get over their initial shock, only a few hours after Kennedy's death. From the stereo of the car beside his came the boisterous, life-affirming 'She Loves You', by the Beatles. It may have been because Walker glanced at the car with such surprise that the driver suddenly turned down the stereo and sped away, perhaps thinking of today's tragic event.

Well, life went on, and its rhythm was becoming ever faster. Oh, Kennedy got killed…well, that's sad, of course. He was a good president. Yet his death doesn't stop us from living our lives. Who but me will make one more payment for the little cabin at White Rock Lake? No one but me will take care of the stern IRS agent, or have their fun with sexy Joanne, or Anna Maria, or, for that matter, that dark-skinned cutie from 51st Street. Everything will be fine, as it is supposed to be in America. Especially since Vice President Lyndon Johnson has already taken the President's oath of office, real fast aboard Air Force One, only two hours after the assassination. He's President now in Kennedy's place. Johnson is a good guy, of course, because our great country cannot be led by someone who's not a good guy. Things happened fast, that's true, but it was done only for our own good – so that we would not be upset about the fact that our country does not have a president. This is it, of course, and no other explanation is possible.

This was Tom Walker's picture of the current thought process of the ordinary American, riding fast in their inexpensive cars next to his humble Toyota, listening to the Beatles. And he was probably right. He had a knack for making generalizations, and for analyzing facts. He could understand human nature well, and he knew much about how people feel. Mostly about things that they usually wouldn't admit to themselves.

Half an hour later he took an exit to stop at a roadside café. Sitting at the bar and drinking his coffee, Walker prepared for his most important phone call for today. It was about time to call the intermediary through whom he'd gotten the Kennedy contract. The intermediary was the only link connecting him with the top man of all, the one taking the President's oath of office only a few hours before on Air Force One. Well, he didn't know for sure, of course, whether the original request had come directly from the Vice President. It could have been someone else. Someone from his entourage, perhaps. What Walker knew was that the intermediary with whom he had been discussing the contract's details was related, one way or another, to one of the government agencies, or rather, to special services. This was as much as Walker had been able to find out through his research.

It was six months ago that he, already known by then as Canadian businessman Tom Walker, a specialist in resolving very complex issues for very high fees, received a special contract for the president of the country. It came via a long chain of intermediaries. There were no conditions and no details.

It had been up to him to figure out all the details, develop a plan of action and pull it off to a T. In exchange, the client agreed to two of Walker's requests. One was to transfer twenty-five million US dollars to a special, numbered account. The second was that, after the successful completion of the contract, a certain person 'sent by Tom Walker' was to become one of the main intermediaries between the weapons manufacturers for the US Army and the US Military Group taking part in the conflict in Vietnam.

Tom Walker had had enough foresight to realize that Kennedy's demise would be followed by the subsequent stepping up of military action in South Vietnam under Lyndon Johnson. And that it would mean billions and billions would be spent on arms and other expenses in the field.

The first condition, the transfer of 25 million dollars to a secret account, had been completed some time ago. The second was to come about very soon.

Walker walked to the phone in the darkish back room, which smelled of spilled liquor and cheap cigarettes. A very young girl slipped away from the room, quickly walking past Walker. She glanced admiringly at his beautifully chiseled features and disappeared at the far end of the bar counter.

Walker dialed the number. The call was answered right away, but they said nothing. The dense silence in the phone was a sure sign that whoever answered the call was listening closely. Walker counted to ten in his head, then said:

'I am done settling my accounts.'

A deep voice responded slowly, with a drawl, obviously speaking through a handkerchief or a napkin:

'I know. We are thankful for what you have accomplished. Is everything alright?'

'Yes. Only the one bunny went crazy at the last minute and started acting up, completely on his own. I mean, the policeman... You must have heard already... It's necessary to deal with it as soon as possible. An avenger is needed to take care of the bunny.'

'I know. He'll meet the bunny in two days. Do you think the bunny might spill anything in the meantime?'

'No. He doesn't know anything. He thought it was some kind of game, just an imitation of the real thing. Besides, he only had contact with some middlemen he'd never met before.'

'Great. I must say again that our country is thankful to you,' the voice became even more veiled. 'What is your news?'

'I don't exist anymore.' Walker's voice took on an ironic overtone. 'This grateful country will hopefully fulfill the second part of our agreement, won't it? So that I can disappear for good and then have no reason to think back to this Event, right?'

'Sure, my friend. Don't worry, the decision was already made. Your man will fill the position in the system as promised. If I'm not mistaken, his name is Weiss, right?'

'Please don't pretend you don't know his name, sir! You know very well that his full name is Martin Weiss. There is one aspect I want you to take into account: Martin has no contact with me. He does not know me, and we have never met. My connection to him exists only via some middlemen; it's a one-way connection, which means you won't be able to find me through him. And I want to clarify one more thing, just in case: if I find out that attempts are being made towards non-fulfillment of our agreements, then...well, to be on the safe side, I will make my information available to the media. And what I know, as you understand, is worse than an atomic explosion.'

'Stop this nonsense, please!' the other man yelled, obviously forgetting to hold a napkin in front of his mouth. 'Stop it! You did your part, and we'll fulfill our promise as was agreed. We don't need anything else from you. Everybody should forget everything now. By the way, what will happen to you?'

'I'll die soon. Drown, I guess. Oh, there's more about Weiss. He won't be bothering you for too long. As soon as he completes his mission, he too will come to a tragic end at some point, in a jungle around Saigon. If you get my meaning.'

'Of course. Such an outcome will be fine with everyone involved, I guess.' The speaker on the other end of the line suddenly gave a nervous laugh and then continued: 'Oh, I hope both you and Mr. Weiss can depart to the other world as soon as possible... You'd better speed things up, my friend. Farewell!'

'Goodbye, sir, and thank you for your warm wishes.'

Tom Walker left the back room and walked along the bar counter, where a dozen customers were staring at the TV screen.

'Police are questioning the man suspected of killing President Kennedy,' the news presenter said in an even manner. 'Lee Harvey Oswald has not pled guilty. He also denies that he had anything to do with the assassination...'

On his way out, Walker met the eyes of the girl who had bumped into him as he entered the back room. She was very young and obviously employed here as a waitress. A fat guy sitting next to her was telling her something, but she turned away from him in order to look at Walker. Her name was Paola; he could see a small name card affixed to the top of her dress.

What a stunner! Walker thought. This girl is incredible. She's a little over twenty. Wow, her eyes... They would drive any man crazy. It's a direct hit, with no chance of recovery. I wish I could take her along, away from here. Go to some islands for a couple of months to catch a breath after all my labors.

Shaking off this sudden fancy in the next moment, he left the café, walking briskly. Ah, but he couldn't help it – after several steps he quickly glanced back. He couldn't miss the pleasure of one more glimpse of Paola. She was standing at the counter, looking after him, holding a stack of tablecloths in her hands. A light, barely noticeable smile appeared suddenly on her lips, but it flitted away immediately, hidden behind a busy person's mask. Or was Walker perhaps seeing things? Anyway, Paola had already turned away her head.

Walker got into his car and started the motor. He looked at the café again, trying to find its name – oh, Mayflower... Then he rode down the narrow street, which soon turned west.

The last rays of the setting sun pierced the side windows, creating mysterious glittering signs around the dashboard. It was as if the sun was desperately trying to stop the hasty retreat of the evanescent autumn of 1963. The last autumn of John Fitzgerald Kennedy.

Soon there was no trace left of Tom Walker. The young Canadian businessman, who had spent two successful years involved in real estate deals, suddenly sold all of his shares, cleared his bank accounts, and stopped answering phone calls.

Three months later, a disfigured body was discovered in Lake Michigan, where Tom Walker liked to go fishing. Well, at least, the documents found in the drowned man's pockets stated that this was Tom J. Walker, born in 1930. He had probably been robbed by local goons, who killed the poor man and threw his body into the lake. Such was the conclusion of the police investigator.

Detailed identification was not possible, since the body was decomposed from being in the water for so long. Walker had no family that could be contacted.

President Johnson, contrary to the pledge given by the late President Kennedy, initiated active warfare in Vietnam in the spring of 1964. He started a swift build-up of the US Army Group there, at the same time doling out enormous sums of money to arms manufacturers.[3] Around that time a 33-year-old man by the name of Martin Weiss began shuttling between Washington, D.C., and Saigon. He owned an intermediary company through which hundreds of millions of dollars passed, money that the State Department had allocated for military spending – that is, for purchasing armaments from specialized companies, as well as uniforms, food, and essential goods. Companies owned by Martin Weiss were delivering most of what was needed for the US military in Vietnam. By 1966 that amounted to billions of US dollars.

Martin Weiss had a very narrow circle of social contacts, always avoiding even minimal publicity, for reasons known only to him. He was maniacally concerned with avoiding any journalists or photographers. Those who had the rare chance to speak with him, however, were always particularly impressed by his gaze: his eyes were at the same time attractive and off-putting. Theirs was a special combination of a deeply hidden, dark threat and a warm flicker of yellow light.

There was another thing about Martin Weiss. At his

---

3. In 1964, the US Congress adopted the Tonkin Resolution, which gave the new President, Lyndon Johnson, the right to use, when needed, military power in Southeast Asia. By the end of 1965, there were around 185,000 US servicemen as part of two full divisions and several brigades. Over the next three years, the US contingent was drastically expanded, reaching 540,000 servicemen at the peak of US involvement.

extremely rare public appearances, he was always accompanied by a slender, dark-haired, very young girl whose name was Paola. No one knew whether she was his girlfriend or his assistant. Martin Weiss never clarified her role in his life, introducing her simply by saying: 'This is Paola.' That was obviously enough for his conversation partners, as far as he was concerned. Anyone who dared ask further questions trying to clarify the matter would only get Weiss's icy stare in reply. The uncomfortable pause that followed would effectively extinguish any curiosity.

In 1967, Weiss came to Vietnam as a member of a military delegation, with the aim of participating in an extended session of the Joint Chiefs of Staff headed by General Westmoreland, commander of the US Forces in South Vietnam. Several days later, however, Martin Weiss suddenly disappeared. Went missing. Officially, he was recognized as killed by the Viet Cong, even though his body was never recovered. After that, Paola was nowhere to be found. Nor could Weiss's money be traced.

Oh yes, and…Weiss was the spitting image of the late Tom Walker. No one, however, could boast of having known both persons at the same time. So, no links between them seemed to exist, nor could any be established. After all, one was killed by some thugs who dumped his body in Lake Michigan, and the other disappeared in the Vietnamese jungle four years later. May the Lord grant His peace upon the souls of both men…

5

The Controller Appears
Paris Again

When Malin got back to his hotel, he started pacing the room from the bed to the desk and back. He was trying to bring things into focus, to figure out what had happened so far. He also felt he had to come to a decision regarding his next steps.

Okay, suppose I really did discover some facts revealing the actual instigators of the 9/11 and, perhaps, even its perpetrators. I immediately became known to whoever wants to keep the matter swept under the rug. They started exploring the situation, telling me those facts were false, and trying to cover up the whole affair. Richard sensed how hot the issue was right away, so he used their delay in taking action against me to immediately send me away from the States. What's next? Those same people who are interested in my staying mum about the issue were probably the ones who killed Philip Marshall because he was somehow able to collect all those sensitive documents. It seems the FBI understands now that I'm not too keen on dropping an investigation of the worst terrorist attack of the new century. By now they most certainly feel that I couldn't have been so dumb as to only glance through a few pages of that major archive, and they guess that I most certainly copied it. Which means…that I've become their next target…

The silence was suddenly interrupted by his ring tone, the room filling with gravelly voice of Louis Armstrong – 'Go down, Moses, way down to Egypt land. Tell all pharaohs to let my people go!' His cell phone, due to its vibrations, was slowly moving towards the edge of the desk.

Malin grabbed the phone and, as he accepted the call, realized he shouldn't have it would only make it possible to pinpoint his exact location. In the next few seconds, a few thoughts tumbled in at once. One, that it was too late anyway. And two: if they needed it, they would have had no problem locating him in his room here at Hotel Lotti. Three: he hadn't even looked at the caller ID on the display, a sure sign of his internal panic, something that could not be permitted in his situation. Malin knew immediately that he had to slip away from Paris quietly, and as fast as possible.

'Speaking,' he said in a flat voice.

'Hi Malin! It's Jane Thompson calling, y'know, from *The Washington Post*. Sorry to bother you during your trip, but you said you could help me, right? Remember? I mean, about the Kennedy assassination. I couldn't identify all the witnesses who were in the vicinity around the time he was killed. Of course, there are lots of photos, but some people in them were never identified.'

'Who do you think they might be?' Malin asked her, more with the purpose of simply saying something. He was slowly coming back to his senses. He felt now that there was no immediate danger for him in her call.

'See, Malin, the FBI questioned most of the witnesses to the assassination. They also gave some interviews… I sifted through the whole archive and found out that there are six people in the pictures and videos who were never questioned, even though they were looking straight at the motorcade. There are no stories from them or about them. Some of them look quite young, so they should still be alive today. Wouldn't it be great if we could find and interview them? Right? Like, about what they felt back then? Can you help me with this? You promised…'

'Fine,' Malin said. He was sure his phone was bugged. He decided he should show calm and composure to demonstrate his lack of understanding of the real situation. That might buy him some time. 'Fine, Jane. Send me the pics so I can study them and run them by my sources. I'll call you back in a day or two. Or write back, depending. Will that do?'

'Oh Malin, you're so sweet! I'm almost in love with you right now… Okay, sending you the pics. That's it. Done! I'm signing off, I'll wait for your news. Bye!'

'Adieu, ciao and good luck, Jane.'

'Same to you, Malin.'

He knew that any sign of his being in a panic would only cause a corresponding reaction in whoever was after him. So, he turned on his laptop and, having opened Jane's message, started going through the old photos she sent over, without haste.

He was revisiting events that had taken place decades ago and wasn't really paying due attention. He quickly scanned the faces of the unknown persons in the crowd. Well, not all were unknown. This one, for example, was Cecil Stoughton, President Kennedy's personal photographer. He looked completely bewildered and very scared. And that was Wes Wise, an ex-mayor of Dallas and a journalist. Oh wow! This guy was Abraham Zapruder himself. Twirling his film camera in his hands, also looking perplexed, he was peering at something, looking above the heads of the people in the crowd. Yes, it was definitely Zapruder, the man who, by complete chance, had filmed the moment Kennedy was killed. The twenty-six-second film had become a historic document of the tragic event. Next to Zapruder, half-turned, stood a young lady who seemed in the middle of saying something to him. To his right, there stood a tall young man, perhaps around thirty. His raven-black hair was combed back, and his glance was piercing. Malin suddenly froze, studying the man's face. He was sure that he had seen him somewhere! He knew that he knew him from somewhere! He had already seen this man with the stern, chiseled features, that strange half-smile that did not, in fact, express any emotion. He had certainly seen those deep-set, severe eyes with a somewhat slithery little glint in them. Oh God, no… Shit, it *was* him! It couldn't be!

The man in this photo was the spitting image of the mysterious stranger who had been with the Russian delegation to the IMF in 1998… And he was certainly the same tall, grey-haired old man on Washington Street, looking on at the World Trade Center attack in New York City in 2001. So many years after the Kennedy assassination, the man was still recognizable.

Some people may not have been able to recognize a thirty-something man in a photograph of a seventy-year-old. But Max Malin was different. He had not even the slightest doubt that all three photos captured the same person – in 1963, in 1998 and in 2001!

Maybe it wasn't possible. If it was, then why would all three photos find their way to me? Malin began his well-trained routine of analyzing even the most unanticipated events. Okay, say this stranger really was there, right in the thick of things? It would almost certainly mean that it was no coincidence. If things coincide twice, it's most probably just chance. But if it happens three times, that has to be a trend, a recognizable pattern. Then are these three important, major events somehow connected? Even by the presence of just one person? But hey, Kennedy's assassination, the theft of Russia's billion-dollar loan, and 9/11…these are no small potatoes – and he was there, every time!

Let's assume that this man represents some international criminal group. A group capable of planning and executing all three events in pursuit of its own goals. Which goals? We don't know anything about that, yet. Maybe he's some kind of a Controller – someone who checks things out, makes sure they're executed according to plan, all the way through to the last stage of the process. Okay, I'll call him Controller for now.

If so, then it's tempting to keep in mind the option that it might have been this Controller who spoke with 'James' two hours before the attack on the twin towers. Wait, but 'James' was talking from inside the FBI building in New York…and the voice of the Controller is available in the recording at the Marshall Archive. Oh, it's all starting to make sense! It's crystal clear, then, why the FBI is pursuing me now. But what if it isn't the FBI anymore? What if they only reported to someone else that I found access to the archive they know is missing? Then this manhunt becomes someone else's responsibility. Why not the Organization for whom the Controller works? Or was working until recently…? Shit! All of this is crazy – and, as always, there are more questions than answers. Nevertheless, it looks like I have stumbled into something beyond all normal reasoning. Something very dangerous.

Still, how come all these pieces of the puzzle related to the Controller ended up in my lap? How is that possible? Malin started wondering. He had already closed his laptop, and was now only lost in thought, sitting in a wide, comfortable chair. Such things do happen, of course. Sometimes you fish for years and net nothing big. But if you hit a whole school of fish, all of a sudden there's a huge catch. Then it means having luck in its pure form... There may be nothing for a long time, but then all you have to do is haul and haul loads of whatever you've got... Shit! Shit! I'll have to disappear into thin air now, there's no question about that. Leave this hotel, leave Paris, cut off all connections, find different ways to communicate... I want to stay alive, too... If I can really disentangle this maze and make my investigation public or, better, write a book about it, then my name will certainly end up in the annals of global journalism. And, well, there's a shitload of money in this, too... Forgive my cynical attitude, O Lord.

The quiet street gradually filled with the noise of voices. Malin, shaken from his deep reflections, felt as if the swelling din was so loud and powerful that it had thrown open one of his windows. He got up and looked outside. The Rue de Castiglione was seething with people now. This was the Gay Pride Parade. Thousands were moving slowly towards Place Vendôme, dancing and making a lot of noise. An unimaginable din rose to the sky. The huge human serpent turned slowly from Rue de Rivoli, filling all the small streets in the area. A motley crowd stopped for a short while before the hotel entrance: somebody had gotten sick. Hotel doormen rushed to a bespangled and beplumed young man who had fainted, and now lay in a rather picturesque pose on the sidewalk.

Malin realized this would be his best chance to slip away. He quickly downloaded all the information he needed from his laptop to a small flash drive. Though no larger than a bone in his little finger, it could hold the Marshall Archive, Oleg Artayev's photos, all the images from Dallas, and much more, whatever Malin might need. Then, acting automatically, he quickly opened his notebook and retrieved its hard drive. He shoved it into the inside pocket of his jacket, adding his passport, credit cards, and cash. He left his other belongings in some disarray around the room, so that his pursuers would have the impression that he would be back soon. He left both smartphones lying around – their SIM cards had been purchased under his name anyway. Malin opened the door gently, making sure no one observed him leaving his room. Then he walked down the corridor and down the stairway to the hotel lobby. He snuck out into the street and was immediately engulfed by the exuberant, motley crowd of the Pride parade.

Paris bustled with life on this warm and sunny Saturday. Relaxed, casually dressed Parisians occupied tables on cafe terraces along the Boulevard des Capucines. People eyed the throngs of tourists aiming their cameras and smartphones at old buildings and bright shop windows. Unhurried French conversation was at times drowned out by the hubbub of Chinese, Russian, and English phrases flying about on all sides, creating a special, unique, and monotonous background sound. The exquisite aroma of good coffee wafting from every café along the way was truly tantalizing. One was tempted to sit down at a free little table between two maples and enjoy life…

Malin, however, went straight to a bank where he could extract cash from his account, everything in it – almost thirty thousand Euros. The ATM whirred quietly, letting him take that amount, plus another nine thousand thanks to the limit on his gold credit card. This was the last transaction that could help his pursuers trace his location. He walked to the nearest electronics shop, some five hundred yards away, where he bought two mobile phones and a small, powerful laptop with a case. He transferred the contents of his pockets into the case, feeling that now he was ready for anything. For now, he was fine. Beyond their reach.

He found a taxi stand, got into a car, and asked the driver to take him to Avenue d'Ivry in the 13th arrondissement. The noisy downtown stayed behind, and in no time, he saw shops and businesses with names written in Chinese and Vietnamese outside the car window. The small shops were surrounded by rather short men. Some wore conical rice hats, and they chatted animatedly. There was a McDonald's at the intersection, its name repeated in three Chinese characters. Malin got off in front of it and started walking the maze of little streets in the area. This was the gigantic Parisian Chinatown. Pretty soon Malin found what he was looking for: a small hotel at the intersection of two quiet streets, with rundown walls, a low bifold door and an obligatory pair of Chinese lanterns hanging outside.

A fat, bald Chinese man sat behind the counter in a tacky, poorly lit lobby. He looked up without haste at the new guest when he heard the doorbell ring. His eyes showed fleeting surprise, but in a moment his expression changed to one of expectant imperturbability. Malin told him that he would like a quiet room for a couple of days. He gave his name as Joshua Irving and said he would pay for his stay in advance. The fat Chinese announced a rate twice as high as was usual for hotels of this class. Malin paid him in cash, and the man tactfully forgot the required check of the guest's papers. A minute later, Malin was ascending the super-narrow staircase to the third floor, holding the room key in his hand. The key was attached to a large wooden ball, on which was engraved the room number.

The room proved minimalist even by Chinese standards, but it was fine with Malin, who had no entourage to mind. Besides, he would have felt equally comfortable at the Ritz or in a tent in the jungle. This square room was almost entirely occupied by a huge and very low bed – rather, a mattress placed atop a wooden frame. The only other item of furniture in the room was a cloudy mirror surrounded by several Chinese prints. The only window opened to the neighboring street.

Malin lay on the bed and, taking out his flash drive, started perusing the photos and documents. He was making every effort now to put his constellation of ideas in some order, using the bits of information that, by complete chance, had come his way. As they had captured his attention, they had of course resulted in some rather unexpected developments.

Looks like I've come across some morsels of information, Malin thought, and they are all related to some clandestine organization. It may have existed long enough to have been behind Kennedy, the IMF loan theft, and the WTC attack, right? Well, it might not necessarily be a terrorist organization… What if it's not even an organization, but one evil genius pulling the strings?

Well, on the other hand, I know some things that seem pretty disturbing. One is the face of their Controller, a man who was present during all three events. Two: they seem to be somehow connected to the FBI and perhaps even the White House administration. Three: even though I've slipped out of their field of vision for now, they will certainly keep looking for me. It might not be the FBI anymore, and not the special services who were unable to get me in D.C. – it might be this Organization itself. Most importantly, they don't know yet that I am aware of what the Controller looks like. Or that I have evidence that the three events are connected…

But what should I do next? I could hunker down here for a while. In the meantime, I could try discovering some links leading to the Organization. Or at least find some more information so I can analyze its activities over many years. It's impossible that it wouldn't give itself away in one way or another.

6

Jia

Day was slowly turning into night. Electrical advertising flashed irregularly on a building roof nearby, creating amorphous light patches inside the room, playing on its whitish walls. Malin sank back against the pillows and dozed, dropping in and out of a sleep so light it was almost imperceptible, soft, and tender, like wispy clouds in early summer.

On the other side of his door, Malin heard a woman's loud shriek in the corridor, followed by a man's screechy shouting the exchange entirely in Chinese. He had barely gotten off the bed when there was a loud banging sound – someone had obviously been pushed against the door of his room. The woman screamed again.

Malin shook off the rest of his sleepiness. His body tightened, and he became like a stretched wire. Had they already found him? He walked noiselessly to the door, looked through the peephole. The door of the room opposite his was wide open, and a young Chinese man was standing there. He looked on as a tall woman struggled with another Chinese man, who held her by the shoulders. In the next moment, the man grabbed her and shook her violently, yelling something that sounded menacing. She looked at him with disdain and spat something in return. His reaction was to let go of her and immediately strike her so hard across the face that she fell, knocking her head again Malin's room door.

This was too much for Malin. Flinging open the thin wooden door, he jumped over the Chinese woman who now lay on the floor and hit straight at the man's face. He fell without uttering a sound. The other man jumped into the corridor and, taking a guarded stance, slowly approached Malin, who could not help smiling when he saw that the scantily clad young man had his eyes made up with eyeliner, eye shadow, and mascara. Suddenly the man jumped at him, hitting Malin hard in the chin. Of course, that was the wrong move. Malin leaned backwards and then, spinning around, sent him hurling against the wall with a powerful kick. Ushiro mawashi worked exactly as it was supposed to.[1] The Chinese man lost all his drive and slid slowly downwards, spreading out on the floor next to the other man.

'Hey, what did you do? You didn't kill him, did you?' The voice came from behind Malin, and he turned around. It was a woman's voice, soft, slightly husky.

She had already gotten up and, leaning on the doorpost, was trying to wipe off the blood that trickled from a split lip, leaving several bright red lines on her tanned cheek.

'No. They'll be fine quite soon. Back to their senses in about five to ten minutes,' Malin said quietly, his eyes glued to the young woman. 'The second guy may have a slight concussion, but not more than that. What about you? How are you?'

Despite the rather awkward situation, when Malin saw this strange Chinese woman, he was involuntarily lost in admiration. She was probably twenty-five, and quite tall, with a very slender figure. Long black

---

1. Ushiro mawashi geri (Karate Kyokushinkai) is a reverse turning kick using one leg against the head area of the opponent.

hair framed her beautiful features, with pronounced cheekbones. Her eyes were like wide almonds, and her straight, thin nose was in ideal harmony with her lips, which even now curved slightly in a light smile.

'I'm okay,' the woman said in a low voice. 'The only thing is…we're going to need to leave, and fast. It's going to become a hotspot for us in no time.'

'First off, I'm Malin,' Malin said, his gaze still glued to the girl. 'And secondly…where did you get the idea that I need to leave this place? I was asleep in my room, by the way, when your friends started banging on the door. I am staying here, you know.'

'I'm Jia. I'm the stepsister of this dimwit,' she pointed at the younger of the two men, both of whom were still lying motionless on the floor. 'Guangming is a ladyboy, a transvestite. I wouldn't care about his private life if he wasn't in danger from selling sex to all these rich party animals. The police will arrive here in about half an hour because an informer tipped them off that a sex and drugs party is about to start here. This animal here,' Jia, with an expression of disgust, kicked the older Chinese man with her leg, 'invited two drug dealers to come over, and they're supposed to be here about now. He wanted to buy a lot of their stuff. So, you can imagine how hot this whole situation is going to become.'

'Hold on, Jia, wait a second! What makes you think I should be leaving here too?' Malin asked as he took the girl into his room, quietly closing the door.

'Oh, you probably think well-dressed Americans often come to France in order to get a room in the cheapest and dingiest hotel in Paris Chinatown?' Her voice was full of derision. 'It's obvious that you have no desire to meet with the police, or someone else, perhaps.'

'I guess you're right. I should beat it, then. I'm not a native-born American, though, by the way, I was born in Russia,' Malin said, quickly throwing his few belongings into the computer case. 'And what about your stepbrother? Do you want him to stay behind here?'

'I already know he wouldn't leave. – Guangming told me that when I talked to him... Malin, hurry up!'

Malin began to collect up her things while she spoke.

'Oh, you must have heard some of our exchange. No, he made his final choice, and he's on his way to the abyss... I've been trying to save him, but this was my last stand. I was the one who told a police informer about today's party. I wanted to take my brother away from all these people, so I told him that he has to leave with me before the drug dealers and the police show up. But Guangming just hit me and told me I was a traitor. So now I should go hide someplace too...'

'Got it, Jia. Let's run.'

Minutes after exiting the hotel, they were walking beneath the pale light of Chinese lanterns, which flickered in the uneasy darkness of the Parisian night. The streets of Chinatown seemed to be slumbering after a busy day, but every side street seemed to be harboring some danger hidden in its pitch-black nooks and crannies. Jia, completely at home here, confidently directed her light steps through the maze of little lanes. Malin kept looking at her and thinking that she looked like a teenager in her skinny T-shirt and dark jeans. And that she seemed a strange participant for the kind of the cruel and brutal incident that had so suddenly brought them together.

'We should find a cab stand,' Malin said in a husky voice. 'Or get a room in some hotel around here.'

'There's no way we could find a cab here at this hour, and as for hotels,' Jia turned towards him and smiled, 'they can be a problem – I mean, those that ask for IDs. I'm guessing you wouldn't be too eager to produce yours.'

'You are amazingly perceptive. So maybe you can direct me to a different place around here? You seem local, right?'

'Let's go to Sue Lee. She is my only friend who Guangming doesn't know. She's a maid at a small hotel nearby which is quite decent. Well, she started as a maid, but now she's managing it, sort of... The owner is her boyfriend now. I'm hoping we can lie low there for a while.'

Malin nodded silently. He had no choice anyway. All he needed was a day or two in a secure place so he could figure out his next moves. He had already cooked up some ideas about how he could proceed with his search for the mysterious stranger whose chance appearance in Malin's life had started this crazy chain of events.

After passing several lanes, Jia rang the bell of a small hotel, the name of which was only listed in Chinese characters. Its door was sandwiched between the entrances to a grocery store and to some undefined office, perhaps involved in currency exchange, or placing bets, or both. A woman answered sleepily over the intercom in Chinese. After a short exchange, the door unlocked, and they entered a decent, tidy lobby.

A moment later Sue Lee appeared, a small Chinese woman wrapped in a morning gown, still looking very sleepy. She kissed Jia and led them to the first floor. As she walked down the corridor, she said there were no rooms available yet, and she could only offer one that had just been vacated a couple hours prior. It was, however, quite tidy, and the room was big, with two beds and a shower in a half-bathroom. She also said that sleeping was more important than money now, so Malin could pay for the room later, in daylight.

Soon Malin and Jia found themselves sitting next to each other in a large, clean, rather nice room featuring two beds, a desk, and an armoire. They were silent for a while, each musing to themselves. Jia was the first to interrupt the silence, asking the obvious:

'Are you a criminal? Are they hunting you down?'

'They are indeed after me, but I'm not a criminal,' Malin answered, leaning back on the headboard.

'I see... So, you're in the mob, and it's your pals who are after you?'

'No, not really. I got into a real mess, so everybody seems to be after me at this point,' Malin said with a slight laugh, opening his laptop. 'You should sleep now. Get some rest. I have to check some things online. Don't worry, I won't peek at you or harass you or anything. Word of honor.'

'I'm not worried,' Jia said, barely audible. She was already sitting on her bed cross-legged, having pulled the plaid cover over her shoulders. She turned off the lights, and the shimmer of the desk lamp in front of Malin gave her face a yellowish hue that made her chiseled features look like an unreal marble creation.

'I'm not afraid of you,' she said, her voice growing husky. 'I have no idea why. But I've been through a lot in my life already, so believe me, I get this feeling inside me if there's some danger around. Any danger. I can sense it in advance. Just as I did in that hotel over there. I don't sense anything about you that's dangerous to me. On the contrary, there's a sense of peace, calm, and silence. Oh, sorry, maybe you need silence...'

Malin silently looked at Jia. She was sitting still, her head inclined to the wall, her eyes closed. A new feeling, which had arisen in him when they entered this room, was spreading in him now. It was an unusual feeling for him, enticing, and bewildering in its unreality. It was a feeling of enormous lightness and ease. All his tension, all the tumult of recent days was suddenly gone, as if they had been dropped into a deep, dark chasm. They were beyond a threshold now, one that only he could step over if he chose to. Here was this woman who had somehow ended up his companion tonight. Strange feeling. Nor was it related to what he had experienced with dozens of other women. Not even with the one and only, his old flame of long ago. This time things seemed much more complex and obscure. Nothing was clear, even though something had come into existence already…

Malin got up and walked noiselessly towards Jia. She sensed it, of course, so she stood up opening her eyes and taking the plaid off her shoulders. She met him midway. He embraced her, feeling a warm current flowing through her body. Time stood still. Then it fell apart into millions of shards and was no more. A police car, sirens blaring and wailing, rushed around somewhere far outside their room.

It was almost noon when the sun broke through the clouds, suddenly flooding the room. Malin stopped peering into the computer screen and was lost in admiration of Jia, seeing her awaken slowly. Neither the loud traffic outside nor the penetratingly shrill chatter of the people lunching on the ground floor café could distract Malin from this woman's unhurried surfacing from the realm of dreams. This was the moment when the unnamed and undefined inherent quality of her charm came out in full force, arresting his gaze again and again.

Malin had spent several hours during the night trying to stir up some evidence related to his theory. He had pored over a multitude of photos online related to major terrorist attacks, to the big events that had influenced global politics since Kennedy's assassination in 1963, changing the alignment of forces around the world. He studied the faces of passersby who had become unwitting witnesses to those events. He was almost eager to see that familiar face again. When Malin returned to the desk, he opened one more file filled with hundreds of deeply disturbing photographs: so many dead, so many buildings blown apart, so many women running from danger, covering their children with their bodies…

Malin reached the files of photos taken during the attempt to assassinate Pope John Paul II in 1981.[2] There were hundreds of high-resolution images there, as well as several videos that made it possible to see quite clearly the faces of those present in the square, both at the moment the shots had been fired and over the next few minutes.

Here was the adoring crowd welcoming the Popemobile, which at one point stopped for a moment. The Pope raised a blonde girl of three high above the crowd and then leaned over the guardrail to hand her back to her parents. Before straightening up, he patted two more children on their backs. Then his car started moving, and shots rang out right away. The Pope fell into the hands of his personal aide and his secretary, who were in the car with him.

In the frame behind the collapsing Pope, Malin saw that several boys were trying to see what was wrong with him. They were standing opposite the place from which the shots had come. Also clearly visible were the faces of three men right behind the boys. The one in the middle of the three was staring at the scene with no emotion, while everyone around him appeared extremely agitated. They were all looking in the same direction, anxiously craning their necks, trying to figure out what had happened to the Pope. Only this man

---

2. Mehmet Ali Ağca, a religious fanatic from Turkey, seriously wounded Pope John Paul II on May 13, 1981, when the papal cortege was passing through St. Peter's Square in Rome.

was impassive, looking on calmly as if he knew full well what was going on.

'Here he is!' Malin exclaimed. He turned around to see if this woke Jia, but she was still sleeping. He glued his eyes to the computer screen again. Yes, the man in this photograph was the same person whose face had attracted his attention in the photo taken during the assassination of Kennedy. The same man who was in New York near the twin towers as they collapsed. The same man in the images sent in from Russia and Monaco related to the theft of the IMF loan and the murder of the Swiss banker...

1963 in Dallas, 1998 in Moscow and Monaco, 2001 in New York...and now here he was in Rome, in 1981. The difference in age did not prevent Malin from clearly recognizing that it was the same man with basically the same features, gaze, and posture. In 1963 he must have been close to thirty, and the 1981 image from Rome showed him to be around fifty.

Malin walked over to the open window and looked down, taking in the morning bustle of the Paris Chinatown. He kept asking himself how it could happen that several of the biggest mysteries of the last century had suddenly fallen into his lap? What crooked miles their binding thread must have followed. The thread's origin went as far back as 1963, and it appeared to be connecting events that could not, at first sight, be connected at all. Who had presented this thread to him, a Russian-born American by the name of Max Malin? Would he be able to get any deeper insight into those events? Despite all the facts he had accumulated so far, he was still far from having a clear understanding of the big picture. Still, Malin could almost physically feel that the big picture was within reach, that it was close by, that it only required some more effort. He already knew that, sooner or later, this crazy mosaic was bound to come into focus, with a unique but comprehensible outline.

Jia came over to the window, too. She was wrapped in her plaid cover.

'Did you win?' she asked, her voice still sleepy.

'Not yet. Right now, I'm probably even more confused than before. I have discovered so much so quickly that I feel a bit overwhelmed. And maybe frightened.'

He grew silent. Looking out the window, he suddenly thought that this mysterious chain of events might have something to do with the image of Jia, now snugly seated in a disproportionately large chair. *What a strange idea*, he thought. Malin had never told anyone any details of his investigations. Except Richard Berwick, of course. This time, with Jia, he felt differently. He thought, for some unexplainable reason, that Jia might unavoidably play a role in his research of this strange affair. Perhaps even a major role.

Malin crossed the room slowly and poured himself some coffee from the pot. Then he sat down in front of the laptop and turned it towards Jia.

'Listen, Jia, I'd like to tell you something. I can show you things here that might seem pretty strange to you. Or even impossible. Even I can't yet grasp their significance. All I know so far are some bits of information I was able to discover…but it all seems so strange that I don't know what to do next. I'm not even sure I should share this with you. What if my telling you these things were to become dangerous for you too?'

'Malin, don't worry about me. All I want now is to share things with you. This may sound banal, perhaps, or like what they would write in those dumb stories they call "women's fiction". But still, here's how I feel: I would like to walk by your side. Do you hear me? That's what I want! I don't know what it'll be like tomorrow, or in a month, but today I feel like I'm bound to stay at your side. And, well, there's a selfish side to it too, because it's something I crave, you see.' Jia smiled and continued: 'I don't really care if you tell me the whole thing or not... That's of minor importance to me. Even if you decided to conceal it from me, I would only follow you without any understanding of what is going on.'

Well, that certainly made Malin talk. He told Jia everything, excluding only some details that he would definitely explain to her later. He started with the appearance in D.C. of the man who had sold the Marshall Archive to his newspaper and told her everything up to his latest discovery this morning. He showed her the documents and photos from the archive, relating in broad detail the stories of events that had happened over fifty years earlier. He felt increasingly surprised upon hearing her comments and questions. He was amused and happy to learn that this woman for whom he already felt some desire was not only very beautiful, but also a smart and introspective companion, a partner.

'Who are you? Where do you come from?' Malin suddenly asked her in a low voice, in the middle of his story. 'This can't be true, right? Why are you familiar with everything I've been telling you about? How can you exhibit the logical capacities of a pro from the special services, or an experienced journalist? And you've already become the only woman I could feel dependent on. Even though we've only just met. Even though I don't know anything about you.'

'Okay, Malin.' Jia's voice took on an edge of huskiness again. 'I will tell you where I come from and who I am, but I don't think you'll like it – you're so righteous, so good...almost a Knight without Fear and beyond Reproach, someone fighting for the Truth...'

'Don't be silly! At this point I'm trying to save my

life. And from now on, yours too, maybe, because both of us are in quite a mess. Shall I continue? You know as much as I do. So, tell me everything. It's your turn.'

'But since you told me your story, Malin,' Jia said, not minding his interjection, 'you certainly have the right to know the truth about me. But it's going to be much shorter than your story. My name is Jia Sheng, I was born in China in 1988, in Chengdu, the capital of Sichuan. But that doesn't mean much, it's only names and numbers.

'Much more important is that my dad was a Lung Tao[3] in London. Lung Tao means Dragon Head. That's the Chinese name for the head of a triad – what they'd call mafia in Europe. My Dad, whose name was Bei Sheng, was head of the Chinese mafia in central London for seventeen years. And I was his little flower and his reason to live. I was able to go to the best schools until I was twenty. I got the best teachers in any subject. From Chinese science and history to the most recent scientific advances in the West. I studied ancient philosophers all the way to, say, F. Scott Fitzgerald and Brodsky. Dad also allowed me to be present at all important meetings and talks, which was against triad tradition – women have always been excluded from such events.'

'Where is your dad these days? Why are you here in Paris?'

'The great Bei Sheng died ten years ago, in the summer of 2008. He may have been poisoned. But no one could find out the real cause of his death, and the post-mortem examination showed no trace of poison in his body…at least, that's what was made public. In reality everyone in his close circle knew Sheng was poi-

---

3. Lung Tao (Dragon Head, 龍頭), also called Dai Lo (Big Brother) is the head of the Triads (Chinese mafia) in a certain region.

soned. Chinese medicine counts hundreds of methods for how a person can be put on the path to death with no residual effects.

'Well, no one could prove anything, and my great father left this world unavenged. I couldn't stay in London where everything reminded me of him – everything around me was suffused with his spirit. So, I told the new Lung Tao that I wanted to leave England. He didn't object, so I left for Paris. I could live here on a small allowance supplied by the treasurer of the London triad.'

'I see. But what about your stepbrother, the one you had that run-in with?'

'Guangming was expelled from the Family. They would not tolerate either his sexual proclivities or his taste for cocaine. This was before my father's death. Guangming was getting paid for sex and used the money he earned to buy drugs. He found me here in Paris sometime later. I felt pity for him, like I always used to – I was the only one in the Family who had shown this good-for-nothing any warmth. He doesn't exist for me anymore... Malin, what does that look mean? Am I no longer within the bounds of your morality as the daughter of a triad head?'

Malin said nothing, only stepped towards Jia and pulled her to him. Silence wrapped around them. Even the cars outside stopped honking. They stayed like this for a long while, all three of them – silence being the third member of their union. They did not know time anymore. Now they knew everything that was needed to take part in such a long silence.

When the Parisian night eventually interrupted their embrace, when the ceiling in this room was once again painted by the soft flares of car headlights and the flickering of neighboring advertisement displays, Malin felt he should start doing something to jumpstart the process, get things rolling. Immediately, not a second later. Like when the subconscious catches a barely audible note, and for a while you try to define this elusive feeling, to keep it in your memory.

He sat down before his laptop and quickly wrote a short note. He inserted into the file the four photographs from 1963, 1981, 1998, and 2001, highlighting the face of the mysterious stranger. This was what he wrote:

I am Max Malin, investigative journalist with The Washington Post (though I may not be employed there any longer). Many of you likely knew my name in connection with my exposé reports. Today my life is in danger. I must hide somewhere in Europe. Yesterday I narrowly escaped an attempt on my life. I know that the danger comes from the US Special Services, which found out that I have very sensitive evidence with regard to their involvement in certain events. There is also danger from an organization, of which I know very little – only that it is responsible for several top-notch criminal acts over the last fifty years. Special Services may in fact be connected with the Organization in some way.

I have serious evidence that tragedies that seem unconnected were initiated by the same people. Here is just one piece of that evidence:

The same person was present at the assassination of President Kennedy in 1963, the attempted assassination of the Pope in 1981, the theft of the IMF's billion-dollar loan to Russia in 1998, as well as related murders of witnesses in 1999, and at the 9/11 attack on the Twin Towers in New York. You can see this person in the photographs I was able to obtain. Look at them attentively and you will see that age does not change his appearance too much. There is no way it can be a coincidence or, for example, image doctoring.

This is only one part of the tremendous and shocking mosaic that may reveal the actual full picture. You can find out the full story from me, journalist Max Malin. Then the whole world will shudder at the cynical misdeeds that have occurred over the last fifty years, and many people who have until now been regarded as VIPs will have to go into hiding or blow their brains out.

For now, I'm the one in hiding, due to a manhunt organized to catch me. If anything were to happen to me, you must know it to be a result of the efforts of special services from various countries, especially that of the USA, and of the mysterious Organization I discovered. A representative of this Organization or possibly even its head is depicted in the photos.

I warn all those who have been trying to eliminate me: I have copied all documents, as well as all the proof I know about, and hid them in several safe locations. If you are successful in eliminating me, all those documents will appear online and become publicly available to all media.

My dear readers, I am respectfully yours.
Max Malin

'Why do you need this?' Jia asked. She was leaning over Malin' shoulder.

'I have to do something. I…we are stuck now, suspended over an abyss. If we don't end this impasse, all that remains for us would be to hide in this blasted Chinatown expecting to die at any minute. I don't know what might happen next, but I expect nothing good. Experience tells me I have to go on with this investigation, but I need to somehow make myself safe from them. Otherwise, our bodies will be found in the Seine within days. There's this method of fishing called live bait…'

'What do you mean?'

'When this information appears on Internet, it will be spread very quickly, all over the place. For a moment, at least, it'll become a sensation. That will force them to take some action, giving us a chance to move forward in our research.'

'Them? We still don't have even the foggiest idea who "they" might be, what they want or what their next moves would be…'

'You're right, Jia. This is exactly why I am about to release some of the facts, make them widely available. Then we'll see what's cooking…'

Malin soon slipped out of the hotel and found a cab a couple blocks away. A flash stick in his pocket contained a copy of his open letter and the photos. After a forty-minute ride, with the Eiffel Tower on the left, the car easily made it through the roundabout at Avenue de Tourville and stopped on Rue de Babylone before a small cybercafé with a rather queer name: B@by Connect.

Usually on a Paris evening there are plenty of people everywhere, but in this café, there were only five or six clients, all of them staring intensely at their monitors. Malin rented the computer for an hour. First, he opened his Facebook page. His page had been very popular in recent years, because it was there that he always placed links to his articles, investigative reports, and official documents.

A few minutes later, Malin inserted his open letter, including all four photos, onto his page. Despite a sudden last-minute feeling of hesitation, he pressed the Publish button. Then he copied it to thirty of Facebook's most popular groups and posted a link to his Twitter account too, making the letter available to the more than two hundred thousand followers of popular journalist Max Malin. Malin estimated that around half a million Internet users would read his text, but he was certain it would spread all over the Internet. Thus, he was counting on millions of readers by next morning before his opponents came to their senses to do something about it.

Leaving B@by Connect, he dialed Jia's number, mumbling a quick message – 'All done. Coming to you.' – and walked quickly to the metro at Sèvres-Babylone.

Warm drizzle greeted him in the empty street. His face got wet immediately, little trickles starting a treacherous journey down his collar. The wind was strong enough to play around with a piece of an old rain pipe, rolling it here and there with a noise reminiscent of a distant crash of thunder. Suddenly an intense, piercing fear went straight into the deepest realms of Malin's consciousness. It pressed against the last limit of the hidden reserves of his will, which had seemed safe, unyielding. He looked back anxiously to check whether anyone was following him. And then he started to run. He felt better only once he was among the crowds of the metro, surrounded by passengers rushing on all sides, or talking animatedly.

A few hours after Malin returned to the hotel, he and Jia discovered that all of his accounts had been broken into, and that the letter he'd posted online had mostly disappeared. However, whoever had been so eager to prevent the spread of Malin's first revelations had acted too late. Thousands of copies had already been copied and shared around the Web. Any serious publication, however, both in Europe and in the USA, had kept mum. Not one had published anything about his sensational revelations...not even one word about 'Malin's sensation'. Nowhere, not on a single major newspaper or information agency site. Even though they all knew the name Max Malin.

Drifting off to sleep, Malin had this thought: the fact that all of his colleagues around the world were silent was a confirmation of this Organization's power. This was the result he had been eager to obtain. His discovery appeared to have startled someone among the most powerful in the world, perhaps someone truly omnipotent. And it was they who ordered all media outlets, even those deemed "serious" and "independent", to remain silent. And his colleagues, alas, had followed orders, waiting for the outcome, the end of the story...

Paris wakes up around six in the morning. This is a rule all over the city, from the aristocratic Rue du Faubourg-Saint-Honoré to the self-reliant Chinatown. Tousled heads lift from warm pillows. Sleepy children try to wave away splashes of sunlight that dart through little openings in blinds rustled by a light morning breeze. Women who looked delicious the night before rush to their bathrooms, seeking to reclaim yesterday's level of beauty. The rising din of the streets, coming through closed windows into bedrooms, fades in the murmur of the air conditioner, but then regroups and grows bothersome, mercilessly stealing the last seconds of anyone's sleep.

Malin woke up to the loud hum of traffic and the growing street noise. He got up from his bed and, stepping quietly in bare feet so as not to wake Jia, went out onto the balcony. Nothing seemed to have changed in the street since yesterday. Still, he felt as if some thin, extremely high-pitched string was vibrating above Chinatown this morning. Oh, shit...no, it had to be nothing... His nerves must have frayed completely. Everything around here was so quiet and nice.

A delivery truck with the logo "La cuisine est délicieuse"[4] on its side was parked at the curb on the op-posite side of the street. One of the many trucks that drives around Paris delivering groceries early in the morning. Hey, wait a minute! The truck was the same one as the day before, only the logo was different. And yesterday there had been two loud young guys unload-ing the truck and taking the goods in to the store. This morning, however, everything around this white truck was strangely quiet, and its cabin was dark. It was sim-ply parked with its engine off. Oh, look, there was the truck that was here yesterday. It's blue, all painted with flowers. It has stopped by the new one, and what did "La cuisine est délicieuse" do? Huh, it started its engine, but didn't go too far, moving slightly off to the side, to a parking spot nearby, close to the next intersection.

Malin could barely contain a desire to rush back into the room. Trying to move quietly, without haste, he stepped inside. Jia was still sleeping. He leaned over her saying:

'Hey, babe, something strange seems to be going on in the street. We'd better leave…and quickly! I'm not a hundred percent sure, but we shouldn't take any risks.'

Jia opened her eyes right away, as if she had been expecting to hear those words from Malin. She got up without a word and started collecting her things. She asked no questions, nor did she attempt to start discuss-ing whether he was right or wrong. Malin felt that this silent trust was his new discovery about the seemingly unreal quality that only Asian women may possess: if he said we must leave, he's right, and that's it.

They were ready to step out of the room when the phone stuck on the small bedside cabinet began to ring. His buzzer sounded insistently and whiny.

---

4. "La cuisine est délicieuse" – French for 'The food is delicious'

Jia answered the phone, listened to the caller for a short while without uttering a word, then said something in Chinese, in a very low voice. When she turned towards Malin, he noted a new, unusual expression in her almond-shaped eyes, as though they reflected flickering flashes of fire.

'It was Sue Lee, Malin. The woman who gave us the room. She said my brother came in a minute ago and that he's asking me to go downstairs and talk to him. Sue Lee said he's drunk and very angry. She felt that it would be better if I could come together with my friend. But there's something wrong here – my brother has never known that Sue Lee exists, and they've never met before. In any case, he couldn't possibly have come to this hotel. Also, her voice sounded different than usual. She never spoke to me in such a manner... And while she was speaking to me in Chinese, she added one word in Korean. She said "dalligi", which means: "run".'

Malin had noticed the day before that their bathroom was adjacent to the bathroom of the next room. Now he grabbed his case and led Jia to the bathroom, where he was able to break through the rather thin wall with a powerful blow of his leg. Luckily, the guests had already moved out of the neighboring room. Malin and Jia slipped into this long, L-shaped room. Its door at the far end led into a narrow, secluded corner, which was 90 degrees to the main corridor.

They opened the door very quietly. When Malin looked around the corner, he saw two men in very long raincoats, completely wrong for the season, who were standing in front of the door to the room Malin and Jia had just left. A third person in the group, a woman, slowly lifted a handgun, ordering: "In there! Go!" In a moment, the men broke down the door and all three disappeared inside the room. Across the corridor, Malin

saw an open door to one more recently vacated gues-
troom. There was wind coming in through the room's
open balcony.

Jia and Malin quickly entered the room, which the
chambermaid had finished cleaning only minutes before: her vacuum cleaner still stood in its center. As they
stepped onto the balcony, they heard a loud voice in
the corridor saying: 'No one's in. But they must have
left only minutes ago. Check the corridors and adjacent rooms. Take 'em alive!' The two fugitives quickly
climbed over the railing, then down the wall, jumped on
the pavement and started running away along a narrow
street, pushing past passersby when they couldn't avoid
them. A gunshot rang out somewhere behind them.

The truck with the upbeat "La cuisine est délicieuse"
logo sped off now but bumped into another parked
car. Still, it attempted to block their path. Malin took
a sharp turn, dragging Jia after him, and they ran into
the nearest alley. Malin, running in front of Jia, bumped
into a young man who had suddenly stepped out of
his BMW roadster. The man kept his balance for a moment, but then tripped on the curbs and fell on the
pavement, cursing loudly. Malin, who by now was in
a kind of trance, smiled amiably and, uttering a very
polite "Pardonne-moi"[5], suddenly grabbed his car keys,
which had fallen onto the pavement. The man couldn't
get up fast enough, and Malin and Jia darted away in
his car, thanks to its powerful engine. Malin managed
to squeeze the roadster past the truck, driving onto
the sidewalk, and then he rushed through the narrow
streets as fast as possible.

'Turn right, Malin! Make a U-turn here and go
down that street!' Jia told him. 'Faster, faster! And now

---

5. I beg your pardon!

brake, please: cops always stand at this spot. Phew…
we're through!'

'Where are we heading?'

'There's someone we have to see, a really special person. He should be able to help us. If he can't, for some
reason, then at least he won't snitch on us. Faster, Malin!'

7

His Holiness Survived
Vatican, May 13, 1981

Having finished a very enjoyable late lunch in the company of his longtime friends, geneticist Jérôme Lejeune[1] and his charming wife Birthe, Pope John Paul II accompanied his guests to the exit of the dining room in the Apostolic Palace, entrusting their further stay to the gentle care of his personal secretary, Stanislav Dziwisz.[2]

The Pope looked at his watch. Almost one hour was left until his appearance before the faithful on St. Peter's Square. The Pope went to his study, slowly lowered himself into his chair and, putting his elbows on the desk, pressed his temples with his hands. He was quite upset after his meeting that morning with Paul Mar-

---

1. **Jérôme Jean Louis Marie Lejeune** (1926-1994) was a French pediatrician and geneticist who made a number of important discoveries regarding chromosomal abnormalities. He was a member of the Pontifical Academy of Sciences and the president of the Pontifical Academy for Life instituted by Pope John Paul II, who was Lejeune's personal friend.

2. **Stanisław Jan Dziwisz** (born in 1939) is a Polish prelate of the Catholic Church. He was a personal aide to Pope John Paul II from 1978 to 2005.

cinkus,[3] head of the Vatican Bank, and Roberto Calvi,[4] chairman of the Banco Ambrosiano.

The two had been exchanging desperate glances, looking mostly at each other, and trying not to look straight at the Pope. Still, they confirmed that billions owned by Vatican had been illegally moved through the Catholic Banco Ambrosiano. It was not this, however, that had upset the Pope, even though it was he who he had recently initiated simultaneous financial investigations into the Vatican Bank and the Banco Ambrosiano. The real shock had come after Calvi, who was nicknamed 'God's banker', had revealed a much more serious fact, which Marcinkus had confirmed. This was that billions of dollars originating from the Chinese triads[5] and the Italian Cosa Nostra[6] had been laundered through Banco Ambrosiano, known in the private circle of the initiated as the 'Papal bank'. Ambrosiano was now on the brink of bankruptcy. This would affect the Vatican's financial institutions. Calvi was imploring the Pope to stop the investigation for at least a few months,

3. **Paul Casimir Marcinkus** (1922–2006) was a Catholic bishop and, from 1971 to 1989, the president of the Vatican Bank (IOR, or Istituto per le Opere di Religione, that is Institute for Works of Religion). In 1982 his reputation was compromised due to the scandalous collapse of the Banco Ambrosiano, the largest privately-owned bank in Italy, which had very close financial relations with the IOR.

4. **Roberto Calvi** (1920–1982) was chairman of the Banco Ambrosiano, the largest Italian privately-owned bank. He was in the focus of financial scandals which resulted in the bank's collapse in 1982. Calvi immediately fled to London and soon was found dead there.

5. Triads (三合會) are Chinese criminal groups, organized as a transnational syndicate based in China proper and having branches in countries with sizeable ethnic Chinese population.

6. Cosa Nostra is a Sicilian criminal organization, more commonly known as Mafia. Lazio, the Italian administrative region that includes Rome, is in the mafia's sphere of influence.

to give him time to siphon off the criminal money. Then the unseemly affair could be terminated quietly, without attracting attention.

When the Pope heard Calvi's suggestion, he flew into a rage, which was very unusual for him. He even banged his fist against the top of the desk.

'Investigations will continue,' he said, 'and all those guilty of misconduct will be punished. That is the end of the conversation!'

'Your Holiness,' Roberto Calvi murmured, inclining his head, 'if investigations are not paused for a while, and Banco Ambrosiano goes bankrupt, then the mafias won't get back their half a billion dollars. Most of this amount is due to the Chinese, as we have almost fully settled our accounts with the Italians. But I have no doubt that they will kill me if they don't get their money. The Chinese are indifferent towards the Catholic faith, but very concerned about their money. They will most certainly go to outrageous extremes. I would not be surprised if both the Vatican and even you, Your Holiness, could be endangered by their retaliation. There can be no guarantees when the triads are involved, because we are all only pawns in their very big games. To them, you are not the Vicar of Christ, Your Holiness, but a simple mortal blocking access to their money...'

'Get out of here, both of you!' the Pope said in a low voice, pointing at the door. 'No one has ever dared threaten me. And you had better acknowledge that I am under the protection of the Virgin Mary and not the Swiss Guard. Your audience is over.'

John Paul's thoughts kept returning to this exchange with the bankers. He recalled every word. It was true that he wasn't afraid – he knew no one would dare raise their hand against the Pope. But if a financial scandal were to become known, the image of the Vatican itself would suffer. To pause the investigations, even temporarily, would be a bit over the top. It would mean the Pope's bowing to the demands of the mafiosi. He could not, he would never do it! But what *should* be his next move? How should he act? Lord, make my spirit firm! Help your humble servant…

Stanislav Dziwisz, his long-time personal aide and friend, and a most serene person, appeared in the door of the study, saying:

'Everything will be fine, your Holiness. Our Lord is with us. Now is the time for you to come out into the square and greet the faithful.'

Paul Morel had never liked Rome. He felt no thrill at its abundant artifacts of antiquity. In fact, he found it rather unsettling – the geographical and temporal continuity set his nerves on edge. Walking through Roman streets made him feel as if he were not fifty-one years old, but much, much older. Now, having left behind him the bend of the Tiber and the somber Castel Sant'Angelo on its shore, Morel moved down Borgo Santo Spirito towards the St. Peter's Square, displaying quite some haste. This tall, well-built, black-haired gentleman was never to be lost on the beautiful Italian women, who were attracted to his chiseled profile, as well as to his dark eyes with the incredibly riveting yellowish spark in them.

'Senti, Superman vuole anche vedere il Papa!'[7] Paul heard two young girls chirp behind him. He only smiled and walked faster. But a minute later, when he was already quite far from these descendants of the Roman patricians, he donned a pair of dark glasses.

The sky was very blue and very deep at this hour – four p.m. on May 13, to be precise. Rare clouds were

---

7. (Italian for:) "Look, Superman also wants to go and see the Pope!?"

moving to the south, disappearing behind the roofs of old, rather somber buildings that stood in an uninterrupted line along Borgo Santo Spirito.

Paul Morel…well, this was the name that this gentleman preferred at this time. A passport and driver's license in the inside pocket of his jacket had indeed been issued to Paul Morel, a French citizen, born in 1930. He spoke French like a true Parisian, without any foreign accent. But the man who called himself Paul Morel now was equally fluent in Spanish, English, and Russian. Oh, Italian too, of course. He knew it very well indeed.

Morel stopped, lit a cigarette, and continued to reflect on what was on his mind before the merry young girls could interrupt him.

The triads have already transferred fifty million dollars. Plus, a hundred more came from the Italians. That's a good price for scaring the Pope, for giving him a serious warning. The old guy should stop getting into the Banco Ambrosiano's dealings. It was actually quite strange that the Pope started this audit, even though he must have known that both the Chinese triads and the Italian Mafia had been laundering billions through this institution they called a 'Catholic bank'. Gigantic interest rates had made the bank management permanently fascinated with the deals. Then those sums arrived directly in the hands of the people at the Vatican Bank, and then…

Well, it's also possible that the Pope doesn't have any idea about all this Chinese and Italian involvement. This would explain his enthusiasm regarding the bank investigation. It was a genius mind that created this scheme. No one would even dare to assume that money laundering was possible through the Vatican. Even I discovered this mechanism, this laundering operation simply through sheer luck when, through a twist of fate, I met Roberto Calvi, who owns the Banco Ambrosiano. Oh, he's a hell of a wheeler-dealer…fine, that's the situation that needs to be corrected. Let everything come out right, as always. So, help me God!

He laughed beneath his breath. Why was he addressing the Lord while preparing a simulation of an assassination of his representative here on Earth? Funny.

Morel got into a phone booth at the intersection with Via de Cavalieri and, looking around, threw a coin into the slot. A male voice answered his call after three rings. The man spoke with a slight Arabic accent.

'Hello, listening, hello!'

'Hey, Amir, speak! I'm the one who's listening here. What's up?'

'Good afternoon, Mister Paul, Sir! They just informed me that the friend of our friends already went to the square in order to get a good location. Our man who is in direct contact with Ağca let me know through Alim that everything goes according to plan. Ali Ağca is entirely convinced that his target is an enemy of Dar al-Islam, the Muslim world, but he is also of the opinion that the target must be given a chance for redemption so that he can revise his views. Consequently, this operation should not have irrevocable termination for the target. Ağca is convinced that such an outcome is much better for Dar al-Islam in general and that Allah is telling him to act this way.'

'Okay, Amir, fine. I hear you. My men will monitor the situation. As for you, now's the time to go to Location B and await my further orders there. You know what your task is afterwards, yes?'

'Of course, Mister Paul, sir! No worries. As soon as Alim returns to Location B, I will cut the thread. And I will immediately call the number you gave me and report back.'

'Another thing. You remember that one of my men

will visit you after you cut the last thread? He'll give you the code for the deposit box where your money is waiting for you.'

'Yes, boss. I do. And thank you for everything.'

Paul Morel continued his progress towards St. Peter's Square, where thousands of people, both visitors to and inhabitants of the Eternal City, were already waiting for a chance to see Pope John Paul II and hear him speak. The crowd became denser with every minute. When he was only some fifty yards from the majestic colonnade of the St. Peter's Cathedral, a stumpy carabiniere,[8] easily moving through the crowd, came up very close to Paul and whispered:

'I am your guide. Follow me. I'll take you closer to the location.'

He walked somewhat ahead of Morel, cutting through the human sea with habitual movements.

This was one of Cosa Nostra's associates, who had gotten the order to accompany the French businessman to the center of future action. He did not know anything about him, except that he was an important person and a friend of the Mafia who was eager to be as close as possible to the Pope as he passed through the square.

Morel and his escort were soon in the square, among a great multitude of people awaiting the Pope's appearance. The crowd resembled a gigantic ant heap: people milled about, trying to move closer to the barrier along which the Popemobile would drive. People were holding their children up so that they could better remember this sunny day's visit to the Vatican, and later tell their children about seeing the Pope.

Paul Morel finally arrived, with the assistance of the

---

8. The Carabinieri are Italy's national gendarmerie and one of the country's law enforcement offices. They are a military force carrying out primarily domestic policing duties.

rather pushy carabiniere, at the spot he had chosen earlier, when he was still preparing the event. Here he was only a few yards from the barrier separating the dense crowd from the corridor of the upcoming Papal progress. His guide left him there, quietly slipping away to become just one of the hundreds of carabinieri roaming the square. Morel immediately felt the push of the immense human multi-organism that filled the tremendous width of St. Peter's Square. Paul kept looking at the people in the festive, lively crowd, once again experiencing that strange sensation that visited him before every important operation: all the nervous tension of the preceding days suddenly eased up in the last hours, transforming into a feeling of conviction that any gambler experiences when they know they hold a royal flush. There was a light tingling in his fingertips. Every little motion of the soft wind, every little ray of the May sun, were beneficial now. All doubts were gone, all fear of inconsistencies in human behavior or uncertainty about carrying out the operation. Complex as the puzzle was, all of its pieces had found their places and stayed put where he expected them to be. He knew now that everything would turn out well.

Turning slightly to the left, Morel saw a slight, black-haired man, his cheeks black blue thanks to a poor attempt at shaving. He was probably Turkish, and he kept staring at the Arch of the Bells, from where the Popemobile was about to appear. Despite the light wind and sun, his face was covered with little drops of sweat moving slowly down his cheeks, looking like tears. No one paid any attention to this man. Everyone was eager not to miss the sight of the Pope, and no one had any interest in a strange-looking little Turk who was already standing right at the barrier, expecting the Popemobile to soon pass him.

Paul Morel, however, immediately recognized the 23-year-old Mehmet Ali Ağca,[9] who he knew from his photos that had accompanied his case file. He had even ordered his psychological portrait, a profile of Ağca, who was a member of the ultranationalist Grey Wolves movement in Turkey. He was a fanatic and an assassin.

Ali Ağca would probably be surprised had he known that a middle-aged man standing some distance behind him, a man with unusual eyes that burned with an internal fire, was in fact the person who some months ago had selected him from a dozen candidates recommended for this operation. This was the man who had ordered a process of Ağca's ideological 'adjustment' and special training, which had been carried out in Turkey, Bulgaria, and then here in Rome. This man had paid a lot of money for it. Not personally, of course, but through intermediaries and trustees.

Professionals who had coached the fanatical Ali Ağca had taken great pains to impress upon him that the Pope must *survive* the attack, though permanent physical handicap would be acceptable. The bloody attempt on his life should be only a dire warning. The head of the Catholic Church must understand how many mistakes and wrong moves he had made with regard to the faithful Muslims. Ağca would become a martyr of the faith. Bismillah! In the name of Allah, or course. At this point Morel's thoughts were interrupted by the roar of the crowd, which began when the Pope's car had barely appeared through the Arch of the Bells. The car stopped quite often so John Paul II could bless the children parents held high from behind the barrier or exchange some words with those who spoke to him; he

---

9. **Mehmet Ali Ağca** (born 1958) was a member of Grey Wolves, a Turkish terrorist group, and a religious fanatic who made an attempt to assassinate Pope John Paul II.

also touched the sick with the palms of his hands and shook hands extended towards him.

The crowd became more vociferous as the procession neared the spot where Paul Morel was standing. The fascination of the huge mass of people reached a high point, voiced as a loud, united cry of admiration. The Pope, the Vicar of Christ himself, was, after all, bending to the people behind the barrier, touching them, sinful as they were, giving them his grace. Absolving them of all that had happened before. Providing forgiveness for everything that would happen in the future... Now, the Pope bent forward to raise a blonde three-year-old girl in the air, then leaned back over the guardrail to return her to her parents (later, this girl, curly-haired Sara Bartoli, would be known as the 'Angel Baby Who Protected the Pope'). Before he straightened up, he patted two more children on their backs. Then his car began to move slowly...

At 5:19 sharp, frightened pigeons flew high above St. Peter's Square, as if anticipating what would happen a second later – long enough, in fact, for the din in the square to die down. Shots rang out! Two of them, one after another, and then one more.

The great crowd of pilgrims to the Vatican roared. No one really knew why, because only very few who were close to the scene could see what had happened. Paul Morel was the only person in the square unperturbed by the events, quietly watching the developments. John Paul II slowly collapsed. He would have fallen if not supported by Stanislav Dziwisz, his personal aide, and Angelo Gugel,[10] his chamberlain, who were in the car with him. Morel could see very clearly that two bullets

10. Angelo Gugel was a personal assistant and valet to Pope John Paul II.

had definitely hit the target, but a nun and a tall man standing next to Ağca lunged at him a second before the third shot, causing the third bullet to go skyward.

The subsequent moments seemed like the quickly changing images in a kaleidoscope. Some plainclothes policemen immediately lunged from all sides at Ağca, who was lying on the pavement. They rudely pushed to the side both Morel and some gawkers standing next to him. They subjugated the Turk, who remained silent and even seemed unconcerned, and then they stood around him, defending him from the attacks of the yelling crowd eager to tear this assassin to pieces.

In the meantime, the Popemobile, with bodyguards hanging on all sides, rushed to the Apostolic Palace, pulling up at the medical facility of the Maltese Order. As usual, an ambulance stood ready, always equipped for intensive care. A minute later this ambulance, accompanied by police motorcycles, quickly left the scene, taking the still conscious Pope to the Gemelli Hospital, a medical institution affiliated with Rome's Catholic University of the Sacred Heart.

Morel glanced once again towards the spot where Ali Ağca had been stretched out only minutes before, behind the wide shoulders of security personnel. The scene had changed fast in the meantime. With the assassin in their hands, security agents were carrying him, running fast to an armored car of the carabinieri, which seemed to have come out from under the ground. Its siren blaring, the car was already leaving the square, moving slowly through the crowd of outraged worshippers, who screamed abuse at the man who had dared raise his hand against the Pope, their idol.

One could even get the idea that there were more people in St. Peter's Square now than before the attack. The cries of grief abated, changing to a uniform hubbub of voices, like powerful waves during a storm, rolling from colonnade to colonnade. Morel felt that people were not in the mood to leave the square, so he turned around and started making his way through the crowd, aiming to reach Piazza Papa Pio XII.

Why did Ağca shoot three times? Morel asked himself some time later when he had left the Vatican. He could finally sit down in one of the open-air cafés, where no music was playing today, due to the latest tragic events. He was definitely told that his task was only to wound the Pope. There should only have been a wound…so why did he shoot to kill?

I wasn't that keen on engaging a fanatic for this operation, but in this case, I didn't have any choice. No professional killer would have agreed to take on such a mission. It was simply too risky. Besides, a professional killer couldn't be used for this. The assassination attempt had to be presented as the act of a fanatic, not as a failed contract killing. Everybody had to regard it that way, except the Pope himself, for whom this whole bloody show was intended. Everyone else, including investigators, journalists and, of course, the general public, are to stay convinced for the rest of their lives that Pope John Paul II was shot by a religious fanatic. The most important thing, however, was to make sure that the Pope would survive this ordeal. Otherwise, my efforts would be fruitless.

Stepping into a phone booth at the corner of the busy, bustling Via della Conciliazione and the silent, meditative Via della Transpontina, Morel dialed a number.

'Ascolta. Parla,'[11] a female voice responded. A great, deep, vibrating contralto. Morel didn't say anything, and when the woman heard only street noise coming through, she said in French: 'Is that you, Paul? On my

---

11. 'Listening. Speak please.'

end, everything is quiet. Speak.'

'OK, Camilla, it's fine here as well. Tell me what your reporters found out?'

'The wounded was taken to the Gemelli Clinic. At first blood pressure was eighty over seventy, or even lower. They even thought it was the end. But things don't look so grim now. The Chief Surgeon of the University Clinic is now operating on the Pope. The surgeon's name is Francesco Crucitti, he was summoned urgently from a different clinic. I was able to engage one of his assistants to report regularly about the patient's condition. Well, I was posing as a journalist writing for the *Corriere della Sera*.[12] It will cost us some…'

'Camilla, get on with it! Talk business. I don't care about unnecessary details.'

'OK, here are the important details: when they opened up the patient's abdomen, they discovered excessive bleeding in the internal organs due to the chaotic movement of the bullet. Altogether they found eight internal injuries. They were able to stop the bleeding, so the blood pressure improved, and his pulse is more stable now. After all major wounds are sutured, the surgeon may need to extirpate a part of his intestines and perform a temporary colostomy. They estimate that the operation may continue another three hours, but currently they're of the opinion that, in practical terms, the Pope's life is not in danger. His condition is "reassuring", as they put it. He'll live, that's for sure. Unless something extraordinary happens…'

'Have you found out, Camilla, when they'll release an official statement to the media regarding the Pope's health condition?'

---

12. *Corriere della Sera* ('Evening Courier') is one of Italy's oldest newspapers (first published in 1876) and is Italy's most read newspaper.

'Of course. At 8 p.m. they will announce that the Pope is alive, but that his condition is not yet completely stable. And around 1 a.m., the Cardinal Secretary of State will reveal the news of the Pope's miraculous salvation.'

'Oh, great!' Morel gave a sigh of relief. 'You bring me good news, as always. That assistant must be properly compensated. What about that journalist lady whose name you were using to get all this info?'

'She'll get very sick in a couple of hours. You know, of course, what comes next...'

'You wouldn't want to follow her, right?' Paul Morel's voice suddenly took on a metallic undertone. 'Right?'

'Paul! Paul...' Camilla checked herself, and her dark, intense fear immediately filled even the deep silence inside the phone booth. 'Me... I... No, I don't. You know that too...'

'Okay, Camilla, that was a joke. Whatever you may know about this isn't supported by any evidence. Hence, I am releasing you. Close out all issues. The money I promised is already in your account, spend it on anything you like. But you must forget everything!'

'Yes, Paul... Of course. Thank you.'

'I mean, I always liked you for your ability to resolve problems in special, non-trivial ways. And because you'd use any means necessary to obtain information. But now we've come to a point when some of what you know may become dangerous, both for me and for the whole business. That's why you have to disappear from this country as soon as possible. And I should never see you again. Nor do I want to know anything about your life or your whereabouts. Okay?'

'Yes, yes, Paul. Thank you!'

'So, what's next today?'

'I'll sort out all the financial issues, check out of my room, get into my car and leave for...'

'It doesn't matter where you go. The main thing is to go far away.'

Paul Morel quietly hung up and, quickly looking around, started down the Via della Transpontina. Away from the crowds of animated Italians and equally noisy tourists, all of whom were discussing the assassination attempt.

An hour later, a very loud bang was heard at the main entrance to the luxurious Westin Excelsiore Hotel on Via Vittorio Veneto. A red Porsche had blown to pieces just as it was about to depart from the hotel. Journalists discovered later that the police retrieved the badly burnt body of a woman from the car. They quickly established that this lady had been staying at the hotel the last few days, that she was around forty, and that her name was Camilla Sartori.

Morel strolled the streets of Rome for a while. At around 8 p.m., he arrived at the busy, noisy Piazza Adriana, which was flooded by the rays of the setting sun. He directed his steps from there to the stone bridge, where several small cars were parked in its shade.

From a distance he could see an inconspicuous dark-blue Fiat Punto parked away from the other cars. Morel opened its door and took the passenger seat. He first closed the door, only then looking at the man in the driver's seat.

Mario Grasso was forty-five years old, dumpy, and balding. He had worked as a killer for hire for fifteen years. Well, in fact, it had been five years since he'd been involved in direct execution of a job, owing to the fact that he had instead established a syndicate under his guidance. It was a rather unusual organization, because even the killers it hired knew nothing about its operations. Well, most of the killers Mario Grasso hired were for one-time-use only – that is, after they were done with their mission, they were eliminated by other, more qualified, and trusted killers called 'cleaners'. Despite also fulfilling Grasso's orders, cleaners had a right to live, for one simple reason: they knew absolutely nothing about their victim or the victim's preceding 'job'. That is, they didn't know who their victims had killed, much less when or where it had happened. So, the chain got broken and no links were left behind. Mario Grasso was highly esteemed as a master of creating interruptions.

'Welcome aboard, Signor Paul,' Mario said, with all due respect to Morel. 'You are as punctual as a Swiss watch. Have you heard about the assassination?'

'Hello, my friend. Of course I did. All Rome is buzzing about it. I say, those fanatics have definitely gotten out of hand... How can they dare lift their hand against the Vicar of Christ?!'

Mario crossed himself slowly and then looked up at Morel, who was staring through the windshield again. Mario may have been professionally cruel, and he may have enjoyed, because of that, quite some respect from the most dangerous criminals in the lower strata of Italian society, but every time he met this man who called himself Paul Morel, he invariably felt skittish around him... Mario could not explain what exactly was behind such an unexplainable, total fear. Today it was caused, perhaps, by the eyes of the man he was talking to. His gaze was fleeting, elusive, but if one could catch it for even a moment, one would feel as if one had bumped into a multicolored, impenetrable wall. The only way one could shake off that feeling was to lower one's head and never look at the man again. This fear may have had something to do with the mysterious aura surrounding Morel: no one knew where he came from or where he would go next. And no one was aware of who he really was. Mario, like many others who had dealt with

Paul Morel, could only sense the following: that he was pursuing some grand, unfathomable goal, and that he would remove any obstruction hindering his progress. He could eliminate anything and anyone in his path, and after careful consideration, he would do so, cruelly, and impassively.

'Signor Paul! My cleaners have completed their jobs. An Arab on Via Torino named Amir departed quietly to the next life after a large dose of heroin. While he still had some of his senses, he kept demanding some code to a deposit box in some bank. What was that about? He must have been delirious, right?'

'Of course. Those drug addicts, they always talk drivel. What else?'

'My guys found one more body on Via Torino, in a bathroom. Not any of us. They found an ID in his pocket issued to a Turkish citizen, by the name of Alim Marzouk. They left everything as it was, unchanged.'

'Great. They did right. What did the Turkish citizen die of?'

'You know someone put a knife in his back. My professionals, hoping for your understanding, arranged for Amir's fingerprints to stay on the knife handle. Plus, they inserted a packet of heroin into one of the Turk's pockets. Now the story is crystal clear: two drug addicts at odds over drugs, so one stabbed the other and then overdosed. Did we do everything right?'

'Of course, Mario. As always, your people made the most correct decisions, and they must be compensated well for their efforts. I would like to add thirty thousand dollars on top of the advance you have already received. Here is the number of the luggage self-storage room, at the same railway station where you usually go to get your money from me, as well as the code for the unit.'

Morel gave Mario a five-thousand-lira bill, on which

some letters and numbers were carefully written by hand.

'Oh, Mario, something else before I forget,' Morel said, still staring through the windshield. 'What about the car of Signora Sartori?'

'That was also accomplished. The car suddenly exploded, and she was not expecting it, so Signora was quickly sent to the best of worlds. No one else got hurt. Is that all for now?'

'That's all for now,' Paul Morel affirmed, looking at the brickwork of the bridge, where someone had drawn a swastika. 'Mario! What's happening in my dear Italy? Muslim fanatics shoot at the Pope, neo-Nazis put Fascist symbols on the ancient walls of Rome... And we two are sitting in your car quietly discussing financial matters – about paying for three murders that happened today...'

And Paul burst out laughing, looking into Mario's eyes. Mario didn't know what to say, so he only shrugged his shoulders. Isn't he strange, this Morel? He might order a couple of killings, lightly, with no scruples, and pay very well for it at that, but now he gets upset over the attack on the Pope and these silly neo-Nazi urchins... Incomprehensible...

Morel shook Grasso's hand and, without another word, left the car, disappearing quickly into the twilight of the ancient city. The Fiat pulled away and a minute later also became invisible, lost inside the evening traffic leaving downtown. Farther and farther from the awful event that had happened in the Vatican today.

Even the weakest, most inconspicuous links were cut now between Morel's participation in the attack on Pope John Paul II. Still, Paul decided that now was the time to implement the rest of his plan, addressing even the most seemingly insignificant details. Paul got into a phone booth at the intersection of some narrow lanes around Piazza del Popolo and, having dialed a number from memory, spoke in English:

'Good evening, Mr. Wan. Am I calling too late for you?'

'Ah, Mr. Morel,' mumbled a high-pitched voice. The man spoke English with a pronounced Chinese accent and his intonation revealed he was a person of advanced age. 'tell me what exactly happened on St. Peter's Square earlier today? I mean, why did it happen the way it did?'

'Mr. Wan, this is a fixed-line phone I am calling you from...'

'My line is clean, don't worry. And I can hear that you're calling me from a public phone, right? That means only you and I can hear what is being said, okay?'

'Okay, then listen to what I have to tell you,' Morel spoke calmly. 'I'd guess you shouldn't really care how I made him terminate the audit at Ambrosiano to make your millions accessible again, right? Calvi and Marcinkus went to see him this morning. They explained to him what might happen if he persists and if, as a result, the Vatican were to appropriate your money – not to mention whatever the Italians have stashed there. But he would not listen to reason – he threw them out, telling them that nothing could happen to him. Well, as you can see, he was wrong...'

'Wait, Morel! The condition was that the Boss should only get some fright if he was unreasonable. And what did he get? Two bullets in his belly...'

'Hey, what's scarier than two bullets in the belly?' Paul Morel smiled wryly into the mouthpiece. 'The target knows very well why he got them... He's smart enough that he'll never believe it was some Muslim fanatic attacking on his own. Everyone else believed it, of course. Except the Pope. He's the only one who understood it all. I guarantee it.'

'Well, fine, you know better,' Wan sighed, becoming barely audible. 'My friends and I just want access to our money. To all of the half billion. And it should be as clean as linens after a Chinese laundry... And remember this: we don't want the Pope to die, and we never did. We don't need that at all, in any case.'

'I know he'll live. This is just an injury. I am very hopeful that there will be no more problems with the Banco Ambrosiano. And that your money, and that of our Italian friends, will undergo the usual process and return to you squeaky-clean, so to speak. But let's change the subject and talk about something more enjoyable. As you know, I am very interested in *The Seven Deadly Sins*. I mean, that chef-d'oeuvre by Hieronymus Bosch[13] that's still at the Prado in Madrid rather than in my collection. I need it, you know. I need it very much indeed. And you did promise it to me if you recall...'

'Okay, now you must listen to me. Why do you need that medieval horror show? Take some of the Impressionists, why not? There are two Monets available. And a Renoir. It's real stuff...'

'No, no, I'm not interested in those Frenchies. Mr. Wan, you know, of course, that I have spent years collecting everything related to Bosch. Everything from his paintings to his sketches and right down to copies made by his apprentices. You may consider it a whim, but for a real Bosch I would be ready to pay, say, the full amount of the fee that I have received from you.'

'Okay, let's do it this way.' The voice of old Ling Wan,

13. **Hieronymus Bosch** (1450–1516), born Jheronimus van Aken, is a great Dutch painter who is considered the most mysterious of all painters in the history of Western art. Only about ten of his paintings and twelve drawings survive. His grotesque imagery is unique and full of symbols displaying various monsters and demons as well as uncanny combinations of parts of human bodies, plants and animals.

head of the Chinese Triad, became louder and more animated. 'All that we have planned should be completed in full. We get all of our money, and we should be able to continue our relationship with the Ambrosiano. If that works out, I will try to do you a special favor. My people in Madrid will, perhaps, be able to exchange the original Bosch for a well-made copy. You'll get *The Seven Deadly Sins*, and the Prado will get a well-crafted copy. We will only do it, however, if my two conditions are met.'

'I understand, Mr. Wan. Let us wait for the final results. I will tell you how you can find me later on. Goodbye.'

'See you later.'

Paul Morel pressed the hook to terminate the connection, but he didn't hang up the receiver until he had first switched off a recording device that had been attached to the phone during the conversation.

I might need it, just in case, Morel thought, walking towards a cab stand through a city slowly drifting off to sleep. *It goes without saying that neither Wan nor the Cosa Nostra people would ever let it leak that they had anything to do with the assassination attempt on the Pope. Not even under penalty of death. Still, it could act as a backstop, in case Pope John Paul II doesn't take this attack as a serious warning – if he decides to continue the investigation of the Banco Ambrosiano, which has been used by the Italians and by the Triads for laundering their billions. And no investigator would be able to close in on me. Only a couple of people know that it was I who invented the whole scheme – using this Catholic bank and the Vatican as its front – but they will be as silent as a grave.*

Two hours later, the body of a man aged around fifty was brought to the morgue at Via Canossa. He had died of a heart attack on a street in the vicinity of Piazza Navona. His documents stated he was a French tourist,

Paul Morel, who had come to Rome specially to hear the Pope's prayer, and to receive his personal blessing.

Shortly before he was discovered lying dead on the street, a black limousine had stopped before a small group of homeless men next to the Basilica Santa Maria Maggiore. Everyone had been surprised when its driver walked up to one of the more presentable-looking homeless and invited him to get into the car, saying the man could help fulfill a certain important task, for which he would be well paid. Anastasio – this was the man's name – never came back to see his pals, but none of them was surprised. After all, it wasn't for no reason that Anastasio's nickname was Rolling Stone: he was prone to coming and going at will anyway, sometimes staying out for months.

Meanwhile, a tall, dark-haired gentleman, dressed well but inconspicuously, was in a cab to the Roma Termini railway station. It was the same man who a short while ago had been using the name Paul Morel, the same person who had happened to be around St. Peter's Square around 4 p.m. that day. Now he was to leave for Paris by train, departing in about an hour. Later, with a passport issued to a different name, he would take a plane, then transfer to another flight. Then there would be another short flight in a private plane, and then half a day on a yacht. The final destination for this gentleman's travel was a small island somewhere in the Indian Ocean. The man who had been calling himself Paul Morel for several years owned both the island and all the structures on it.

He looked out the side window, leaning back in the backseat of the cab. Rome at night was sliding back, looking like an old movie. It was mentioned already that he had never liked the Eternal City, just as he would never admire the grandeur of the Colosseum or the

Sistine Chapel. Rather, today he was thinking that if today's shots did nothing to change the Pope's attitude – if he was not directed to the only correct decision – then he, formerly known as Paul Morel, would really be very sorry that Bosch's chef d'oeuvre, *The Seven Deadly Sins, and the Four Last Things*, would be unable to join his private, secret art collection. Well, somehow it seems that one can survive without moral virtue, while it is so much more difficult to live without sin.

8

First Names
Paris Once Again

René Duchamp, 40, had worked with money all his life. For him, however, the money was not an end in itself. He liked working with all kinds of transactions, accounts, companies, and offshore destinations. He experienced a gambler's thrill and, at times, even a feeling of rapture close to the feeling of a musician whose violin soars skyward in Vivaldi's *Seasons*. He adored the process of transforming millions of dubious and uncertain origins into beautifully legalized rows of numbers in bank accounts. He loved the financial finesse of the process, and he was always on the verge of breaking the rules. Well, in fact, he did break the rules, quite often...

Tall and athletically built, tanned, with a light sprinkle of grey in his head of hair, Duchamp was well known in criminal circles. And in police institutions across Europe, for that matter. Police inspectors who constantly monitored his activities, however, now held the view that René was not, formally speaking, breaking the law, at least not at the moment. He had just spent two years in prison for money laundering, and he was now leading a quiet and lonely life, residing in a swanky six-bedroom apartment on Avenue Montaigne and spending away an inheritance that was also of dubious and obscure origin.

Four years ago, René Duchamp, a well-heeled and self-confident man, had met an enigmatic Chinese woman, Jia Sheng, and completely lost his head. He had showered her with flowers and expensive gifts, but she had always returned them, explaining to him scrupulously that it would not be possible for the two of them to develop a relationship, owing to the simple fact that she had no feelings for him other than an inclination to become his friend. A year later he had surrendered. Since then, theirs had become a rare case when a relationship between a man and a woman evolves into a real friendship, one of openness and mutual trust. And even though they had seen little of each other recently, each of them always knew that the friend was there. This feeling was a comfort to them both.

When René Duchamp was arrested, it was Jia who had managed to delete the data in his computer that was so important to investigators. Eventually, the prosecutors were unable to prove the main charge against René. Thanks to Jia's interference, Duchamp spent only two years at the Paris's high security La Santé prison, rather than the ten that had been expected.

Malin and Jia left the stolen BMW on Avenue George V and walked down the street, towards the elegant apartment building on Avenue Montaigne where René Duchamp, Jia's trusted friend, had his domicile. He was the one she had said would not snitch on them, even if he was unable to help them.

Dinner in Duchamp's large drawing room lasted over two hours. This gave Malin enough time to tell their host the entire story (or at least most of it), starting with Philip Marshall's archive and culminating with their escape from Chinatown. René was so fascinated with Malin's story that his Havana cigar went out perched on the edge of his ashtray, and he didn't even touch his glass of cognac, which spent two hours spreading yellow reflections from the table lamp around the room.

'Hey, this would be a disaster for the US, Malin! And not only for them,' René said pensively, all of a sudden. 'This would affect hundreds of millions of Euros, US Dollars, Yuan, British pounds, Russian Rubles, Swiss Francs and other happy, shiny paper bills. I'm ready to help you guys as much as I can. And I will surely be able to do a couple of things for you…'

'What would you like to get in return?' Jia asked casually.

'Well, first of all, your thanks would be welcome.' René smiled, but he was looking straight at Malin with eyes that betrayed not even a shadow of a smile. 'Secondly, Malin, all I want would be your promise that when you are done with your research, you send me a copy of your text shortly before the book is published. The full text, with every detail. Three days prior to the publication date. I can guarantee to you that no one but me would know of the book's contents!'

'You guess right, Rene, that I hope to write a book. Indeed, if I manage to stay alive in the process of unraveling this mysterious web, I will publish not only a series of articles, but also the full investigation report – many, many pages. But I don't understand, why would you need my manuscript three days before publication? Besides, I don't think this will happen in the near future… Would you try and sell it to someone?'

'Don't you understand, Malin?' Duchamp chuckled, finally turning his attention to his cognac. 'Judging by what you've told me, this should be a bombshell! A real big one, too! It would affect the heads of some states, the biggest banks, and leading global companies. It would shatter all the exchanges, send plummeting the quotes of American and European companies alike.

Exchange rates and stock indices would take quite the tumble. With such insider information I would be able to load up on Real Money! We're talking billions here, Malin! Billions! Oh, by the way, I can guarantee that you and Jia would get ten percent of my catch. That would make it possible to live out the rest of your life in your own villa in the Maldives. Agreed?'

'I hope I understand what your offer is about,' Malin said slowly, casting a questioning look at Jia. 'And you would still guarantee that my information would not be leaked anywhere before the book is printed, right? In this case, I agree. Anyway, we've told you so much already... That alone would be a guarantee for you that you would get my text. You understand, however, that I can give you no guarantee that I'll stay alive until that moment...'

'All right, Malin, let's not go there.' René smiled again, and this time his eyes had real warmth in them, with crow's feet enhancing the impression. 'Now that we're partners, I suggest that we analyze the situation one more time.

'When I think of the command that that lady gave...' René said, waving around his dead cigar, 'I mean, you said she commanded them to take you alive. Your pursuers, whoever they were, obviously had instructions to deliver Malin safe and sound to their employer. Of course, we have no idea who that could be. However, my gut feeling says those guys were not from the FBI. Their style was different, everything was too much in the open, plus the FBI never conducts operations abroad. Besides, Mr. Malin, the FBI would probably prefer you dead rather than alive. So, it must be someone else. Someone who wants to talk to you. And this 'someone' is certainly directly connected with the Organization whose 'Controller' was present during all those major assassinations and terrorist attacks.

'They want you because you found out their organization exists, in the first place. And has been in existence at least since 1963. My guess is that they understand now that you will be able to find the string connecting a whole number of other tragic events that happened over the last fifty years.'

'Well, René, here's what I think,' said Malin, ice clinking in his glass. 'We have no new leads for now. But there is this information from Artayev, the Russian journalist who dug out the photo of the false Igor Larionov. I'm referring, of course, to this 'Larionov' who was onsite during the '63 Kennedy assassination, in '81 in Vatican when the Pope was wounded, and in 2001 when the twin towers were destroyed. May I use your Skype to call Oleg from here?'

'Of course. I understand you have no communication devices that would help anyone monitor your whereabouts. And my calling Moscow won't attract anyone's attention.'

A few minutes later, sitting in Duchamp's lush study-cum-library, Malin connected to Artayev via Skype, using audio only, no video.

'Oh, I'm glad to hear you, Malin!' Artayev boomed in his very deep voice. 'How are you? What's up? I saw your sensational text on Facebook, the one about some 'Controller' in 1963... But you know what? Some miracles started occurring soon after: any mention of this story started somehow disappearing from the net. Or mentions of your name, for that matter. Can you imagine that? The material was there only an hour ago, but if you follow the link now, there is nothing there anymore! It's the same all over. Someone in charge has been cleaning it up around the world...like magic...'

'Hey, Oleg! Hello! I already know about all this,'

Malin interrupted Artayev. Looking at Jia and René, who were standing next to him, he told the Russian journalist: 'Listen! I can't talk for long, but I just want to ask one thing: can you help me?'

'Oh, Malin, you know I'd love to... Of course!'

'Then listen carefully. First of all, don't tell anyone that I called you today. We last spoke a few days ago, got it? Okay? Secondly, could you please tell me everything you know about this mysterious Larionov. Everything you were able to dig up on him.'

'All right, Malin, but I already told you everything when I sent you his photos. The only thing I can add is that nobody really knows how it happened that he became a member of the Russian delegation... I mean, the one that came for the talks re: the IMF loan. I mean, the $4.7 billion for Russia that later disappeared just before Russia's default in August '98.[1] Igor Larionov was not someone holding any executive or ministerial position. No official could even confirm to me that the man ever existed. As for the photographs and the list of delegation participants, everybody told me – I mean, everybody who is still living – that they were fakes...

'You know, of course,' Artayev went on, 'what some people think: that that money never even made it to Russia. I must have told you already that it was supposedly dispersed to various accounts and only successfully stolen later on. It disappeared from The National Republic Bank of New York, which was owned by Edmond Safra. I mean, this was done at the direction of the then-deputy minister of finance: the money was redirected, and it disappeared after that. And when Safra

---

1. On July 20, 1998, the Executive Board of the International Monetary Fund approved a $4.781 billion loan to Russia. According to some information, however, this loan never made it to Russia because it was stolen.

got scared and decided to testify to the FBI, our billionaire Boris Berezovsky paid him a visit. Their conversation scared Safra out of his wits, to the point that he immediately left for Monaco – where he soon burned to death in his mansion under mysterious circumstances.

'Berezovsky came to see Safra together with – oh, you must have guessed! – our man Larionov. One of the security cameras captured Larionov in Monaco a day before Safra died. He was staying for two nights at the Hotel de Paris, where he checked in as Russian businessman Igor Larionov. And he left that hotel one day after the banker died. Oh, and you know what? Later on, the video recording of Larionov disappeared. Can you imagine that? It simply got lost!

'Something else. I was able to discover, using my connections in our border guard service, that no Russian citizen of the surname Larionov left Russia during this period, nor entered the Schengen Area! Also, using every trick in the book, I was able to get some info from the Ministry of Finance about Larionov's Russian travel passport, which he used for his trip to Washington to attend the IMF talks. You probably won't be surprised, but here's the thing: no travel passport with such data and such codes was ever issued in Russia to a Larionov… It was a fake. But that's all I know. I couldn't find out anything else about Larionov. Dammit, what kind of a Larionov is he?'

'Thank you, Oleg! This was a great help. I must cut this conversation short now, but I promise you I'll get back in touch with you when everything is over…'

Malin switched off the connection and cast a meaningful glance at René and Jia. There was a gloomy silence in the room for a while. Duchamp was the first to speak:

'As far as I can figure, the person who was assumed

to be a 'Larionov' was directly related to the disappearance of billions from the IMF loan in 1998. Looks like he had connections with both the mafiosi among Russian officials and international criminal syndicates that were interacting with the IMF and the World Bank. And it looks to me like he is indeed the key person who organized the whole mess, acting as principal liaison between corrupt officials in Russia and in the West. Well, this is where I might help you a bit.'

Hearing this, Malin leaned forward, pressing his armrests so hard that his knuckles turned white. Jia walked up to him and put her hands on his shoulders. René was silent for a little while. He looked at his guests sharply, then continued, still speaking in a low voice:

'Some time ago, in 1997, I had a major partner, with whom I was working to make Russian money legitimate via the Bank of New York.[2] He was Russian or, rather, he had some hellish mix of Jewish, Russian, and some Asian blood. His name was Semyon Levine. He's an old mafioso who was involved in all kinds of illegal business since the Soviet era. He's had very reliable ties with organized crime groups around Russia and in the West. Semyon was also directly related to the fate of the IMF loan that vanished into thin air in 1998. As far as I know, some of that money was moved through his financial structures.

'But, when all those related to that money started mysteriously dying off, Semyon decided to go and lie

---

2. Citing information received from some contacts inside the FBI, both The New York Times and Newsweek released a statement on August 19, 1999, claiming that the Russian mafia laundered $10 billion through the Bank of New York (BoNY). Later, in 2005, BoNY acknowledged that a number of its employees were taking part in implementing schemes aimed at tax avoidance and legalizing money used by Russian importers for an amount of about $7.5 billion.

low. He's seventy, he's no fool. So, no one can find him anymore – except me, and some other very close, trusted friends. There were other unresolved issues too, besides the loan story, so he has to step very carefully these days. He lives in a large country house in a small village outside London, practically isolated from the outside world, but he still keeps track of all the latest financial and criminal developments using modern means of communication. His name is Sam Levine now.'

René fell silent and then reached for the cigar box on his desk. Moving it closer to him, Malin said:

'Please continue, René, keep going!'

'So, when we talked, Semyon would intimate that an omnipotent organization existed, which, in his opinion, has been responsible for the most famous crimes of the last fifty years. I know him pretty well, so I am sure he hasn't gone senile. I think he must know quite a lot about your Larionov, and about much more. Believe me, my friends, this old man told me many stories similar to what I heard from you. But they were never established facts, only his assumptions and conjectures.'

'Will Mr. Levine talk to us at all?' Jia asked in a low voice. 'Why would he want to be candid with us?'

'Okay, I'll say this bluntly: Mr. Levine has been living in fear for his life. He would love to go out, stay in the open, even return to Russia, perhaps, and continue his commercial activities that were interrupted there. He thinks that some organization – which must have sent your Mr. Larionov to Russia and Monaco – intends to snuff him out, too. After all, Semyon Levine is a man who knows too much. But if you can make this story public, heads will roll all around the world, and then no one would care about Semyon anymore. My guess is that you might be his best chance at returning to Russia, at getting back to his big deals and his big money.

Alright, now I have to make a few calls so I can send you to London.'

Malin laughed out loud, saying:

'What's the idea – us, travel to London in these circumstances? Even as we're hunted down by the FBI, maybe the CIA, plus the mysterious, omnipotent criminal organization? What about our passports? Or our faces, for God's sake! It's not possible!'

'Wow, what a surprise!' Duchamp said, also laughing. 'It seems to me, Malin, that you're still thinking along the lines of what's expected from a decent American citizen who pays tax on each earned cent, imagining that any other type of behavior exists only in Hollywood thrillers. My God, what a baby! You should get it into both your heads that if Semyon sees your meeting as something important for accomplishing his ends, you'll get new, reliable passports in three days. Issued to other names, of course. You would have to change your appearance, of course, but not that much. You'd have to get a different hairstyle and dye your hair. Malin should get rid of that stubble on his cheeks or, on the contrary, grow a beard. And that's that. Well, you see, Malin, the thing is that I need money. Big money. And I believe that you will win. Which means that, in accordance with our agreement, I believe I'll be receiving a lot of money from you. Alright, guys, please stay here in my study for a bit, wait till I've talked to Semyon.'

Duchamp left the study and dialed a number in his drawing room. When his call was picked up, he spoke quickly into the mobile phone:

'Hi Semyon. I feel quite daring to be interrupting your proud solitude. How's your health?'

'Hi, you risk-taking apache!' Semyon said, voice muffled; he seemed to have some difficulty rolling his R's. 'I know that when you call me, it's always for a reason. Just as I know that my health isn't of any concern to you. Okay, putting two and two together, I can arrive at the conclusion that you need something from this old man... so speak up!'

'You see, Semyon, here's the story...'

And René related to Levine everything that Max Malin had told him that day. He particularly stressed the point that if Malin could successfully complete his investigation, and make its results public, then Semyon would be able to live without fear, stop hiding, and even return to Russia. Levine listened attentively to René, and then, after a brief pause, he said:

'What can I tell you? You know well enough that I'll say yes to this. This is of interest for me. But I know your ways, boy. What might be your conditions, your lion's share, eh?'

'Oh, Semyon, what are you talking about? It's no big deal for me. If all comes out right and you end up free to go anywhere, you would only waive my debt to you, the two million dollars. Plus, you would pay me one million. It's not much money for you, not at all. And the current situation is so weighing on me.'

'Oi, René, René... I've known you for so many years and you never change. But it's all right. It's a deal, I'm fine with it. Still, I doubt very much that your Malin will find success in his quest... Well, he had some luck with those photos, of course...but even I know too little about this Organization, and one thing is clear to me: it's not possible to defeat it. Well, anyhow, one should try doing something, at any rate. Let them come over to me. They should make sure, however, that they are not shadowed. You know how to arrange such things. So long, my friend.'

So, Malin and Jia had to endure three long days confined in René's luxurious apartment: going out would be dangerous for them. René put them up in an exquisite guest bedroom with a fireplace, an enormous, canopied bed, and a desk with a powerful laptop, set up right in front of the window that overlooked Avenue Montaigne. Such accommodation was all that they needed. Also, Duchamp preferred it this way. He didn't want Malin and Jia roaming around in his study, for obvious reasons. He apologized that Malin had to work in their bedroom, but intimated, on the other hand, that since he was a financier, after all, well…

When Duchamp told them on the last day that their documents were ready, he left his apartment to meet the courier who was delivering them. The sun was merciless, and Paris was sizzling in a red-hot summer spell. Even Jia, who had come to like sitting and reading on a small patio that could be reached from the drawing room, preferred to dip in the cool water of the whirlpool bath, enjoying an hour among the pleasant and slight prickling of air bubbles.

In the meantime, Malin sweated over the laptop. The day before, he had gotten the idea that he could install software that would allow him to search for identical images among specified photographs. He took the risk of connecting to a remote server that René allowed him to use, and contacted one of his old pals, a hacker whose nickname was Elvis. Malin asked Elvis to suggest the best available facial recognition program.

'Malin, baby, despite all the buzz, I don't care about your adventures,' Elvis said, speaking through an audio connection. 'All I really care about is the size of the "thank you!" I receive from your latest advance. By the way, being an honest kind of guy, I haven't taken anything from it yet…not a dime!'

'It should be your usual rate, only take double,' Malin said. 'And I don't need any primitive shit like VO-

CORD FaceControl,[3] even with all its updates, but a real cool software, you know, something the special agencies are using these days. Can you do that for me?'

'Got you. Of course, such stuff does exist. Though, by the way, they said they would cut off the balls of the hacker who successfully swiped it, but since they couldn't find him, his balls are still safe and in place,' Elvis laughed. 'I named this software Hecate. It extracts just what's needed out of billions of faces. Here, I just sent it to you. Meet Hecate. I'm sure you'll love it.'

Malin launched the application and loaded images of the four faces into it: the mythical Igor Larionov, the young Controller in Dallas in 1963, the older man from the 1981 photo in Rome, and the face in the 9/11 photo.

The program performed with amazing speed, sorting through hundreds of millions of faces online and selecting only those whose likeness was closest to the specified images. Then it did a second pass, throwing away the least likely ones and leaving only the truly most similar faces. It even took into account possible changes due to age. Damn! What great software! Elvis, you great guy!

Malin tensed up when Hecate went through its last pass, removing any images it considered as least similar to the original four. The air conditioner suddenly started, loud and clear in the completely dead silence of the room, and Malin heard soft steps – Jia, in a white terry robe. She came up to Malin and stood behind his chair.

'Any news? Did you get something?'

'Yes, baby, I did. Here's today's catch. Let's see what we've got.'

Hecate had chosen only two photographs from a

---

3. A remote biometric face recognition system with gender and age identification

very great number of images available online. Two faces looked at Malin and Jia from the computer screen. And they were identical to the images of Larionov and the two Controllers from 1963 and 2001.

The first image, which Hecate labeled as being 89 per cent similar, was a rather old photo of a Luis Cristobal Santana, from Yale's 1954 yearbook. It had been posted on a site called Friends of Yale, which collected all kinds of archival images related to the school's alumni over the years. Santana's year of birth, 1933, was also indicated.

Malin eyed Santana's face keenly. The young man had only been twenty-one when the photo was taken. Oh Lord! Of course, it was the same face. Very similar to both the false Larionov and the Controllers. As for the 1963 image, it was almost completely identical to that of this Yale alumni.

'It's done, Jia! Now we know for sure,' Malin croaked, –he was losing his voice— 'His name is Luis Cristobal Santana. His age fits, too: he was thirty when Kennedy was shot. Bull's eye!'

'Okay, first we search for Luis Santana, born 1933, and then look at the second photo.'

Malin had been so impressed by the first result that he had forgotten about the second image! He started the search, and they had a result in no time: Luis Cristobal Santana had graduated from Yale in 1954, majoring in Law. Only a year later, the 22-year-old lawyer, who had only just started his career, suddenly became a partner of a large legal company – Yodel, Marcos & Santana, located in Washington, D.C. According to the search engine, its lawyers specialized in counseling US government organizations in their dealings with Egyptian authorities, as well as with all kinds of commercial structures in the vicinity of the pyramids.

At first, the Washington office where young Luis Santana acted as the company's chief partner had been providing legal support for the financing of the construction of the Aswan Dam,[4] which was supposed to be erected using a loan provided by the US and Great Britain. But on July 19, 1956, the USA suddenly walked back its decision to loan Egypt $140 million.

A miracle had occurred, however: $25 million of the loan money was nevertheless sent to Egypt from the U.S. Bank – but then mysteriously disappeared. The money never made it to Cairo... Journalists reported later that the law company Yodel, Marcos & Santana was directly involved in the deal. When the FBI started its investigation, it soon found out that no one by the name of either Yodel or Marcos had ever existed... Instead, the company was run solely by the 23-year-old Luis Cristobal Santana, an American citizen. It was also established that none other than Luis Santana, who had created dozens of entities, as well as invented stand-ins using false documents, was moving around millions of dollars that the US government had allotted for countries in Africa and the Near East.

After a major uproar, which became known as the Aswan Affair, Santana disappeared into thin air. No one had ever seen him again.

A year later, on November 9, 1957, a plane was lost over the Pacific Ocean. This Boeing-377 Stratocruiser, serial number 15960, which had the romantic name of Clipper Romance of the Skies, was flying from San

---

4. The Aswan Dam is a very large and complex hydrotechnical system of facilities on the Nile River in Egypt, close to Aswan. The construction financing was secured by the US State Department decision, on July 17, 1956, that it agreed to provide the necessary loan to Egypt. The loan was for $200 million, to be effected via the World Bank. The USA, however, very soon retracted its decision.

Francisco to Honolulu.[5] Five days later bits of debris belonging to this Romance of the Skies were found in the ocean, but not all the passengers' bodies could be recovered. One of the passengers who had registered for Flight 7 was Luis Cristobal Santana. The FBI press release stated that he was on board the plane that had borne this meaningful name: Romance of the Skies.

This was the official version of how the life of new millionaire Santana had ended. This was the person whose eyes were looking out at Malin from the digitized photo.

'Now what's this? Isn't this an interesting puzzle?' Malin said slowly. 'I wasn't expecting so much information from our search. Now we know that both "Larionov" and all the "Controllers" went by the name Luis Santana, when he was still rather young. Let's look at the second face now, okay? One more name might emerge, why not?'

Hecate labeled the second image as 84 per cent similar to the specified original. It was a small, digitalized photo from the archives of the New York Times. It showed, in 1966, apparently the same man who could be seen in the photo taken when Kennedy was shot. His face, taking into account certain age-related changes, was identical to the other images.

The caption said, however, that this was one Martin Weiss, one of the main lobbyists of the largest corporations supplying weapons, equipment, uniforms, food, and essential goods to the US military in Vietnam. The

---

5. Pan Am Flight 7, a Stratocruiser 10-29 (registered N90944, serial number 15960, named Clipper Romance of the Skies), left San Francisco for Hawaii with 38 passengers and 6 crew. The 377 crashed around 5:25 p.m. in the Pacific Ocean. There were no survivors and the entire wreckage has never been found. Only 19 bodies and bits of debris were recovered five days later.

newspaper also reported that his commercial structures were the main intermediary between the large companies and US authorities spending billions of dollars on these purchases.

Malin got up, mumbling to himself, and started pacing around the big bedroom. Then he grabbed a cigar, clipped its end, and squeezed it between his teeth without lighting it.

'Oh my, he is Weiss, on top of it all... Martin Weiss...' Malin spoke out loud, but to himself. 'If we consider the years, then the sequence is as follows: Santana – Weiss – Larionov. I have no doubt they were the same person. Oh hell! How is that possible? I can't figure out how they're connected, though. Shit, my brain's on fire. Jia, could you please look up online what's available on Martin Weiss?'

Information about Weiss was rather scarce. Malin and Jia were disappointed that they could only find out that Martin Weiss had arrived in Vietnam in 1967, as part of some mysterious military delegation. It was quite unusual that Weiss, a civilian, a businessman, and a lobbyist, was suddenly there to participate in an extended session of the Joint Chiefs of Staff headed by General Westmoreland, commander of the US Forces in Vietnam. What kind of authority must have been vested in this person if he was allowed, in the middle of active military operations, to join that holy of holies: a secret meeting in the highest military quarters?

Jia could only further discover a short announcement in the Vietnam War Almanac that businessman Martin Weiss, who had been involved in supplying the US Army in Vietnam, went missing there in 1967, only a few days after that session of the Joint Chiefs of Staff. And only much later on was he officially recognized as killed at the hands of Viet Cong.

'Was his body recovered?' Malin asked sharply.

'Of course not.'

'Then it must be our Controller...'

Steps on the stairway sounded, and seconds later someone knocked on the open door. Duchamp's cheerful voice interrupted their quiet conversation.

'Hey, lovebirds, ready for a visit to the United Kingdom? Her Majesty has grown tired of waiting for you two. Check out the magic I have in my hands!'

René produced two new US passports from a large yellow envelope, setting them by the laptop, along with credit cards and driving licenses. Two new mobile phones followed, as well.

'Okay, let's see... Newlyweds Mr. and Mrs. Murphy are to proceed from Paris to London, continuing their honeymoon journey. Malin...oops, sorry, Mister William Murphy, please make a reservation for Eurostar,[6] and in a couple of hours you'll already be in the Channel tunnel...'

'René, I am so thankful for everything...everything, past and present,' Jia whispered her thanks.

'Oh baby, baby,' Duchamp chuckled, before his voice changed to a labored joviality. 'You must realize that mine is a very rare case when a man in love was able to remain a good friend despite having been spurned. Apologies for my directness, Malin. You should know, Mr. Malin, I have been doing all this only because of the money I hope to be able to get from you at some point in the future. That is, if you can conduct your investigation in full, if you remain alive, if you do not cheat me, and if you give me the copy of your text prior to the publication of your book.'

---

6. Eurostar trains traveling between Paris and London cross the English Channel via the Channel tunnel.

'You bet!' Malin smiled. 'Too many "ifs", of course. Still, I would never have counted on all this – that you, such a shrewd financier, would join such a risky affair as a Samaritan venture…'

'Sometimes such things happen. Even with me. Okay, enough of this sentimental nonsense! Get ready and go! My friend Semyon Levine already has copies of your passports so that he can identify you both. He's waiting for you. His address is with your documents, as are his phone number and directions how to get to his place.'

9

Mr. Levine and New Names
for the Controller, London

T he train emerged from the brightly lit exit of the tunnel, and into the English morning haze at lightning speed. Though the weather was warm, fog clung to the ground, holding onto the trees, clutching at their long branches. The fog flew back in a rush from the train, as it hurtled forward.

Surfacing from his light sleep, Malin tried to stretch, but couldn't – he realized with some surprise that he was in a train seat. A moment later he was completely awake. Jia was sleeping in the window seat next to him. Her exquisite outline was so filled with light that it seemed as if she could dissolve into the wisps of fog flying past the window. God, she was beautiful…

Malin took a small laptop out of its case and started scanning the news, hoping that nothing bad had happened of the kind that might hamper their progress. Seeing the latest news from *Le Parisien*, however, he felt as if an icy wave had hit him somewhere beneath his ribs, spreading through his body. Malin reread the short, dry report:

> *Paris. Last night René Duchamp, a former financier who had spent two years in prison for money laundering, was killed in his luxurious apartment*

on Avenue Montaigne. He was shot in the head by a silenced pistol, so no neighbors heard the gunshot. According to Marcel Fridoux, Commissaire de Police of the 8th Arrondissement in Paris, signs on Duchamp's body indicated that he had apparently been tortured prior to being killed. The Commissaire rejected robbery as a motive, as valuables remained untouched, including a large sum of money in cash, jewelry, and paintings belonging to the victim. The perpetrators allegedly took only the hard drive of Duchamp's desktop computer, as well as two laptops, according to investigators.

There was a hushed sobbing behind Malin: Jia was trying to suppress her tears. She had woken up and looked at the newsfeed over Malin's shoulder. They must have read about René's death at the same time.

'Oh, God! Malin! Malin, I killed Duchamp,' she whispered, pressing her wet cheek to Malin's face. 'Why did we go to him at all? Why did he agree to help us? René was my best, my very best friend. The most faithful one, the only real one...'

Malin started stroking Jia's cheek, tenderly and carefully, at the same time wiping off her tears. This Frenchman had earned a place in his heart over the last three days. Malin had even started to feel something he wasn't quite familiar with: he had started to trust René, that cheerful and self-composed man who, on top of everything, had been in love with Jia. At first Malin had reckoned that René was mostly pursuing his commercial interests, and that his warm feelings towards Jia were only second to those. But that was obviously wrong: Duchamp could have turned them in to their pursuers and that would at least have spared him torture.

'There, there, Jia... Don't cry, talk to me...'

'Wait a minute, Malin. Listen to me.' She looked up

at him, and her tears were suddenly gone, replaced in her eyes by a bright cold spark. This spark was one of the things that had made such an impression on Malin when they first met. 'I understand, of course, that we had nowhere else to go in that situation. And that he was the only person I could think of. I also understand that René was pursuing his financial goals when he decided to help us. But you have to keep in mind that he was in love with me all this time, both when we were together, when I was on my own, and even later on, when I came to him with you. It was a hopeless love, but still, he stayed my best and closest friend. That's why I started crying when I saw the news… I'm sorry…'

Embracing Jia again, Malin started thinking aloud:

'But how could our pursuers have figured out that we were staying at René's? Our devices were new, and they weren't registered to your name or to mine… Wait! I've got it! Before we left for the train, I checked my pages on Facebook and Twitter a few times to get a feel of the general situation. I also used search engines to look for materials on 9/11 and on Kennedy's assassination. If they had started monitoring traffic to my pages, they could have immediately gotten Duchamp's IP address and tracked our location that way. They must have compared all search queries from that IP address, and that must have given them the clue where we were. That we were hiding at René's on Avenue Montaigne.'

'Malin! It seems like it's only chance that they didn't make it to René's while we were still there – they came over some hours after we left. But whoever they are, they tortured René, so it's quite possible that they could find out…'

'Exactly, Jia. Now that you started it, I'll say the rest. They could have gotten all the info about our passports and where we were going. René could have told them this under torture. Plus, my booking of the tickets to London was still there in his computer. That's dangerous…very dangerous.'

'But no, no! That can't be true!' Jia smiled suddenly brushing her tears aside. 'René was always a great conspirator. I know this about him quite well. He might have told them most of it, especially while they were torturing him. Our destination, even our new names and passports. He also knew, of course, that the train booking was in his computer. But he would not have told them anything about Semyon Levine – not a word. I also know that he always kept important phone numbers and addresses memorized, just because he was counting on the possibility of another police investigation. Besides, he loved money and so he was hoping, until the last moment, that those intruders would spare his life in exchange for cash. You know, even in such a critical situation, he must have had in mind that he would later earn billions using information from your future book. I know this René Duchamp… I mean, I knew him… By the way, I have no doubt that he would try to get some financial gain from Semyon Levine, too. As a referral fee, sort of, for bringing us over to meet with him.'

'Are you saying that our pursuers would only know our new names and that London was our final destination?'

'I do hope so.'

'Then it might be sensible for us to take a chance,' Malin said, after a short pause. 'Let's not get off in London, we can travel a little farther. When we get to London St. Pancras, we change immediately for a local train to Brighton. It's eighty kilometers from London and about fifty from Levine's home. We'll take a cab from there to get to him.'

The Eurostar sailed beneath the gigantic glass roof of St. Pancras. Malin and Jia walked behind a group of Chinese tourists. At a glance, it seemed no one was there to shadow them, but Malin knew it was practically impossible to notice signs of professional surveillance in a crowd without years of experience doing so.

They were lucky: only ten minutes later, Malin and Jia were already sitting on the train between London and Brighton, pretending to be just one more lovey-dovey tourist couple. All around them was the hubbub of groups of merry travelers. Some men behind them were chatting in Spanish. Three young guys next to them, apparently American students, laughed without stopping. Malin felt somewhat relieved. He breathed more freely now, feeling relatively safe.

Three hours later, a slow-moving taxi they hired at Brighton station brought Malin and Jia to a small village completely buried in greenery: everything was so lush here in the far outskirts of London. Branches of old oaks hung down, almost touching the car's window shield. It seemed that they were about to knock on the roof of the vehicle. The cab soon stopped at a tall, wrought-iron gate with magnificent chestnut and oak trees behind it. These trees grew so close to one another that one could see no buildings at all.

They paid the driver and walked to the gate. Before they even had a chance to touch the bell, they heard a deep male voice speaking in a strong Russian accent. The man was having some difficulty pronouncing his R's:

'Hello there, I can see you guys. After the cab drives away, I will open the front gate. Walk over to the main building and I will meet you there.'

Seconds later the door opened with a slow, smooth movement. As soon as they stepped inside, it started closing again. The park was enormous, and looked unkempt, but both Jia and Malin felt a special aura from its deep greenness, even in its abandoned condition.

One would want to walk beneath its cool canopy and never leave it again. As they walked to the mansion following a wide passage, they once more had a feeling of entering a tunnel, this time made up of sky-high oak trees with branches intertwined high above their heads.

'What a great place, Malin!' Jia whispered, smiling happily. 'This is the first time in days I've felt calm and secure. Why don't we stay here?'

Malin hugged her shoulders and whispered back, speaking very close to her ear:

'With you, I would have stayed anywhere, even in Chinatown in Paris. But…'

'Yoo-hoo, lady and gentleman!' The host's loud voice boomed from a loudspeaker hidden somewhere close-by. 'I must let you know that my security can both see and hear you very well.'

Malin only laughed in response. Picking up the pace, they soon arrived in front of a structure that seemed to be a strange cross between a Victorian manor house and a newly erected Gothic castle.

Mr. Levine welcomed them at the entrance. There was a mountain of a bodyguard by his side when they walked in, but he immediately left, walking away through a side door. Semyon turned out to be a fat, bald, and rather short man of around sixty-five, looking something like a massive ball of flesh. He was dressed in an expensive bathrobe made of sueded silk. It was open in front, showing blue jeans and a light-colored shirt beneath it. His bottlebrush moustache, thick and bristly, was matched only by his large eyebrows, which hung down over his eyes. It was these large, colorless eyes that scanned the new guests attentively. They had a hard and tense expression in them, despite the host's amused laughter and the merry crow's feet that danced around his temples.

'Hello! Hi there!' Levine spoke fast, and frequently changed the topic of conversation. 'René sent me your photos… God rest his soul…' Levine definitely had a problem rolling his R's, which was even more noticeable in person. 'Oh, what a good boy he was! He was my pupil, by the way. But many good boys end their lives in exactly the same way… It's so sad… Oh, well, do come in, make yourself at home.'

Semyon suddenly changed to Russian, without showing any interest in how his guests might respond:

'Do you speak Russian?' He asked Malin. 'You were born in Russia, right? Oh, I'm going mad here with all this English…'

'Of course, I do, Semyon,' Malin answered in Russian. 'Russian is my tongue as much as English, perhaps more so. I must apologize, though, I am sorry, but the only Russian word that Jia knows is "vodka", so, I guess, we should better be talking in English, okay?'

'Okay, guys. Let us use the tongue of the local tribe. When I speak English, by the way, my Jewish blood doesn't show that much: here, they don't have those hard Russian Rs… Come to my drawing room… Where the hell is my butler? Hey, hello, Michael, can you bring us some whisky and some tea?'

Semyon, Malin and Jia were soon seated comfortably in enormous leather chairs in front of a cyclopean fireplace, which looked rather like the gaping, horrible mouth of some mythical monster. The host told them proudly that it was a rare chef d'oeuvre from the seventeenth century. The atmosphere was set nicely by a very good single malt whisky, which Michael, the butler, poured into their glasses, exhibiting the utmost dignity. His powerful build betrayed his probable second occupation as another bodyguard for Semyon.

'So, what's up, my dears… Oh, or what should I be

calling you? Fugitives? Runaways? Escapees?' Levine asked Malin and Jia, turning playful as he nosed his whisky. 'No, really? What's your mood? Give me the full picture of the situation you've ended up in. René gave me the short version, plus I got a little bit from the Internet. But I must hear it all in your own words. Then I can get an idea whether I might be of any help to you.'

It should be mentioned at this point that Semyon Levine's life story wasn't just *like* an adventure novel – it might as well have been one. This genius entrepreneur-adventurer had been born in 1940 in Soviet Russia, to a Jewish family. They lived in Kiev, capital of Soviet Ukraine, but theirs was a low-lying part of the city called Podol, close to the Dnieper, where many poor Jews had lived historically. Semyon, or Syoma, as everyone knew him there, took up a profession as a dental technician in the fifties, but by the time he turned twenty, the only link between him and dentistry was that he was heavily involved in buying up gold in bulk and reselling it, at a great profit. This was completely illegal – gold was distributed by the state only to state-certified and state-employed dentists, who were supposed to be using this material for dental crowns. Later, Semyon created an illegal organization that managed and controlled a whole network of card sharps who worked rich clients, mostly illegal entrepreneurs, who were staying in the resorts of the Crimea and the Krasnodar area. Semyon's business grew fast. It functioned like a Swiss watch, bringing in tens of millions of Soviet rubles. And one man ran it alone with hands of steel – he who was known under oh-so-many names: Syoma, Senya, Seva, Papa, Semyon Izrailevich, Uncle Izya… Well, eventually he had been arrested and prosecuted, of course, for another activity that was strictly prohibited in the Soviet Union: buying up American dollars. He had been convicted and sentenced to ten years in a high-security prison. Six years later, Levine had been paroled, due to good behavior and to his strong, actively formulated attitude towards his plans for the future. This had allowed him to leave prison and move on to Moscow, where he brought his stashed-away millions of rubles in cash, as well as his gold.

Later on, in the late eighties, Semyon had been successful in organizing one of the first pyramid schemes. Not in Russia, but in the US of A, during his occasional trips across the pond. Having cheated gullible Americans of almost two hundred million dollars, he made it to the international most wanted list. During Russia's 'roaring nineties', Semyon Izrailevich Levine created a semi-legal financial empire, using his powerful intellect and enormous influence on Russia's criminal leaders. They were all criminals with an honor code. Crime lords all right, but they bowed to his special talents as a financial adventurer and to his steel will, which allowed him to unite the illegal business of three largest criminal groups in Russia. By then, Semyon was able to launder billions of rubles, so that he could buy up shares of many former Soviet enterprises en masse. Suddenly he was an honored guest in the offices of the highest Russian authorities – all the way up to President Yeltsin's close circle.

Once they had settled in, 'Mister Levine' sipped his whisky and puffed at his short cigar, listening for about an hour to Malin and Jia's story, which included the mysterious 'Santana-Weiss-Larionov', the identical faces in the photographs, and all the tragic events during which this same person had appeared. Malin explained that he and Jia had become the target of a manhunt involving both US special agencies and some unknown groups of gunmen. Malin told Semyon everything. Almost everything. He said nothing about Jia's backstory, but it was clear she was of no interest to Levine anyway.

'Hey, but this is fascinating! It simply can't be true!' Levine laughed heartily, interrupting Malin mid-sentence. 'This can't be true because such a thing should never have happened! Just think of this! A simple American journalist, once a US marine, a man of Russian origin, did it! He…I mean, you…were suddenly able to crack the wealthiest, most secretive criminal group on the planet. And I'm not kidding you, my dears. No one really knows of its existence. Maybe some thirty or forty people all around the globe have guessed that it exists at all. I came to this conclusion because of some knowledge I have, following certain logic and deductive reasoning. I may have been right in arriving at my judgment and, lo and behold, I am still alive, but I've been hiding here in this lair for the last seventeen years as a result. Could you show me the photos?'

Malin started his laptop, and soon he was presenting, one by one, all the photos in his collection: Santana, Weiss, Larionov, Kennedy's assassination in '63, the Twin Towers disaster, the attempt on John Paul II's life in the Vatican in '81.

'What can I say?' Levine said, looking at the photos. 'This is definitely one and the same person. I have known him as Igor Larionov. I can vouch for that. But it is also possible that his other name is…Sergio… And I have a reason for this…'

'Please, Semyon, tell us more!' Jia said pressing her hands together and looking straight at Malin. 'It's a matter of life and death for us.'

'Listen, Jia, I have no idea what binds you to this young man, but I can guess you aren't his sister,' Levine smiled. 'I understand your anxiety, but all I can say is this: those whom Malin was able to pinpoint will not let you live, neither of you. Perhaps I won't be spared either. There's only one case in which you might survive. That's if you can do the impossible – find out everything and tell the world the whole story.'

'Okay, but now it's time for you to tell your story, Mr. Levine,' said Malin, who changed to Russian, for whatever reason.

'I didn't know anything of what you just told me. I mean, not about Kennedy, nor 9/11, nor the Pope. I mean I only knew what was generally available. However, I knew Igor Larionov quite well. I almost said, "very well", but he was definitely not the kind of man one could say that about. Okay, let's go back to 1998. At the beginning of the year, it became clear that a crisis was slowly approaching, threatening the whole country. This was due to slumping oil prices, to financial problems in Southeast Asia, and to overinflated, deficit-ridden budgets that the State Duma was passing frivolously, and which merry President Yeltsin was equally lightly signing off on... But they were trying, at the same time, to rein in inflation through rejecting monetary financing and supporting the overvalued ruble. Can you imagine that? My partners, however – and I had those on all levels, from big criminal bosses to high government officials – my partners had invested heavily in dollars and in Russian state securities, which they would sell at the right moment, following a nod from some insiders with the Ministry of Finance. Do you understand my explanation?'

Malin nodded and Semyon, taking a drag at his cigar, continued:

'Okay, so it was early June. The Deputy Minister of Finance, his name was Matvey Assianov, invites me to his office. He and I had some deals in common at the time, not all of them were always within the, ah, legal field, so to speak. For example, I would buy up Russian state securities, following his advice. I got them from all kinds of foreign companies, who were desperate to sell those papers because in the moment they seemed almost hopeless. So of course, I was getting them very cheap, for a quarter of the price. But then, at some later point, Assianov would suddenly announce that his Ministry of Finance was able to find some way of buying back this state debt. Which I would have gotten for a song, you see. They would buy it back at, say, eighty percent of the price of the securities. Okay? Can you imagine that? So, I would cash in the difference, which was huge, about forty or fifty percent, and those sums were quite large too. They came to thirty, forty or fifty million dollars! I would send half of what I got to offshore accounts belonging to Matvey and his cronies.

'Now, one time I came to Assianov's grand office, and there was this man there who seemed to be in his mid-sixties. Tall, distinguished-looking, well-groomed, his black hair brushed back, and oh, he had remarkable eyes, they were really special – they had this yellowish spark deep inside, which had a strange kind of glimmer, or a flare. Yes, yes, this man here in your photo. The one in all your photographs. Assianov introduced us. Here, he said to me, meet Igor Mikhailovich Larionov. He has worked for a long time abroad, has developed very good relations with people from the International Monetary Fund, but now he is back to Russia, as it is his home country. Well, the USSR had been his home country, you know – Matvey said he renounced his Latvian citizenship and had already received the Russian passport by a special decree of our President.'

'Could Larionov speak Russian freely?' Malin asked interrupting Semyon's narration.

'Yes, indeed. He spoke Russian as well as you and I. Only if one paid very close attention to his pronunci-

145

ation – then an attentive listener might say there was some slight accent, sometimes. A strange accent, definitely not Latvian, nor anything else Baltic. Oh, by the way, Larionov spoke practically without accent in English, Spanish, and maybe Italian. I found this out later, during the talks.

'Well, back to my story. We were speaking at the Russian Ministry of Finance, mind, and Assianov was presenting the following plan to me. The country is to going to the dogs, he said, so the crisis will be at its peak within the next few months and there will be a default on payments. That is, Russia was bankrupt. Everybody knew it: we knew it, the IMF knew it, and most Western bankers knew it, too. "We, however," Assianov told me on that day, "are organizing, with Larionov's assistance, the receipt of the next scheduled tranche of the IMF loan. It will be in the amount of four billion seven hundred million dollars. But it should be siphoned off via a complicated scheme." Americans would simply disregard the upcoming default, which was imminent, Assianov said. Larionov would be clearing everything with them.

'I realized immediately that whoever had invented this scheme was a genius. Here we have the crisis, a gigantic loan, its disappearance, and a default on the state debt. That's that! No one will be searching for anything. And it will be declared that Russia was bankrupt. We three discussed all kinds of details that day, for quite a long time. Larionov showed some of his cards. He said that he was representing a powerful international organization that he kept calling "The Office", always with a tone of great respect. Larionov said the top manager of The Office was someone whose name was Sergio, but this person was so high up and powerful that even he, Larionov, had never seen him: they only communicated

146

via a secure channel. Sergio made decisions regarding all loan issues in the USA, and he, Igor Larionov, was supposedly only following orders by this head of The Office. That is, he presented himself as a small fry…

'Later on, however, when I could analyze all developments, I arrived at a conclusion there was no mysterious Sergio at all! Sergio and Igor Larionov were the same person, and this person had invented this duality for his own security. Your photos were final proof of that, by the way.

'My part in this whole story was that all our guys – oh, I mean those financial structures associated with me and my colleagues – would be able to pick up, at a specific moment, the four billion seven hundred million dollars and paint them a different color. That is, we had to transform these "disappeared" billions into money that had no relation to the IMF, and then disperse it in accordance with all agreements.'

'And what were those agreements?' Malin interrupted Semyon's monologue. 'Between whom? When did it all happen?'

'Oh, you're moving fast… Okay, fine… We had everything ready by June, just before Assianov and Larionov went to America. The lending chain was supposed to go like this: money would first go through the Republic National Bank of New York owned by Edmond Safra, after which it would be my turn. I organized the subsequent path for the flow of these funds. One billion was to go back to the IMF boys, who were taking great risks when they decided to get involved in this Russian affair. After all, they were providing guarantees for a huge loan to a country that was basically just a step away from financial meltdown. Everyone in the game knew very well that no one would ever see this money again. Nor get it back. Still, they were all talking smart, pretending to be clever while they deliberated urgent aid to the ailing Russian ruble…'

'Are you sure, Semyon, that the IMF accepted a bribe of a billion dollars for granting a loan despite knowing it would be a bad loan, and knowing of the planned embezzlement?'

'Oh, now you've really surprised me, young man… You, who were able to follow the whole "Larionov-Sergio" link all on your own! Why are you asking me such stupid, infantile questions? Of course, they did! I made the transfers with these very hands, sent the money to eight different accounts at banks in Cyprus and the Cayman Islands. I'll share documentation on all these accounts and transfers, so no one will have any doubts later on. You will certainly need this for your story about "Larionov-Santana-Weiss-Sergio" or whatever the name was.'

Levine started tapping at his keyboard, and ten minutes later he handed Malin a memory stick.

'Here you are! I have nothing to lose anymore. In here is all the account data, all transfer records, all payment postings, whatever was due not only to those IMF assholes but also to the other participants. I sent seven hundred million to Assianov, and he told me that the main part of that was sent on to President Yeltsin's family and to some top officials. I broke up those sums into five parts, which were channeled to accounts that are also listed on this stick. Larionov took a billion and a half, because he was the originator of the whole scheme, plus he had provided guarantees for its completion. He maintained that he could buy favors from not only the IMF but also US government officials, all the way to some big guys at the White House – but of them I don't know anything at all.

'But I'm telling you that this mysterious Larionov was absolutely right. Nobody has ever seen such a green wave for doing what we were doing. My guys and I received three hundred million bucks, and the remaining billion was distributed to foreign accounts belonging to the Russian Ministry of Finance, where it vanished without a trace. In other words, it was torn apart into smaller pieces by Russian officials and oligarchs who found success the same way I had, buying up state securities using Assianov's info. Oh, and I shouldn't forget that around two hundred million got lost somewhere in Safra's bank. We'll deal with that later today.'

Semyon Levine grew silent and then looked straight at Malin, who was downloading data from the memory stick into his laptop.

'Hey, Malin, you understand, I hope, that this stick has info on everyone but me, right? Remember that you have never met me, never talked to me and you don't even know my name! Right? Right?'

'I'm not a baby, Semyon! I know my shit.'

'All right then! It's settled. And let me put things straight so as to avoid too many questions. I'm telling you everything I know because I have one single goal: I'm hoping that with my help you will be able to get to this Larionov-Sergio, make it back in order to tell the whole truth, and destroy their damned Office. Only then can I live in safety. There's only a slim chance of success, of course, but I have no other options. I wish I could stop hiding. I want to go back home. To a place by Moscow where I still have a house.'

Malin was surprised to see Semyon in this mode. This powerful, brutal, and even dangerous man sank his head into his shoulders, slumping. He had turned suddenly into a very tired old man, someone who had lost something important over the course of a long and complex life.

'All right, all right, my friends.' Levine roused himself after a minute or two of tense silence. 'Hey, let's not be sad. You'll be fine, you'll do all right, and this means that I'll be fine too!'

'We would love to hear more…' Jia spoke in a timid voice after first looking at Malin, who was undecided as to whether it was a good idea to make Semyon return to his story.

'Well, dear lady, here are some more details: Larionov was appointed as Special Counsel to the President's administration, and, as I already said, he arrived in the USA in this capacity, as a member of the team of Russian negotiators who were visiting the IMF for some special talks. Assianov was head of this delegation, but he was, in fact, present only as a front: this shmuck, this cheap con man could not do anything, as all issues were coordinated and resolved by Larionov. Assianov was there only as a figurehead, a dummy, just like the rest of the team. His function was basically to nod in approval and sign documents.

'On August 14, 1998, the money authorized as a loan to Russia left the Federal Reserve Bank of New York. It was transferred to Edmond Safra's Republic National Bank of New York. From where the whole amount, billions of US dollars, was distributed through my people in accordance with all agreements. Well, I already mentioned that. Safra and his partners appropriated two hundred-odd million as their bonus for rendered services. We also got what we wanted. But later on, crisis hit Russia terribly when it defaulted on its payments. People were taking their lives. Old people were starving… Oh, don't look at me like that. You shouldn't hold it against me. The thing is that those dollars, even four or five billion, could not have saved the country. It wasn't possible anymore; don't you get it? It was a drop in the bucket…'

'Okay, but what happened next? Why are you hiding here? Why did bad blood brew between you and this Larionov-Sergio? Was it something else?'

'Oh God, so many questions at once… The full sum was transferred to Safra's Republic National Bank of New York, right? And we re-directed its portions to the right destinations. I'll always remember that outgoing account number: 608555800. A simple number, so easy to remember. As soon as the money left the account at Safra's bank, I managed all postings and payments, so only Larionov and myself knew the true paths of those billions. Assianov, being no fool, quietly distanced himself from the whole thing. He didn't want to know anything anymore. And why would he, why would he want to know what sums went to what bank? Sort of like, "What's done is done, I got my share, why should I care?" Well, right… He got promoted soon after and became Russia's Minister of Finance. As for Larionov, the man left town as soon as all the money reached all the accounts. There was no trace of him left: no contact information, nothing. He came from nowhere and returned whence he came – into thin air.

'So, things went off smoothly, or so it seemed. When the default hit, everything tumbled down. There was a lot of confusion, and in the chaos, no one was paying any attention to the IMF's billion-dollar loan that we had redirected.

'One year passed. Then one night, that was in September '99, I got a phone call. None other but Igor Larionov. The guy who had gone with the last year's snow, so to speak… He told me in his low and calm voice, hissing like a snake, that the FBI had started an investigation into the disappearance of the four-billion-dollar tranche of the IMF loan. So, they, together with the Swiss prosecutor's office, were looking for evidence.

That is, they were trying to find us. Nothing terrible has happened yet. The FBI almost hit a wall, but...there was this "but" ...'

'It turned out, Larionov told me, that those Yanks and the Swiss had followed somebody's advice and spoken to old Safra and frightened him out of his wits by pretending they knew quite a lot about some of our dealings. They were faking it, of course, but Safra was already suffering from Parkinson's, and he got ready to testify. Well, he would tell the FBI and the Swiss prosecutors what he knew about the IMF tranche, which actually wasn't too much, but what he did know would have been enough to start disentangling the maze.

'At that point, something happened that I wasn't expecting at all. Larionov said that he had received information that it was, in fact, I who had ratted on Safra to the FBI about his bank's activities related to our project. And that I had supposedly done it for guarantees of immunity from persecution. Larionov's next move was, first, to demand that I return all the money I had received as a result of the project. He phrased it this way: "Money should be given back for temporary safe-keeping, and also as a safeguard." Second, he insisted that I fly to Paris to meet with him. Larionov said I could prove my innocence to him only during a personal meeting. And then, following that, we two would agree on the right moves to achieve a good solution. As for the banker, Larionov said, he would take care of him and send our mutual friend from Moscow – Boris Berezovsky – who was both a billionaire and a skilled negotiator. Well, if Borya wasn't able to resolve this matter, then Larionov was ready to take more extreme measures... Yes, Larionov called that powerful Russian billionaire not Boris, but Borya, as if he were a little boy...

'Of course, it goes without saying that I never had any

contact with the FBI. Nor would I have had. At the very least because I'm still on their wanted list due to some matters in the past. I realized Larionov was shocked by Safra's decision and must have decided to start a major mopping-up. He obviously intended to take away my money and get rid of me when I came to France. My initial reaction was that he couldn't do anything to me if I stayed in Russia. I was at home, after all, and that meant a lot. Local police were eating out of my hand. My buddies, all thugs, were all around me. Plus, I had a well-trained security service. Taking all this into account, I showed him – excuse me, ladies – my middle finger, and decided to sit it out at my place near Moscow. He tried contacting me a few times more, but I didn't respond. Which was dumb, because…what happened soon after was the most awful thing of my entire life.'

Semyon took a sip of his whisky. Then, as he started lighting a cigar, he lowered his eyes. Still, both Malin and Jia saw something like tears glistening in them. Perhaps they were mistaken. Regardless, the old man suddenly seemed barely able to speak. He was trying to push out the words, but they came out in a croak. Malin gave him a glass of water.

Levine drank it slowly, puffed at his cigar, enveloping them all in thick smoke. Then he was at last able to continue:

'The son of bitch tried to kill me twice. The first time, they blew up my car, but I was lucky: I was sitting in the back, and I got off with a slight concussion. When they made a second attempt, they mixed up the cars – so they shot dead the driver of the other car and one of my security men. But then…then they blew up my wife and son. Because they thought I was traveling with them in that bulletproof car… My son had just turned fourteen…

'What next? Oh, I fled Russia. Sold all my shares and real estate there for a song. I transferred all the money to numbered accounts, lost my passport, got a new one changing my name…that's how I ended up here. Those guys, whom Larionov-Sergio sent over here, they were looking for me for about ten years. Then it seemed maybe they decided to end the search: they either thought I was dead anyway or that I wouldn't be able to tell anything to the FBI or whoever. As far as I know, they're off my trail. But I haven't dared leave my lair here, anyway.'

'Tell me, Semyon, was Safra's death in the fire… I mean, was Larionov-Sergio to blame for it? That's how Artayev, the Russian journalist, presented it to me.'

'Of course, Malin! I am convinced of it. I can see it as clearly as these lines on my palms. Larionov started cutting off all leads that could have led anyone to him. Assianov, for example, could be spared. First of all, he didn't know about the sensitive transfers. Second, he would surely keep silent as the grave about the rest, so he wasn't dangerous. I knew too much, and I was aware of it, so I had to hide in order to save my life. The only one out there who was visible was Safra, and he'd expressed willingness to talk to the FBI and the Swiss prosecutor's office.

'Oh, by the way, Borya Berezovsky was one of Larionov's cronies, but he knew as little about him as I did. Boris was a man of rare intellect, but he was trapped in some kind of state of awe – he was enchanted by Igor Larionov, even believed him to be almost omnipotent. Boris told me that himself. He said that at times he felt a panicked fright because of Larionov. He explained that throughout his life he had only ever been afraid of that which he could not fathom, and Larionov was exactly that. The unexplainable. The unfathomable. Well, a live person, that's for sure, but… At some point Boris departed to a better world, too, of course. Just like so many others who have had contact with Larionov… Shit! With Sergio-Weiss…or whatever his name was?'

'Oh, Santana is another,' Jia said. 'And who knows how many others…'

'So, here's what I was told,' Levine continued. 'Safra and Berezovsky met and talked at the banker's villa on Cap d'Antibes. I have reason to believe that Larionov was also present. Safra seems to have started trying to weasel his way out, telling some tall tales. After which, I guess, Larionov simply burned him to death in his own house in Monte Carlo. Not with his own hands, of course, no, he would never do that, but it doesn't matter much. In fact, none of us had anything against it. All of us needed this old banker to leave the scene – and he was very ill anyway – but only Larionov could act in such a skillful and clever manner. I am too old to believe in coincidences…'

'Do you remember any special features of this Larionov-Sergio?' Malin interrupted him. 'Any character traits? Habits? I would need any links to reality, rather than to his mystical side.'

'Wait, Malin, here's something for you, perhaps!' Semyon exclaimed after a momentary pause. 'I'll mention something perhaps insignificant, but you might be able to use it somehow. Larionov and I met several times to discuss details of our project, both at the Ministry of Finance and at my summer place by Moscow. I noticed that his laptop featured an unusual screensaver. It was The Garden of Earthly Delights, that Hieronymus Bosch painting.[1] Specifically, it was the right side

---

1. *The Garden of Earthly Delights* is the famous triptych by Hieronymus Bosch, which received its name after its central part dedicated to the sin of lust: Luxuria. The actual original title of this creation by Bosch is not known.

of the triptych, which depicts Hell. I asked him once why he liked Bosch. And why in particular he liked this nightmare vision, reminiscent of the worst, most horrible apparitions? Do you know what his answer was, Malin?'

'No. What?'

'Larionov was silent for a while, looking straight at the image on the screen and then he said, clearly, with conviction, something like the following: "Bosch is my God. He showed the world exactly as I see it. Ugly, petty, and wretched. This condition is unavoidable and unchangeable, because we've gone so far down the road that it cannot be improved. This is why there is no sin in doing what I keep doing. I've been using my intellect and my knowledge of the basic human behavior in order to control this gigantic brothel, and to take what I want to take. That might be billions of dollars, or the lives of those who are most important for the rest of you… I make your superiors fulfill any of my wishes. For I am – God! Or this: I am like Bosch!"

'Having said that, Larionov laughed and turned his notebook screen to face me, so that I could see every detail of that awful vision called *The Garden of Earthly Delights*. Perhaps it's some nonsense. But it really sank deep into my mind. Oh, another thing – his gaze was uncanny. Deep in his pupils, one could see eerie yellow flames flaring up. Today I can think differently about it – I understand that it must have been an optical illusion of sorts. Perhaps Larionov simply had an expressive gaze, and his eye color just had a strong yellowish hue, but back then I really got scared looking at him. I was scared! I, who others were always scared of!'

A hush fell over the room. Malin turned around his empty glass. Jia, who had her head supported by her intertwined palms, was looking straight at Semyon

Levine, an old man sitting with downcast eyes, seemingly hypnotized by his cigar, which by now was almost out. Suddenly the first peals of thunder came through the window from outside. A nocturnal thunderstorm was coming up, a severe and uproarious one: the kind when thunder comes only seconds after a violent flash of lightning...

'We already have a unique compilation of information on our hands,' Malin spoke broodingly, 'something that would seem able to shatter this world. But it doesn't provide us the main clue. We're still roaming around like blind kittens, not knowing how we could get to this Santana-Weiss-Larionov-Sergio. Where could he be, this elderly Bosch fan?'

Jia, who had been silent for a long while, suddenly raised her head high and began to speak quickly, as if trying rid herself of some visions from her past:

'I've had this feeling lately that we're circling around an important point – a correct one, but one we keep passing by. In a way, it's like being in an intricate labyrinth. Why don't we get through the whole story, step by step, and try to pay attention to all of the tiniest details. I would also like to ask you, Mr. Levine – what would you do next in our stead?'

'You may be surprised, my dear girl, but I would turn to your countrymen. To the Chinese. Don't act so surprised. You were the ones who told me that "Martin Weiss" was a lobbyist for a military corporation supplying American troops in Vietnam, right? And he supposedly died at the hands of the Viet Cong in 1967. Correct? His body was never recovered, so there is a strong hint that that person was something like a phoenix, reborn into a character in the next part of your story.

'Well, I happen to know that, even at that time, the Viet Cong could not have organized such an ideal disappearance and later rebirth without the participation of either certain Soviets or the Vietnamese mafia, the so-called Snakes.[2] I don't think it would be possible to get any information about it from my Russian fellows. But perhaps it would be possible to talk to some of the longtime snakes? What if someone from those days is still around?'

'Oh, I see what you're talking about!' Malin perked up. 'Since we won't be able to get closer to the Vietnamese, we could try the Chinese triads – they had very close connections with the Vietnamese Snakes after the war, in the 1970s. In fact, I wrote an article about it a couple years ago.'

'You're right. I have been working with some guys in the US Triads recently. That's why I know a little bit about their cooperation with the Vietnamese. Unfortunately, we parted ways before too long, so I'm not sure I can find any of their people here in London. What if—'

'I can talk to the triads here in London,' Jia interrupted. Both Malin and Semyon raised their heads at the intensity in her voice; her offer was loud and clear. Both men looked at her, waiting for an explanation. After a pause Jia offered: 'Perhaps we could even meet the 489…'

'Wait, wait, Jia.' Malin looked at her in total bewilderment. as if seeing her for the first time. 'Hold on, my dear. First of all, who is this 489? And secondly, you told me your late father was head of the local triad, but that was quite a long time ago, right? And now you're telling

---

2. The Vietnamese mafia is sometimes called "snake" due to its pattern of transnational activities: first a "head" shows up somewhere – this is a person who establishes contact with local authorities – and later on the "body" follows, this being the main forces of the organized criminal gang. Vietnamese "Snakes" cooperate regularly with Chinese Triads.

us you could arrange such a meeting.'

'Everything is fine, Malin. Don't get upset. 489 refers to the current head of the Triad here. He's also known as Lord of the Mountain. And speaking of my contacts with the Chinese in London, I should have mentioned that my dad was one of the *most* venerated Lung Tao. Lung Tao means the same thing as 489 or Lord of the Mountain. After my father died, his connections with others in those circles remained unsevered, according to the old tradition. They would stay there even if I wanted to break them off.'

'Okay, girl, do your part!' Semyon said in a muffled voice. 'Perhaps this will be the smartest move that would take us to Sergio. Or maybe it's a dead end, who knows? But it's certainly worth a try.'

Jia found her mobile and dialed a number – from memory, it appeared... Then she spoke in Chinese for quite a long time, calling around and talking to a number of different people, sometimes laughing out loud, and once even raising her voice. Both men were silent, trying to catch at least one familiar word in the rapid flow of Jia's confident singsong.

When Jia finished her phone marathon, she downed whatever remained in the glass before her and said:

'Everything seems to be all right. Lung Tao Guang Lan is expecting Malin and me in London tonight at nine. I already explained that the Lung Tao is head of the triad in a certain region. Lan is responsible for Great Britain. He's a little over forty, but despite his relative youth, he is one of the most powerful Lung Taos anywhere in the world. Guang Lan considers himself my father's pupil. He said he would try to help, in memory of my father.'

'But you had reason to believe, you said, that your father was killed so that someone could replace him,'

Malin said casually. 'Would you suspect Lan as someone who might have arranged that?'

'Listen to me, Malin,' Jia's voice was low, but rough. 'My suspicions are none of anyone's business. I will have to come to terms with them using my own reasoning, my own logic. I have no evidence against anyone. Such suspicions have no reason to exist. My father taught me that any idea, any thought may be spoken aloud only if it can be confirmed by solid facts. In this case, however, my dad would have been on my side. Especially since Lan didn't become the head of the London triad right after my father's death. It was Yun Han who stepped into my father's shoes, so if anyone, he's the one who may have had some connection to dad's death.'

'I'm sorry, Jia. I didn't mean to touch a sore spot,' Malin tried to apologize. He was quite embarrassed about his insensitive blunder, so he changed the subject. 'We still have time before we leave for London, so, if it's all right with Semyon, I would try to use this Hecate again. I suddenly have a crazy idea.'

'Semyon is certainly not against it,' Levine smiled. 'Still, could you first explain what it's all about?'

'We used this special program for searching faces, right? And we were using the images of so-called Larionov and the two "Controllers," from 1963 and 2001. This helped us find Luis Santana and Martin Weiss. Plus, Semyon, you gave us a new name, Sergio. So, what we know today is that, between 1963 and 2001, the same person used the following names: Luis Santana, Martin Weiss, Igor Larionov, and Sergio. There is a blank space, however. There is this photograph taken on September 11, 2001, and the same Controller is there. But we have no idea who he was at that time, what name he was going by, or what his function was.

'Why don't we start a search using only this one

photo from September 11? We could also ask Hecate to do its search using only certain parts of the man's face. For example, using the area around his eyes. After all, eyes are the most striking feature, and we remember someone's eyes better than anything else about him.'

'OK, let's do it, Malin. We do have time before our evening meeting.'

Malin opened his laptop and started the software. Then he put only one photo into the search box, the one in which a stranger stood on Washington Street half an hour after the second plane hit. Malin highlighted the man's eyes and, cropping this part of his face in Paint, he inserted it as a second search task. With the search request containing just the one item for reference, Malin entertained a slight hope that Hecate would find it easier to ferret out other, similar images from the vast global archives online.

The program started going fast and faster, zillions of images flitting past at incredible speed. Malin sat down on the windowsill and grew still, waiting. Thin, transparent rays of the sun cut through the space between ancient oaks and were refracted in the glass, creating an intricate lacework of light around the room. Semyon and Jia were sitting next to him, somewhat off to one side in cozy chairs, their images reflected several times in the windows. They were talking about something, but Malin could not make out what they were saying... He turned around. Jia's exquisite fine profile seemed to be floating in the air again, this time surrounded by the interlaced cobweb of sunbeams.

An image from thirty years prior suddenly came to mind. Why did it surface now from the warm, long gone past of his childhood? They were all together, he and his parents, riding a local train to their summer place in Tarasovo. Pines were flitting past the car windows, and a silvery patch of some lake was appearing for short moments between their tall trunks. That was happiness. Such happiness that it was overwhelming to his soul; its wave was gigantic, too big for the small child who could now only drown in it, feeling only it. Thinking about nothing else. Well, perhaps anticipating that their station was to come soon, and that his papa would put his backpack onto his shoulders, and his mama would take Maksim by the hand when they started out towards the forest. They would walk for a while under the canopy of so many trees, stepping on a little sandy path littered with pine needles. And then they would come to a small house that they rented for the summer from Uncle Anton, who was always somewhat tipsy. Anton wasn't really his uncle, of course, just as this dacha that they called 'our dacha' was not really theirs. But it did not matter, because later they would go out mushroom hunting and swimming in the lake with little Vitya, their neighbor. In the evening, around the hour when the still bright yellow-red sun was falling behind the tops of the pines, Maksim's mama would read him a book.

This sudden train of memories was interrupted by a melodic sound: Hecate was signaling that its first task was complete. Malin approached the laptop, feeling, he thought, like a hunter about to check his snares. The box labeled 'Result' showed two almost identical photographs. Both were obviously taken for IDs. The only slight difference was their size. Most probably they had been taken for a passport and for a driver's license. The faces were very familiar, the same as that of Santana-Weiss-Larionov-Sergio. Beneath both photos were the texts of newspaper articles. Malin read them out loud, even though both Jia and Semyon were standing just behind him, looking at the screen.

The East Orange Record[3] reports: The Silver Stars Motel burned down last night. It was located two kilometers from East Orange (a town 10 miles from New York). Firefighters discovered the badly burnt body of one victim, Eric Novack, born 1931. A retired banker with no family, he was addicted to alcohol in recent years. The motel fire may have been due to Novack's cigarette, which was still burning while he was intoxicated. Pictured is the man's ID photo, which miraculously remained intact. Burial will happen at Bishops Cemetery tomorrow noon.

The same article was printed in a second local newspaper, only they had used a different photo.

Both publications were dated September 12, 2001. That is, the day after the destruction of the skyscrapers in New York.

Max Malin was the first to break the silence:

'Okay, here is one more name for our Controller. When the planes hit the World Trade Center, our Controller was watching quite unperturbed, and his name that day was Eric Novack. Later things followed a well-oiled scenario: Novack died next day in a fire, his body was badly burnt, but some of his official documents were, miraculously, only singed. Our Controller, in the meantime, got a new identity. Still, as for his age, it all fits. Luis Santana would have been 68 in 2001, and Novack's age, as per his ID, was 70. There's no doubt it's him! I'm convinced.'

'How old is the Controller today?' Levine asked. 'He must be of a venerable age, but it seems like he is still pretty active, doesn't it?'

'Let's count. We're in 2018 now. If we take the earliest reference to this person, that would be Santana's birth date. In this case our many-faced hero must be

---

3. This is a regional daily newspaper from East Orange, New Jersey.

eighty-six years old. But I wouldn't trust these search engines too much. In my opinion, his age could be between eighty-three and eighty-eight.'

Semyon nodded and suddenly left the fireplace lounge, quietly closing the door behind him. He came back with a large envelope in his hands. Holding it out to Malin, he switched to Russian once again:

'Malin, of course I understand that you may protest what you regard as "dirty money", put on a show of injured innocence and tell me why you cannot accept even a penny of it. But let me assure you that the money in this envelope has had nothing to do with any illegal operations.'

'That's interesting. How do you determine the quality of your cash, Semyon?'

'Very simple: I took this one from a special shelf inside my safe. Yes, I have in fact allocated a special shelf for good clean money.' Levine beamed, all smiles. 'There's not much in here. Thirty thousand Euros in small bills. You can use it for your research. You must find Sergio and continue spreading information about him. Let the whole world know about him. For Sergio, this might mean his end. And for me, a new start, a new life…'

'I'll take the money,' Malin said without hesitation. 'For one, I don't have much choice. In this situation, any money can and must be used well. And secondly, I may find some solace in the thought that it won't get back to its original owner anyway.

'And I would like to say something else,' Malin went on, sitting down on the chair in front of the fireplace. He turned towards Levine who was standing close to the fire. 'I understand your dream. You want to return to Russia, to take your revenge for losing your son and your wife, and also simply to stay alive. But all that you have here in England is positive. You've got all of life's comforts – a lot of money, a great home, a relatively quiet existence. The only negatives are your age and some health problems. Maybe you should ignore this Sergio-Larionov thing? Forget about it and enjoy your life? Wouldn't that be much easier? Or if you wanted some excitement, you could easily stir the pot by writing a book about your life. It could add some zing to your existence to write a tell-all, and you could publish it in Russia or the US under a pseudonym, or even anonymously. Then you could rest comfortably here at your fireplace with your whisky and your cigar, following the international scandal and the ballyhoo from here. Wouldn't you love that?'

'Well, my young friend, let me first say this. You must already have some idea that this story related to the IMF loan and the banker's death is only one episode of a gigantic maze. Only you might be able to put together the pieces of this huge puzzle. I'm not religious, you know, but I am, sort of, mystically inclined. So, in your case, I have a mystical, intuitive feeling that you should be all right. That you can do it. Too much has already fallen into your lap all by itself. And already you can establish some links along this special chain of events.

'Secondly, no one would be looking for me at all unless I started leaving my lair and acting up. If I were to tell the world only a small part of what I know, everyone would realize that I'm still alive, and that my memory is as intact as my desire to take revenge. It would be a very different situation from your publishing the results of your investigation, telling the whole story of this Controller from the sixties up to now. If you do it, universal panic will ensue, and my enemies will have more urgent things to care about. This is the only good option for me. Anything else would be deadly. It's strange but the older I get the more I desire to live. With every new day

I feel my list of unaccomplished deeds grow longer and longer. You'll understand this later in your life.'

'At the same time,' Malin started, taking a cigar, but not lighting it, 'you are quite willingly sending me to meet what you consider to be certain death. And you don't seem to have any qualms about it...'

'That's not true, Malin. It's not about meeting your doom. It's your life. And now, to be exact, this is your only chance to stay alive: unravel the most mysterious, serious events of the past fifty years. That would be your only chance to survive and to save her life, too,' Semyon nodded his head, indicating Jia. 'You're up shit creek in this. To put it more politely, you're already so deep in trouble that no other options are left for you. It's either you get them, or they get you. Do you agree with me now?'

'I guess I do.' Malin got up slowly and walked up to Levine's chair. He gazed straight into the old man's eyes for a while. Then he started towards the next room, where he and Jia had left their things.

'We'll get going, okay?' he said.

'Fine. It's time to go. I'll take you to the cab.'

10

The Lost Billions and a Banker's Death
Monaco, 1999

S eptember '99 on Côte d'Azur, the French Riviera, was unusually rainy. The small resort town Ville-franche-sur-Mer, fifteen kilometers away from Nice airport, had been completely drenched over the preceding week. The weather improved only by Sunday, when the tender flecks of sunlight reflecting off the surface of the sea once again started playing their eternal, happy game of hide-and-seek around the light-colored house walls all along the Quai de l'Amiral Courbet.

It was early morning. A tall, dark-haired man with a chiseled aquiline profile and deep-set piercing eyes stepped out of a rented Bentley, which had brought him from the airport to this quay. The man, looking much younger than his actual age of sixty-odd years, walked at once inside a building with a rather unpretentious name: Welcome Hotel. He got the key for a deluxe suite booked in his name, which, in this period of his life, was, according to his Russian documents, Igor Larionov. Though he was a citizen of Russia, he nevertheless spoke Russian with a very slight accent that many thought probably hailed from one of the Baltic countries. His French and English, on the other hand, were perfect, with no accent at all.

Larionov went up to his floor and left his small, lightweight case in the anteroom. He walked around his suite, inspecting both the rooms and the balcony that opened to the sea with great care. Outside, one could hear the voices of some vacationers, exuberant with their first sunny day on the beach.

Larionov took off his coat and got a small bottle of whisky from the mini bar. He looked at it with some suspicion at first, but soon he settled into a chair on the balcony with a glass in his hand. Putting on his thinking cap, as they say.

His trip to Villefranche-sur-Mer had been organized following the insistent request of Russian deputy minister of finance, as well as that of some Russian billionaires, all of whom had successfully pilfered a part of the IMF loan to Russia. The loan had been granted in the amount of almost $5 billion just before the Russian financial meltdown in August of 1998. Why did they get only a part of it? Because a sizeable sum of that loan amount had also been transferred to Larionov's own offshore accounts... After all, it was he who had both masterminded and directed that tremendous financial plot.

Well, Igor Larionov mused to himself, why is it that now, a year after the Russian default crisis, this banker Edmond Safra decides to speak to the FBI representatives. He has been the owner of the Republic National Bank of New York, of course, and the main postings and transfers of that IMF loan were done through his bank. Recently, God knows why, Safra told the FBI guys that he was ready to give testimony about his relations with the Russians. What testimony? What would he testify about? Was it possible that this ailing old banker really decided to tell the Americans what he knew about the lost Russian tranche? What a strange move! Especially since he had smeared himself in a big way through his own participation in that affair.

Or could it be related to a different affair of laundering Russian money through his bank? If that's it, then there's nothing to worry about. That story is already over, plus any connections that would have led to Larionov, and his business were already mopped up quite thoroughly. The FBI has all the information – they received whatever they wanted to know a year ago, and that investigation is most certainly over by now. So, what more could Safra want to tell them? Well, today Boris and I will hear it from Safra himself.

There was a soft warble of the phone from the outside line.

'Hello?'

'Hi, Igor, hello! Here is Boris Berezovsky. I got the news that you'd already checked in at the hotel.'

'Great, Borya. Did you come to an agreement with the banker?'

'Is there anyone with whom I can't make an agreement?' Berezovsky tittered, and Larionov could easily picture Boris, all smiles, rubbing his hands together, as was his custom.

'What I meant was when shall we meet him? Be more specific, please.'

'Here's what we've got. Safra expects us today at four p.m., at his Villa Leopolda,[1] not far from where you're staying. I'll come and get you in an hour. We can discuss things on our way there. Is that alright?'

'Yes, fine.'

Larionov tipped back in his lounge chair and started

---

1. Villa Leopolda is one of the most expensive private residences in the world. It is located in Saint-Jean-Cap-Ferrat, that was a part of Villefranche-sur-Mer on French Riviera until 2015. Net area of the villa is 1700 sq. m. /2033 square yards/. It is surrounded by a private botanical garden having an area of 14,2 hectares /35 acres/.

thinking that, at his age, it wasn't right that he should rush around the world managing and monitoring projects for other people, even if they were really important. He was, after all, already a multi-billionaire – why should he care about any issues, whether global financial fraud or contract killings or terrorist acts. However, it seemed that he could not exist in any other mode or live a different kind of life.

Over the last forty years he had always personally controlled all major projects, and that was why they had always been successfully completed. *And that means*, Larionov thought, *that the time has not yet come to transfer the reins of power to someone else, even a most trusted accomplice. Besides, I've found no one of the kind in the whole world. No one has become big enough to match me. I must do everything with my own two hands.* To retire and lead a quiet life, without developing new ideas or forging any plans, seemed to him to be a dreary and pathetic end. He could, of course, spend the remaining years of his life on his own island in the Indian Ocean, which only a few people on this planet knew about, but that would only be for the final chapter of his life, which would promptly culminate in a visit from the grim reaper. And that particular visit had nothing to do with Larionov's plans for the foreseeable future, which only included more playing of intricate games, more being involved in the action – enjoying only the active, aggressive element of existence, something he couldn't live without!

Soon the buzzer sounded, and the receptionist reported that a car was expecting Mister Larionov downstairs. Igor put on a light sports jacket that showed off his trim, sporty look, put his phone and his wallet into its inside pockets and descended to the ground floor. He didn't bother to lock up his suite. There was nothing in there that would betray anything about him.

Exiting the hotel, a bodyguard popped out of a Rolls-Royce Phantom just in time to open its back door for him. Larionov found himself inside the car beside a dark-eyed man with a starkly receding hairline. This fellow started shifting around his large seat in jerky movements, as if, despite the overwhelming spaciousness of the car's interior, his guest would need more space to sit. Larionov immediately recognized the habits of his long-time acquaintance. It was Boris Berezovsky, a member of the first batch of Russian billionaires, and a man from the closest entourage and confidants of President Yeltsin's family.

'Greetings, Igor! How was your flight?'

'Hi Borya! How do you know that I was on a plane? Is someone monitoring my routes?'

'Oh no, no! What are you talking about? Who is capable of following you?' Berezovsky started bustling about again, trying to conceal his uneasiness, but his manner betrayed a strong internal fear. The Rolls-Royce's owner could do nothing about it: deep inside, Boris always felt a throbbing of sheer panic whenever he was in Larionov's presence. And panic was not a feeling with which he was familiar. 'I only asked the receptionist to let me know when Mister Larionov arrives. That was it. Nothing more, Igor, my friend...'

'It's all right, Boris. I was joking. In fact, I drove here, all the way from Marseilles,' Larionov said in a low voice, looking Berezovsky straight in the eye. This was not true: he had in fact flown into Nice, but that had been on one of his private planes, which were registered as the property of an offshore company. Larionov said what he said because he was trying to figure out whether Berezovsky knew about it. Judging by Berezovsky's behavior, this time the man was speaking the truth. Which was great:

the less they knew about him, the better.

'Borya, let's go over the present situation once more. What does Safra want to tell the FBI? Why does he need it? Which specific information he would like to reveal? Most importantly, if it's about our IMF tranche, what offer could we make him? Tell me what ideas you have, my friend.'

'Well, Igor, the situation isn't clear. But I have managed to learn that Edmond decided to reveal how the funds were passing through his channels last year. Only the funds related to the IMF loan, of course, the ones that were meant to go to Russia but never made it. A trusted source from his entourage told me that Safra became horrified that his bank could be implicated in laundering Russian money, not to mention in having contact with the Russian mob. This is why the old man decided to tell the FBI about his lesser sin: helping us out with the tranche project. Because, you know, it was only assistance, just a little help – and only because of his own stupidity, supposedly, because he couldn't be aware of the whole picture – anyway, I think that would be Safra's line. If he were to present things that way, he wouldn't be that heavily prosecuted, but our role in the whole affair would become immediately clear. His testimony would make transparent the system you created, which worked so well. And that would lead to more investigations, to criminal actions, etc.'

'Boris, this only means that we must make one thing perfectly clear to him: he absolutely cannot do any of that to us. Let's first listen to what he has to say, of course. We can draw our conclusions later based on his words.'

'Sure, sure. Whatever you like. We'll be there in a couple of minutes. Our friend lives here, you know, at this amazing villa that he owns – La Leopolda. Oh, this villa is my dream. I wanted to buy it, twice I made him offers, but Safra said "no" both times.'

'Oh, you poor fellow. I guess you'll live. Anyway, looks like we're here.'

Villa La Leopolda was a vast complex of yellow-red structures surrounded by a fence with dozens of security cameras on it. Its resident was 67-year-old Edmond Safra, billionaire, and owner of the Republic National Bank of New York. The guests were expected: the gate slowly opened just as the Rolls-Royce came to a stop in front of it, and the car rolled smoothly onto one of the many terraces of La Leopolda.

Larionov and Berezovsky, accompanied by a security man who came out to greet them, walked first through a cypress path, past marble lions atop a parapet beside a very large swimming pool, and entered the house. There, a grey-haired major-domo greeted them, telling them drily: 'Monsieur Safra is expecting Mister Berezovsky and Mister Larionov on the veranda.' After a long walk through all kinds of passages, after climbing many flights of steps, the guests finally arrived on a wooden veranda that might remind one of a hunter's lodge. There was Edmond Jacob Safra himself there, coming towards them with arms outstretched in a welcoming gesture. He was round-faced, bald, and wore expensive, glittering spectacles.

'I am very glad to see you, my friends! Please take your seats. What would you like to drink?'

A short exchange of greetings followed. Berezovsky started fidgeting again. Larionov's face expressed no emotion, except for maintaining a polite smile. All three were sitting in low chairs around an ebony table. Larionov, tasting a Le Montrachet 1978 that Safra offered, closed his eyes in appreciation. He sipped more of the exquisite wine, but eventually broke the prolonged silence:

'What a great wine, Mister Safra! If I'm not mistaken, Le Montrachet of that year was selling at Sotheby's recently at twenty-four thousand dollars per bottle. It's definitely worth this much!'

'You might be surprised, Mister Larionov, but it was I who bought all seven bottles in that lot. I have two compliments for you: not only are you a true connoisseur of wine, but also your French is truly excellent.' Safra said this looking at Berezovsky, for whom Larionov translated into Russian what he felt was necessary for Boris to understand. 'Quite different compared with many of your compatriots!'

'Thank you. But let's talk business.'

'Of course, Mister Larionov!'

'Let us be frank with each other, Mister Safra. That would help us understand our positions correctly. And, perhaps, allow us to avoid any rash acts on either side. There was a strange piece of news that we received from across the Pond. We were told that our reliable partner, a banker named Safra, had supposedly decided to talk to the Federal Bureau of Investigation. This despite the fact that he'd made a lot of money on our transactions August of last year. They say he's supposed to be giving testimony. Is that true?'

Safra's eyes, which had been nervously scanning his guests' faces so far, immediately froze, narrowing into little slits. Larionov, however, noticed the first flashes of panic in them. After a short pause the banker said, in a low voice:

'Well, yes, my friends, your sources were right. Indeed, I did give my consent to provide some testimony to the FBI. It's scheduled for this coming December. However, it would not have any bearing on the subject of last year's IMF loan, or on our deals around it. None, zero – please do take this into account! The Americans have pressed me quite hard, so I will have to tell them *some-*

thing about legalizing money via the Bank of New York. Only some part of those operations, and only showing some documents related to those parts. I mean certain transactions in which your countrymen were involved, but those are a completely different story, so you have nothing to do with it. Right? Besides, this will just be a deposition, so nothing would go to court. It's just meant to give the FBI some idea about how to look for launderers. Again, your money has nothing to do with it!'

'My dear Monsieur Safra, it's not just about our money, but also yours. You were given your share, after all, and a pretty big one, too. You can't deny that, right? But most important is this: can you provide some guarantee that everything will happen exactly as you have just told us? And how can you prove it to me?' Larionov spoke very slowly, looking Safra straight in the eye. The banker slumped in his chair, as if it suddenly felt too big and uncomfortable. Larionov's eyes had become two bottomless pits, with ghastly little yellow fires flickering far below. Edmond Safra, already 67, was a weathered man who had seen a lot in his life – but he was overwhelmed by fear, animal fear that grew into a terror he had never felt. Never before had he seen such eyes as these: his death sentence was clearly written there.

'But why, Mr. Larionov?! Why would you have any doubt about my word? Please don't. I built up my business from the start on the basis of being honest about everything with my partners. Please, let us leave this topic and never return to it. All three of us made a lot of money on that project, so I would like to raise my glass to our cooperation. Please have some more of this wine that you liked so much. Mr. Berezovsky, take another sip!'

The guests held up their glasses, and Larionov stood up. Berezovsky followed suit.

'Mr. Safra, please excuse us, we have one more important meeting in an hour, no less important than this one. Thank you for your sincerity and your excellent wine.'

Safra got up heavily from his chair. Shaking his guests' hands, he said in a tired voice:

'I was glad to be able to meet you both, my reliable partners – and, I hope, my friends. Maher will take you to your car.'

A middle-aged man emerged immediately from behind the door. His hair was carefully combed back, and he had the tight appearance of a former athlete or soldier. Larionov noted that Safra had not pressed any call button, which meant that Maher had most certainly been listening in on their conversation: he appeared as soon as the banker mentioned his name.

'Gentlemen, please follow me. I will see you out,' Maher said in English. His pronunciation was American. Walking past him, Larionov looked straight at him and smiled slightly with a strange smile.

Several minutes later, the softly purring Rolls-Royce brought the two guests beyond the gate of Villa La Leopolda.

'Igor, my dear! I must have missed quite a lot of your exchange. Could you please explain what happened?' Berezovsky asked, rubbing his hands. 'I got the impression that Safra was frightened to death...'

'You're right, Boris. What he was telling us is a pack of lies, from the first word to the last. I am convinced that he's already decided to tell the FBI the full story of the IMF loan. His sweet tales about the Bank of New York were meant as a distraction. Safra must have already told the Americans all that he knows about the bank, but in December he will tell them everything about us too, in order to protect himself. So, what would you suggest? What options do we have for dealing with him?'

Waiting for an answer, Larionov looked straight at Berezovsky, and Boris felt a cold shiver go down his spine. Berezovsky, who was used to being the master, the lead, had ceded leadership to Larionov from the first day they met. With him he felt better in the role of a subordinate. Every time they met, Berezovsky caught himself feeling a strange wish to become small, insignificant, and preferably, to find someplace to hide. Perhaps the reason for this was that Berezovsky had obtained, two years ago, disturbing, completely non-verifiable information: that Larionov was not what he pretended to be, and that the scope of his activities was much larger than anyone could imagine, even with the most fantastic assumptions.

'You see, Igor, the situation is close to becoming a dead end, both for me and for my Russian partners, including those surrounding the top man in the state. If Safra were to testify to the FBI, telling them how we handled those billions from the IMF, the shit will hit the fan – it would fuck everything up!' Berezovsky cursed as if for some relief, but only felt more nervous than before. He continued: 'This would mean both the Americans and Europeans – primarily the Swiss and French, in the latter case – laying their hands on our assets, alleging that they were all stolen. And they can do it because it's an international issue, not some internal affair of Russia's. This is how they would squeeze us. It would be a very tight situation, even if later we might be able to convince them that Safra was lying, and that our assets were honestly earned. Actually, perhaps we could resolve this by giving them something...interesting...but in any case, we would first have these hellish problems and also lose quite a lot – billions, even... I know you will disappear to the nowhere from which you came, but as for us...we'll lose everything. Or almost everything. What is to be done?'

'Then this problem has to be resolved, Boris. Definitely and conclusively.'

'Will you be able to do it?'

'Yes.'

'So that the banker would not testify? He would… fall silent?'

'He will.'

Berezovsky paused for a while, thinking. Then he sighed and said:

'How much and when?'

'One hundred million. And the problem would be resolved within a month and a half.'

'I'm sorry, Igor,' Berezovsky mumbled, as if all of his energy left him, 'but you have already made over a billion on this affair. Why do you want so much more now for this issue?'

'Because if the problem with Safra is not resolved, you will all lose much more. Billions of dollars. And that would be a real problem. As for me, as you so correctly put it, I would simply disappear. So, share this information with your colleagues and your partners, please. Let them decide.'

'Personally, I have nothing against your conditions. I have no choice anyway – but I'm only one of many who would be interested in Safra staying silent. I need time to talk to all the others. But I think a positive decision might follow in around a week's time.'

'That's fine. Take me to my hotel now.'

It was Thursday, December 2, around the time when Monaco's late evening becomes the beginning of its night. At this hour even the most seasoned promenaders desert the Avenue d'Ostende. A black Mercedes, outwardly no different from dozens of its brethren parked close by, drove slowly up to the luxurious Hotel de Paris, which was drowning in bright yellow lights.

Stepping out of the car, Igor Larionov said curtly to the driver: 'Tomorrow's your day off. I'll call.' He entered the building accompanied by a porter, who put his suitcase and small briefcase onto a trolley. A few minutes later, he went up to his deluxe double room. When his luggage finally arrived, he took out his laptop and several mobile phones, spreading them around a dainty table. Then he sat down in a deep armchair and, closing his eyes, remained motionless, musing.

Tomorrow at five in the morning, Ted Maher,[2] Edmond Safra's nurse and bodyguard, has to carry out certain actions, he thought. Yes, the same man who looked so unfriendly to me and Berezovsky last September. He will act because some others convinced him that these actions were absolutely necessary. And Maher trusted those people implicitly. Just as I trust them, only my trust in those people cuts off at a certain line, limited by a certain large sum in US dollars.

A month ago, one Axel Forsh had come to Monaco. He was Ted's old friend from their years in the military. Axel had told Ted that he was connected with some lawyers and revealed to Ted that Safra was so impressed by his professional care and loyalty that the old man intended to include Maher in his will. Axel Forsh showed some proof of that to his old buddy Ted, who was in fact in dire need of money. It was a draft of the will taken down by the banker's lawyer, with a sum of one million dollars right by Maher's name, in Safra's handwriting. Naturally, it was a fake, but it was very well done – plus

---

2. **Ted Maher** (born 1958) entered Las Vegas Police Academy in 1979. Then he served in one of the most prestigious units of the US Army, the 82nd Airborne Division, and several years later he was transferred to Special Forces, also known as the Green Berets. Towards the end of the 1990s Maher left military service and became a nurse with a hospital of the Columbian University. In 1999 he started working for Edmond Safra after the latter's grand-daughter spoke in his favor. Maher took the position of nurse and bodyguard, with an annual salary of $180K.

Ted Maher believed his friend, who had served with him in the 82nd Airborne Division, after all. How was it possible to distrust his friend? Besides, people have a tendency to believe what they would like to believe. This was something known all too well to the older gentleman presently going by the name Igor Larionov.

Soon a man who was Larionov's proxy, and who turned out to be an acquaintance of Forsh, suggested to Maher that he could stage an attack on Safra, and then make a spectacular entry 'saving' the old banker's life. That would surely impress Safra, especially since he had lived in fear for his life since Larionov and Berezovsky had come to see him. And supposedly, after his 'miraculous rescue', the billionaire would most certainly make a new will in which the sum left to his rescuer and trusted bodyguard would be much larger. Logical, and convincing, too...right? Right.

The laptop beeped, indicating a message coming in, and Larionov had to take his mind off his musings. A minute later he was dialing the number that had just been sent to his mailbox. Of course, his mobile was new and had never been used before.

'Listening. Tell me quick what's up,' Larionov spoke Spanish this time.

'Everything is fine. Yesterday the banker's bathroom door got jammed shut. Thanks to a friend's effort. They called in a locksmith, and he was also our professional.'

'All right, what next?'

'A new lock was installed in the bathroom door. Now it's possible to lock the door from a remote location. This armored door will be blocked so well that it can't be opened from inside or outside the bathroom. It can only be unlocked from an external control panel, which can be used from a distance of up to two kilometers. Walls are not a problem. The same specialist installed hidden cameras in the bathroom, in the bedroom, and in the corridor. He did it together with Ted. All cameras have encrypted connectivity.'

'What about the passwords, so that I can get the feed from the cameras?'

'They are with our man, who will stay in a hotel close by. He'll block the bathroom off and then unblock it when he can see that everything is all right.'

'I see. But I also want to see the result. Send me the passwords.'

'Okay, boss.'

'When everything is over, a beautiful lady will want to see you. She will give you the second part of your payment for this job. Send me your new phone number to the same address, and she'll meet you tomorrow night in Paris. Your name for her is Étienne. What about other people? How are the friends who were advising our bodyguard boy?'

'Both had contact only with me. Yesterday they were offered a chance to sail along the coast on a yacht docked close by. Well, they took a boat to get to the yacht, but something went wrong. They must have drowned, I guess.'

'Okay, fine. What about the locksmith?'

'Oh, he went home to Brazil. He wasn't in on anything, you know. Did his job, got his payment, then off he went.'

'I see. Signing off. Farewell, Étienne.' Larionov laughed after he pressed the 'off' button. Then he took the SIM card out of the primitive phone, wrapped it in toilet paper, and flushed it down the toilet.

Soon the camera passwords arrived in his inbox, so Larionov poured some more whisky, added a couple of ice cubes, and got comfortable in front of the computer. Outside, the lights in others' windows were going out, the city slowly getting off to sleep. Monte Carlo is especially sad in winter, somehow resembling an old man who had gambled everything away.

So it was that early in the morning of December 3, 1999, at 4:20 a.m. to be exact, a large trashcan filled with discarded papers suddenly burst into flames in Edmond Safra's office, on the fifth floor of his plush villa. Only minutes later, the fire started consuming documents outside the can, and then the draperies and silken wall upholstery also caught fire. By 4:35 a.m., the fire was already burning in the corridor leading to the banker's bedroom. The fire in the trashcan did not start all by itself, of course. Someone poured out some petrol intended for cigarette lighters, then threw in a burning match... This was the doing of a bodyguard – that same slim, darkhaired Ted Maher who had closely scrutinized the banker's Russian guests only two months before.

When the fire had spread quite far, Ted stepped closer to Safra's bedroom door, then took a small knife out of his pocket, closed his eyes tight and – struck himself with the knife, trying to do it carefully, aiming at his abdomen and side. He had barely had time to put the knife away when the next door was thrown open and an elderly woman in a nightgown ran into the corridor, ramming into Maher. This was Vivian Torren, another nurse taking care of the ailing banker. She was yelling 'Fire! We are on fire!' and then, seeing Ted, switched to 'Ted, save us! Where should we run?'

'Vivian, stop it, don't panic!' Maher tried shouting louder than she was. 'This is not only a fire, but also an attack by some intruders. I was wounded. Take Safra with you to the bathroom and lock it. There are two strangers in the building. I'm calling firefighters and the police!'

Ted Maher yanked bedroom door open. Edmond Safra was already standing there, and even bumped straight into Ted. The banker, his eyes wide with the utmost fear, was trying to run. His mouth was wide open as if trying to scream, but no sound came out. He was choking.

'Ted! Vivian! We're on fire! What should we do?'

'Monsieur Safra! We were attacked. I am wounded,' Maher shouted, pressing his hand against his bleeding side. Now he forced both the banker and the nurse towards the open door of the bathroom. 'Go in there, quick! Lock yourself inside! There's a phone there! I'll take care of the situation!'

Once Maher made sure that the two elderly people had locked themselves in the bathroom, he grabbed a mobile phone and, having dialed emergency service, he shouted:

'There's assault and arson! Belle Epoque Penthouse, fifth floor!'

'Emergency services are already on their way. We got the smoke alarm signal five minutes ago.'

'Call the police! There are two unknown persons in the building. I am Ted Maher. Bodyguard. And I'm wounded.'

'They are on the way already. Can you hold out a few more minutes?'

Meanwhile, Igor Larionov was sitting at his computer, wearing headphones, and switching from one camera to the other. He calmly monitored the events unfolding amid the blaze Ted started, including his invented assault on Safra's residence. So far events were unfolding strictly according to plan, stage by stage – to the point that Ted Maher was no longer the subject of Larionov's interest. The bodyguard dreaming of getting millions from Safra's will had already done his part, so he wasn't needed anymore. As Larionov switched to the camera concealed inside the bathroom where Safra and Vivian had locked themselves in, he heard a loud click:

now the armored door was blocked remotely. In the meantime, thick smoke, dark and deadly, started seeping into the bathroom through microscopic slits and a few small, specially drilled holes. There was no way out from the hell of this smoke-filled bathroom – the two elderly people sitting on the marble floor could only huddle together. Suddenly the phone rang right above the head of the banker, who started weeping quietly. He got the phone by a long reach, picking up the receiver.

'Hello, Monsieur Safra! Maher speaking. The house was taken over by some thugs, and we all, including the police and the firemen, were taken hostage. Do not open the door to anyone! Can you hear me? Let no one in! They will be telling you that the fire is out and that the intruders were detained. But they will only be trying to make you come out of the bathroom. Don't trust them! Oh, they're about to take away my phone…I'll save you…'

A gunshot was heard over the phone, then someone screamed, and the communication was lost. Safra repeated to the nurse all that he had heard over the phone, adding in a whisper as he started choking:

'The voice didn't sound exactly like Maher's. Or maybe it did…and there was a gunshot and this scream…'

Only Larionov knew that it was not Maher who had called the banker, but the man he had dubbed Étienne late last night. Ted Maher, in the meantime, was welcoming the firefighters and policemen. He was sincerely convinced that Edmond Safra was about to be rescued and that he, a luckless Green Beret, would soon become heir to a few million in the banker's will.

Several minutes later, someone banged loudly on the bathroom door. Safra felt as if acrid smoke had filled every cavity in his body. They were shouting something, those people outside, but he couldn't really make out the words due to the thick, tightly shut door.

'Vivian, don't open the door. Maher told me those are the intruders,' Safra croaked. He didn't know that no one would be able to unlock the bathroom door anyway. Opening his eyes with difficulty, Safra looked at the nurse, who was lying on the floor surrounded by smoke. He immediately realized that Vivian Torren was dead. There was something strange about her face and the position of her body characteristic only of the dead. Then Safra started asphyxiating too, with a terrible, deep-seated cough.

Someone was banging against the door and many voices were heard, but all this barely reached the old man's consciousness as he slipped away, sitting there in the bathroom, leaning against the edge of the bathtub. Time was quickly slowing down its progress for him, becoming palpable – this elusive substance, time, was gradually dissipating and disappearing, dissolving inside the dying man. The door of the bathroom was finally broken through at 7:45 a.m. But when the police and rescue workers rushed into the bathroom, the 67-year-old billionaire and banker, Mr. Edmond Jacob Safra, was already dead.

In his deluxe suite at the Hotel de Paris, Igor Larionov cut the transmission and switched off his laptop as soon as the hidden camera showed the image of medics pronouncing Safra dead on the scene. He went up to the bar, poured some whisky into his glass, and stepped out onto the balcony, holding an unlit cigarette. It was done. This chapter was over: Safra the banker would never give any testimony to the FBI, and Larionov's Russian clients had already sent the sum of one hundred million dollars to an account at an offshore bank he owned. All that was left was to cut off any links that could lead someone to him – to the person using the name Igor

Larionov, for now, and who spoke Russian with a slight accent, with perhaps a Baltic ring to it.

Later that same evening, a rather short, grey-haired, middle-aged man entered the inexpensive Hotel Esmeralda in the Latin Quarter, not far from Notre-Dame de Paris.

'There's a lady waiting for you, Monsieur Étienne,' the receptionist told him. 'She's very beautiful and... oh, *très gai*...very jolly.'

'Thank you, my friend,' Étienne said in his muffled bass voice, easily recognizable as belonging to the man with whom Igor Larionov had spoken by phone late the previous night. The man whom no one in Paris knew.

A dainty brunette was sitting in a large red chair in the hall. She was in a provocatively short black dress that hugged her body tightly. A cheap manteau of artificial fur adorned her shoulders. Her gaudy make-up was certainly proof that this girl was not exactly a part of Paris's higher society, and that she was most probably approachable for a relatively modest amount. At least, this was certainly the opinion of the night receptionist, on whose round face this opinion was writ large as he watched with a smirk the exchange between Étienne and the girl, who was saying:

'Oh chéri, but you're so late! You told me you would come around nine, and now it's already—'

'Please shut up!' Étienne told her gruffly. Nevertheless, he took her by the arm, directing her to the lift.

'Order something to drink, Étienne. I'd like some whisky!' she said.

As they passed by the receptionist's desk, Étienne told him:

'Please bring a bottle of Chivas Regal to Suite 202, plus some fruit...'

Minutes after the strange couple entered a small,

comfortable hotel room, a servant rolled in a trolley with a bottle of whisky, glasses, ice cubes, and a small bowl of fruit. Étienne paid in cash, and when the boy left, he gave a lingering look to the girl who, without saying a word, had already lain down on the bed. He filled the glasses a third full and at last said:

'Tell me, first of all, what's your name? Secondly, why are you so outrageously dressed? And thirdly, where is my money?'

'Oh Chéri, so many questions at once... My name is probably Marie, and I came in this outfit simply because there are no business meetings at this hour anymore. Let everybody know that you ordered a call girl to your hotel room so you wouldn't feel lonely at night. As for the money, you shouldn't worry about that: the three hundred thousand is here in my bag, and I'll solemnly hand it over to you right after we drink this glass of whisky.'

'Will you stay for the night, then?' Étienne asked her, his voice suddenly growing husky. He felt a sudden desire to shag this floozy, right away...probably the result of his nervous stress of the last few days.

'We'll see... Here's to you!' she said, raising her glass.

'Okay, let's first do the money thing, and then the rest.'

Marie got up from the bed and, moving smoothly, walked over to the desk where her large bag was sitting. She took out a thick envelope and threw it onto the bed.

'Here's your money...'

Étienne got up from his chair. As he reached for the envelope, Marie, with a lightning-fast movement, took out of her bag a compact Beretta Nano pistol with a silencer and shot at his head without aiming. Spreading his arms, he fell heavily onto the bed, an expression of bewilderment frozen on his face. Having made sure he was dead, Marie put both the pistol and the envelope back into her bag and then sat comfortably in the chair, taking up her glass again. She spent almost an hour in this position. Closer to midnight, she broke in the window and tore the curtain to imitate how some supposed intruders had gotten into the room. Then she poured almost all the whisky from the bottle into the toilet. Leaving the room, she closed its door tightly, making sure that the lock produced a loud click.

On her way out, leering drunkenly, Marie chirped to the receptionist:

'Oh, Monsieur Étienne is so very tired… He had a lot of whisky, you know, among other things… Now he is asleep. He asked me to tell you not to disturb him until he wakes up on his own.'

That same night, when it started raining in Monaco again, Igor Larionov left Hotel de Paris and, instead of calling for his Mercedes, got a cab to Nice airport. There he showed his Canadian passport, proceeding to the VIP area. An hour later he was on board a luxurious Gulfstream G500 that belonged to some offshore company, which wasn't really known to anyone.

Thus, Igor Larionov was no more. Just as if a person by this name had never existed. His passport, as well as his biography, were only a most sophisticated fake, down to the smallest details. And the man who had appeared for quite a long time as Igor Larionov now gazed tiredly through the plane window, seeing the lights of the seafront promenade recede into complete darkness.

11

The Triad in Search of Paul Morel
London

The sun rolled over London at a leisurely pace, aiming to tumble down somewhere beyond the Docklands. A taxi crawled forward slowly, getting stuck in the congestion of downtown traffic, but still making its way through the eternal bustle of Soho, aiming to get to the red lanterns and colorful latticework of London's Chinatown. he driver, a young Arab, turned his head to his passengers – a beautiful Chinese woman and a middle-aged man – and asked several times through the transparent partition that they repeat the exact address of a Chinese restaurant on the edge of the quarter.

They soon arrived at an inconspicuous business sporting an unsophisticated name: Imperial China. It was located next to a hairdressing salon on the ground floor of a four-story residential building. A tall young Chinese man met them at the entrance. When he saw Jia, his seemingly inscrutable face immediately changed to a beaming smile. They hugged, speaking in Chinese, and then they entered the restaurant. Malin paid the cabbie and followed them.

Inside the restaurant, Jia turned around, telling Malin in a low voice:

'This is Jian Rong. We grew up together, and we ha-

189

ven't seen each other for almost ten years. Now he's become *hung kwan* already, that is, he is the so-called Enforcer, head of the security team that ensures the safety of the Lung tao, the head of the triad.'

'Have they invited us for a Chinese cuisine tasting?'

'If you're hungry, they'll give you food later. But now we'll walk through this restaurant to the residence of Guang Lan, who is the Lung tao of the triad that operates in the UK.'

They crossed the dining area, where some twenty Chinese were eating. Malin noticed that they were all men. Some of them stopped eating and stared at the new guests, scrutinizing them. Jia and Malin walked up the staircase, which was draped with rugs, and arrived on the first floor, where two Chinese men politely asked them if they had any arms on them, and then asked them to pass through the arch of a metal detector. The two men were obviously clad in armored vests beneath their jackets, and both wore pistols that were concealed, but bulged out to make it clear that they had them.

Guang Lan was a young-looking, rather short Chinese man, whose age might have been anything between forty and sixty. His skin was like ivory parchment, tightly stretched over his sharp cheekbones, and his dark eyes were well-hidden, lost among the many small lines flowing to his temples.

'How many years have passed, *qīn'ài de,*[1] since we last saw each other? My dear girl, I am very glad that you and your American friend have come to see Lan.'

'Thank you for your warm welcome, Mister Lan. You're such a busy man, *xiānshēng,*[2] I'm very flattered

---

1. My dear, 親愛的

2. *Xiansheng* (Chinese: 先生) is an honorific term (same as *sensei* in Japanese), literally "one born before" (or "elder"). It is used to address a Teacher, also as a title when addressing persons of authority

that you found time to see me and my friend Max Malin.'

'Your father who was in this role before me, the great Lung Tao Bei Sheng, he did so much for me...please sit down. Tell me more of what made you come to see me.'

They sat down at a narrow table, which was immediately attended by two Chinese menservants: quickly and noiselessly, they served tea, along with bowls of sweets and goji berries.

'Malin, tell what you have to Mister Lan, please.'

Malin opened his laptop and told the short version of his incredible story, illustrating his words with photographs. When he presented the first images of the man who called himself Santana, Lan moved closer and took a long, hard look at the face of the young man from the long-gone sixties. The way he scrutinized the images suggested that he was trying to figure out whether he had ever known the man or not.

But when the faces of Martin Weiss and Igor Larionov emerged, the Lan's imperturbable mien changed to a strained mask. He put his hand on Malin's shoulder, trying to get him to stop changing photos so quickly.

'Wait a minute! That's him! Him!'

'Who is he, Mr. Lan?'

'Well, this is Paul Morel. I thought he'd been feeding worms for a long time. Somewhere far away on another continent, where he ran to hide from us and from the Cosa Nostra. He got off with millions of dollars – hundreds of millions, rather. You don't need any Vietnamese to confirm his identity. I'm telling you: this is Morel for sure! At least that was his name in the seventies and early eighties. He led to a conflict of interests between us and the Italians when he stole huge amounts of mon-

---

or showing one's respect to someone who has achieved a certain level of mastery.

ey from us both. Others died because of his exploits. Plus…well, he was also connected to that attempt on Pope John Paul's life in '81. We think…'

Jia and Malin exchanged looks, both realizing the same thing at once. Yes, everything was taking shape, becoming clearer. Now there was a logical explanation for that photo in which Larionov-Santana-Weiss was shown standing on Saint Peter's Square, looking at the wounded Pope John Paul II. Now the man with that familiar face had a name, one more of his many names: Paul Morel.

Malin felt a little vein vibrating deep inside, with further waves expanding and echoing throughout in his body. *I've got it now! We've got it!*

Guang Lan got up, bowing his head slightly and murmuring, 'Kĕnéng de.'[3] He walked over to the window and started dialing someone on his mobile phone. Lan started speaking as soon as the call was answered, his voice taking on a tone of respect. He was obviously explaining something and mentioned Morel's name a few times.

'He asked us to wait a while,' Jia whispered to Malin. 'This is an important conversation related to us.'

'I see. Still, I can't believe that we were able to hit the nail on the head… Everything looks too good to be true.'

'How come it looks "too good" to you?' Jia suddenly raised her head, looking straight at Malin. Her gaze was cold and alien. 'For whom was it "too good"? For René Duchamp, perhaps, who ended up dead because of it all? Or, maybe, for Marshall, who is also dead and whose archive fell into your lap?'

Malin could not have answered anything to this, be-

---

3. Possibly (Chinese: 可能的)

cause Guang Lan interrupted their exchange. He came back to the table, stepping softly.

'You got very close to Paul Morel and, as far as I can understand, you are very eager to find him. We could help each other in this respect, perhaps. Is that so, Mr. Malin?'

'Of course, Mr. Lan.'

'Fine. We'll go to the Great Tai Lo, the Big Brother.[4] Ling Wan himself! He is already close to ninety, and has been enjoying his restful years, but his mind is clear and deep. He is still my teacher and my top advisor. He knew Morel well, so he might be able to help you in your search. If he feels like it, of course.'

'Ling Wan is a living legend,' Jia said, leaning closer to Malin. 'He was one of the Triad's top bosses starting in the sixties. He's so high up that even I have never seen him.'

Malin, Jia, and Lan went down to the restaurant, where several sturdy bodyguards joined them, all Chinese. The group took seats in two dark-tinted SUVs, and soon the mini-motorcade left behind a London that was close to melting due to the heat.

An hour later, the cars were riding through the splendid suburb of Kingston-upon-Thames, and soon arrived at a property with a three-story mansion, which was hidden behind a high fence, obviously of very old make, but still sturdy, and heavily overgrown with ivy. The cars rolled into a very large yard, protected from the scorching rays of the sun by some huge old syca-more trees. When the guests walked over to the front entrance, two Chinese men greeted them, exchanging a few sentences with Lan and Jia before accompanying

---

4. Big Brother, or Dàgē (Chinese: 大哥) is the highest boss of the Chinese Triad.

them inside the old Victorian building.

An old Chinese man, small and wizened, came out to meet them in the drawing-room. He stood as straight as if he had swallowed a stick. A muscular young man supported him, holding him by the arm. When Malin saw the great tai lo Ling Wan, his first impression was that very old age seemed not to present him any problem. In his gaze, and in each of his leisurely movements, one could readily see enormous energy capable of mastering everything around him.

'I'm happy to see guests in my home who have brought good news,' Ling Wan said slowly, with impeccable pronunciation. He inclined his head slightly. 'I am glad to be able to see the daughter of my brother Lung Tao Bei Sheng who, unfortunately, left us so early. Please sit down. Have some tea.'

After an exchange of greetings everyone sat at a low and long table on which tea and sweets had already been served.

After a pause for tea drinking, Ling Wan broke the silence and started to speak. But he spoke in such a low voice that one could hear how the tea utensils jingled softly in the server's hands.

'Lan told me, dear guests, that you could clarify some details about my old acquaintance Paul Morel. He disappeared a long time ago, in 1981, and we thought he was dead. I would like to hear your story directly from you, with all the details. We cannot make mistakes in this case. If Morel is alive, I must be aware of it, and then I can take certain steps. Please, Mr. Malin, I would like to hear your story.'

Malin related all recent events with all the details, showing Wan the photos from different years, as well as some documents. He spoke for quite a long time. He had told the story many times now, but this time, for

194

some reason, he was quite nervous and even getting off the point, sometimes saying the same thing twice over.

As he listened to Malin, Ling Wan's face was immovable, not unlike that of a Buddha. Not a single feature on his face changed as his dark eyes keenly scanned each new photograph appearing on the laptop screen. Only when he saw Santana-Weiss-Novack-Larionov standing on Saint Peter's Square during the attack on Pope John Paul II did the brows of the Triad boss quiver, almost imperceptibly, moving slightly towards the bridge of his nose.

When Malin was done with his story, again only Wan's voice broke the silence, though it became, if possible, even less audible, close to the rustle of foliage in autumn:

'I have no doubt that this photograph shows Paul Morel, whom I knew a rather long time ago. The photos were taken at different times, so the age is different, but it is crystal clear that it's him in all the photos. I will tell you what happened a long time ago. This might be a long story, but it might show you, I think, the caliber of his personality. And perhaps…well, who knows, maybe it will help you find Morel, if you compare my story with what you know.'

'Thank you very much, Mr. Wan,' Malin could not help replying. 'I am ready to listen to you for hours, for days, if needed. Especially if we can use it in order to get out of the dead end, we're in right now. We're all ears.'

'I knew Morel for a couple of years starting at the end of the seventies. Well, it would be a great overstatement to say so. I didn't really know him. No one knew Paul. Not a single person! He would come and go, like a burst of flame when one throws new dry sticks on the fire. But he would appear only when he needed to. We only knew that Paul was rich and that he moved constantly, all around the world. Where his home was, or who his family was, those were things no one knew. Did he have a home at all? Or family? Today he was a Frenchman, tomorrow an American, the day after to-morrow he may have become a Russian. Morel could speak many languages, almost without any accent, all of them close to sounding native. There was always a feeling of threat about him. Anyone who dealt with this Paul Morel, or whatever his name was, would feel that air of threat coming from him. Even when he would speak to you about trifles, or when he was discussing business issues. I never knew where that came from… that threat seemed to sort of live inside him constantly, in his dreadful eyes, which seemed able to change color. Not only color was in them, but also an abyss. Okay, but I'm straying from the point….

'Morel knew everything – the scope of information that was available to him was astounding. What he did not know, for whatever reason, he could usually find out in no time at all. This was his other line of business, by the way: providing information against very large sums of money. And I mean really big money, sums that seemed too much even for us. But Morel never made mistakes, and this was why his services were sought after.

'He told me at one point, in a joking manner, that we were like dinosaurs in his eyes, as we had no clue about the necessity of using the latest technology – all those electronic gadgets for monitoring and extract-ing information, or military technologies. A lot can be done only with those new things, he said. It's only when those don't bring the expected result that one should turn to using big money, offering bribes, or making ma-jor threats. There is no chance, under the circumstanc-es, that anyone could withhold any information. Morel said that if someone doesn't want to sell what he knows for one million, then you should offer him ten million. If he wouldn't take ten million, then you should kill him. Also, there is never just one person who knows a piece of information. There are always more people in the know: two, three or more. And this means that the second or third person will sell the information we need. If he feels that we won't budge, if we keep insisting, then he'll sell it for ten million, no problem.

'Believe me, Malin, we have quite some resources at our disposal, so I had tried many times to find out who this person was who presented himself as Paul Morel. Alas, no details became available, but in general terms I got the idea that he was in charge of a very special, powerful organization that resembles the mafia, but functions differently.

'In our case, everyone knows our hierarchy and venerates it. In Morel's case, on the contrary, the structure was there, but at the same time it was, in one sense, non-existent. There were separate groups of agents who performed various tasks, but none of them knew anything about each other, nor about other groups. Some people were responsible for gathering information, others for acts of violence, including killing; still others took care of legal business. Some dealt in illegal business, some interacted with outside organizations, and some were in charge of terrorist acts. Et cetera. But only one person knew it all. And that was Paul Morel.'

Old Wan grew silent, taking a cup of tea in his hands.

'Mister Wan,' Malin said, unable to restrain himself any longer from asking some questions, 'please tell me whether Morel had any normal human traits. What was he interested in? What were his passions? Women? Drugs? Anything? Something?'

'No, Malin, none of that. Nothing. Well, perhaps this, maybe...he was very interested in painting. And above all, in that painter from the Middle Ages, ah – it was Hieronymus Bosch. Morel was always looking everywhere for his work. He would even buy sketches, even work by painters who had been Bosch's pupils. He was so maniacal about it that he would pay anything for what he wanted to get. He almost never bargained, so art collectors and antiquarians were always flocking to him. He even asked us once whether we could do him a favor and arrange the theft of one of Bosch's paintings from the National Gallery in London. It was *Christ Crowned with Thorns*. He was offering tens of millions of pounds for it. We tried to accommodate him, but we found it an impossible task, in principle, so Paul was very upset. That was the one moment when I could see at least some emotion on his face.'

'If I may ask, Mr. Wan – what kind of business did you have together?'

'At the time, I was able to organize a great cooperation with the Italians. Thanks to their assistance, we could start delivering cocaine to Italy and then on, to the north of Europe. And that was only the beginning of our relationship. Cosa Nostra was especially good for us because they had a unique channel to the Banco Ambrosiano, a bank that was directly connected to the Vatican's Secretariat of State. That is, they had protection and security at the highest level. Who could think of that? The Pope's closest circle and dirty money, all rolled into one. With our friends' help, we were able to legalize over two billion dollars in 1979! Can you imagine that?'

'No, I'm not sure I get it,' Malin said, as he got the impression that Wan was about to explain the most important part of the story. 'What does our Morel have to do with it?'

'Why, it was he, of course, who organized the whole

scheme for Cosa Nostra, and then brought us in as a major client. Morel was at the root of the necessary financial arrangements: it was he who had brought together, at the right time, Toto Riina,[5] who was head of Cosa Nostra in Sicily, and Licio Gelli,[6] head of P2, a Masonic lodge. By the late 1970s, Gelli was controlling the main financial flow of Banco Ambrosiano. Later on, it was Morel again who talked with the bank's chairman, Roberto Calvi, who had already gotten the nickname "God's banker" at that time. He was able to convince the latter that it was necessary that he work with the Cosa Nostra. He impressed upon Calvi that such a joint business with the mafia would be greatly profitable for the Holy See. Well, Morel was right, as always.

'The thing was that the main shareholder of Banco Ambrosiano was the Vatican Bank and thus, due to Paul Morel's involvement in the whole process, the money laundering scheme involved even Paul Marcinkus, then the head of the bank. Morel later turned to us, inviting us as a major client who would be interested in laundering especially large sums of money.

'As it happened, Paul Morel was able to tie together the Holy See, the pontiff's bankers, the Cosa Nostra, and us. Each member of this scheme was pursuing its own interests: we were legalizing the billions we earned

---

5. **Salvatore Riina** (1930–2017), called Totò 'u Curtu (Sicilian for "Totò the Short"), was a chief of the Sicilian Mafia, known as "the boss of bosses". He personally killed around 40 people during his career as a mobster, and he was connected to hundreds of contract killings. His nickname was Shorty (Italian: Il Corto) due to his height of 158 cm.

6. **Licio Gelli** (1919–2015) was an Italian financier who in 1967 became the head of the clandestine masonic lodge Propaganda Due (P2) that controlled almost the whole territory of Italy via its 17 branches. He was sentenced for his role in the Banco Ambrosiano scandal, which included schemes involving the mafia as well as the banking system of the Vatican.

through drug trafficking, the Italians were laundering their money *and* getting interest on the deals with us, Banco Ambrosiano was going strong, making its money while profiting off the movement of funds, and as far as Calvi and Gelli were concerned, they may have received rather large bonuses in cash both from the Italians and from Morel. The largest interest on all the deals, naturally, was that which Paul Morel was receiving. As per my sources, he was getting close to ten per cent off all operations. And this was an enormous amount of money!

'I don't know if they were sharing their bonuses with Marcinkus, the head of the Vatican Bank, but one thing I am certain of is that Pope John Paul II was totally unaware of what was going on. He was convinced, for a while, that his bank was simply a very successful operation, bringing in a lot of income for the Vatican.'

'Excuse me, Mr. Wan,' Malin said, abandoning his tea and checking the recorder under his jacket. 'As far as I know, there was a huge scandal in the early eighties related to Banco Ambrosiano...'

'We shall touch upon this as well. At the close of 1979, the Vatican's budget deficit became a chronic ailment. It was the result of some financial malpractice, and this mini state was, for all practical purposes, close to financial collapse...and this despite the fact that the assets of the Vatican Bank alone were counted as being over two and a half billion US dollars in 1978. The Pope must have known this and, being hardly an ignoramus in financial matters, he ordered a secret internal investigation into discreditable practices of the Vatican Bank and, respectively, Banco Ambrosiano. Calvi and Gelli panicked, but we were not aware of this, and neither were the Italians from the Cosa Nostra. Morel kept telling us that all was proceeding normally, and that he was resolving any upcoming issues on his level. At the time,

I did not have any reason to disbelieve him.

'Later on, however, it became known that Paul Morel, assisted by Roberto Calvi, had siphoned off almost 1.5 billion dollars of Cosa Nostra's money from Ambrosiano and its offshore branches. That was only in the period between December 1980 and March 1981, and all this money was sent to several small, but reputable banks in Switzerland. I don't really know if he was doing this all on his own, behind the back of the mafia, or together with Cosa Nostra. I still have no idea…as for us, we were completely unaware of these problems with the bank. We were blissfully ignorant of all that, so to speak, because both the investigation and later actions were conducted in full secrecy…'

There was a pause. Wan was resting now, sinking back in his comfortable soft chair. After about a minute of silence, the old man opened his eyes, continuing his tale:

'Towards the end of March, in 1981, Morel told me that there were very unfortunate events developing around the Ambrosiano and the Vatican Bank. He told me about the secret investigation that the Pope had initiated and that was still going on, uncovering ever more mismanagement and wrongdoing. The Pope seemed to be very keen on discovering all there was to discover, *ad finem*, so to speak, down to the last detail. And then, perhaps, handing over all of the results to the procurator's office. But we had about half a billion dollars stuck in that bank. And that wasn't just our money, but also that of our suppliers, over a rather long period of time. Thus, it looked like a catastrophic financial dead end for us. And then Morel offered his solution.

'He said that he would find a way to turn up the heat on the Pope, in order to make him stop his investigation for a period of time. During that pause we could siphon off our money. Morel said this service would cost us fifty million dollars more. I found out much later that he also charged the Italians for doing this: they paid him almost one hundred million dollars. Morel also gave us this condition: that we should not know any details of his operation, and that all we had to do was wait for the desired result. Well, I had trust in him, you know because he had never made any mistakes. This was why we agreed to his condition. The Italians did the same, by the way.'

'I guess I know what happened next,' Jia said, somewhat haltingly. 'Was it the assassination attempt on the life of His Holiness? Are you leading up to that?'

'Yes, my daughter. On May 13, a month, and a half after my last meeting with Morel, and after he had received money from us and from the Italians, that assassination attempt occurred. Morel called me that night, right afterwards, saying that everything would be all right now and that we would be able to get back our investment. That was the first time I started yelling at him. I said that this was not the manner in which even we would resolve issues. That it was an impossible development for us, and that we would need to hide from police forces around the world forever. And that no one would want to work with us anymore. In response, Morel only said quietly, "Wait," and then hung up on me.'

'Later on, I found out that Cosa Nostra also knew nothing in advance of Morel's actions, and so immediately declared a manhunt for him. To no avail, however. I was told some details of what happened: prior to the attack on the Pope, Morel had sent Calvi and Marcinkus to see the Pope. Those two had tried to convince him that it was important to temporarily halt the investigation and to unblock accounts: they insisted to him that continuing the audit could come to a sticky end. They mentioned threats from the mafia and the imminent

scandal, but the pontiff simply showed them the door…
I also was told that that fanatic, whose name was Ağca,
was only supposed to wound the Pope lightly, in order to
frighten him and show him the threats were real. Still,
I don't know exactly what happened there on Saint Peter's Square, or why Ağca started shooting to kill… Perhaps his religious fanaticism got the better of him…'

'As far as I know,' Malin said, trying to clarify the
story, 'the end result was sad for all involved, right?'

'Yes, indeed. Morel's plan didn't work that time. The
Pope survived the attack and went on with the audit of
both banks, even more resolutely than before. He probably figured the attack was the peak, and that after that,
nothing could threaten him. Only one week after the
attack, on May 20, Roberto Calvi, who was the head of
Banco Ambrosiano, was arrested. It was revealed that
he had been performing banking services for the P2, the
notorious masonic lodge. Calvi was sentenced to a huge
fine and four years in prison, but he was released from
the detention while his defense lawyers were waiting
for the court of appeals to convene – no one knows
why. A year later, on June 11 of 1982, Calvi left Italy for
London. And then you may know the most publicized
development: a week later, on June 18, Calvi's body was
found hanging under London's Blackfriars Bridge.

'One more important detail: within the next year, all
other intermediaries were liquidated. Anyone who had
had any contact with Paul Morel and the Pope's bankers,
even accidental contact. And neither I nor our Italian
partners ever got to see Morel in the flesh, not a single
time. Nor have we or the Italians received our millions
back, whatever we paid for that attempt to influence
John Paul II. And one more sum, amounting to almost
one billion dollars, also disappeared. It was Morel who
siphoned it from Banco Ambrosiano to his Swiss banks.

We looked for it, but there were no traces left. None whatsoever. Do you understand what happened? Morel could have been in collusion with the Italians, of course, but I can't prove it. They kept telling us that it was not so. But we have been at odds with Cosa Nostra since that time; our relationship is still tense. Suspicion is a poor preconception to have when it comes to sharing territory with others.'

Malin was listening attentively to Wan's story. Almost every phrase spoken by this old Chinese man was filling in the existent gaps in the mosaic. Now the full picture was finally emerging of how this Santana-Weiss-Novack-Larionov-Morel entity had acted in Italy. It was becoming real, and it already showed the related contours of events. Suddenly an internal warning signal in Malin's head made him aware that Guang Lan, who was sitting diagonally from him, was looking at him with a strange expression on his face. And that Ling Wan had produced an answering smile, obviously in response to that. Was something wrong?

Well, there was indeed. How could he forget? These people had not searched him when he came to see them. But they were wise men from the Far East, and as Orientals it must have been on purpose that they did not pat him down. They had known from the start that he was secretly recording their conversation – and still let him do it. Why? Well, it wasn't important to know why right this minute…first he had to find a way out of this embarrassing situation with minimal losses.

'My dear sir…' Malin started, before suddenly being overcome by a coughing fit, which gave him enough time to arrive at his ultimate decision – to confess. 'Mister Wan, your story has helped me in a major way to reconstruct Morel's Italian period, so to speak. And to understand the real reason for his presence on Saint Peter's Square on the day of the attack. Well, at this point I have to admit to behaving unethically today. I am a journalist, you know, and as such, the task I see before me is to find out the full story of the man you have known as Paul Morel, and to tell it to the world. Which might also be how I save my own life. I have only one life, and right now I've become the target of a manhunt maintained by Morel's people, as well as the FBI, which has to cover the asses of all those politicians who are probably connected to him. This is why I need real evidence and precisely recorded facts and acknowledgements. This is my way of making a confession to you that I have been so bold as to capture our conversation without your permission...'

'Well, young man,' Ling Wan started, in a somewhat husky voice, 'if you mean the recorder or your mobile switched on to record our exchange, whatever you have inside your jacket, I knew it was there from the start, as soon as you appeared in my house. But I am glad that you made this unexpected confession. It is something that inspires my respect and only increases my good feelings towards you.'

'Tell me, please, whether I may continue recording, and later keep it for my purposes?'

'Yes. Mr. Malin, my understanding is that the money Morel stole from us can no longer be retrieved. But if he is still alive, I would very much like to eliminate him. My path towards this goal may lead, at this point, through you, through your exposure of this man. So yes, I am very aware of the fact that your recording, if you publish it among other pieces of evidence, would also constitute evidence against me. But I am not afraid of that.

'The truth is that I live here under a different name, while international intelligence agencies are convinced that the great tai lo, old Ling Wan, left this world a year ago. We had some problems around that time, and Interpol started looking for me very actively, hoping that I might be able to give them some testimony. But I am an old man, so "Ling Wan" had to pass away very quickly. Not unlike Morel...' the old man beamed for the first time. 'So, you may record and have no worries about it.'

'Thank you, Mister Wan. I think I have one more question. It may be a bit unusual, though.'

'I have grown accustomed to being asked strange questions. Let me hear it.'

'The information you shared with me so far is priceless. But what can we do next? Where should I look now for the next step to get to Morel? How can we find him by following the tracks we've already discovered? If he is still alive, of course...'

Ling Wan took several sips of his tea. Then he closed his eyes and seemed lost in thought. The drawing room filled with a kind of a resounding silence. Several minutes later the old man spoke:

'I think he is alive. I think the proof of this is in how excellently the manhunt is organized. I am also quite convinced that Morel, or whatever his name is, will find you himself. Because he must find out what you were able to discover about him thus far. That's how dangerous this information could be for him. He is most probably convinced that you must have hidden your findings somewhere safe to insure yourself against him. I would guess that not only are you trying to find him, but he is also looking for you. Yet would you survive an encounter with him? I don't know. But I'm not sure that you would.'

'What should we be doing, then?' Jia joined in the conversation, taking Malin by the hand. 'What should our next move be?'

'You must go to Italy. To Rome. You should see Don

Domenico Radore there. I will give you his phone number and notify him of your arrival. He is an important person within the Cosa Nostra. Despite our problems with that structure, he remains my close friend and confidant. Why? Oh, you don't have to know my reasons for that… Don Domenico is convinced that it was Morel who stole their money, and he was also totally against the idea that we could have anything to do with that attack on the Pope. He might be able to give you some hint as to how you get one step closer to Morel. I cannot guarantee it, it would certainly be worth a try. Tell me, Lan,' Ling Wan turned to Guang Lan who was sitting close by, 'do you have any idea what the best way from here to Rome would be?'

'I can offer our friends my own car, tai lo,' Guang Lan said, getting up and slightly, deferentially, bowing to the old man. 'They can take it to St. Pancras Station. From there, they would leave for Paris on Eurostar, and in Paris they can change for a train to Rome. This would be the safest and least traceable route.'

Half an hour later, Malin and Jia bid their farewells to Ling Wan and left the mansion, accompanied by Guang Lan and his bodyguard. The gigantic sycamores were already drowning in the faint light of dusk. A deep stillness seemed to be ringing all around them, their steps echoing as they tread over the fine gravel of the footpath. Malin turned towards the bulky black SUV they had arrived in.

'No, Mister Malin, sorry,' Lan said, touching Malin's shoulder. 'This car is too noticeable. Our driver will take you in that small one.' Lan pointed to an unremarkable grey Honda parked a way away. 'You must vanish quietly, and my SUVs are too well known in the city. Plus, you will ride without any escort, so you can vanish into the highway traffic more easily. Oh, by the way, I am sorry to enquire, but I was curious why you deleted everything on your hard drive before we left Mr. Wan?'

'The thing is, Mr. Lan, I've been on the run for many days now. Since I feel like a lure for some people who are out there looking for me, I prefer not to have such a large object with me that I can't throw away and run for my life. All the data was copied onto smaller data carriers that I carry around on my person, with my passport and money. Thanks to that, Jia and I can always leave without any luggage. I can always buy a new toothbrush later, anywhere, even at a gas station. Oh, I mean petrol station...'

'You have everything figured out,' Lan smiled and then turned to a small Chinese man who had gotten out of the Honda to greet them: 'Here are your passengers, Gang. Drive them carefully. Don't break any rules on the way. Don't hurry, go with the flow. Take them to St. Pancras and then call me.'

Gang nodded without saying anything and opened the back door for Jia. A minute later the Honda exited the property's gate and started rolling smoothly upon a narrow lane towards the London highway. They were the only car on the road, but within less than ten kilometers they would join a never-ending flow of traffic, a big highway where they would be quite inconspicuous. This lane went through the forest on both sides, and it was so narrow that two cars traveling in opposite directions would have a hard time passing each other. A red sun was slowly sinking beyond the treetops, some place far away where they touched the sky.

Malin felt the fresh night air. He took Jia by the arm. 'Are you cold?'

'No, it's not that. I suddenly feel very much afraid. I have been more or less all right today, but when we were driving off from Wan's place, I was surprised to suddenly feel this strong wave of fright. Where are we heading? Why? What's going to happen to us next? But...well, I'm sorry. Please forgive me. I'll gather my wits in a moment...'

'Oh, my darling, everything will be fine...' Malin started to say, but he checked himself, feeling right away how phony and stupid the words must have sounded. 'Hey, Jia, you can leave at any moment. Why don't you stay here in London and live among your people? The hunt is for me only, but my only option for staying alive is to go all the way to the end of the road. I don't see any other solution. In your case, however, it might be better for you to get off their radar. It would make sense, indeed, to meet again later when things are back to normal. We would be together later, that's all.'

'Oh, you fool! I love you, Max Malin. When does our train depart?'

12

Farewell, Jia

With only one mile left to the wide motorway, Malin noticed that Gang had started to look frequently into the rearview mirror.

'Is something wrong?'

'This Range Rover is following us and has been for about a mile already. And when I slow down, it slows down too. It's strange. There are two people inside it.'

'Oh, come on, Gang,' Malin said hesitantly, but nevertheless he turned around and looked back. 'We're on a narrow road, so this car simply doesn't have anywhere to go around us. Plus, how could they have traced us?'

'Not a problem, Mr. Malin. If you or one of our guys made even one call using a mobile phone, that would be it: voice recognition systems do work here, and quite well. Let's not forget who we are – the police are always interested in what's going on with the triads. And British cops are as bribable as anywhere else.'

'Maybe you want to scare us, Gang,' Jia smiled, 'but we are not afraid. This is probably some local gent returning from his country estate...'

Her words were interrupted by a gunshot. The bullet hitting the boot lid ricocheted into the rear window, which caved in instantly, showering them with an avalanche of glass fragments. With a lightning-quick movement, Malin pressed Jia's head down to her knees, so that she would be out of the line of fire.

'Step on it, Gang! Head for the motorway! There are people there, and cameras, too… They won't dare attack us there.'

It wasn't necessary to say this to the driver: he had already floored it, the car taking off with a roar and tearing forward to the main road, gravel raining out from under its tires. Shots popped at their back. The motorway was already quite close, but the Honda suddenly jolted to the side of the road. It came back on track, and continued forward, but now weaving from side to side.

'Shit! They hit one of our tires!'

With only about fifty yards left to the motorway, suddenly another Range Rover rolled across the narrow country road, stopping in front of the Honda, and completely blocking the way. The sun, on its last path to the murkiness beyond, was directly behind it. Its windows were rolled down, and two silhouettes raised their guns and started a hail of gunfire.

The many gunshots were so deafening that Malin felt as if everything was happening in slow motion: seconds turned into minutes, and each movement was split up into separate frames. Now he and Jia and were lying crouched on the car's back seat. Now the front window was slowly disintegrating under bloody mess. Now Gang's face was hitting the steering wheel as bloody scraps of his brain flew all over the car interior. Now Malin was opening the back door and, grabbing Jia's hand, falling into a roadside hedgerow, hiding behind it, pulling Jia after him. Now they were rolling down into a ditch and crawling fast towards the forest. When Malin chanced a momentary look back, he could see their Honda sandwiched between the two cars of their pursuers, who were still shooting.

Malin came back to reality only when they were already running between the trees. Time returned to its normal course as low-hanging branches slapped him hard on the face, which made him turn around again. Jia was right behind him. When he glanced backward for the last moment, he caught a glimpse of four people leaving their cars and starting downhill to catch up with their prey. The runaways were soon surrounded by thick forest growth, but they could hear their pursuers' voices somewhere behind them, as well as occasional gun shots.

When Malin and Jia had run a couple more minutes, they came to a slight clearing before an almost impenetrable thicket. They had to stop under an old, gigantic, wide-branched oak-tree to try and catch their breath. They felt as if every little vein in their bodies was vibrating, each muscle stretched and strained to its limit. They scanned the growth around them, trying to figure out where the killers might be. But everything was quiet. Very quiet. Until a branch snapped somewhere to their left, immediately followed by a gunshot.

Malin turned around and was almost overwhelmed, seeing a man in dark overalls running straight towards them. His eyes were wide open, and his mouth was open wide, yelling a victorious 'Gotcha!' Malin's Green Beret reflexes kicked in, lightning fast. With his left hand, he managed to draw the man's pistol aside and, at the same time, he hit the attacker with his right hand, delivering a tremendous blow to the man's throat. The black shadow croaked, his eyes rolling up, and he slowly sank to the ground. Blood streamed out of his mouth.

But it was in the next moment that the worst possible thing happened.

That was when Malin turned around to Jia: he saw her lying on the grass, curled up with her knees touching her chin. Her eyes were closed, and a thin trickle of blood was running from the corner of her mouth.

'Jia! Are you wounded, Jia?'

There was no answer. Malin bent towards her and took her hand, pulling her slowly up. Her legs suddenly convulsed straight out, and then she slid limply to the side, lying motionless in the wet grass. A large blood-red stain was spreading across the front of her white T-shirt. She had stopped breathing. Jia Sheng was dead.

Malin stood helplessly above her body. A heavy silence suddenly fell in the forest where everything had been so full of movement and noise only minutes ago. No sound came from anywhere, and no cars even drove past on the motorway which was, after all, very close now. Malin just stood there frozen, overpowered by a very strange and very cold thought: Jia was no more for this world. His next thought was that there were other people close by who had killed her, and who would still try to kill him. He knew already that there was nothing that could bring Jia back to life. He also knew that he was the only person in the world who had this unique information in his possession. The only thing he could do now was try to save his own life. If he did, then he would be able to preserve the memory of this young woman who had joined him in such a simple and natural manner, despite the fact he had been all alone and on the run. She was the one who had said, of her own volition, "I will stay with you till the end."

Malin suddenly heard a light, barely perceptible sound somewhere to the left of where he was standing – it must have been a branch snapping under somebody's foot. Malin drew into some dark shade, crouching behind two big tree trunks. Luckily, they were so thick and grew so close that their low-hanging branches had created a kind of improvised shelter. Malin was securely hidden here from the searching eyes of his pursuers. Then he could see them: two men in dark overalls stepping carefully through the thick growth, with pistols in their hands. They froze when they discovered the two bodies on the ground. Disregarding the girl's body, one of the men, who was taller and sturdier than the other, leapt to his colleague's body spread on the ground beside Jia. He put his hand to the man's neck and then said in a very low voice:

'Michael is dead. Shit, this son-of-a-gun Malin can really use his arms. Check if the girl is still alive.'

'Nah, there's a hole in her chest. What should we do with the body, Nicolas? Looks like Malin has already abandoned his hussy in order to get away from here. Didn't I tell you I could have gotten him when I had him in my sights? I could have taken him down neatly, with a single shot.'

'Shut up, Robbie. You know that we have to deliver the bastard alive. I have no idea why, but that was the order. We do what we're told.'

'Don't I know shit? But I had such an urge to take him down… We've been after him for how long? I'm sick of it already!'

'Okay, shut up now. Let's go to the freeway, he might be there somewhere. Where else would he go?'

They turned around and, carefully moving through the bushes again, started slowly towards the motorway, suddenly loud again with the sound of caravans of roaring trucks. Malin stayed a while longer in his hideout, remembering that there should be one more pursuer around. But once he was convinced that no one was following the two men, he walked up to Jia's body and bent over it again. His mind was incredibly clear now, perhaps due to the pain of loss that he carried, and to the huge wave of adrenaline that had smashed into his body a short while ago. He felt like an analytical machine, a computer that had to instantly assess the situation and look for an optimal escape route from this specific, difficult situation.

Jia was not here anymore, she was gone, she could not be retrieved… Malin touched her hand, thoughts flitting through his mind: *Ling Wan will certainly take care of her. He will do what must be done. And when my quest is over, I will come back to where she is buried and stay forever next to that place. Yes, I'll live next to wherever she finds her last refuge in the dark depths of the earth, beneath the ground… But now I must tell the Chinese about Jia, and then find a way to get to the train station.*

Malin checked if his small thumb drives were still in his pockets. He retrieved a smartphone from one of the pockets but threw it far in the bushes. He had a second mobile, a simple old one, the push-button type, small and reliable. It was snugly tucked away in his other pocket. Malin switched it on and dialed Lan's number: Lan had given it to him before they said farewell.

'Ni hao.[1] Hello!'

'It's Malin. Bad news.' Malin spoke fast, trying to be done within one minute. 'Listen to me, please. They followed us. They probably figured out where we were using connection information. Jia was killed…Gang is dead too. He is in the Honda, half a kilometer before the motorway. Jia's body is close by, but it's in the forest, on the left side of the road. I am asking you and Wan to take care of her body and her soul. When I am done with my investigation, I will find you and you will show me where she was buried.'

'Roger! Everything will be done as it should. Will you still follow your plan?'

---

1. Hello! (Chinese: 你好 *nǐ hǎo*)

'Yes, as promised. Will you do everything?'

'Don't worry. Of course, we will. Now you must leave. Take care of yourself.'

'Thank you, and goodbye.'

Malin took a last look at Jia's body and then started walking slowly along the road. He used the trees as cover, carefully monitoring all around him to detect his pursuers. It was starting to get dark, but on this clear June night, it was still too early to walk beside the motorway. In his thoughts, Malin was gradually creating an optimal plan for escaping to London.

The night was rather cold, but Malin, turning up the collar of his jacket, kept stubbornly moving forward. He stepped softly, with no sound, like a cat of prey. He could not think about anything anymore, and even if he were to lose his direction at times, his deep-seated instincts helped him get back on course as he made sad progress away from where Jia's bloodied corpse lay on the cold ground, ever closer to St. Pancras station in London. Moving off the motorway, behind the trees, he walked some ten kilometers or more in this manner, until around dawn the green colossus of Wimbledon[2] emerged in the distance. One could already hear human voices and the noise of traffic from that direction, a clear indication that a new day had begun. Around eight in the morning, Malin, trying to display a natural ease and smooth gait to any casual observer, came out of the bushes and joined those Englishmen eager to start their workday early.

The green walls of the stadium were already lit by rays of morning sun, and the air was filled with that intoxicating fragrance that one can only experience ear-

2. Centre Court of the Wimbledon Tennis Tournament has the capacity of 15 thousand seats. It is located in Wimbledon, the south-western suburb of London.

ly in the morning at the height of summer. Malin preferred to avoid groups of tourists who had already come to gawk at the world-famous tennis courts. Finally, he found the objective of his long stroll: a taxi stand. A minute later, a red-bearded cabbie, who was obviously used to anything and would not be surprised even by Malin's shabby appearance, was driving his first client of the day to St. Pancras Station.

As the cab gently rocked Malin, the stress of the night was slowly easing off, so that he could begin assessing his new situation. He knew now that he was walking right at the edge of a precipice, but also that he could not quit. It was do or die now. He had already lost everything: the woman he loved, his dream job, his home. He had become a fugitive, a person with a fake passport, someone whom omnipotent people were trying to catch. And for some reason, those people wanted him alive. Malin knew there was only one solution to his quandary: collect all the information, analyze, and systematize it, prove every little detail, and make the results of his findings available to everyone around the globe. Only that, in his opinion, could save him. Only that could destroy the powerful enemies, whose recent actions proved, in his eyes, that he was on the right track.

He would bring his quest to its conclusion, and he would reveal the truths of all the mysteries around the worst crimes of the last sixty years. Malin knew that he would be able to write a great book that would become a worldwide bestseller of the century! Then no one would be able to destroy him because they would all be too busy trying to save themselves.

As the cab approached Regent's Canal, Malin, unwittingly, started an imaginary conversation with the person he had been trying to find for about a month now:

Hey   you,   Santana-Novack-Weiss-Larionov-Morel!

Whoever you might be, even if you are the Devil incarnate, I will find you. I will find out your worst secrets, the ones you've kept hidden for decades. When I publish that book, Watergate will seem like baby talk compared to those crimes… Then there will be no place on Earth you can hide, Santana-Novack-Weiss-Larionov-Morel. All of mankind will be after you and those around you.

Getting out of the taxi, Malin edged quickly into the station building. Stepping forcefully through the crowd, in the manner of an exceedingly busy person, he walked straight to the ticket office and bought a ticket for the next Eurostar to Paris. It was leaving in half an hour. Malin used this time to change into whatever he could buy at a small but very expensive boutique: grey trousers, a wide sports jacket; he also picked up a baseball cap and sunglasses. On his way to the train, he got a new smartphone and an English SIM card. Soon he was sitting comfortably in the Eurostar, which was ready to rush at great speed into the tunnel under the English Channel.

When the train began to roll, Malin switched on his new phone and, connecting to the Wi-Fi, he was able to check several of his secret emails for the first time in a week. These emails had been specially created for communicating with some of his closest colleagues and trusted sources of information. No new messages anywhere, not one email. Only the last one, dedicated to communication with Richard Berwick, his longtime friend, and head of the *Washington Post* investigation department, had a single message, which had been there since the night before:

Hello, my friend! The case re: the murder of Charles (the source who sold us the archive) was closed. They found some junkie who confessed to it and then he got thirty years. What a load of hooey! Everyone knows the informer wasn't killed by some loony dope fiend. Your Facebook post went viral all over the infosphere. They panicked in a big way, all the way up to the White House: they were eager to know who was in the photos and what materials were in your possession. "Malin's Letter" disappeared from Facebook quickly, and all of our "colleagues" started saying that whatever you wrote was just crap, that the photos must have been doctored, and that you must have run away to somewhere in Africa. They cleaned up almost everything online.

They gave me the ax, too. Kicked me out of the Post, that is. I continued collecting some information related to our topic of interest, but then I was forced to leave the US. I'll share particulars when we meet. I'm living in Switzerland now, with Elsa and our kids.

I found something important. We should meet, by all means possible. And soon. Where are you? Please do the crosscheck before you answer.

Malin immediately recalled that they had agreed some time ago on the necessity of crosschecking each other in critical situations to help assure that there was no trap set for them. Malin thought for a short while and then wrote: *Could you remind me which brand of wine was on the table during our last meeting?* The answer came back right away: *We didn't have any wine, my friend. We drank Russian vodka that you brought over for some reason, despite the late hour.* Now that Malin was convinced that he was really communicating with Richard Berwick, he wrote back: *Arriving in Rome tomorrow morning.* Five minutes later Berwick's message was: *I'll go there too. Let's meet tomorrow at Harry's Bar on Via Veneto,3 at our usual hour.* Their usual meeting time, as

---

3. Via Vittorio Veneto is a street in Rome leading from Piazza Barberini to Porta Pinciana. It is one of the most famous, elegant, and expensive streets in Rome, featuring the best and smartest hotels,

Malin knew, was noon. Back in D.C., it had been during lunch break, from twelve noon to twelve thirty p.m.

The train slowed somewhat before diving into the Channel Tunnel. It went tearing through the seemingly endless corridor, filled with light from the many lamps that flashed past the coach windows. Suddenly two British policemen appeared in the car where Malin sat in the last row. What were they doing, for God's sake, in this express train rushing towards the French side of the Channel? They proceeded slowly down the aisle, looking attentively at passengers' faces, obviously trying to find somebody. They moved ever closer to where Malin was seated. He had already grown used to his role as a runaway, and tensed up inwardly, trying hard to look nonchalant, just a normal person sitting transfixed by his smartphone screen.

After a few tense moments, the policemen walked past him, heading for the next coach. Malin relaxed, leaned back, and closed his eyes. He started thinking about everything he knew at this point. This was quite a lot at this point, so it was worth breaking down the information he had collected so far and putting it in some order for himself. And he had time for it now.

Between 1954 and 1957 someone by the name of Luis Cristobal Santana, a young venturer of outstanding abilities, stole 25 million dollars from the US government and then organized what was supposedly his end in a mysterious plane crash over the Pacific. Looks like this name, Luis Cristobal Santana, was indeed his real name.

Let's go farther. The same person, this time under the name of Martin Weiss, or, perhaps, some other name that we don't yet know, appeared, in 1963, at the lo-

---

US embassy as well as Café de Paris and Harry's Bar, which were shown in Federico Fellini's film *La Dolce Vita*.

cation where President Kennedy was killed, and was standing right there when the bullet struck Kennedy. Later on, Weiss became a lobbyist for gigantic corporations providing ammunition, facilities, food, and uniforms to US troops engaged in the Vietnam War. Weiss, however, mysteriously disappeared in the Vietnamese jungle in 1966, probably at the hands of the Viet Cong. Officially presumed dead, he had most probably been directly involved in organizing Kennedy's assassination. Still later, he appeared in the 1970s under the name Paul Morel, this time in Italy. He was manipulating money via multimillion dollar schemes while laundering vast sums of money through the Vatican Bank, the money itself coming in from the Triads and Cosa Nostra. In 1981, however, he organized an assassination attempt on the Pope that was a stillborn affair from the start. And when Pope John Paul II, despite this attempt on his life, had fearlessly continued with the audit, Morel had preferred to disappear – but first he disposed of several main actors who knew details of the failed assassination, and disappeared a few hundred million dollars belonging to the Mafia.

Next time this character turned up was in '98 in Russia, under the name Igor Larionov. At first, under the guidance of the Russian Ministry of Finance, he used his connections within the International Monetary Fund to arrange a large loan of almost five billion to Russia. This money, naturally, got lost along the way, and never made it to its destination. And then this Swiss banker, Edmond Safra, whose bank had been chosen as the transfer point for the loan, died in a mysterious fire, trapped inside his own home in Monte Carlo, right after he had decided to talk to the FBI. Larionov visited Safra several days before this tragedy, with one of the Russian oligarchs. When Larionov got his billions, he simply disappeared. Vanished into thin air. Oh, and the Russians were also saying that Larionov may have had one more name – Sergio.

What next? Next was September 11, 2001, in New York, when someone took a picture of the same man at the same time that the Twin Towers were collapsing. As far as is possible to ascertain, his name at the time was Eric Novack. It was most probably he who had been on the phone to an officer of the US secret service, whose name I don't know yet discussing the upcoming attacks. And, among other things, this was all happening close to the moment when the first plane was already on its path to hit one of the towers. Oh, and the photo of the retired banker "Eric Novack," who allegedly died in a motel fire not far from New York on September 12, had the same face yet again – good God, he's used a lot of names! How much blood, how many dead bodies, and how much money! All related to one and the same man, who has always stayed alive. He must be over eighty now... And now it seems that this is the very man who started a manhunt trying to get me. And, for whatever reason, he wants me alive, only alive and kicking... One more thing: he's a fan of that medieval painter who created horrifying images...what was his name? Oh, yes, Bosch...what nonsense! Why Bosch, of all people?

13

Hieronymus Bosch as a Lure
Don Domenico. Rome

I n Paris, Malin transferred to the Thello[1] train for
Rome, and fourteen hours later arrived, with no problems, in the capital of Italy. It was around noon when
he got off the train at the Roma Termini station. Everything was so drenched by the sun, and so colorful,
that he suddenly felt, for the first time in several weeks,
relatively safe. Malin could not explain why this feeling
of ease and comfort descended on him. Perhaps it was
symbolic, a feeling of being far from England or France
where the manhunt for him would still be on. Or maybe it was just the general atmosphere in the Eternal
City, a city he liked very much. Perhaps it was working
its usual influence on him: in Rome, he always felt as if
he were taking a sedative, ambrosia.

Deep in his soul, however, a needle was stuck, constantly wounding him, the memory of Jia constantly attaching herself to any new, current experience. It
smarted even now, during this relative and probably
temporary bout of serenity. The ease and calm had
been bestowed on Max Malin right when he saw the

---

1. Thello is international train service for trains between France and
   Italy.

223

Baths of Diocletian[2] and the neighboring Piazza della Repubblica, sporting its excessive number of pillars. *Jia, Jia, Jia… Where are you, Jia? Where are you, my invincible-yet-delicate Guardian Angel?*

After a long walk through many narrow streets, after an hour spent buying yet another laptop, mobile phones and other things, Malin took a taxi to a hotel. It was a small hotel of only 33 rooms, the Hotel Trevi, located basically around the corner from the famous fountain of the same name, and quite close to Via Veneto. The medieval building allowed a tired Malin into its air-conditioned lobby, and minutes later, having checked in using his fake passport, under the name of William Murphy, he could lie down and relax in a comfortable room with carrot-red wooden panels on its walls. Yet he could not fully sleep to recuperate, because in an hour's time he was to meet Richard Berwick – his former boss, colleague, and old, tried-and-true friend.

Harry's Bar, located at the end of Via Veneto, close to the entrance to Villa Borghese, had long been a favorite of the in-crowd of Hollywood stars, whose photos lined its walls. This was why on a sunny day it was usually close to impossible to get a little table in the dark, at the back of the parlor. That is, unless you're a DiCaprio or Pitt, and not surrounded by crowds of fans. Still, it was exactly there, at the back of the bar, that a short and rather plump Richard Berwick was already seated, expecting Malin. Richard had flown in from Switzerland only two hours before.

'Ah, hello, here's the little friend who abruptly cut my career short,' Richard Berwick greeted Malin jokingly. Malin had been expecting this kind of joke, espe-

---

2. The Baths of Diocletian (Italian: Terme di Diocleziano) are the ruins of enormous public baths in ancient Rome, located close to today's Piazza della Repubblica.

cially since Richard was already in the process of tasting his first cognac. The friends hugged, and Malin sat down across the table from his former boss.

They drank a double Courvoisier for starters, then spent about twenty minutes on short updates about their current lives. Malin, of course, was especially eager to lead the conversation, since he had ended up in the thick of things, but Berwick would not lag behind.

It emerged that Richard had been dismissed from his position as head of Washington Post's Investigations Department right after Malin left for Paris. And when Malin had published his Facebook post, with its sensational information about the mysterious Controller, Richard had had to leave Washington. Things soon got worse: someone had started a fire in a part of his house, and that in broad daylight! Lucky that Richard and Elizabeth had been visiting friends that day. Then their dog had been killed... In short, some of those who knew the situation suggested it might be best for the Berwicks to go away for a while, not just from D.C., but preferably from the country altogether. Luckily, the Berwicks had inherited a rather nice chalet in the Swiss Alps, in Samnaun – the property had belonged to Richard's mother-in-law, who had died only a year earlier. Using Richard's contacts in Canada, he and Elizabeth had been able to move over there without attracting undue attention. Over thirty-five years of journalistic work, the Berwicks had been able to save some money, so the older couple lacked nothing. Except adrenaline, without which Richard Berwick's existence had become rather dull.

'You know, Malin,' Berwick started speaking in almost a whisper, abruptly changing the subject, 'I think I have found, or almost found, your Santana-Weiss-Morel. And your recent adventures are one more confirmation of the fact that I got very close to him.'

''Oh, come on, Richard, don't keep me in the dark! Spit it out!'

'Let's not rush, my friend,' Berwick said: he was obviously savoring his sudden success, so he was certain to provide the full story with every detail. 'Hopefully you remember I've been investigating art theft for over thirty years. I was looking into stories of how great paintings were stolen. I did it at first only as an investigative journalist, but later on I really became an expert on this topic. You may know that I was able to track down not only the theft of Picasso and Magritte,[3] whom I personally like best, but also that of two paintings by Renoir, a Rembrandt and even a Leonardo!' Richard could not conceal his pride. 'And I still follow all the art auctions, even now. I take notice of the old canvases that suddenly appear there. Plus, I hate to say it, but the black market needs special attention as well. I was always very much aware which anonymous collectors had been using serious art dealers. Because, generally speaking, it is a separate world, like some kind of underwater kingdom.

'I have known one of its actors for quite a long time. In certain, quite narrow circles, he is a very well-known dealer, and he is indeed a legendary illegal dealer and buyer of masterpieces. He is an Italian, and his name is Luca Lavallieri. He's been involved in shadowy business of this sort for fifty out of his eighty years in this world. As far as I could establish, all the stolen Rubenses, Rafaels, Bruegels, Gaugins, et cetera, et cetera went through him. Luca selects a masterpiece when it's ordered by collectors known to no regular art dealer. Those guys are ready to pay tens or hundreds of millions of dollars for a stolen masterpiece, or for pieces that disappeared a

---

3. **René François Ghislain Magritte** (1898–1967) is a Belgian surrealist painter.

long time ago and were never recovered. They pay this much because they want to admire, let's say, an original Van Gogh in the solitude of their private office, secure in knowing that the same painting in the museum is simply a perfect copy of what they own. Or that this painting had officially been declared missing after half a century on the search list.

'Okay, so this old Lavallieri has been providing his services to such collectors all around the world. He knows everyone. He's stinking rich and owns homes in Rome, Paris, Lausanne, and Los Angeles. He's a rare bird, too, you know, one in a million: he himself doesn't own one single piece of art. Whatever he has in his possession is only for sale. He's also a loner, with no family and no children. He says one shouldn't get attached, neither to a painting nor to a person, because it would only be painful to part with them. And in any case, his task is to sell.'

'Richard, could you please get to the point. I'm already expecting you to say the name Hieronymus Bosch at some point.'

'Yes, my friend, you're right, but please bear with me. Thing is, Luca Lavallieri has been looking for works by Bosch over the last thirty years, and he does so with amazing regularity. Bosch, you may know, is this somber genius from medieval Netherlands – he was practically a surrealist. Only twenty-five of his paintings are known to exist, and all of them are in large museums. Well, Luca has been focused on anything related to Bosch, paying any money in the world even for sketches, drafts, or works by Bosch's apprentices. He was also offering over a hundred million dollars to professional art thieves for any of the twenty-five paintings that hang in museums. To be exact, Lavallieri was offering up to a hundred and fifty million bucks per painting.

Even now, Luca keeps making his offer known that he's interested in anything related to Bosch. They say that Lavallieri doesn't even haggle if a Bosch comes up – which is completely uncharacteristic for him.'

'I'm convinced that his client, that mysterious Bosch aficionado, is our Controller Santana-Weiss-Morel,' Malin nodded. 'Didn't I tell you he was asking the head of the Chinese Triad to arrange a theft of Bosch's *Christ Crowned with Thorns* from the National Gallery in London? And Levine—that Russian Mafiosi—he told me the screensaver on Larionov's laptop was the right side of Bosch's triptych *The Garden of Earthly Delights*, in which the painter depicts Hell.'

'You see, Malin,' Berwick said, pushing his glass away and resting his elbows on the table, 'I decided to go as far as I could to find out the identity of Lavallieri's client. You know, I've never known any collector to be more wacko than their client. And for some reason I made a connection between your Controller and this Bosch nut – some subconscious guess, an intuitive decision. All those years working as a journalist, I guess…

'Luca has known me for many years, so he trusted me to some extent. So, when I told him I had undergone a long search and found two sketches by Bosch, he swallowed it almost at once. Plus, I told him they were sketches for *The Garden of Earthly Delights*. And that, as I'm now retired, I need to make a couple million for playing middleman in this case – Switzerland is great, but expensive, so I could certainly use the money to make life more comfortable. Lavallieri offered me ten million dollars without even seeing the sketches. Assuming proof of their authenticity, of course.

'But that was not all. I convinced Luca it was my first time doing such a deal, and that I was actually afraid to get involved, almost to the point that I was considering dropping it entirely. He got quite agitated when he heard this, so much so that I asked him to tell me something about his client. I said I needed it for my own safety and peace of mind. Luca wouldn't budge for quite a long time, but when I told him I was dropping my offer and wouldn't be selling those sketches, he became almost crazed, perhaps with greed.

'Then Lavallieri did tell me a few things. It turned out that the name of his billionaire client was Sergio, and that he is already over eighty years old. Luca didn't know where his home was or what he did professionally. He had seen the guy only once, twenty years ago in Geneva, where Sergio came to buy two works and a sketch by one Jan Maes, a pupil of Bosch. They met in a café on the lakefront and in just thirty minutes Sergio was gone.'

'Did you show him the photo?'

'Do you think I'm a nincompoop? Of course, I did! I told Luca that my friend had a client who was also a Bosch aficionado, so that if I didn't like something about this Sergio of his, I would certainly switch my deal to the other client. I told Lavallieri I could show him a photo of my friend's client that was on my iPhone – I used the image of our Morel, the one from '81, taken at St. Peter's Square, but I had doctored it to remove the crowd around him. I wanted Luca to see only the Controller's face. Luca recognized him right away, and acknowledged that it was indeed his client, and that his name was Sergio. This sly fox Luca was quite happy to tell me that we were obviously talking about the same man and asked that I allow him to be the one to close this Bosch deal. He also insisted that he would transfer money to my offshore accounts within ten minutes of seeing the sketches.'

'But how could I become part of this game?' Malin interrupted Richard's tale. His excitement was rising, like what a hunter feels, exhausted as he might be, feels upon seeing a desired animal. 'Oh, maybe you could present me as the owner of the sketches, who wants to sell them. That would be rather stylish: since Lavallieri exposed his client to you, your reciprocal move would be to bring in the man who's selling the Bosch. Just because you trust Luca so much...what do you think about this idea?'

Old Luca Lavallieri answered Berwick's call right away, and they quickly made an agreement about their meeting. Luca was overeager to get sketches of the great Bosch for his most important client. He was also quite happy to meet directly with the seller: for Luca, that meant having a chance to negotiate the conditions of the deal himself, and thus pinching off a bit of Richard's own middleman fee. They agreed to meet at one in the afternoon the next day, at the luxurious Westin Excelsiore Hotel,[4] which is in the same neighborhood. Berwick had found out that Lavallieri was residing permanently in a deluxe suite there, in which he conducted his negotiations and closed his deals. This was where they agreed to meet.

Before they parted, Berwick made Malin promise he would go straight back to his hotel and rest properly, spend twenty-four hours doing nothing before the meeting. Malin nodded in agreement, but did not tell his friend, who always wanted to be in the center of the action, that someone from Don Domenico Radore, Cosa Nostra's boss, would be waiting for Malin in the lobby of his hotel in an hour. Malin had called Radore earlier that day using the phone number Ling Wan had given him. Upon hearing what Malin could say over the

---

4. The Westin Excelsiore Rome is a luxurious five-star hotel on Via Veneto in Rome.

phone, Don Domenico had agreed to meet, saying he would send his assistant to Malin's hotel.

The summer heat was stifling in Rome. It was omnipresent in the Eternal City, so that drops of the splashing Trevi Fountain evaporated mid-air, and even the most indefatigable tourists from the Land of the Rising Sun had to flee to their air-conditioned hotels.

Malin walked to his hotel, trying to keep to the shadier alleys to evade the merciless, scorching rays of the sun. The deserted streets, immobile cars at the curbs, even the air itself seemed to have condensed into solid mist due to the heat – to Malin it all seemed to be the setting of some surrealist film in which he, for some reason, had agreed to play the main role. He was the only moving object in this petrified world. This strange picture was made complete by a total silence that suddenly reigned all around him. Feeling dead tired, Malin stopped at an intersection, leaning against the ancient stones of a building on the corner, thus becoming a part of the immobilized world around him.

He suddenly perceived light steps not too far behind him. He raised his head, slowly turning around: lo and behold, two persons, a man, and a woman, were closing in on him. Despite the heat they wore leather jackets. They were walking almost in step, and their large sunglasses playfully reflected the blinking beams of the sun. The woman started unbuttoning her jacket as she went, carefully retrieving a pistol with a silencer on it. Malin quickly turned around, looking for getaway options, but only saw two more persons emerge from the next alley. He recognized them at once: tall, sturdy, obviously well-trained, they were the same two he had seen in the forest by London where Jia had been left dead.

Time froze. Knowing that the worst might be about to occur, Malin, in a knee-jerk reaction, suddenly ducked and delivered a side kick, his leg hitting the face of one of the pursuers, the man who had come closest to him. The man fell to the ground, sending the woman flying as well. She pulled the trigger as she fell, firing off an almost inaudible shot – ka-ching! The same slow-motion effect began as the bullet resounded against the wall – a sound that could be heard crisply clear only because of the general dead silence – and ricocheted into the shoulder of one of the men in the second pair of Malin's pursuers. He had been running towards Malin, but now fell on the pavement, stretching his arms cinematically, and his buddy immediately stopped, leaning over him.

Suddenly time returned to its normal rhythm, and Malin was able to deliver a blow to the woman's arm, who was already getting up, though rather slowly. He managed to strike the gun out of her hand, then jump over some low fence that he only now noticed, running through a couple of congested back yards, and darting out a minute later into a perpendicular alley. Gasping for breath, Malin dashed through an open-air café, knocking over a table as he ran, then made it through an archway into the area behind a restaurant, full of empty beer barrels and rubbish bins. He pressed his back against the warm wall and slowly squeezed himself into the narrow space between the wall and a high pyramid of beer barrels, which provided Malin with a small opening through which he could watch what was going on in the yard. A ringing silence descended once more all around him, except for a lonely church bell that could be heard faintly, chiming very far away.

A minute later, two of his pursuers appeared in the yard. It was the leather-jacketed woman from the first pair and the tall tough guy of the pair who had been pursuing Malin in the London suburbs. The latter's partner must have stayed behind to get the wounded man someplace. The two spoke in low voices, but Malin, pressed against the wall, could hear every word.

'He's not here either. Got away, the son-of-a-bitch. Why did you take out your piece? Nicholas's order was to take him alive, anyway.'

'I wasn't going to shoot…well, maybe wound him a little. But he…quiet!'

She pressed her earpiece to her ear for a short while.

'Yes, Nick! Got it. Roger.'

'What's that, Bella?' her pal asked impatiently.

'It's over. Nicholas sounded the all-clear. From now on, this numbskull isn't our responsibility anymore. Others will deal with him. Let's get out of here.'

'Thank God it's over. I got so sick of it: first they want him alive, then dead. Then it was alive again…let others take on this headache now.'

'Oh, cut the crap! They pay us, so we do our work. Let's go. We'll have to resolve things with the doctors because Neil's arm has a hole in it…'

Both started resolutely towards the archway. Now they were no longer on guard. Bella, tall and slim, clad in her black leather outfit, moved with such grace that Malin couldn't help but admire her smooth movements, combining a feminine gait and barely concealed aggressiveness. Suddenly, when Bella was already inside the archway, with her partner walking in front, she turned and stopped. Her dark eyes scanned the yard one more time, and then she gazed intently for some time at the pyramid of barrels behind which Malin was hiding. He could swear their gazes locked. But then Bella smiled a strange smile and tossed her head, as if she were fending off an illusion. In the next moment, she turned and quickly followed her partner. Soon they disappeared around the corner.

Malin slowly started retreating, weaseling himself

out of the narrow space behind the barrels. He made one step, then waited. Another step. He wasn't sure they had really left. It could have been a tactical move: they might only pretend they were leaving, while their accomplices checked out the neighborhood. *Why not?* Malin thought, making one more step out of his hiding place. *Shit, this heat is too much! Well, it seems they may really have left for now. But hell's bells, why did this Nicholas tell them I'm no longer their target? And that some others would be dealing with me from now on? What others? Shit! Fuck! What's going on?*

Malin disentangled himself finally the barrels, and, walking slowly and cautiously through the back yard, he went into a café's back room, then into the café itself. Finding an exit, he found himself in the lobby of a small hotel where a big group of noisy American tourists was milling about. Sticking with the group, he exited to Via Veneto and then started walking to his hotel.

To tell the truth, Malin was thinking, *I shouldn't bother hiding anymore. It seems anyone who's interested in me knows quite well that I'm in Rome. On the other hand, it would be better to play it safe, because I have no idea who these "others" might be who were ordered to "deal" with me just now. There is no doubt, however, that these agents who were after me in Paris, London, and now Rome, are by no means representatives of the US special services. They belong to some private army, probably that of the "Controller" whose many names I already know. So now I must get quietly to my hotel, and then, at least for some time, my safety should be assured by Don Domenico Radore.*

Malin walked through a couple of quiet alleys and then entered the Hotel Trevi through its staff entrance. He went straight to the receptionist, but before he could say anything, this young gentleman with mascaraed eyes and an affected manner eagerly told him:

'Oh, Mister Murphy! You have a visitor waiting for you in the lobby. He is sitting over there, in that chair by the big window.'

The youth became obviously nervous when he looked in the direction of the man at the window who was expecting "Mister Murphy". *Mister Murphy? What Mister Murphy? Why Murphy?* Malin was bewildered for a short while before he realized something. *Oh, right, that's me! I registered at this hotel using the documents of US citizen William Murphy. Lord, I must be out of my mind with exhaustion...*

'Yes, thank you. I'm coming.'

A man of about forty got up from the chair to greet Malin. He was rather corpulent, and he was dressed formally despite the heat. His black curly hair hung down above black eyes.

'Hello Malin! My name is Amato. Don Domenico is expecting you at his place.'

'Hello! I'm ready to go.'

As they walked towards the exit, two more Italians in similarly styled dark suits got up from chairs close by and exited just before Malin and Amato; one of them nodded to Amato. Soon a black Maserati Quatroporte drove off from the main entrance of Hotel Trevi, Malin and Amato comfortably seated in back. A large SUV car with the two attendants followed them closely, basically only three meters behind their Maserati.

Both cars were rather big, but they moved quickly through the narrow streets, heading towards the suburbs of Rome. Malin, who was a big fan of Rome, kept looking out both sides at the mix of gorgeous Renaissance buildings and much earlier structures, the remaining fragments of the ancient Eternal City. As always in Rome, this mix would present itself unexpectedly, creating a natural setting that provided a uniform, unique impression that cannot be seen anywhere else in the world.

When the sun was already starting its downward path, leaning towards the horizon, the cars arrived at a large estate located about thirty kilometers away from the capital. They rode through the park, stopping in front of a gorgeous late Renaissance villa.

Malin was led to a large reception room featuring huge medieval tapestries that hung down from wooden transoms fastened close to the high ceiling. Malin at first felt uncomfortable there. It was as if he had found himself standing on the set of a film about medieval knights. But his mood changed when he saw a tall, tanned man who was walking quickly towards him. The man seemed to be about seventy, or perhaps a little older. His gorgeous head of grey hair made his very dark eyes stand out – an effect enhanced by silvery cold sparks glimmering in his irises. Perhaps they were simply reflections of the large candles burning brightly in candelabras placed atop the large dinner table. Both Amato and the two attendants, the latter so much alike as to appear to be twins, now stood at attention at the entrance to the room.

'I would like to welcome you, Mister Malin, to my humble home,' said Don Domenico Radore in his deep, rich voice. His English was perfect. This was one of the most influential and dangerous Italian mafiosi. 'My dear friend Ling Wan told me about your quest, and I must say your intentions coincide completely with our own. Sit down, Malin. May I call you by your first name? You are, after all, much younger than me, aren't you?'

'Certainly, Don Domenico,' Malin nodded, and decided to reciprocate the host's florid style. 'I am very pleased we could meet today, and I would like to thank you for your hearty welcome, and for providing what's needed for my safety upon my arrival.'

'What would you like to drink, Malin? We're in Italy, and that means I can offer you some excellent chianti. Or being an American, would you prefer whisky? Oh my, I almost forgot, you were born in Russia, right? Perhaps you would like some vodka?'

'Wow, you know about my Russian heritage! Impressive! Still, I would prefer whisky.'

As soon as Don Domenico has completed a detailed discussion of the upcoming dinner with his tall, haggard personal chef, he and Malin settled into chairs around a large table before the fireplace, ice cubes clinking faintly in their glasses of whisky, and unhurriedly started their conversation.

'Malin, I only know as much as my friend saw fit to tell me,' Don Domenico said, lighting a thin cigar that made the room fill with a rather sharp fragrance. 'He and I head very different organizations, we have different goals and different methods of achieving those goals, but over the last forty years Wan has become very close to me. Someone I can almost fully trust. Why "almost"? Because I can fully trust only myself.

'Okay, I know you're looking for a man whose name was Paul Morel in the '80s. Wan told me you have a lot of information on this man, and that Morel would not like that very much. So, you want to find Morel, right?'

'Of course. Otherwise, I would have been at home today in Washington, D.C.'

'Then you must know, Malin, that the man who used to call himself Paul Morel meets only those whom he wishes to meet. For others who become too curious or try to find out any details of his existence, oh, that means only one thing: disappearance. You know what I mean? Disappear for good, forever. Do you understand that?'

'Yes, Don Domenico,' Malin said with a measured tone. 'I do understand that, as no other person would.'

'Tell me, Malin, what would you do, when and if you can meet Morel?'

'I would interview him,' Malin smiled, suddenly realizing very clearly that, in fact, he had no idea what his actions should be when and if he were to meet Paul Morel.

'Amen,' Radore burst into laughter. 'Amen, my friend. In all honesty, I very much doubt that you will find Morel. But I would like to offer you the only available option for staying alive if you really do meet him. You should first collect all your records, all photos, all videos, all documents related to Morel, make copies of it all and entrust them to someone very reliable, and known only to you. This person's task would be to act if you do not contact him within, say, three days after you left to interview Morel. Then he should send everything he has to the media and leading intelligence services around the world. And tell each of them that this information was sent to the others as well. Why? Because one special service can be bribed into silence, but bribing five or six at the same time, well, that would be quite a challenge. And you must tell Morel about this arrangement during your first encounter with him.'

'I think that in this case Morel would have two options. One would be to try reaching an agreement with you – when such an agreement is reached, that is, a solution optimal for you both, then he would let you live and release you. His second option would be to torture you in the worst possible way until you tell him where all the information about him is hidden. Then he would send you to kingdom come, and your trusted friend to boot. As far as I know Monsieur Morel, this second option would be preferable for him, as well as much easier. But there might be a third option. Something neither of us can imagine. This is how Paul Morel would have acted in the times when I used to know him... If he is alive, I doubt he would have changed too much.'

'May I ask you, Don Domenico,' Malin said, with some caution in his voice, 'why you agreed to talk to me? I don't want to say anything inappropriate, but my guess is that a request from your Chinese colleague and friend wouldn't be enough on its own. You might be taking a risk if you were to tell me anything confidential. I am a journalist, after all.'

'I've been taking risks all my life, dear Mister Malin. There have been many times when I could have lost my life or ended up behind bars. But you should understand that today, I am officially a thriving businessman. Well, everybody understands everything here, but the authorities don't have anything against me these days. And it goes without saying that if you mentioned me in some unfavorable context, I would deny that we have ever met and talked. Much more importantly, however, would be that you would get yet another enemy in me. That's number one. As for number two, you must know that digital gadgets are electronically suppressed in this room. You won't be able to record our conversation. So, I would recommend that you put your gadgets aside and then we can start talking business. On the other hand, I understand quite well that you must document everything to do with the target of your research. So, if our discussion goes well, I mean, if I like its outcome, then you'll get an audio file of our conversation, only with my voice changed so drastically that no one would be able to recognize it.'

'My interest in your research is very simple: I want to know whether Morel is alive or not. I also hope for your success because, if you find Morel, and if you stay alive in the process, then I would love to enjoy the greatest exposé of the last couple centuries... I have my reasons for that, and I think you might have an idea what's in it for me.'

Malin looked at this mafiosi with great interest. He suddenly realized that over the last couple of weeks, he had spoken with the highest bosses of the largest criminal clans: the Chinese triads, Russian mafia and the Italian Cosa Nostra. *Even if some of them aren't active anymore*, Malin thought, *the possibilities seem to be endless. Or almost endless. At the same time, this "Controller", a man of many names, was able to fool them all. They hate him, they wish he were dead, but at the same time they are obviously afraid of him. Plus, at a very deep level, they admire him. And in the end, all these very powerful people, who have whole armies of thugs and enormous sums of money at their disposal, were not able to "resolve the issue." It was me, Max Malin, a simple journalist, who was able to figure out this much about Santana-Morel-Novack. Maybe I can stay alive, and even win this battle. Well, I simply have no other option...*

'I am grateful to you, Don Domenico, for your frankness,' Malin continued aloud to his host, 'and I trust your information can clarify many things about the questions I have about Morel. So, could you please explain to me what exactly connected you to Paul Morel, and why you no longer hold any warm feelings for him?'

'If I'm right, Malin, Wan has already told you the part of the story in which he himself was directly involved. In that case, I should continue with my side of the story, so that you understand what my relationship to Paul Morel was. Well, I should rather say – to the person for whom "Morel" was one of many names.'

'Paul laundered almost a billion and a half US dollars for us through Banco Ambrosiano. He made that money legal and brought it to successful businesses. He was truly a financial genius... Well, not only financial... But in early May of 1981 some problems began: Pope John Paul II decided to audit his Catholic bank, as well as his bankers. Paul was able to take out seven hundred million for us – taking his huge percentage, of course. But about three hundred million was left suspended because the audit had already started. Plus, we were expecting some new income to arrive that was meant to pass through Banco Ambrosiano and its branches. Everybody got nervous except Morel. He told us he would find ways to influence the pontiff and that it would resolve all issues. To tell you the truth, for some reason I was convinced at the time that Morel was omnipotent, and that brought me to believe that he could actually influence even His Highness, perhaps using some device or approach not within my comprehension.'

'Believe me, I am Catholic, as is everyone in our Family,' Domenico Radore crossed himself, and all the Italians present in the room did the same, 'so I would not allow a single hair to fall from the head of the pontiff. I did not know at the time who was involved in Morel's plan, and I understood only after May 13, 1981, when that man attempted to assassinate our Holy Father. My people saw Paul Morel on St. Peter's Square that day. As we found out later, he had in fact directed all of Ağca's preliminary training, plus managed his later statements when Ağca was in prison. He was doing it secretly, and everything was so cunningly set up that Ağca did not even suspect he was being led by the nose...

'As you already know, this was when Paul Morel made the first mistake of his career. The attack did not frighten John Paul II. The audit was not stopped, but on the contrary, continued even more actively and thoroughly.

'Our three hundred million dollars, plus a pretty large sum that was provided to Paul Morel as a premium for "resolving the issue" – all this was transferred from our Virgin Islands' offshore facility to Morel's bank – from there the money was supposed to go to Banco

Ambrosiano and then emerge into the world as clean and beautiful money. However, nothing arrived at the bank in the Vatican. It was all absorbed into financial structures owned by people controlled by Paul Morel.'

'He called me some time after the fact to tell me that that money did, supposedly, get to Ambrosiano, but "perished" in the audit. But that was a lie. In June of 1982, my people apprehended none other than Roberto Calvi, the fugitive head of Banco Ambrosiano. You may excuse me for putting it this way, but they tortured him quite well so that he would talk. Calvi told them our money never made it to his bank. It all remained in Morel's financial structures…'

'Calvi, as far as I know from press reports, did not survive too long after this, right?'

'Oh, yes. They had to hang him under the Blackfriars Bridge. Well, he knew too much, so he would have died anyway. Because of Morel, for example…'

'Have you met Morel since?'

'Alas, never.' Don Radore smiled sadly. 'I knew how powerful Morel was, and I knew that he could become really dangerous, but nevertheless I did try to find him, though taking great care about it. But it was useless. However, nineteen years later, in 2000, my friend and brother Don Cesare Bologna, who was working for the benefit of our Family in New York, recognized Paul Morel in one Sergio Esposito. At least, everything about the man was very much like Morel: his facial features, his manner of speaking, his shrewd and devious mind, plus his lack of boundaries when it came to his methods of achieving his goals. We started seriously suspecting that it might really be Morel.'

'But Don Bologna couldn't prove anything, and there was no way we would be able to check on Sergio Esposito, because he was, you know, working with

Jacky Nose[5] and Little Nick Corozzo[6] from the Gambino Family. He also had some serious deals going on with the Genovese family.[7] So we had to put a stop to our search so as not to run into any problems with our American partners.'

'We were able to find out, however, that Sergio only rarely appeared before the Family. He mostly communicated via electronic mail or dealt with issues through intermediaries. His special capabilities were used only in extreme cases. I mean, only for the most serious and delicate missions – anything from big financial deals to dangerous contract killings and far-reaching political games. Oh, it's important to consider that Sergio – who was most probably Morel – was not a Consigliere, a counselor to the mafia boss. No, this man never acted as an underling. He appeared when he chose, to execute an order or organize a consultation, create or manage needed structures or links – and then he would disappear.'

'I beg your pardon, Sir,' Malin interrupted the Italian, 'I am sorry, but my understanding is that Cosa Nostra couldn't find out anything about Sergio's whereabouts, right?'

'We were able to establish certain connections, certain contacts, but in the end, we were always sorry we

---

5. **John "Jackie" D'Amico** (born 1937) is a New York City mobster who served as street boss of the Gambino crime family from 2005 to 2011. Gambino family is one of "Five Families" which control organized criminal activities in NYC. Nose was D'Amico's nickname because of his "Romanesque nose."

6. **Nicholas "Little Nick" Corozzo** (born 1940) is an American mobster operating in New York. He had a rank of "caporegime" ("capo"), or "captain" in the Gambino crime family. In the 1990s Corozzo was elevated to acting boss of the family.

7. Genovese family is one of the "Five Families" that control organized criminal activities in New York. Only Gambino family has more members than Genovese family.

got involved. Anyone who got too close or too curious would simply vanish… The only thing that we could discover was that Sergio had good contacts with the Arabs or, rather, with Al-Qaeda, and that those contacts were at the highest level of that organization. And also, this: Sergio was able to resolve many issues with the top officers of special agencies, for example from the National Security Agency.

'Sergio would always appear and disappear like a shadow… No one knew his permanent address. Nor who he worked with. And his possibilities seemed so boundless that it was not truly feasible to assess them in their entirety. It was Cesare who told us about his suspicions that Esposito was, in fact, an older Morel. Their ages were very close: Paul Morel's year of birth was 1933, and Sergio Esposito was around 66 or 68 years old in 2000. I couldn't fly out to the USA, because I'm on the wanted list there. The guys from the Gambino family said they would not help us in this respect, because they had known Esposito for a long time, and he was a born American, while Morel was a Frenchman. I didn't believe them, by the way: they were simply too interested in continuing their business with Sergio.'

'And what happened with this Sergio-Morel later? I mean, after 2000?'

'Same thing again: he vanished into thin air. He was last seen on September 8, 2001, a few days prior to the 9/11 terrorist attack. I could establish, through my various channels in the US, that Sergio seemed to have been under investigation by both the FBI and the NSA. But they were looking for him in a sluggish manner, without haste and without any desire to go too deep… Oh, by the way, there were government agents questioning guys from both the Gambino and the Genovese families. And those pals of ours got the impression that the goal of these "conversations" was only to convince the higher echelons that Sergio was dead... This led me to conclude that Sergio-Morel was this time in charge of some very special projects for some very big wigs... Since this seemed to be related to the destruction of the Twin Towers, Sergio was to be liquidated. At least officially. At least for reporting purposes.

'Well, because of all this, Sergio Esposito, alias Paul Morel, was gone, disappearing without trace. I have had no further information about him. Now the next move is yours, Malin. And now, hopefully, we can have our dinner. Be my guest...'

'Thank you, Don Domenico,' Malin responded automatically, obviously thinking about something else. Putting on the table his glass, which still had some whisky left in it, he said: 'You connected some dots in the story that I wasn't able to connect so far. I was only guessing, but you made it happen for me: Paul Morel, who was also, as I now know, Sergio Esposito, is linked to the 9/11 attack. This is a very important part of the general picture, which I've been putting together like a jigsaw puzzle. Now I really must find this main person, the key player, in the flesh...and try to remain alive while I do.'

'Here's to you, young man!' Don Domenico Radore announced, raising his glass, the fifty-year-old Chivas Regal sloshing around it in little golden waves.

14

Failed Sale of a Non-Existent Bosch

When Malin came to his hotel he eased into a big armchair and as was his habit started thinking about his latest discovery. Odd bits of information were slowly emerging as parts of the larger picture, so that a first bit was already definitely followed by the second, with the third attaching itself to the first two without any problem.

It is crystal clear, he thought, *that the Controller, who has received one more name by now – Sergio Esposito – was directly related to the 9/11 terrorist attack in 2001. Just as there is no doubt that he was not just another gawker who was accidentally caught on camera that day...*

Malin poured some mineral water into his glass and started pacing the room. He could sense that a link between several important points was close. *Keep up the good work, Malin. Think hard. Push a little bit more. Rack your brains a bit harder. What was it? Oh, what if... Shit! Bingo! I've got it!*

He suddenly remembered that in the Marshall archives, among many other documents, had been the transcript of a recorded phone conversation. That conversation had been recorded by special services at 6:50 a.m. on September 11, 2001, and for some reason had not made it into any official report about the attack.

Wasn't that strange? So, one hour and fifty-four minutes before the first plane hit a tower, there had been this conversation between someone called James, who seemed to have been an unidentified official – this was probably not his real name – and another person labeled "Unknown" in the transcript.

Yes, indeed! This "Unknown" was certainly our Controller of many names: Santana-Novack-Weiss-Larionov-Morel. And now we must add Sergio Esposito to them. Malin switched on his laptop and started the audio file. Now he had a different appreciation for the deep, muted baritone, with its metallic, domineering overtones. For him, it was not a voice of some "Unknown", but the real, live voice of someone about whom Malin had come to know quite a lot already. Finding him had become a matter of life and death for Max Malin... He listened one more time to the whole recording:

James*: Hello! Is that you, my friend?*

Unknown*: Yes... Were you expecting someone else to answer? And why are you calling me now? It's five minutes earlier than scheduled.*

James: *There are changes to the plan. Boss just made a new decision. Suddenly. But his decision is not up for discussion.*

Unknown: *What new decision? With less than two hours left before the event... The birdies can't be stopped anymore.*

James: *Let all three birdies fly on. They are needed and eagerly expected. The decision was made, however, not to destroy the two big nests completely. Whatever the birdies can do is fine. It'll be good enough. But as for the third, the smaller one... Let* *it fall after the birdies arrive.*

Unknown: *Are you crazy? That's impossible! The system runs on its own, so the two nests will collapse on their own. Probably within an hour after the arrival. And the third will do the same, a little later. So, nothing can be changed at this point. Nothing! Everything is already set up and there's no way anyone can change anything. Millions were shelled out to set it up. Besides, no one who rigged the system is around anymore. Only they might have been able to do something this late in terms of introducing changes, but, as I said, they are not around anymore...*

James: *What do you mean?*

Unknown: *They aren't around anymore. They were expendable...*

James: *Listen! I don't give a flying fuck about those people. All I know is that the destruction of the first two nests must be avoided. I mean, the two large nests. There should be no complete destruction! The third one may disappear... This is what the Boss decided. All other agreements are still in force. No money should be paid back. Let the birdies strike, but that's it!*

Unknown: *This is what I can tell you. We can do a lot. But I'm not God, and I can't stop the mechanism that's already started working. All three birdies will arrive in about two hours, and all three nests will fall down. First the first two, then the third a little later. And that's that! Of course, no one would mention anything about money in the end. And no one would pay any-*

*thing back anyway. What don't you get? All of the
job's details were discussed in advance. You paid,
and I got the job done. And now you're telling me
that the final stage, something we've been working
on for two months, should be called off. And that
only at the last minute when, technically speaking,
nothing can be done. Nothing!*

James: *Hey now, let's not put it like that. Let us...
listen, the only thing that has to be called off is the
complete demolition of the two big nests. For the
simple reason that their total demolition would be
the only point we won't be able to explain away.
Because they're too big and too stable. The Boss
may have some other reasons, too. You have, after all, received everything you've asked for, so you
may disappear, no problem. All you have to do is...*

Unknown: *James, why don't you and your moron
of a boss go and fuck yourselves? Why can't you
grasp the simple fact that the bomb is falling, and
can't be stopped midair? It is not, I repeat, NOT
possible, since it was already dropped... In short,
everything will happen the way it was agreed on
earlier. With all due respect, I do not think that
you and I will ever hear of each other again. And
I don't even exist for you anymore...*

James: *Hold on, my friend! Hold on... (The call
is dropped.)*

Everything seemed to fit now. If this was really the
voice of Sergio Esposito, the man of many names, then it
meant he was indeed one of those who organized 9/11,
and that his interlocutor was, in fact, some high-level official in the US special services acting as a point
of contact between Client and Contractor. What was

emerging was quite gruesome: it meant that the tragedy had been contracted by circles within the country.
Probably at the highest echelons of power. Or, hopefully, at somewhat lower levels?

Oh Lord, this cannot, should not be true... Malin's
thoughts raced feverishly in his head, which he held
in his hands. But there are facts here that cannot be
denied...this, then, was, why the FBI was trying to convince me that the Marshall Archive was a bunch of crap.
And why they later must have decided to liquidate me
and started their manhunt. Just in case. They were planning to get rid of me, just as they got rid of Air Force
Captain Philip Marshall, who was conducting an independent investigation. Or CIA operative Simon Kotz,[1]
who announced that 9/11 was a staged terror attack
organized by special services. Or the many others who
looked beyond what was in the pages of the official reports.[2] It's all the work of the devil! What a devil he is!

Suddenly Malin heard Jia's voice from afar. It was so
hushed that it almost dissolved in the silence of the room:

Malin, you have gotten entangled in a very bad affair...too terrible to be believed. So bad that you will
probably not be able to survive...

---

1. Simon Kotz was a CIA officer. In July 2015, he came out with a
   sensational statement announcing that the tragedy of September
   11, 2001, was, in fact, a monumental special operation. Kotz was
   about to go public in September 2015 presenting some documents
   that would, as per his statement, shed light on the cause of the
   tragedy, but on September 3 he was found dead in his London
   apartment.

2. For example, **Michael Ruppert** (1951–2014), an American
   investigative journalist, writer and political activist. Ruppert was
   found dead in his home on April 13, 2014. It was announced that
   he committed suicide. When he was researching documents about
   9/11 terror attacks, he found information that the CIA was involved in drug trafficking, with the support of major oil companies,
   in order to finance its covert operations.

Malin knew no such thing was possible. He knew Jia was dead, and that hearing her voice was most certainly his own imagination, his subconscious mind transforming his thoughts into the voice of the person he most craved to hear speak to him again – any words... saying anything...

Yet you have no alternative, Max Malin. Do you get it? There are no options left for you except one. To go all the way and get this guy. The only way to make your life safe again would be to use the information you were able to find. If you abandon your quest any sooner than that, they will destroy you. In this case the information would become a grenade with its pin removed, a grenade you'd be holding in your hands. You would be destroyed for having looked where no one is allowed to look and stay alive...you see, Malin...

And then Malin woke up... The early twilight was still being dissolved by the many automobile headlights outside. Malin sat down at his laptop robotically, so that he could do, in a measured and consistent way, what had to be done. One action after another. He created several folders, distributing all the data he had collected into relevant folders. He checked up on everything he had, making sure that all files were still available and readable. Then he copied everything to three flash drives of different colors – red, blue, and black. He gathered his things and gadgets into one bag, putting it away into the closet, placed the flash drives in his pocket, and left the room. He walked toward the service rooms at the back, rather than the staircase on the opposite side.

Malin descended via the fire exit to the ground floor, arriving at a door with a sign that read "Staff Only". One of its leaves was slightly open, banging about due to a draft of air. Malin looked around for surveillance cameras, but none were installed, so he went into the staff room.

In the narrow corridor, wearing a polite smile on his face, he was barely able to get past a pretty raven-haired housemaid who glared at him with her black eyes.

'May I help you, signor?'

'Thank you, no. I know my way.'

Malin took several steps forward, then turned around and, having made sure that the housemaid had disappeared behind a partition at the other end of the corridor, he slipped quickly into the staff bathroom. He locked its door and looked around again. Then he stepped up on the toilet bowl and, slightly raising the suspended ceiling, put his red flash drive, wrapped in a piece of toilet paper, behind the metal bar holding the deck panel. Putting the ceiling back in order, Malin left the bathroom and walked straight to another staff exit that exited to the hotel. His first item was hidden securely: no one would figure out that something so important would be concealed behind the suspended ceiling of a staff bathroom. Malin was convinced this flash drive could easily stay a year or two in such a safe place. Well, it had better not be a hundred years, of course, when the building might eventually be demolished.

Exiting through the service door, Malin found himself surrounded by a darkness that was filled with the incredible air of Rome at night: it was light and somewhat tangy in the old quarters of the Eternal City, as it almost always is at the end of a hot summer day. Such air descends onto the city, becoming palpable with darkness, shrouding the yellow streetlamps in the narrow lanes, which arch and dip.

Malin stopped a cab and asked it to take him to the nearest DHL office. There, he sent the blue flash drive to Canada, post restante, addressed to his own name. His third flash drive stayed in the pocket of his jeans. It would stay on him and thus continue into the unknown with Malin.

Ten minutes later Malin walked down to the Pantheon, where he was immediately surrounded by rambling, promenading crowds of noisy youths and tourists taking up tables at open-air cafés around the square. A large group of Chinese tourists was running around taking pictures of the beautifully illuminated structure of the Pantheon. Some loudly discussed when the building was constructed, while others announced the names of the geniuses buried inside. A tall Chinese woman, standing apart from her countrymen, with her back to Malin, was looking intently at something at the far end of the spacious square. Her black hair was trailing over her shoulders, and her sensitive back was covered only with a light T-shirt bearing the image of Pope John Paul II…

'Jia!' Malin said, without realizing that was speaking aloud. 'Jia!'

The woman turned around and glanced at Malin inquiringly.

'Did you say something to me?' she asked, and her unfamiliar face, even though it was beautiful, immediately brought Malin back to reality. He was in Rome. It was the Pantheon over there. And Jia…she was far away, she remained forever in the forest by London. Forever.

'I'm sorry, I mistook you for someone else. I beg your pardon.'

'No problem,' she responded, turning away with a somewhat demonstrative movement, and continued watching the square and the milling crowds.

It was at that moment that Max Malin knew precisely where he should be going – indeed, where he was now about to go. But first he walked into the next best café, ordered a double whisky, then another. A couple of minutes later, he found a cab at a stand somewhere close to the Capitolium.

'Take me to Atlantis.[3] It's on Via Prato della Corte.'

The cabbie, a young skinny Italian, nodded respectfully, presumably because this client, obviously a man of means, and looking like a somewhat exhausted superman, knew by heart the address of this expensive gentlemen's club.

'Okay, boss,' the cabbie saluted, and the car sped off, moving swiftly down the middle of the lively night traffic, with honking cars driving the guests of Rome around in search of night entertainment.

Soon Malin was sitting alone at a table in the low light of the dark blue hall of the famous club, sipping his third shot of whisky. An amazingly beautiful biracial woman was on the stage, in a strange performance space full of cages. The woman, drowning in a deep blue light, moved smoothly, bending, and curving and arching her nude body, following every turn and twist of a slow melody from the eighties. A female voice, high-pitched, enticing, taking one to the clouds with it, sang:

The time will come when I will go and visit my old city Led by memory's magic to the magnet of its fall, Where yellow mountains of its leaves exude a smoke so sweet And sunlight flutters all around from pools on to the walls...[4]

'How about a lap dance?' a young Italian girl asked Malin as she passed by his table clad only in a couple of wide white ribbons that hugged her breasts and thighs. Ribbons gleamed ghostlike in beams of bluish patches of light.

'Thank you, no. Not now, honey...'

Malin was slowly descending into a deep, silent, in-

3. The World of Atlantis is an elite private club in Rome, featuring erotic entertainment.

4. Copyright Oleg Lurye

ternal space. Perhaps it was due to the influence of the – by now – many shots of whisky. Malin was drifting off into memories that swung like a large pendulum inside him: from the far-off flurry of images related to his past life to very recent gusts of feeling.

…Summer on the Vasilyevsky Island in Leningrad – he plays in the coolness of a courtyard that looks like a well, then the voice of his mother calling from the window: "Maksim, time to go home!" …

Washington, first snow. Malin, stepping behind his father's coffin, cannot really hear the words of solace or condolences expressed by his father's students. He is deeply involved in talking to his dad, promising: he would certainly realize whatever his father's expectations had been. Snow crunches under his feet. Well, he never made it to St. Petersburg, during the many years that he lived in America…

Now it's London on his mind… Smiling, Jia extends her hands towards him: 'I love you, Max Malin. When is our train departing?' Our train, oh Jia, it has already departed, without us… Forever…

And the voice sang on, sounding sweet from afar:

Oh, impossible fall, through the windows look inside A lone saxophone at the corner stays lonely The reflection of the red leaves freezes beside God smiling at us through the branches of the trees

A tall, slender Chinese woman in cut-offs and a semi-transparent tank top came up to Malin noiselessly, looking questioningly at him, a lonesome gentleman sitting with a glass in which the ice had already thawed some time ago. Malin glanced up at her and then, on a whim, said suddenly:

'Sit down, please. Where are you from?'

'From here. I work at Atlantis. My name is Mei.'

'Oh, I understand that much,' Malin said wearily,

trying to sound as if he were trying to tell a joke. 'I'd guess you're from Atlantis, Mei, and not the competitors across the road. But my question was where you come from to end up here at all?'

'Oh, from Shanghai. But I've been living in Rome for twelve years already.'

'So, how old are you?'

'Twenty-four.'

'Well, you're big girl now, that's good!' Malin laughed. 'My name is Malin. Nice to meet you. Well, I'm not really interested in lap-dances. Would you rather stay here with me and keep me company? Would you like something to drink?'

'Champagne. Waiters know they have to bring champagne for the girls. Because it costs a lot...'

'It's all right. We'll survive that, somehow,' Malin responded, and gave his order to a waitress in a nominal mini-skirt who happened to be flitting by: 'Champagne for the lady, please, and whisky for me.'

Then they two simply sat there saying nothing, watching how the stage became immersed in differently shaped puffs of colorful smoke, and listening to the soft and deep sounds of music, with some thumping drums in the background for support.

'I would like to ask you if you could do something for me, Mei. Could you speak Chinese to me, please?'

'Signor Malin understands my native language? What do you want me to say?'

'No, I don't understand Chinese. Which is a big pity. But right now, I just want to hear its sounds. What should you say? Doesn't really matter. Say anything, whatever you want.'

Mei straightened her back, put her hands between her knees and started speaking in a sing-song voice, rocking slightly from side to side:

'*Piǎo yǒu méi... Qí ji shi... Dài qi ji shi... Dài qi ji shi...*'

Closing his eyes, Malin listened to the girl's soft voice, which at times was drowned out by the loud music. A minute passed. Then another...

'What were you saying, honey?'

'The song says that ripe plums keep falling in the garden, and that fewer and fewer are left on the tree. Also, that someone who has been looking for me will be happy when we meet. And—'[5]

'Thank you, Mei. I should go now, I guess.'

Malin took out several large bills and gave them to Mei. Then he paid for the drinks and, walking slowly, stepped out into the night. A light, warm Roman wind greeted him outside. His feeling of intoxication was soon gone, and when Malin returned to his hotel, there was a strange lightness in his body, something he had not experienced for quite a long time. He felt a sudden surge of energy, seemingly out of nowhere. Oh, thank you, Jia...

Malin woke the next morning to the merciless sun streaming through the open windows of his room, and the din of early traffic on nearby Via Veneto. Outisde, a woman yelled: 'Idiota! Perché hai lasciato?'[6] In other words, this street too was already full of life.

Malin had his breakfast quickly, and then left the hotel with all his belongings: he had fit everything into a rather small bag along with his laptop. He exited onto the sun-drenched street and started moving towards

---

5. This song is from Shi Jing, or The Book of Odes, the oldest collection of Chinese poetry dating from the 11th to 7th centuries BC. The first stanza of The Song About A Girl Gathering Plums, is:

   Dropping are the fruits from the plum-tree;
   There are [but] seven [tenths] of them left!
   For the gentlemen who seek me,
   This is the fortunate time!   (translator: James Legge, 1871)

6. 'You, idiot you! Why did you leave?' (in Italian)

Villa Borghese, to which filled tour buses were already making their way through the busy traffic. Walking past the US embassy on Via Veneto, Malin could not repress a smile, thinking that some FBI men might be waiting there for him. Fifty meters further down the street, he turned into the sparkling bronze of a revolving door, which was the entrance to the luxurious Hotel Westin Excelsiore. Once inside, he found himself in a gigantic lobby featuring pretentious paintings and sculptures and adorned with frescoes.

Dozens of hotel guests were hurrying from the bars to the hotel concierge stand and the reception desk; one more tour group of well-off Asian tourists was checking in early. Several businessmen were sitting in nearby armchairs, talking discreetly and importantly into their phones. Richard Berwick got up quickly from a little sofa in the corner: he was, as always, quite disheveled, and looked busy.

'Hi Malin! Everything should be all right. Lavallieri is already waiting for me, expecting me to come with you to sell those Bosch sketches. He called me twice... he's probably concerned that I might take him in...'

'And where are the sketches? What shall we tell him?'

'The sketches are supposedly stored in a bank safe not far from here – two streets down. Thing is that once we get everything settled, Lavallieri will want to look at the sketches. What then?'

'I will try to get as much information as possible about his client Sergio. Then we'll see... Perhaps we could put some pressure on him...what do you think, Richard?'

'Yup, we'll see. Let's play it by ear, right?'

'Okay, let's go.'

The two friends walked across a long room filled with frescoes. Turning around a grand piano placed in the middle, they entered a lift and went up three floors. Then they walked over a soft, thick rug in the corridor and arrived in front of a large door. Richard knocked cautiously. The door was thrown open right away, so that Malin even thought their host had probably been waiting for them behind it, peeking eagerly through the spyhole.

The man who opened the door for them was certainly quite old, perhaps near eighty. He was of average height and had on a light linen blazer. His moustache was certainly tinted, and his long hair was carefully combed back. As soon as the door was open, he took several steps back, inviting his visitors to come in. In a way, he looked like the neat and tidy creation of an artist of the late Renaissance, like a miniature page, perhaps, if somewhat aged.

'Do come in, signori! Please feel at home in the humble dwelling of this poor art collector. Hello, Richard! And you, Sir, must be the happy owner of the sketches by the great Hieronymus Bosch, right?'

'Yes, hello. I am Malin Gorin.'

'My name is Luca Lavallieri,' the old man said, shaking hands with his guests now. His hand was soft. It was like shaking hands with a cat. 'Oh, you must be Russian. At least because of the last name.'

'No, I'm American. But I've got this name from my ancestors.'

'Please come in, friends, and sit down. Would you like whisky? Oh, perhaps, coffee?'

This hotel room was like a seventeenth century palace chamber. The furniture was all dark wood and brocaded in gold. The table had fanciful cabriole legs, and everywhere there were hassock poufs, old chairs, and paintings. The ceiling was painted with frescoes. The drawing room was a rather large space with two huge windows, a fireplace, and a balcony. A double-leaf door to the right was closed tight; it probably led to the bedroom. The bathroom was on the left.

Lavallieri got no answer to his question, but quickly mixed whisky and soda, added some ice and handed Malin and Richard two cold glasses. Despite his age and the early hour, he got himself a bottle of beer out of the fridge.

'Here's your whisky, and do sit down, my friends.'

The old man was fidgeting and looked quite nervous. He made small, sudden, quick movements, and the bottle in his hands was tossed around so much that one suspected the beer to be ready to foam up and stain the fancy carpet below. Lavallieri finally sat on the couch once his visitors had comfortably installed themselves in two capacious armchairs. He took several deep draughts from his bottle, then jumped up again, saying:

'I must excuse myself for a minute, my friends. I'll be right back, sorry. You know, I drank a bottle of beer before your arrival. So now nature is calling…it's my age, sorry…'

Luca Lavallieri moved towards the bathroom with strange, mincing steps, and stopped in front of the door. For some reason he glanced back at his guests, and then disappeared behind the door. Malin and Richard looked at each other, and with a taut smile, Malin asked his friend:

'Is he always like this? Is something wrong? Why is he so nervous?'

'No, he's never been like that. He might be out of whack, and quite a bit so. His occupation is certainly very stressful. Maybe something is not going according to plan. But honestly, I am quite surprised.'

'Make no sudden movements or I'll shoot!' a male voice announced harshly. The man standing right behind Malin. Malin looked up and saw in the mirror in front of him that the bedroom door was now open, and that a dark-haired man of average height, clad in a leather jacket, stood aiming his gun at Malin's head.

Malin recognized him right away as the one who had almost gotten him yesterday, not far from Via Veneto. Yes, he and the beautiful Bella. Today, there was nothing Malin would be able to do, and a moment later the gun barrel was touching the back of his head. The unexpected visitor could shoot fast and without any qualms. No doubt about that...

Malin looked to the right, checking out Richard's situation: he was sitting stooped in his chair, his head tucked into his shoulders. Bella was standing behind him, tall and also clad in leather like a biker. She was aiming her gun at the back of Berwick's head. She must have quietly slipped out of the bathroom to where the frightened Lavallieri had disappeared, and she must have done it at the same time her partner came out of the bedroom. Two more men whom Malin had not seen before came out of the bedroom, both carrying multi-charge Glocks. One of them also held what looked like a small medical bag.

The situation was hopeless: Luca Lavallieri had lured them into this trap, perhaps because he feared for his life, or perhaps wishing to get the Bosch sketches for free. Here he was, by the way: he moved slowly out of his bathroom and stopped in the door, pale with fear, his lips trembling. Suddenly Malin had a reassuring thought: Bella had said yesterday that their order was not to kill Malin, but to take him alive. That is, he had a chance for living a little longer. Malin coughed, clearing his throat, and spoke in a choked voice:

'We cannot provide any resistance and we are ready to fulfil any demands. All I am asking is that no one get hurt and that you let us live. What do you want?'

'Just stay where you are,' Bella responded, speaking with a strong Italian accent. 'There is nothing else. Put your arms on the armrests, so that this nice gentleman can put handcuffs on them and chain you to the chairs. Your lives are safe for now. Some very influential person needs you, Signor Malin, and he wants you to be safe and sound. Or at least partially sound. Execute orders now!'

The two new men put handcuffs on Malin and Richard. Then, with a gesture of their pistols, they ordered Lavallieri, who was still scared out of his wits, to step away from the front door, which they double locked.

Putting the medical bag on the coffee table, Bella opened it and got out a syringe. She filled it with the contents of several ampoules, walked up to Malin and held his head with her left arm. Slowly tilting it to the side, she made a light movement with her right hand, sticking the syringe into Malin's neck. He didn't feel anything as she gave him the shot, but a few seconds later a sensation of tantalizing, cumbersome heaviness filled his legs, slowly expanding upwards. Thighs, abdomen, and breast followed. It went ever higher.

Bella bent to Malin's face, looking at him with that dark gaze that he knew from the day before. Then she gave him a peck on the cheek.

'Oh, cutie pie, what a bother you were! Never have I run after any guy as long as I have run after you...Lord, a whole month!'

Malin knew he would become unconscious in a few seconds, but he concentrated all his willpower to look up at Richard, who was still sitting in his chair. It was then that one of the intruders came up to Berwick from behind and hit him on the head with his gun, exercising a practiced, precise movement. Richard went limp immediately, losing consciousness.

Malin could tell that the blow had been administered with all necessary caution: it was certainly not meant to kill Richard. He felt relieved that his friend was going to live, at least for a while...but then, all of a sudden, Bella's leather-clad partner, who was standing at the bathroom door, grabbed old Lavallieri, who was obviously terrified and could not utter a word. Pushing the old man away slightly, he shot him point blank in the chest. This was the last image that froze for Malin.

He could not move anymore; his lids had grown so heavy he could not lift them. His consciousness was still fighting this condition, trying not to let in the awful, tremendous heaviness that was taking over his body. He could still hear somebody talking, but the words were coming from very far away now, and the voices were very low:

'Why did you get the old man?' Bella was asking.

'Do you think I would do anything without coordinating with Nicholas first? He told me to do it. Luca isn't needed anymore. He's lived for too long now. Plus, he saw too much today, and he might talk if somebody were to push him up against a wall.'

'Hey, wait a minute, but we also know too much... will they do away with us, too? I heard that Nicholas's boss always does that with those who work for him.'

'Honey, when you were applying for this job, did you think you'd be tending flowers?'

'Oh, piss off! Let's pack our shipment.'

'We should take our guy with us, of course. As for this fatso from Switzerland, let our men carry him out of here like a drunk and put him in a cab to his hotel later. He should sleep a lot after so much cognac...by the way, fill him up with cognac properly, and give him one more shot.'

'What about Luca? Will he be staying here?'

'Yes. Put up the "Do not disturb" sign outside. They might find him in a day or so...'

A few seconds later, the enormous heaviness pressed down on Malin so that all sound muted completely, disappearing like the last rays of the Italian sun.

This was when the leather man and Bella took off the handcuffs, sprayed Malin's shirt with quite a lot of whisky, and raised him up, holding him under the arms. He hung down limply, his arms around their shoulders, his feet sliding along the thick rug. A minute later, all three were moving to the exit across the hotel lobby, in which several hotel guests, some security men and a smiling receptionist stared after them: it was obvious that this signor had gotten drunk to the gills, so now his wife and a friend were taking him home after a night of heavy carousing.

'You creep, you!' Bella was loudly lamenting in Italian. 'It's only noon and he filled up like this again! Vincente, why did you give him those drinks? Don't you know he can't take much alcohol? Let's put him in the car!'

15

When Skyscrapers Fall
New York. September 11, 2001

A vigorous New York morning gripped the waking Manhattan. At this early hour the fresh air felt somewhat chilly. No one was rushing through the streets yet, and the city was waking slowly to an average Tuesday, which the forecast said would probably be one of the last sunny days in September. It was six in the morning. The first wave of eternally busy clerks had not yet arrived from all sides to flood the cool crystals of the skyscrapers that pierced the heavens. It seemed the buildings themselves were still slumbering, trying to prolong the happy condition of these last minutes of calm.

An older gentleman who called himself Eric Novack sauntered along Murray Street towards West Broadway. He was tall, and athletically built. His head was thrown back a bit and his was black hair with streaks of grey, he had regular features and only a few wrinkles lined his face. His eyes, set fairly widely apart, were looking up at the sky. If one did not know that Novack was going on seventy-two, they might guess he was sixty at most. He had on blue jeans, a casual light jacket, and sports shoes of a matching color. An expensive Canon camera hung on his shoulder. One would assume he was a rich tourist who had decided to admire the World Trade Center towers, with their hundred-and-ten floors, early in the day before the bustling, noisy crowds arrived to start their working day.

How come I feel it again, just like before? Novack was wondering. Today is the final stage of ten months' exhausting work, but I'm completely calm inside. Why? I fear nothing, I have no worries. Such overconfidence is great, of course, because I know I thought of all the details and made provisions for every, or nearly every, contingency. On the other hand, overconfidence always leads to partial relaxation, to slacking and loss of control. Which isn't good…even though I know I took everything into account and did everything right.

So, all actors are ready to step onto the stage, and the script is ideal. And I shouldn't be blamed if some spectators are to die during the performance. After all, they came into this theater of their own free will, Novack thought, lighting a new cigarette without breaking his stride. We're talking fate here. It's their fate. How can one blame the wind for turning into a hurricane and uprooting a tree that killed a passerby when it fell? The deceased happened to walk by at the exact moment it started falling. How can we accuse the wind for what happened? Same here. It's fate that these people were born in or moved to New York, got their specialized education, and then got a job in a company with offices in one of these buildings…

Novack's thoughts were interrupted by a phone call. He knew his number was known to only one person. Someone who had asked to be addressed as James.

'Hello! Is that you, my friend?' The voice of the caller was quite muffled, so that one got the impression he was talking through his handkerchief.

'Yes…were you expecting someone else to answer?' Novack asked sarcastically. 'And why are you calling me now? It's five minutes earlier than scheduled.'

'There are changes to the plan. Boss just made a new decision. Suddenly. But his decision is not up for discussion.'

'What new decision? With less than two hours left before the event...' Novack was speaking in a calm manner, but deep inside him, little, loud strings had tensed up and started to quiver. 'The birdies can't be stopped anymore.'

'Let all three birdies fly on. They are needed and eagerly expected. The decision was made, however, not to destroy the two big nests completely. Whatever the birdies can do is fine. It'll be good enough. But as for the third, the smaller one... Let it fall after the birdies arrive.'

'Are you crazy? That's impossible! The system runs on its own now, so the two nests will collapse on their own. Probably within an hour after the arrival. And the third will do the same, a little later. So, nothing can be changed at this point. Nothing! Everything is already set up and there's no way anyone can change anything. Millions were shelled out to set it up. Besides, no one who rigged the system is around anymore. Only they might have been able to do something this late in terms of introducing changes, but, as I said, they are not around anymore...'

'What do you mean?'

'They aren't around anymore. They were expendable...'

'Listen! I don't give a flying fuck about those people!' the person on the other end of the line screamed. 'All I know is that the destruction of the first two nests must be avoided. I mean, the two large nests. There should be no complete destruction! The third one may disappear... This is what the Boss decided. All other agreements are still in force. No money should be paid back. Let the birdies strike, but that should be it!'

'This is what I can tell you,' Novack said in a low voice. 'We can do a lot. But I'm not God, and I can't stop the mechanism that's already started working. All three birdies will arrive in about two hours, and all three nests will fall down. First the first two, then the third a little later. And that's that! Of course, no one would mention anything about money in the end. And no one would pay anything back anyway. What don't you get? All of the job's details were discussed in advance. You paid, and I got the job done. And now you're telling me that the final stage, something we've been working on for two months, should be called off. And that only at the last minute when, technically speaking, nothing can be done. Nothing!'

'Hey now, let's not put it like that. Let us...' The person at the other end must have moved his handkerchief off the phone: the sound of his voice suddenly became very clear. 'Listen, the only thing that has to be called off is the complete demolition of the two big nests. For the simple reason that their total demolition would be the only point we won't be able to explain away. Because they're too big and too stable. The Boss may have some other reasons, too. You have, after all, received everything you've asked for, so you may disappear, no problem. All you have to do is...'

'Oh James...,' Novack suddenly burst into laughter. 'Why don't you and your moron of a boss go and fuck yourselves? Why can't you grasp the simple fact that the bomb is falling, and can't be stopped midair? It is not, I repeat, NOT possible, since it was already dropped... In short, everything will happen the way it was agreed on earlier. With all due respect, I do not think that you and I will ever hear of each other again. And I don't even exist for you anymore...'

He ended the call even as James was still shouting,

obviously growing more furious. Then he took the SIM card out of his phone, broke it into pieces and threw it into a water gully. A hundred meters down, he also hurled the phone into a rubbish bin.

Boy, what idiots! Novack was talking to himself now as he turned onto West Broadway. They ordered a gigantic project, they gave me almost a billion as an advance, and I have spent six months preparing everything. Hundreds of people were involved, and none of them were really aware of what was going on... And look, here we are now: suddenly the buildings cannot be demolished, they must stay intact... Let the planes hit whatever they will hit, but let the two big buildings remain whole...why? Does the boss want them kept whole as a memento of the event? They want the third building destroyed, oh yes, I can understand that: they want everything inside that building to disappear. Stupid morons! How come they don't get it: the machine has already been set in motion, and there's no way back. Hopefully this fuckwit pretending his name is James understands that much. But it doesn't matter – it's not my problem anymore. Everything will happen according to plans they coordinated in the first place... Besides, all sums of money have already been transferred, so there's no cheating. Perhaps they simply shat the bed in some major way. I wonder what crackpot idea got into whose top-level brain this time.

Morning finally conquered the whole of Manhattan. The sky was especially bright and transparent, with a bluish hue, and vibrated slightly from its own coolness. The gigantic twin towers were happily reaching heavenward, their tops already splashed by the first rays of the sun. Novack felt his point of view dismissed their immense, oppressive hugeness, and they turned into an amazing succession of intertwining, long and clear lines ideally matched to the austere facets of the smaller cousins standing around them.

Novack turned into a very small café crammed between a huge bank building and a ponderous post office. Several bank clerks in immaculately ironed clothes were seated around two little tables, hastily finishing their breakfast. They ate silently, staring at the pages of morning newspapers. A strange song played over the PA system. Novack had never heard it before:

I'm a black dog running, down by the sea, Past all feeling, passing sound and light To that Lady from all those old stories Who's magic like an ancient amulet.[1]

Novack took a window seat. Raising his head, he could see most of the towers' panorama. He suddenly felt a craving for cognac, heavy-bodied and tangy, oak flavored. He wanted each drop to envelope his throat and create echoes in his head like light and soft impulses. Novack smiled: well, it looked like he had developed a second idiosyncrasy. His first was an old, overpowering desire to be present at the scene of the global events he participated in arranging. Now he was becoming addicted to drinking cognac in the morning, too – which could attract attention, of course. Oh, so be it! In this city, no one is interested in other people. Plus, something was going to happen soon on such a grand scale that no one would think back to some old gentleman ordering Hennessy at an early hour.

Novack soon finished off the contents of his squat glass. Deep inside him vibrated a tensely strung cord of anticipation. He looked at his watch: nine twenty. He retrieved another mobile phone from his jacket, dialed a number, and asked in a flat, steady, expressionless voice:

'How's everything?'

---

1. Verses copyright Oleg Lurye

'Two Boston birdies are already up in the air and the third, in Washington, is taxiing to take off,' someone reported. His voice rang with a noticeable Eastern accent, sounding like a boy's. 'Our clients are all on board. Their relatives told me they were praying fervently before getting on the plane. One was, by the way, very concerned whether the money transfer reached his family. He was very nervous about it.'

'Which birdie is he in?'

'In the third. I was told that the plane is ready for takeoff. This can be seen from the airport building.'

'All right,' Novack said. He was silent for a moment, then said: 'Five hours should be enough for you to get here from Boston. Meet Moses at the usual place. You'll get the rest of your money there. Oh, something important: when you get here, stay under the radar. Just keep low and go straight to the meeting, okay? And... well, you must forget all this and get out of the country, as far away as you can. You must rest, you know...'

'A deal is a deal, boss,' the man laughed. 'Now that I am well-heeled, no one could drag me to the States for a couple years, minimum. I'll be someplace in the ocean, under palm trees...'

'All right, that's it!' Novack cut short their conversation. 'Do your work now. And give my regards to Moses.'

When Novack got off the phone, he realized he was alone in the café. The working day had begun. The waiter turned the music a bit louder and went back to the staff room: he was probably bored when there were no clients. Novack's mobile rang loudly.

'Okay, speak, my girl, what's cooking?' Novack said in a low voice.

'Could you please smile, boss?' enquired a muffled female voice, sounding as if the caller was speaking from very far away. 'Our Arab middlemen had major problems.'

271

'Which ones, exactly?'

'The ones who helped us find very religious flyers. Men who could convince the pilots that they were the chosen ones, so they could take vengeance on America and thus go straight to Allah… Anyway, these middle-men, they got into a very nasty situation themselves. They were the first to go to Allah, somewhat earlier than the flyers…'

'Oh, don't be wicked, please. What happened?'

'Last night they had a car accident. Both of them. It was awful. Their Cadillac was rammed by a speeding truck. Both were killed instantly. The driver of the truck took off, of course, and my understanding is that no one will be looking for him…'

'Have you seen these poor devils? Did you make sure it was them?'

'I could see what little remained of them…it was awfully convincing…'

'All right, then. That's it for now. You've warmed my heart. Don't stay there. Fly home and then don't leave Europe. I'll find you.'

Novack switched off his phone and opened it with a practiced movement. Then he took out the SIM card and, upon exiting the café, threw it into a rubbish bin. He walked unhurriedly to Washington Street, looked up once again at the towers, and walked on towards Barclay Street. He could still hear the song, which the waiter was playing at full volume now: *I'm a black dog running, down by the sea.*

This was a usual work morning in the city; nothing foreboded the coming tragedy. Only the man who called himself Eric Novack, who was slowly moving towards the World Trade Center, knew about it. Plus, those at the top who had ordered and paid for the impending nightmare. They had never met Eric Novack, nor did they even know who he was, where he came from or where he would go after today's events. He was only called The Contractor, and for them, for the purposes of their agreement, this was good enough.

When Novack was already about a kilometer from the twin towers, he heard the slight, mosquito-like drone of the oncoming plane from somewhere in the distance. It got ever louder, more and more vibrant. Novack stopped and turned towards the gigantic towers. For him, time now froze. It was a moment of anticipation not unlike what a gambler feels watching the marble, thrown with a flick of the dealer's hand, rolling around, slowing gradually in the roulette wheel.

The city, however, took no notice of either the increasing noise of the plane engines or of a tall man standing in the middle of the sidewalk. A large clock mounted above the entrance to a nearby building showed it was forty-six minutes past the eighth hour. That was when the impact was heard... The huge Boeing 767 hit the North Tower of the World Trade Center slightly above its middle. A powerful explosion thundered forth, and huge flames immediately blazed up high above.

Soon the downtown of the gigantic metropolis was seized in a major paroxysm. Hundreds started running, shouting, but not hearing each other. They rushed in all directions, bumping into trash cans and streetlights. Taxis ripped forward and braked hard, hitting each other with their bumpers. A woman lay on the asphalt, twitching in an epileptic fit. And only Eric Novack, who stepped to the side of the street and took up a safe position close to an archway, was looking up attentively, expecting further developments.

After seventeen minutes of panicky crowds destroying everything in their path, Novack could distinguish, despite all the chaos and hellish noise, the slight buzz of a second plane. He started counting to himself, watching the blazing inferno at the North Tower: *One, two, three, four, five, six, seven...*

The second Boeing glided into the South Tower, WTC-2, and it seemed to Novack that this plane was flying slowly, that its impact was a soft one... Due to the pandemonium all around, the impact itself seemed not to be as loud as the first hit. Still, in a moment the second twin was also blazing.

Both skyscrapers were on fire now. Novack looked up again at what had happened a minute before: the terror attack of the century. Then he started walking fast down Church Street, away from the huge buildings that were now on fire. He knew that in about an hour, the South Tower was to collapse completely, and half an hour after that, the same was to happen to the North Tower, which was also weakened by the impact. He knew there were tons of powerful Thermate in both buildings. Over the course of the previous two months, some fake repairmen had brought loads of it into the towers and put them in designated places around the trusswork. It was meant to make buildings collapse like card towers, which would only happen when the flames reached a certain point. The planes had started an unstoppable countdown as soon as they hit the buildings: these were the last minutes of their existence.

Next in line was the third building: 7 WTC, which stood north of the Twin Towers. It counted forty-seven floors, and it too was stuffed with Thermate. Novack started getting concerned, however, that the third plane seemed to be late.

Where's the third plane? Why is it late? It's already fifty minutes after the first impact, and they were supposed to hit the three targets with a time lag of about twenty minutes. Where are you, birdie number three? You are no less

*important than the first two, and you were also promised
to my clients...*

People were still running in all directions, shouting,
and bumping into each other. Sirens wailed loudly, heart-
rendingly; ambulances were rushing around, giving way
only to firefighters and emergency rescue teams. Suddenly hundreds of policemen appeared on the streets,
but it seemed that they didn't really know what they
were supposed to do. They mostly ran around, yelling
into their walkie-talkies. At Thomas Street, Novack
walked into a parking lot: the gate arm was up, and the
security guy must have left, for the door of his booth
stood wide open.

Novack ascended to the third floor, got into an unremarkable grey Camry with tinted windows, and started
the engine. He looked at his watch again and put on the
radio. All radio stations seemed to have gone mad. An-
nouncers were shouting, talking over each other. They
were all explaining to their listeners what was currently
known about this unimaginable, devastating terror attack. That two passenger planes had hit the skyscrapers
of the World Trade Center. That both buildings were
now on fire, and that people were being evacuated from
them. That the explosions had probably been organized
by Al-Qaeda operatives, and by the main terrorist of the
planet – Osama bin Laden. Yet there was nothing about
the third plane. Just one report saying that one more
Boeing had supposedly hit the Pentagon.

As Novack drove around the last ramp, there came
the loud sound of an explosion, somewhat dampened
by the concrete walls of the parking building. The car
shook slightly. That had to be the South Tower collapsing. All right, the system worked fine. Half an hour later,
as the grey Toyota Camry slowly made its way through
gigantic traffic jams, through the congestion of many

rescue vehicles and fire engines, and by the time it made it to West Houston Street, the earth shook again. This time it was because the second skyscraper had collapsed: The North Tower of the WTC, WTC-1, had crumbled.

When Novack got to the streets of a deserted, quiet Upper Manhattan, he heard news on the radio that made him slow to a crawl.

'We got a report just a few seconds ago,' the announcer spoke incredibly quickly, 'that a third Boeing 757, Flight 77, whose departure was delayed at the Washington, D.C. Airport, was also hijacked by terrorists, and hit the western wing of the Pentagon at 9:37 a.m. The wall of the building collapsed twenty minutes later. Firefighters are putting out the fire. The death toll is not yet known.'

Novack's hands, which were lying on the steering wheel, clenched so hard that the ends of his fingers turned white. He moved the car sharply towards the curb and stopped there. With his motor still running, Novack leaned back in his seat and started thinking hard.

What's that? What could have happened? Why was there this snag in such a carefully planned event? Why did the Boeing flying from Washington turn towards the Pentagon? It was supposed to hit the third building in New York, 7 WTC, a little after nine in the morning. And where was this Flight 77 for over an hour, if it departed at 8:20 and hit the Pentagon only at 9:37? The distance between the airport and the Pentagon is very short, so where the hell was it? I don't understand what happened. What about the third skyscraper? It must be destroyed in any case, otherwise my contract will not be fulfilled. And that's out of the question. In principle. The building is stuffed as well, just like the other two.

Novack's brain went into overdrive, and in no time at all he had already calculated and accepted the most probable version of what had happened.

All the hijackers, recruited via Lebanese middlemen, were religious fanatics from the poorest stratum of society. One of Novack's conditions was that all the men would be from different countries, and that they would have no prior knowledge of each other, even in a roundabout way. All of them were offered an opportunity to kill enemies of Islam, in praise of Allah, but at the expense of their own lives. In this way they would provide for their families as long as the family members lived. One hundred and thirty men declared that they were willing to die for the glory of Allah, even though they had no idea what their task would be. After a very careful screening, fourteen men had been selected for the operation and distributed among the three airplanes. The suicide attackers underwent the necessary training and were made completely ready for the hijacking and their own subsequent deaths, which would take them immediately to the realm of Allah. Their training was both technical and ideological.

But it was true that, on the last call he took, the one about making sure all the terrorists boarded the plane and that the planes took off, the man had told him that one of the hijackers on Flight 77, named Salem, was behaving somewhat unsatisfactorily: he kept praying too fervently, acting on edge, and asking about the money for his family, even though he himself had transferred it to his family the week before.

This was why Novack made the only reasonable assumption: Salem and his pals had become overly exuberant after their success in hijacking the plane – or perhaps they had even taken some drugs, either before carrying off this big feat of theirs, in order to keep their spirits up, or after it, to celebrate their achievement. So, when they realized that no one was controlling their route in the air, they may have decided not to destroy some office center in New York, that is, the 7 WTC, but rather to direct their righteous rage at their main enemies in the Pentagon.

In the end, it wasn't important anymore why that plane had ultimately hit the Pentagon. As he sat in the car with his eyes closed, all Novack's logical reasoning removed this issue into the background as something of little immediate significance. Pentagon here or Pentagon there, it had already happened. Something else was of more significance: that the 7 WTC was laden with a huge load of Thermate load, and that a great fire inside the building would be necessary to activate it… Otherwise something else would have to be done, something his plan had not foreseen. Novack felt that something uncalled-for was taking place and, correspondingly, something highly insulting for him: this was an option that his powerful brain had not foreseen… What was needed now would be at least some official reason for destroying the third skyscraper. Otherwise, there would be no plausible explanation for the building to collapse in such an orderly and precise way, all on its own, without any assistance from certain specialists….

Someone was knocking at his car window. When Novack opened his eyes, he saw a policeman trying to look inside in order to figure out what was going on. He lowered the window.

'Are you okay, Sir? Your car is parked in such a strange position…I could see that someone was inside, but you weren't moving.'

'Oh, I'm all right. I drove up here from Lower Manhattan. After I saw that nightmare, I couldn't get back to my senses. So, I felt I'd better stop and wait till I get back to normal, at least a little…'

'You saw it all, did you?' the young policeman asked

Novack, looking horrified. 'Oh my...you did...'

'Yes, it was awful,' Novack said wearily. 'And unreal. Like in a movie. Do you have any more information?'

'Yes, we're getting constant updates,' the policeman nodded at his radio. 'But they say that nothing can really be seen too well because of all the dust. Oh, they just said a third building is on fire.'

Novack experienced a sensation like a hot wave flushing down onto him from above, quickly rushing all the way to his feet. Was fate fulfilling his contract all by itself? He asked gently, as if afraid that his feeling of ultimate success would be disturbed:

'What do you mean by "third building"? Which one? Was there another plane?'

'No, it caught fire after the Twin Towers collapsed. The Seven is ablaze from its seventh floor up... You really should go home, Sir. You look very pale. How do you feel?'

'Relatively normal, I guess,' Novack smirked. 'Thanks for your concern. And good luck to you.'

He put the car into gear and drove off with caution. The time was slowly rolling just past noon, and the city remained deserted and scared. Cloud patches rushed across the pale sky, looking like dirty, tangled pieces of fluff. His car moved forward steadily. Sometimes its reflection could be seen in the windows of rare oncoming cars, all of which were cautiously aiming for the West Bronx. Novack could accelerate a little bit when he turned onto Amsterdam Avenue. This was when he laughed softly. *Oh Lord, can it be true that You were helping me today, together with Krishna, Buddha, and Allah?* he thought. *Oh my, the Seven is on fire! Thank you, Lord, for this miracle!* He turned up the radio.

'The Building Seven of the World Trade Center is on fire,' a reporter was saying, probably in a direct live transmission: his voice was very hoarse. 'The blaze has already engulfed five…no, it's seven floors now. Firefighters told me just now that there is a chance that they will be able to put out the fire, because it's not as strong or extensive compared with the Twin Towers. Plus, the building itself has a sturdier structure. Still, there is some problem with getting enough water because the water supply was severed during the collapse of the North Tower.'

A bit later, as Novack drove up to a nondescript hotel bearing a proud name, New York Deluxe A, he looked with unexpected delight at this dreary grey building that could otherwise elicit no feeling but sadness… He usually preferred such ordinary hotels for occasions when he was present at events he had orchestrated. He found them to be quite comfortable, having a large number of identical rooms with prefabricated furniture. There were several hours left until some further events were to occur that Novack intended to manage in person, so he left his car in the parking lot at the entrance to the hotel and walked through the almost empty lobby to his room on the third floor.

He turned on the TV set and lay down on the bed, closing his eyes again. Not much was left to do, but he already felt tired: the vein in his temple was pulsating, and it boomed like a heavy echo through his entire body. He stretched his legs, relaxing completely. Novack knew that three hours of deep, uninterrupted, and dreamless sleep would fully restore his energy level. This was his usual procedure, and his trained body, forgetting the day's tribulations and physical stress, dropped gently into sleep.

This time, however, there was a dream. Simple and consisting of short episodes, as if he were watching a newsreel.

Paola, tall and slim, runs through some corridor inside one of the towers. She is in a colorful crop-top and her favorite, worn-out jeans. Her long black hair is swept to all sides, and its strands are stuck to her wet face. Gigantic glass panels crack and burst behind her, falling down with a shower of shards. Metal pieces and beams can be seen falling behind her, beyond the gaping space where windows used to be. She keeps shouting loudly... Her eyes look straight at him. But Novack stands frozen, he does not feel his feet at all, cannot make a single step, even though he must get to Paola, must grab her hand, and take her away from this building, which is obviously about to collapse...besides, she's running in the wrong direction! Don't go to the lifts! NO! Run to the stairs! To the stairs...!

In the next second Paola is already running down the stairs, taking the several steps at a time. Thank God! Run! Run, my darling! You will make it. Suddenly flights of stairs start collapsing just meters behind her. Just as she runs around this corner, the stairs fall. One more turn, one more. Paola shouts something, and Novack knows that she is addressing him. But he is dumb, he cannot speak. Not a word, not a sound... Only a horrible roar of the falling flights of stairs can be heard, and the terrible groaning of metal being torn apart...

Then there was a strange, clear realization that all this was a dream. Whatever he had just seen – both the collapsing skyscraper, the running Paola, and himself, mute and paralyzed – was only in his dream. Oh, this was like a gulp of cool water during an infernal heatwave – he could feel it all around his body, starting in his throat. This was a dream. Of course, what else?

Paola, his amazing Paola, had died in the summer of '76, in a hospital in London. She was only thirty. They had been together for thirteen years before, since the day he saw Paola in a café in Dallas in 1963 – on the day

Kennedy died. Thirteen years together before the ghastly oncological process destroyed her, the most beautiful creature there was, in a few short months.

Then the dream rushed again into his consciousness, shutting out reality and presenting Novack with a vexing question: *Why is Paola still running down the stairway of a slowly collapsing skyscraper? The building could not be taking so long to come apart – the blast was calculated to be enough for it to fold in just a moment. Floor after floor.*

Paola, however, reaches the ground floor. All alone. There is no one around. She runs through the lobby and gets out to the street, where she will be saved. It is then that the giant mass of the building makes a seemingly slow and unstoppable downward slide, with dust clouds shooting up and expanding to all sides, accompanied by the eerie, swelling screech of folding floors that overwhelms any other sounds. Paola keeps running forward, in slow motion now, but gigantic pieces of debris, also in slow motion, cover her over completely.

Novack was trying to shout, but again he could not. Well, yes, this was only a dream. An idiotic, a stupid dream…

He woke up when three hours had passed, on the dot. Refreshed, full of energy. The rest of his sleepiness vanished in a moment, as soon as he perceived what the CNN news anchor was saying, in a peculiarly metallic-sounding voice:

'Due to the fire that engulfed more than twenty floors, Building Number Seven of the World Trade Center collapsed completely, all forty-seven floors. According to unconfirmed reports, there were no casualties, because all fire teams were evacuated from the building two hours ago. Building Seven of the World Trade Center is now completely destroyed...'[2]

Novack looked at his watch: 5:22 p.m. Now his contract was fully executed. He closed his eyes again and smiled. All he had to do next was to personally take care of some details of the final mopping up. After that, Eric Novack could die in peace. After all, the man lying on a large double bed in a room at New York Deluxe A Hotel knew very well that his favorite island was waiting for him. An island where white sand warmed fast in the mornings, so warm that small crabs in their metallic-shining crust outfits preferred to rush to the long, hissing wave of the oncoming tide, while the ocean kept counting its unending, monotonous sighs, now swelling up, now retreating.

Even with his eyes closed, Novack kept pressing buttons, going through the available TV channels.

CNN...ABC...CBS...NBC... Suddenly Novack jumped up and stared at the screen. This news anchor was, for some reason, frowning as he droned on:

'The fourth hijacked plane was Boeing 757-200 Flight 93 by United Airlines, registration number N591UA. It was flying from Newark, New Jersey, to San Francisco, California. Radio contact with the plane was interrupted at 9:28 a.m. and its transponder signal was lost at 9:40 a.m. Around this time, the plane turned around and changed course for Washington, D.C. Experts believe that terrorists who hijacked this plane were planning to crash into the White House and destroy it altogether. The plane, however, did not reach its goal, crashing at 10:03 a.m. in a field close to Shanks-

---

2. Building 7 of the World Trade Center (7 WTC) was, per the official version of events, damaged by the falling debris of the WTC Twin Towers. This started fires inside the building, on its lower floors. The collapse of 7 WTC happened at 5:20 p.m., almost five hours after the North Tower collapsed.

ville, in southwestern Pennsylvania. The site of the crash is approximately 240 kilometers north of Washington, D.C. All those on board have died.'

Novack smiled as he understood. Oh Lord! What idiots! His men hijacked only three planes. Only three! Idiots! Novack was not even upset that his client had barged in on pre-agreed developments. He knew immediately what had happened. He was amused by how primitive their attempt was to change the rules of the game.

Well, there it goes, right? Novack said to himself. These imbeciles realized that they could not go back on the complete destruction of the skyscrapers. And they figured out, too, that it would be difficult to explain the collapse of all three buildings due to fires that started after the planes' impact. So, they decided to scare the world with a terrorist attack attempt on the White House, to sidetrack everyone's attention... But first things first, what those twits got into their heads was redirecting this unfortunate flight to Washington, then cutting off communication with the plane and destroying it at Shanksville, so that the plane wouldn't reach its supposed aim... How can one explain the fourth Boeing that went down two hundred and forty kilometers from the President's residence? Especially since it departed later than the other three planes and went down only after ten in the morning. One should expect that questions will be asked anyway. How come those skyscrapers collapsed completely, if by all accounts, plane impact alone wouldn't be able to damage them so much that they fall apart neatly like that. Well, this was what they wanted, that was their requirement, so I did everything per client's orders. Now, this fourth plane will not save them, it cannot clear away all the sticky questions that will be raised.

Jesus, again, what idiots! Why not make investigations top secret and hire the right experts to do what's needed? Also, why not tell journalists what to write? That would be all. That would have been enough for Americans to start hating anyone labeled as an accessory to the terror attack. Then Americans would support invasion into any country their president singles out.

He left his hotel carrying only a small leather shoulder bag. He walked up the Riverside Drive. A warm wind was blowing the first yellow leaves off the trees on the other side of the street, hurling them under the wheels of the few cars slowly moving north, eager to get farther from the hell of Lower Manhattan. Faces of oncoming passersby showed subdued, quiet fear. Everyone was walking with eyes lowered, trying not to look trying not to look into each other's eyes. Two African American guys sat on the low wall around a sports field, just sitting around, not talking in loud voices or throwing their arms around as they usually would, probably in imitation of some rappers. No, they were only watching pedestrians pass by, saying nothing. Even the bulky boombox sitting between them wasn't producing any sound.

Novack felt like he'd ended up on a production set of some strange arthouse film where people were still walking, sitting, and riding in their cars like normal, but all in complete silence, without uttering a word, studiously executing each pre-agreed movement. It was certainly hard for them – they were torn apart by a fear so deeply entrenched in each of them that it might turn to panic at any minute, manifest itself as a loud scream. Still, they were trying to contain themselves for now, even if they wanted to leave the film set as soon as possible, to stay away from the all-seeing eye of the camera – so that they would be able, at last, to scream, to run as far from there as possible.

When Novack turned right at the intersection with

285

Payson Avenue, the silence was suddenly cut by the blaring of police sirens. After a hundred meters more, he saw the police cars parked on the pavement, close to the entrance of a small café, as well as ambulance backing up to it. Looking at the address, Novack realized that this was his destination. He stopped, lit up a cigarette, and took a drag. Several gawkers were eyeing what was going on with great interest; they paid no attention to the tall policeman asking them to step farther to the side. Two young men, coming out of the café, joined the gawkers. Novack, who was standing right behind them, heard their conversation.

'That cop in there, he was really a pain in the ass. Asked me why I'm not at work and how I can drink beer on such a day... And what should I be doing if I don't have a job and if I don't give a flying fuck that some Arabs blew up half of Manhattan? What do I care? I care so much more about the fact that I've got only ten bucks left in my pocket...'

'Come on, buddy,' one of the gawkers asked him, 'tell us what the hell happened in there?'

'Not like I have any clue. That cop already asked me about it, too. In a nutshell, two men were in there. One was wearing a hood, sitting with his back to us, facing the wall. We could only see the other guy's face. I mean, I could certainly see him well, from where I was. Tanned skin and with memorable features. At some point this guy, the one with his back to us, he got up abruptly, put up his hood, and left so fast that no one could see his face. Five minutes later the other guy, the one who had stayed back, suddenly started wheezing horribly and foaming at the mouth. So that was it. He fell face-down on the table and then he was gone. We ran up to him, checked him out – but nah, he wasn't breathing anymore. We called the police right away and they got here five minutes later.'

'Look, here he is. They're taking him away.'

The doctors carried out the body. The face of the dead man was covered, but Eric Novack knew exactly who was there under the thin plastic cover. The same man with an Eastern accent, of course, the one who had reported to him from Boston this morning about the readiness of the terrorists and the plane departures. It was he who had gotten the order to come over to New York and meet someone named Moses to get the remainder of his huge fee for completing his very complex task. Moses, who worked for Eric Novack (though he had no knowledge of that fact), had fulfilled his dreadful mission nice and easily, and now he was already far away from here. To cap, Moses had no idea who Eric Novack was... In this way, the last link connecting the collapse of WTC skyscrapers to the man by the name of Eric Novack was neatly cut off.

Eric Novack walked some two hundred meters more and stopped at a long row of parked cars. When a silver-colored Dodge flashed its lights, Novack walked straight to it. Its front door opened, and Novack eased into the passenger seat next to the driver, a middle-aged man, grey-haired and quite corpulent, who was happily smiling at Novack and looking at him with respect.

'Glad to see you, Mister Novack!' the man said in a deep bass, turning to Novack in an agile manner despite his girth. 'Please have my sympathies for the loss of your business. But life must go on, right?'

'Yes, thank you. Good afternoon, Peter! Even though there's nothing good about it today. Do you know how many people have died? Those damned terrorists!'

'Right. It's a big tragedy. I got a terrible shock when I saw it all on TV. But then I told myself: Peter, I said, this is not the end of your life. What is really important is that our deal with Mister Novack does not fall through. My guys, they did a great job, by the way.'

'You know, Peter, I'm a banker, but now that my small bank is gone, no events, even the worst imaginable ones, could prevent my bankruptcy. This is why Eric Novack must disappear from the land of the living... once and for all. Well, all right, let's talk business. What do you have?'

Peter heaved a deep sigh and explained, feigning sadness:

'Last night a lonely elderly gentleman died suddenly, mysteriously. Well, he was seventy years old, and he's been a great fan of liquor for over forty years. He kicked the bucket in a small motel a hundred kilometers from here. He went to that Silver Stars place yesterday, together with my guys. When they checked in, they registered him as Eric Novack.'

'And what next?'

'Oh, only two hours after you give me your documents, as well as the remaining fee, a fire will start in the motel room. It's full of empty bottles and cigarette butts anyway, so it will easily catch fire from an unextinguished cigarette, for example. And it will burn down together with a newly appeared Mister Novack, who's dead anyway. His body will burn beyond recognition, of course, but some parts of your documents will be legible and that much they will certainly find.'

Peter chuckled, looking at Novack with anticipation. Novack got a large, bulky envelope out of his bag and, holding it forth, rested his eyes on Peter, slowly announcing:

'Here is my driver's license, my corporate cards and the remainder of your fee. It's fifty thousand, right? I hope I heard you right.'

Peter, who had been quite boisterous and talkative so far, looked at Novack, but meeting his glance, checked himself, answering in a somewhat husky voice:

'Yes, Mister Novack, of course. Everything is all right. Would you like me to give you a ride someplace?'

'No, thank you. That isn't needed. Okay, so Silver Stars Motel in two hours, right?'

'Yes, Mister Novack.'

'Great. My guys will check things out. Thank you, my friend.'

Novack opened the door with an abrupt movement and slipped away. The big man remained motionless for about a minute, looking after the tall figure walking towards the intersection. Suddenly Peter felt a strange fear spreading inside him, creeping all around his body. It had started the moment he met Novack's eyes.

The man who was no longer Novack crossed the intersection and stopped a cab in the next street. He told the driver to take him to LaGuardia, then sat back, closing his eyes, and inhaling and exhaling deeply several times. Night was slowly spreading over the gigantic city, the darkness highlighting the pale glow of illuminated ads, and thousands of windows that looked like tiny fireflies.

A minute later Novack got a mobile phone out of his pocket, dialed a number, and asked curtly:

'How's it going?'

A high-pitched, ringing voice coming out of the phone hit his ear and made him frown:

'This is unbelievable! How could you have foreseen today's events, all this disaster? On September 6, as per your orders, we put options[3] on United Airlines and

---

3. Put option is a right, but not an obligation, to sell an underlying asset at a fixed price (the strike). A European option can be exercised only at a certain moment (time T) rather than at any time until T, while an American option allows the holder of the put to exercise it any time until the option's maturity date T. Buying

American Airlines...plus Morgan Stanley. And I still can't believe we got twenty thousand options on Boeing! Buying options with the right to sell at a predetermined price only three days before the disaster, that is, just before a total slump...wow! This is the work of a genius! You must be a visionary, a true grandmaster!'

'Stop yelling, Michael. What are the results?'

'Results are stunning, it's a strike, ten pins down! And the beauty of the thing is that everything went immediately offshore! It's just stellar!'

'How much is expected?'

'You got richer by three hundred and fifty million, and this is by the most conservative estimate. And it's only the beginning. Oh, I have also become a millionaire.'

'Okay, fine,' Novack sighed wearily. 'Keep up the good work...I'll be in touch.'

He closed his eyes again and started some more calculations. At times he felt his brain was a perennially functioning mechanism, constantly analyzing and combining hundreds of thousands of situations, complex eventualities and making the only possible, correct conclusions. A kind of a perpetual motion machine that could transform any task, even one that seemed unsolvable, into a desired and always successful result.

Well, let's see. After all expenses, two hundred and fifty million was still left for me from the fee the client paid for my organizing the event. Plus, I got about three hundred fifty million using my foreknowledge of the upcoming disaster, because I bought put options of those companies in advance of their shares slumping. Well, not bad. There were foul-ups of course, especially with the third plane, but

---

put actually means predicting that the underlying asset price will fall by the exercise date and become lower than the strike. After the 9/11 terrorist attacks, US companies' shares lost $1.2 trillion within one week.

in such situations it's the end result that counts. The rest are overhead costs. And now I should get out of here! Away from this country that considers itself the center of the universe, but which can be so easily stricken with horror... It's all done, it's all over now. I must go home...

The cab drove up to the airport. Three hours later, the man who had for some time been calling himself Eric Novack was sound asleep in the luxurious flat bed of a private Gulfstream IV, flying over the ocean through the night. New York was now very far behind, sleepless and in mourning, a city where all people would shudder to hear planes flying in the sky... And somewhere else, much farther, close to I-80, tired firefighters, combating a blaze at the small Silver Stars Motel, found a human body charred beyond recognition. Using some scraps of the victim's documents, which were in part miraculously intact, the coroner could, however, establish that the name of the deceased, a seventy-year-old American, was Eric Novack. May the Lord have mercy on his soul...

16

Sergio. First Encounter
Somewhere in the Indian Ocean

Colorful blots pulsated under his closed eyelids. They grew bigger and smaller in a smooth, flowing manner, then flowed together in all kinds of patterns, as in that toy for children: the kaleidoscope. At times the blots combined to create murky images that moved jerkily, as if in an old movie. A silent movie, of course. For example, here he was, for some reason seated in a wheelchair, being pushed across the spacious hall of an airport terminal. He could not see who was pushing the chair, but Jia was walking beside him, and for some reason she kept wiping his mouth. She talked to him continuously, anxiously explaining something in the manner usually used with children or the mentally deranged. Oh no! It was not Jia at all! It was Bella, who had given him that shot in his neck in the Excelsiore in Rome. Suddenly he felt nauseated. Was it due to sea sickness? Now he was in a cabin. It was sunny outside, but the blue surface of the water rippled with the grey crests of waves. The ship rolled about quite a bit. Lying on a bed close to a porthole, he tried to move slightly, but his body was not responding to any of his attempts to stir. His arms and legs were leaden. *What's wrong with me? Am I paralyzed? I can't even shout.* Then emptiness all around him once more, sticky, and deep.

Then at some point Malin sensed light. Not just color-ful blots, but real light as sunlight, penetrated his eyelids. Cautiously, he moved his fingers, then his toes. His body was relatively obedient now, and free of pain. He badly wanted to stretch, to arch every immobilized muscle, every joint. He decided not to, however. Instead, he opened his eyes just a crack, and found he was lying on a large bed, covered with a light and immaculately white bed sheet. The room was large. Through the window he could glimpse exuberant tropical growth outside. A blue pan-orama of the ocean was visible between wide leaves. The sun beat down on the large windows, but the room was cool, air conditioned. Detecting a light movement of air in the room, he guessed that someone else was present.

Oh, come what may...there was no escape in any case. Malin opened his eyes fully and raised himself up a little bit, pulling the nice-smelling bed sheet over his naked body. A rather small brown woman in a short white coat got up from her chair and, putting her smartphone aside, walked up to Malin. She appeared very beautiful to him.

'How are you feeling?' she asked, speaking English in that soft accent specific to people from East Africa.

'I'm fine. But where am I? And who are you?'

'My name is Aina. I must care for you. You are a guest of the Master. He is a very good man. He told me to go and report to Alex as soon as you come back to your senses. I'll be right back, very soon.'

And she started towards the door, moving smoothly and gracefully.

'Wait, Aina! How long have I been here? What's the name of the Master?'

'Goodbye! Mister Alex will come soon, and he will explain everything.'

Aina left, quietly closing the door. Malin came back

to his senses enough to notice two things, both very important. One was that the door was not locked, but only closed. And two, the windows had no bars. Did that mean he was not a captive? Strange… Malin remembered all that had happened in that hotel in Rome. He suspected that they had brought him somewhere far away, first by plane and then by ship. What did it all mean? Could it be that he would indeed get to see the person he had been so eager to find? But why did they not keep him in shackles, why were the doors unlocked, and the windows without bars? Why were there no security guards at his side? Or were they, perhaps, stationed right outside the door? Ah, now he noticed the blue egg of a surveillance camera stuck in the corner.

'Hello, Mister Malin!'

Malin started and turned towards the door, which had opened without a sound. A tall black-haired man came into the room. He had regular European features, piercing blue eyes, and combed-back hair. He looked to be around forty. The man wore a light shirt with the top buttons undone and white jeans that accentuated his well-trained body. His movements were smooth, as if he were in a lazy mood, reminding Malin of a dangerous predator who, for the moment, happened not to be hungry.

'Hello,' Malin responded in a low voice, getting up from his bed and wrapping himself in his bed sheet. 'You must excuse my state of undress…'

'Don't worry about that. I took the liberty of providing you with clothes much more suitable for the local climate – they're there on that chair. And you'll find your belongings on the table. I mean, whatever you had in your pockets, your personal items. Make yourself at home, everything here is at your disposal. You were so eager to get here, so now you have become our guest. Please, dress at your leisure.'

Malin got up and stood behind a screen. He put on the same light-colored jeans and loose, short-sleeved shirt of the same cut as what the other man wore. And as he put on the jeans, he noticed a featherweight metal bracelet around his ankle. It had no lock of any kind, but it was about half-an-inch thicker on the outer edge. This explained why there were no locks or guards. Without a word, Malin scooped up his belongings from the table – money, credit cards, his ID, and the flash memory stick – and put them into his pockets. Then he stepped from behind the screen and faced the man, giving him a quick glance up and down.

'Why don't you sit down? What would you like? Whisky? Coffee? Water?' the man asked in a measured tone. 'Let us introduce ourselves properly.'

'Water, please,' Malin said, suddenly hearing how hoarse his voice was, and feeling a desperate thirst. A minute later, he was seated facing the man, drinking from a tall glass of ice-cold water in his hands.

'My name is Alex,' the man said with an easy manner. 'I represent the man who owns this house as well as the whole island where we are at the moment. The master's name is Sergio and, as far as I know, you have been looking forward to meeting him for quite some time – and quite tenaciously, I might add.'

'Is it the one who went by aliases Novack, Larionov, Santana, et cetera?' Malin blurted out. 'Or am I wrong about any of these names?'

'I don't know, Mister Malin. For me, he is simply Sergio, and I am not entitled to know more than that.'

'Tell me, Alex: what's this thing on my leg? Simply an adornment? Or a souvenir?'

Alex laughed, throwing his head back, but his eyes displayed no mirth: in fact, studied Malin's face attentively.

'I assume, Mister Malin, that you know very well

whose guest you have become. And I am sure that your guess is correct. You're about to become one of a very few people who have had the honor of being introduced to Mister Sergio personally. All around the world, there are probably ten or, at most, fifteen people who knew who he was when they contacted him. We took this precaution with the anklet because we are aware of your physical strength and mental capabilities. It's merely a precaution.

'We are currently on an island in the middle of the ocean. The island is well guarded by both trained professionals and all kinds of electronic systems that block and control any and all messages. All telecommunication links, by phone or via internet, are controlled by special filters. It is not possible to trace anything from any continent outside, because all of our traffic occurs via a number of remote access points. As for the bracelet: it's an ingenious and effective device. If you were to go beyond a pre-installed perimeter – in your case it would be this house and a one-hundred-meter radius around it on all sides – this toy would first inform you that you should stop, and if you did not, it would simply explode, so that you would lose your leg. Well, I don't think you're so reckless as to try testing whether it works as I said. Am I right?'

'You could call me reckless, perhaps, but I'm not an idiot. I understand your message. Thank you for your caution. Can anything else threaten my life here?'

'No, nothing. Well, come to think of it...you know, our master Sergio is quite old, so his manner can provoke negative sentiments. But if there were any aggressive gesture from you, I mean, if there were any danger to his well-being, I would have to press a certain button on the remote control I always carry with me, and then, too, the bracelet would blow up in a controlled, local explosion that would only leave you maimed. There are backup buttons in some other locations as well. But I'm quite sure that, as a journalist, you should be much more interested in finding out the truth, and in receiving unique information, rather than in behaving aggressively or wishing to take vengeance. Am I correct?'

'Of course, Mister Alex.'

'Okay, let's drop the formalities. There are no "misters" or "sirs" here. I'm Alex, and you're Malin. Do you agree? We're around the same age, besides.'

'Agreed, Alex,' Malin said, stressing the other's name. 'Now could you please tell me what happened with my friend Richard?'

'I think your friend is very much alive and quite healthy. He was only upset that you disappeared during the drinking party you'd both enjoyed at the hotel. As far as I know, he woke up in his room, in his nearby hotel, by the next morning, when he found he had a huge hangover and that he felt completely out of it. Most probably, he couldn't even remember what happened the day before… As of today, to the best of my knowledge, he is already back home in Switzerland.'

'Thank you, Alex. Now, what happens to me? When do I meet Sergio?'

'It's noon now. You should rest for an hour or so. You'll find drinks at the bar, as well as fruit. Mister Sergio has invited you and me to share his lunch today. I will come and get you when it's time.'

Alex nodded and left, once more without a sound. Malin took a bottle from the bar and was surprised upon seeing what it was: in his hands he held the legendary Glenfiddich 1937, a whisky that cost twenty thousand dollars per bottle. Then he came across a Hardy Perfection, a 140-year-old cognac…plus several bottles of Cheval Blanc 1947. Wow! This bar contained liquor probably worth as much as two hundred thousand dollars. Had he found himself in Aladdin's cave?

Reviewing this collection, Malin decided to stay away from the bar, at least for now. Drinking hard liquor or, in fact, any liquor could be dangerous for him: after all, he had been given some shots, and this was to be his first meeting with Sergio. Consequently, Malin poured himself a coffee and sat down in a chair. He was trying hard to stifle the many feelings rending him apart – a complex mix of fear, of excitement about reaching his end goal, and, for some reason, of deep sadness and despair, resulting in a pain developing under his shoulder blade. *No, no! I should stop that! I must figure out my next steps, and arrange them in order, and choose my line of behavior. Oh Lord! What is this: "line of behavior"?! What rubbish! I'm about to meet the greatest criminal of recent centuries! A man controlling a vast and invisible criminal empire, whom any special service or criminal syndicates in the world would love to meet...*

There was a knock on the door at 1 p.m. sharp. Alex came into the room and nodded to Malin, inviting him to go out.

'Are you ready, Malin?' Alex asked.

'Ready for what?'

'To meet the man you wanted to see so much.'

'Do I have a choice?' Malin asked sarcastically.

'I guess not.'

'Then let's go, Alex. At least because I'm really very hungry,' Malin smiled, getting up from his chair.

They walked through a very wide, long passage paneled in dark wood. Paintings hung in shallow, evenly lit recesses. As excited as Malin was to see Sergio, he could not refrain from slowing his pace, trying to see what those images depicted. He soon realized that these were all original canvasses from the Renaissance. If only

Richard could see them!

'Are you interested in these things?' Alex asked, turning towards him. 'There are two Rafaels around here that the world is unaware of. And this here is an early da Vinci... Giorgione here. And Caravaggio.'

'Does anyone know about these masterpieces?'

'Of course!' Alex laughed. 'Sergio does, I do and now you do, too. Oh, a couple more people, very few because guests rarely come here. The security knows, and the servants. You won't find these paintings in catalogs, or sometimes their photos are provided with a note that they were lost or, maybe, stolen.'

'Where's Bosch?'

'Oh, the great Hieronymus... That's a different story. His works are only in Sergio's private quarters, or in the parts of the building where he spends most of his time. This is simply the Renaissance corridor...'

'Well, this is not "simply a corridor", it's a real gallery. Do you have other "simple corridors" as well?'

'Yes, there are others with paintings from the Dutch Golden Age, and one that's all Impressionists... We also have a special passage with sculptures from Ancient Rome, and another with Russian icons. Here we are, by the way.'

They had arrived in front of a high, carved door. Alex knocked on it and then, slightly opening the door, let Malin walk forward. Beyond was a small chamber, awash with sunlight coming in through a row of windows on the left, but the room was designed peculiarly so that its right side was entirely left in a soft shadow, a semi-darkness. A long, heavy table was set up there, with three places set.

Malin heard a deep, confident voice.

'Come in, my friend! I'm happy to see you in my home.' It came from a tall figure at the other end of the chamber, who emerged from a door hidden deep in the shadows. The source of the voice was still concealed for a few more seconds, even as he said: 'My name is Sergio.'

When light fell on the man, Malin could at last see him clearly. The person walking towards Malin with a steady step was a well-built, gaunt man, an old man wearing a dark, buttoned-up shirt, and dark trousers. He had exquisite facial features, a perfectly straight nose, and tight lips. His black hair had just a little grey and was combed back. And as for his eyes…his eyes projected a strange yellowish glint from within, bursting out from unfathomable depths, as startling as headlamp of a train rushing through the dark night. The light from this man's eyes could be seen clearly even in the presence of the sunlight coming in through the windows.

He extended his hand, and Malin was surprised by the warmth of his handshake. An amazingly beautiful, very large blue diamond, framed in white gold, flashed on Sergio's ring finger.

'My name is Sergio,' he repeated and then went on: 'As far as I know, you are aware of my other names, at least most of them. May I call you Malin? I am already eighty-six, you know, more than twice as old as you.'

'Of course, Mister Sergio…'

'Just Sergio. Please be seated.'

While Malin looked on at this man whose age did not show at all, only one question came to mind, surfacing from his subconscious at a truly inappropriate moment. It was simple: how was Sergio in such good shape at his age? After all, this man was guilty of terminating thousands of lives, crushing millions of destinies. Why did so many of Malin's relatives and close friends, all great people who had done so much good for mankind…why did they get old so early, and pass away in the prime of life?

They were seated with Sergio at the head of the table, Alex to his right and Malin across from Alex, his back to the windows.

'Listen, Malin! Since you are my guest, I would like to make a suggestion for our next steps,' Sergio said. 'We should first eat, and after the meal, you are welcome to start satisfying your curiosity. Agreed? After all, you have been seeking a way to meet me for exactly this purpose, right?'

'Not just curiosity, no,' Malin glanced up at him and blurted out a question that felt unexpected even to him: 'Why did you kill Jia?'

'Please accept my most sincere condolences, Malin,' Sergio said, leaning against the high back of his chair. 'Please believe me: I gave no such orders with regard to your girlfriend. I wanted you both in one piece, safe and sound. It's Nicholas and his oafs who are to blame for her death. They were hunting you down when they were supposed to do nothing of the sort. I always assign jobs only to the best, the most talented professionals, but even they can make mistakes, unfortunately. The human factor, you know… Forgive them, if you can… but, by the way, the one who did that was punished.'

'What happened to him?'

'He died. Oh, just by chance. He died not because he had killed that young lady, but because he did not fulfil my directions… Well, let's have lunch. What do you prefer? Beef? Fowl? Fish?'

'I have one more question, Sergio. Though I'm on an empty stomach…'

'Yes, please.'

'Why am I alive? Why do you need me alive? And why, if I am not mistaken, does it seem I might live a while longer?'

Sergio laughed. Very quietly. It was like the rustling

of foliage. Then he put his napkin to his mouth and, quickly removing it, he said:

'My respect, Malin. You could have asked me this question in the first seconds of our meeting, but you held out for five whole minutes. So, I'll answer it right away, rather than after lunch. Don't be concerned about your life. I have grand plans for you. If we can agree on certain points, which should be interesting for both of us, then you will live as long as you may, and perhaps even have a happy life. Unless, of course, you get hit by a car crossing some road, or a brick falls on your head. You will become famous as no other journalist in the world ever has. Are you satisfied with my answer?'

'In a way, yes, Sergio. I do not understand, however, what you mean under "our agreement", but your guarantee to keep me alive for some period seems enough for now. As for lunch, I prefer a good steak. Medium rare.'

Alex pressed a button on his side of the tabletop, and a minute later two waiters entered the room. Both were dark-skinned, tall, and wore identical white coats. One served hors d'oeuvres with quick and elegant movements, while the other offered drinks. Malin was hungry, but he also felt a craving for some strong alcoholic drink.

'Whisky, please, with just a little bit of ice,' he said.

A few minutes later, an incredible eighty-year-old astringent beverage was giving him a feeling of light both knocking about in his head and plunging somewhere to the bottom of his belly, accompanied by a nice ticklish sensation. His inebriation was very light, and he felt able to think clearly, perhaps more clearly than usual. Certainly, he had a much clearer understanding of what was going on.

Sergio and Alex were savoring Chateau Mouton Rothschild 1945, discussing its aftertaste and the nuances of this rare wine's flavor. Suddenly Sergio interrupted their exchange and turning towards Malin, asking him in Russian:

'Do you remember your childhood in Russia? I mean, in Leningrad?'

His intonation was almost native, but carried a very slight accent, as if he learned it from someone of the Baltic states.

'Yes, I do,' Malin said, a bit surprised.

He suddenly felt that someone was barging in, trying to step across a boundary separating the most intimate part of his soul, something he cherished deep inside. He felt something like a chill shaking him inside. He curtly repeated:

'I do.'

'Okay, Malin, just relax,' Sergio changed to English again. 'I wasn't intending to pry into your most personal memories. I know these lines by your great poet and bard: "I hate it when they pry into my soul" ... Vysotsky, right? My friend in Russia used to listen to his songs whenever we were driving somewhere in his car.'

Oh God! Now Malin knew why Sergio's voice had seemed so familiar from the first moment of their encounter. He had first heard this voice in the recording he had found in the Marshall Archive! In that conversation that had taken place between some "James" and some "Unknown" at 6:50 a.m. on 9/11! It was impossible to mistake that voice. "Unknown" and "Sergio" – were the same person! And right now, that person was sitting to Malin's left...

They conversed easily about wine and music over several courses. Sergio expressed his opinions on Russian literature of the first half of the twentieth century – surprisingly, he knew it quite well.

'You know, Malin, I am fascinated with Babel and Bulgakov. I count the latter among the most magnificent, superb writers of the twentieth century. Compared with his universal, fantastic realism, all the other greats of world literature pale... Bulgakov is an artist who can paint with words. He combines the delicacy of Vermeer[1] and the madness of Hieronymus Bosch.'

'Did you say Bosch? It was he who helped me find you,' Main said, changing the topic.

'Oh, my dear friend! You are mistaken. It was the other way around. The great Hieronymus lured you to this place, because I knew from the start about the research your friend Richard had undertaken. It's thanks to him and his idea about Bosch that you were able to become my guest. But since we touched upon Bosch, I can't help but boast a bit... Alex, please!'

Alex took a remote control that was lying at the edge of the table next to him and pressed a button. There was a light buzzing sound at first, then Malin saw dark curtains on the opposite wall move to the sides, while a long lamp lit up what had been behind these curtains all along... Malin stood up, flabbergasted, and then sat down in disbelief. Before him was the famous triptych by Hieronymus Bosch: *The Garden of Earthly Delights*...

It was the very same triptych in which the great artist had presented all human experience, showing both earthly life and afterlife. Paradise spread its mysteries on the left panel, while Hell raved madly on the right. In the middle, between these extremes, one could see the puzzling, frightening garden of earthly delights... Each detail of this painting attracted the viewer's gaze as if by magic. It seized all attention and would not let go. Malin slowly got up, walked up to the painting, and froze, focusing his eyes on the horrifying medieval surrealism of Hell.

---

1. **Johannes Vermeer** (1632–1675) was a Dutch painter of the 17th century, regarded today as a master of genre painting and exquisite portraitist.

'How strange,' Malin said, barely audible. 'I saw it at the Prado in Madrid, that is, I saw the original, but it did not impress me as much as this here. Over there, perhaps, there were too many people around me in the museum. The environment was different, while here I'm one-on-one with the images... My God! Sergio, who made such a great copy for you?'

'Wrong again, my friend,' Sergio smiled, also coming up to the painting. 'This is the original! And what you can see at Prado is a brilliantly executed copy created at the end of the sixteenth century, a hundred years after Bosch's death.'

When Sergio saw Malin's surprised expression, he added some more explanation:

'You can't imagine how much energy and money I had to spend in order to make that restorer shut up, the man who accidentally found a great copy of *The Garden* under the top layer of some other old triptych. The copy was made by a follower of the Bosch school. Well, I also had to spend tens of millions of dollars for a smooth and seamless exchange of the original at Prado for its copy! And even if you write about this in your book at some point, no one will believe you, that's a given...'

'How do you know about the book? And if you do, why are you talking about it without any concern? That book would expose what you were involved in through-out your life. It would be the end of you. It would mean your death.'

'Dear Mister Malin,' Sergio said, smiling one more time and raising his glass, 'I know quite a lot about you. And as for your book, which is supposed to ex-pose me as well as all those around me over the last several decades, oh, I need this not less than you do. It would not mean my death. It is my life. And yours too, by the way...'

'What do you mean?'

'Our lunch is over for now. And we also had a chance to admire my favorite Bosch. So, I would like to suggest that we pour some more and continue our fascinating conversation. Among other things, we can discuss your future book...'

Malin was so dumbfounded by what he heard that he virtually fell into a soft chair nearby.

'I should probably say it again. Sergio, Alex, I don't get it...could you please explain further?'

Alex stayed as impassive as he had been throughout lunch, obviously disinclined to break his silence. He only smiled, almost imperceptibly, pouring drinks: whisky for Malin and wine for Sergio and himself. Sergio started speaking after a pause of a minute. His voice was expressive, and his eyes, with their yellow, almost orange hue (some might call it Judas-colored), were glued to Malin's face:

'Indeed, you were able to find out more about me than anyone on this planet has known, with the possible exception of Alex. But let me tell you, Malin – what you know about me is only a small part of my life history.

'The fact is, as you know, that I am Luis Cristobal Santana. I – that is, he – was born in 1933, but perished in an airplane crash in 1957. You also know that I am Tom Walker, who was present in 1963 during Kennedy's assassination, and who died that same year on Lake Michigan. Are you surprised, Malin? Ah, you did not know this name: Tom Walker? Take a note of that: when I was in Dallas, that was my name at the time.

'I am also Martin Weiss, who made billions after Kennedy's assassination. That happened because some people around President Johnson helped me become the focal point for delivering all military supplies to Vietnam. And, yes, I did vanish in the Viet Cong jungle in

1967. You know, of course, that I became Paul Morel for a while, the financier who acted as a go-between for the Cosa Nostra and the Vatican's Banco Ambrosiano, and who was present on St. Peter's Square when there was an attempt on the Pope's life. Later on, that Morel was gone, of course, and no one knew where the hell he disappeared to. Shall I carry on telling you what you know?'

'Of course, Sergio. This is truly interesting for me.'

'As you undoubtedly know,' Sergio took a small sip of his wine, slightly smiling, 'I have also been Igor Larionov, that mysterious Russian from some Baltic state, who achieved the disappearance of the IMF's almost five-billion-dollar tranche in 1998, even though it was meant for helping Russia.'

Malin could not help but interject: 'Wasn't it also around that time that Edmond Safra died under strange circumstances, right before he was to testify before the FBI?'

'Yes, my dear friend, this is correct. Moreover, you were able to figure out that I was Eric Novack, who was present during the destruction of the Twin Towers on September 11, 2001. I have also obtained information that you were able to find that this bad-bad guy Novack was talking earlier that day with an unidentified representative of the American special services and telling them that the "birdies" had already flown, so that nothing could be done to make any changes to the plan. You must have recognized that voice by now, I guess. Correct?'

'Yes, Sergio, I did. What's next?'

'Oh, by the way, I should mention something, Malin. Your gadgets are back in your room at the moment, but don't be upset. Our conversation is being recorded, and you will get an audio file later on. You are a journalist, and you will need all such recordings for your book. Later on, I will provide you with all the irrefutable proof necessary regarding everything I tell you. Now, let's get back to the list of some of my names and achievements. Needless to say, all of the above was organized and managed by me – the Kennedy assassination, the attack on the Pope, the disappearance of the five billion for Russia, Safra's death, and the destruction of Twin Towers in New York.'

'I understand that already,' Malin said slowly, looking the old man straight in the eyes.

'I know. This is why I can speak with you now,' Sergio continued, without displaying any emotion. 'This is what you must understand as the gist of the matter, Malin: I did not shoot anyone, and I did not blow anything up. None of that. I only did what others needed. And they needed it so much that they were willing to pay for my skills in organizing whatever they wanted. Yes, I did receive huge sums from them, amounting to billions of dollars, but those were only dividends on my having the brain of a genius – forgive my immodesty. In a nutshell, it's all just business. And a big business, based on two main human passions: avarice and lust for power.'

'The world is crazy, Malin, it's a madhouse! It turned long ago into that nightmarish hell Bosch foreboded. This world has become an abyss – an abyss of sin, corruption, perfidy, lies, money mongering, and power games. I am simply a mirror above that abyss. Nothing more. Do you understand my point?'

'I'm not sure…and what's next, Sergio?'

'For now, my friend Max Malin, born Maksim Malinin, I would like to suggest that we end this conversation, so that you do not drown in a flood of information. We can continue talking tomorrow. At around lunchtime, just as today. Now you can take a walk around this island, as you are my guest, and I would like you to see everything with your own eyes. Do you agree? Oh well, you don't have much choice anyway...'

'You're right,' Malin said, getting up.

Alex stood up, as reticent as he had been all this time, and then whispered to Malin standing next to him:

'We'll walk around the premises, Malin, but don't forget about the anklet. And please keep in mind that all communication links go only via networks we control – very efficiently, I might add. And there are surveillance cameras all over, and security guards, too. You'll get all information in detail, whatever Sergio wants you to have, at any rate. You'll get audio files, documents, photos, et cetera. So don't start doing anything on your own, please. And there's more: it won't be possible to determine the island's location. All I can say is that it's in the middle of the Indian Ocean, with thousands of miles of water on all sides...'

'Okay, Alex. Promise!'

17

Sergio
A House on the Island

They walked through the same corridor that Malin already knew, Alex walking in front of him and Sergio.

'Why do you need my book, in which you and all your partners will be exposed?' Malin said, unable to leave this question unanswered. 'Why do you want that?'

'How come you don't understand? It's so simple!' said Sergio, stopping in front of a small painting in a gilt frame showing a young man from the Renaissance period, looking at the viewer but only half-turned towards them. 'Just look, Malin, at this masterpiece. His eyes and his faint smile – all the acclamation for *La Gioconda* is for naught, in comparison... I am reminded of the eternity, of the infinite, when I look at a countenance of this sort, something that cannot be fathomed. I will probably leave this world sometime soon – just as you will, much later on, I guess. But someone else will certainly stand in front of this image and study this youth's face, trying to understand what he might be thinking, or the secret meaning of his smile, or what his gaze conveys...'

'Hey, but this is Raphael, right?' Malin halted and stepped closer to the painting. 'Right, and this is the priceless *Portrait of a Young* Man[1] considered to be irretrievably lost. Am I right?'

'Correct, my friend. Only it was lost for everybody else, while for me, on the contrary, it was gained... Well, I must say, Malin, that you have a pretty good knowledge of lost chef d'oeuvres.'

'Indeed. I had great teachers,' Malin said drily, thinking of Richard Berwick.

'Anyway,' Sergio said, disregarding Malin's emotional response, 'I would like to spend the rest of my life in serenity, having achieved peace of mind. In the last hours of my life, I would like to be looking at this young man of Raphael's, cherishing his smile and his gaze, rather than at Bosch's turning inside out all the entrails of our lives... I would like to die quietly, peacefully, slipping away while trying to fathom his radiant mystery – that is, I would like to surrender myself to infinity in his presence...'

'But what does this have to do with my book?'

'Don't you understand? No one – well, almost no one – knows me better than you do. Many are convinced that I am already pushing up daisies. Others think that, for example, Weiss or Larionov died long ago, but Novack and Morel are still alive and still pose risks, fatal risks for them. But none of them can identify me. They do not know that all those names are of the same person! So, they have been trying to hunt me down, under my different aliases... And that never ceases for even a second. This carries on not for some primitive revenge – it's fueled by their fear of discovery. Thing is, what

---

1. Raphael's *Portrait of a Young Man* was lost in 1945, and its whereabouts is still unknown. This masterpiece was created in 1513-1514. It is thought to be the painter's self-portrait. The museum in Krakow, Poland, offers a reward of 100 million US dollars for its return.

I know about them is known to nobody else. So, if I start talking, if I tell everything that I know, the whole of their sleazy, insecure world will crumble. Now, my friend, you will be the one who will reveal those secrets that can still be told... Those that will make me safe until the end of my days.'

'But how is it possible? How come disclosing your own dreadful secrets would protect you, who has been mastermind and supervisor of all these events?'

'This is very simple! All those who live in fear of exposure, dreaming about my annihilation, will be exposed! Then, correspondingly, liquidating me will no longer be of immediate importance for them, because their biggest immediate issue will be how to save their own lives, their billions, pull their own disappearing act, get lost, fly under radar... That is, they will have other things to worry about. It won't be about me anymore...'

'Will people believe this information?'

'Those who know certainly will! They will recognize the details and circumstances you mention. They'll have no choice but to believe that I suddenly started talking, backing up my testimony with evidence contained in audio recordings, documents, facts. Today, there are probably about forty or fifty persons left around the globe who will understand your text fully, and who will trust that you really know the source of your information. Your book should be written, in fact, for them, for the few dozen who will know exactly what you're writing about... This is why your book will become the bomb of the century, the grandest, most sensational exposé!'

'The remaining audience, your two or three hundred million readers, they will certainly doubt this or disbelieve that, and they might even contradict you. But none of that will matter: even if they disbelieve you, they will still buy your book, the book of the greatest investigative journalist of our time. They will buy up huge print runs, because Watergate will seem like child's play compared to your revelations. Are you getting it now?'

'I guess so. But why do you reckon that they will stop searching for you?'

'Well, I will not be dangerous for them anymore, since I will already have told everything I know and which I was involved in. I mean, that would be their assessment, but we will certainly not tell everything there is. Not by far. Still, what you reveal will be quite enough for them to think that I am no longer extremely dangerous for them. You must know, Malin, that there are some very influential persons, who have been defining the great political games until now, who will have to resign after your book is published... Some might even need to escape to a different country or shoot themselves... Will you be afraid to write your book after such an introduction?'

'What can I do? This is a part of my job, after all,' Malin smiled. 'Oh, tell me this. What about various special services? They will have to open criminal cases and start investigations, right? Since they will know quite well who they should be after and what to look for.'

'Don't make me laugh, Malin. They will be debunking you in the first place... They will call you an air-monger and a seeker of halfpenny sensations. As a last resort, they can even find the corpse of some old geezer and announce that these are the remains of the worst criminal of all ages. Me. Are you ready for this?'

'It was a long road to get to you, and I lost too much along the way. There is no turning back for me now. Though, I should mention one point that's really important to me personally: am I still alive only because of this possible future book?'

'I guess so,' Sergio smiled. 'But let's not think of sad

things. Let's walk around a little bit. I would like to show you my data center. This might convince you how much I trust you.'

They walked into a long corridor with glass walls which revealed the amazing panorama of the tropical forest beyond a tall fence with movement sensors flashing their searching thin red rays. The corridor terminated at the blind metal wall, which featured only the eye of a surveillance camera looking at them in a definitely unfriendly manner. Alex, raising his hand, touched a dark rectangle close to the window. The wall turned out to be an armored door, gliding slowly to both sides so they could enter a large room divided into office cubicles.

Here was heard the monotonous hum of servers, and perhaps other electronic equipment, as well as the ripple of many voices. Suddenly these quiet sounds were obscured by the powerful low-frequency chords of a ZZ Top[2] song…

"I'm running out of time, I'm about to lose my mind," the voice of Billy Gibbons yelled into the room. The fact that it was playing on an island somewhere in the middle of the Indian Ocean, at a place unknown to anyone on Earth, left a sense of fantastic unreality. On an island ruled by a dark genius of recent centuries. Suddenly the music stopped abruptly, and a young, almost boyish voice was heard in silence:

'Shut up, all of you. The boss is here.'

There were six young men in this room sitting in large, comfortable chairs at desks lined with several computer monitors. None looked older than twenty-five. When they noticed the visitors, they got up and greeted them politely. A burly, red-haired youth wearing glasses – he

---

2. ZZ Top is a cult US blues-rock group. Its lead vocalist is Billy Gibbons.

was the first one who had noticed Sergio and his guest –
came up to them extending his hand in welcome.

'Hi Isaac,' Sergio said shaking his hand first. 'Please,
Malin, meet the head of my data center. His name is
certainly biblical.

'This young man is twenty-three years old now, but
he is probably the greatest hacker on this sinful planet,'
Sergio told Malin in a low voice once Isaac had shuf-
fled back to his cubicle. 'He was born in Russia, and
when he was a kid, his parents brought him to Israel.
By the time he was 18, which is of age in Israel, he was
smart enough to hack a couple of US government servers. Then he was able to crack the servers of the Russian banking system, and also messed with Swiss banks,
making them lose many millions. A couple of times
Isaac even helped Arab terrorists, just for the fun of it,
for the sheer achievement in this sport of hacking...
The result is that they're all looking for him: FBI, FSB,
Mossad, Interpol... He can get so reckless it's almost
insane, but he is also a coward.'

'The other five are the best professionals, hackers
and programmers from the US, Europe and Australia,'
Sergio said proudly. 'Each of them committed many,
many sins against some state or another.'

'How can you be sure they will stay faithful to you,
and won't betray you at some point?' Malin could not
remain silent when he heard Sergio's words. 'Perhaps if
they are paid a really large sum of money...'

'It would be absolutely pointless for them to betray me. These boys have complete security here, and
they live like kings. They have everything: fashionable
homes, amazing booze, cannabis, and LSD, girls, or boys
– it's their choice. They can keep company with whoever they want to, or they can live all on their own.
Most important for them is that they are all millionaires

already. Each signed a contract with me to stay here for five years, during which time they will live comfortably and in complete security. They will be doing their favorite work while getting, in practical terms, all the pleasures of life. Plus, each of them gets two million dollars each year to a secret personal account, and they don't have to spend a cent of it! Which means their money stays safe and keeps accruing interest... Five years later these young geniuses will be able to leave in the same manner as you. They can go to any country. There is only one condition: they must teach the people who arrive to replace them. And, by the way, they can start a new life with no problem because we supply them with new documents confirming their previous whereabouts and job history. If they want it, they can even surgically modify their appearance...'

'I think,' Sergio continued, 'that this arrangement should be quite all right for them. And, of course, each will have those ten million dollars in his pocket, money that is completely "clean": one will receive this sum as an inheritance, some others get it as a bonus for a unique invention, or maybe through some other arrangement. If any one of them wishes, he can get a highly paid job with one of the larger, completely legal companies I own as a shadow partner. They won't even know that they remain within a part of my empire... Anyway, with all the above, would it make any sense for them to betray me, even for a sizable sum of money? This is the mode in which all operate who have direct contact with me, or who are directly subordinated to me.'

'With regard to your concern, one more important detail is that I have collected all available evidence against each and every one of my employees. None of them, you know, is an angel, and that means that each has a pretty dire background featuring all kinds of criminal activities. God forbid they even think of betraying me or start blabbering too much: all this information will go straight to a specific security service that would be unspeakably happy to have pinpointed one more criminal who had long been wanted. So, no one will leave paradise in exchange for hell. But let's walk further on: I want to show you something even more interesting than what you have seen so far.'

They entered another corridor, its walls adorned with paintings made in the twentieth century. Malin could not stop and look closer, but he noticed canvases by Kandinsky, Picasso, and Dali. Once again, all of them had been lost or stolen from museums or private collections over a period of decades.

'Tell me, Sergio, since you have internet on this island, isn't it possible to contact the outside world from here? Plus, people elsewhere should be able to find you, no?'

'No, this is not possible, my friend. All incoming and outgoing signals pass through a succession of several remote servers, where they are recoded, and only after that do messages get to us on the island. The same happens on the way out. My young geniuses created a unique, one-of-a-kind system – it has no close analogues anywhere in the world. The system provides complete protection from any electronic surveillance, even from satellites. Anyone would sell their soul to the devil in order to get such a system: I'm talking about the Pentagon, NATO, the CIA, the FSB, Arab terrorists – the lot! Now, please come into my humble library.'

Malin and Sergio, still accompanied by a silent Alex, walked up to the second floor, and stopped briefly in front of a pair of grand oak doors which, of course, moved slowly aside, obviously at someone's command. The wood-paneled room beyond was huge and split across two levels. The second level was a balcony run-

ning around the room which could be accessed via
several stairways. There were many gigantic bookcases
lined with books. Tens, no, perhaps hundreds of thousands of volumes stood on shelves behind glass doors.

Utterly surprised, Malin could say nothing for a
while, and finally it was Sergio who broke the silence:

'Today is the age of the Internet and e-books, of
course, but I keep collecting books for my library. I am
an old man and I like books. Books – they are made using paper, you know. Their pages rustle when you turn
them – books should also have that special aroma. Did
you notice that only money and books have a special
aroma like nothing else? But money is only the means
for making my wishes come true. Books, on the other
hand, are much more than that. They are one of my
cravings. Just look at them!'

Malin had never seen anything of the sort, so he started walking forward, looking at the rows of books on the
shelves. Sergio called to him suddenly: he opened one
of the glassed-in bookcases and took out some bulky
old volume:

'Turn around, young man! Since you have Russian
roots, this might be of special interest to you. The first
Russian book carrying an exact date was printed in
March of 1564 in Moscow. It is known as *The Apostle*,
or, rather, *Acts and Epistles of the Apostles*. It was a real
masterpiece of typographic art. This date is considered
to be the start of book printing in Russia.

'You must excuse me for lecturing you but collecting
unique editions of books is my other hobby. After collecting art, of course. The Apostle was printed by Ivan
Fyodorov and Pyotr Mstislavets in the first government
print shop, which was located on Nikolskaya Street in
Moscow, close to the Kremlin. Here is this book! They
say that fifty-nine copies of The Apostle exist today. To

be correct, it is sixty. But only you and I know about it. Here it is, the sixtieth copy. It is, by the way, in much better condition than any of the other known copies. Do you want to hold it in your hands?'

'Yes, I do,' said Malin, carefully accepting the almost five-hundred-year-old book.

'Let us continue,' Sergio said, opening the next bookcase. The blue diamond on his right hand emitted a shower of little lights under bright lamps. 'As is known, Harvard's library asserts that they have the only existing copy of the *Azbuka* (Alphabet Book), also by Ivan Fyodorov,[3] who printed it in 1574. Bollocks! Here is the second copy of the *Azbuka*! Please take a look.'

They kept walking around the balcony, and Sergio showed Malin his other treasures. A rare copy of *Hamlet* published in 1611, during Shakespeare's lifetime. And one of the earliest editions of Dante's *Divine Comedy*, published in Brescia in 1487. Or the first edition of Petrarch's *Canzoniere e Triumphi* (Songbook and Triumphs), as well as an exquisitely engraved, 18th-century volume of Leonardo da Vinci's drawings.

While Malin was making himself familiar with Sergio Santana's unique library, he could not forget that this was the man who had masterminded the most awful criminal acts of the last century. Correspondingly, a straightforward, simple question was bothering him quite a bit. How was it possible that this tall, educated old man could combine in his brain and soul such seemingly incompatible qualities: his exquisite, tender love of the beautiful, and actions that led to the deaths of thousands, from rank-and-file employees of the Twin

---

3. The first ever printed copy of the Russian alphabet called *Azbuka* was published by Ivan Fyodorov in 1574 in Lvov. Officially it is known that the only extant copy of this book exists in the library of the Harvard University.

Towers to the president of the United States of America? How was it possible that a connoisseur of art and rare books would be planning and executing the most incomparably criminal acts?

Yet as soon as Malin was able to catch Sergio's gaze and see those smoldering yellow sparks in his eyes, he felt that he was able to figure it out himself: such people as the master of this island could fit no preconceived standard. They are unique, and probably born into this world only once every few centuries. And they are indeed evil geniuses.

'Would you like me to guess what you have been thinking about just now?' Sergio's deep bass voice interrupted Malin's train of thoughts. 'You were thinking, how can it be that an educated intellectual, a lover of art and fiction, a person who seems overall quite mild, became, by your reckoning, a monster? Because after all, it was I who organized the assassination of President Kennedy, the attack on Pope John Paul II, the destruction of the WTC towers and many other atrocities, right? Do I guess correctly?'

'Yes,' Malin nodded, standing in the middle of the library, facing Sergio. They were very close to each other, eye to eye. 'This question is easy to predict.'

'Well, my friend, I am neither a killer nor a sadist. I never wanted to kill anyone, and I still don't. Killing is a senseless and idiotic action if it is done only for the sake of killing. I was only executing complex orders, really special jobs, and I received billions for it because I am probably the only specialist of this scope in the world. In my case, all those perished – oh, they were like expendable material, like operating expenses. Those people had tough luck, that is all. Some may have made fatal decisions earlier in their lives, and when they eventually became a president or a pontiff, they may have undertaken some actions better avoided… Others may have simply been in the wrong place at the wrong time and became a victim by accident. And then there were those who were trying to obstruct my plans or to interfere with my fulfilling the task I was entrusted to complete.

'Please understand something, Malin,' Sergio continued, his gaze glued to Malin's. 'I have never done harm to anyone of my own will or out of whimsy. I am a peaceful art and book collector, I like great art and unique books – it just so happens that I am also keen on doing my work properly and effectively, because this is what they pay me for. When I say "they", it refers to those whom, in your line of work, you may at times greet in a friendly manner, or whom you interview. Okay, fine, maybe not you personally, but your colleagues or your predecessors…and then you consider *me* the enemy of mankind, right? Am I expressing myself clearly, Mister Malin?'

'Quite clearly, Mister Sergio, alias Santana,' Malin smiled. 'AKA Weiss, Morel, Larionov et cetera…'

'Well, you have certainly learned my names very well,' Sergio smirked dryly. 'Why don't we continue our little promenade through my humble domain?'

'Wait, Sergio,' Malin said, not moving. 'I have a personal question: are you married?'

'No. Love was probably the only luxury I could ill afford these many years. There were women in my life, even quite a number, but mostly only with the purpose of satisfying certain cravings. Well, I am a man like you, only much older.'

'But what about loving someone for real?'

'I should say it one more time: I am the same as anyone else. Yes, I was in love, only once, but that was true love. But it was so long ago…probably forty years back.'

'Who was she, Sergio?' Malin could not keep himself

from asking questions. 'What happened to her? Is she alive?'

'No. She died very young: it was cancer. Her name was Paola. But could you please stop asking questions about my private life? You are here for a different reason. All right?'

'Yes, indeed, my task is different. But I wanted to understand you a little better.'

'Let us move on, and our major interview will continue tomorrow at lunchtime,' Sergio said, smiling only with his lips. His eyes remained, as always, like two deep, cold wells with flashes of yellow fire within. Malin thought, however, that when Sergio mentioned Paola's name, something in his eyes had changed very much: his gaze had been different for a couple of moments, something like a deeply hidden sadness suddenly surfacing in them. Or had it, perhaps, only been his imagination?

18

Sergio
Day Two

A dark-skinned parlor maid woke Malin the next morning, rolling a table nicely set with breakfast into his room. The spread included poached eggs, black and red caviar, cheese, freshly baked bread, and many other delicacies in cut-glass bowls. Sunlight flooded the room, which was pleasantly cool thanks to the air conditioner. Outside, beyond the windowpanes, the wide leaves of palms swung slightly in the ocean breeze.

Though Malin had drunk quite a lot of whisky during a rather long dinner last night, he was in an upbeat mood. But deep inside, a little bell was ringing, signifying some obscure anxiety: what should he expect today, on his second day of this strange captivity on an island owned by the most dangerous criminal on the planet? Although, it had to be said, this same man was showing him such incredible hospitality.

Sergio's aims are relatively clear, Malin thought, downing a sandwich, and chasing it with some excellent black coffee. *I think I also understand why he wants this book. Sergio wants to explode the situation so that he no longer presents any danger to "interested parties". But his logic is strange to me. Why should he use such a loud and bombastic event to create such defenses for himself? What if in reality he's playing a different game that he wants to conceal behind my writing about his exploits? And what about my own release from captivity? I cannot see through to what the situation might become. Okay, let's wait and see what happens. So far, the most important thing is that I'm still alive, and that I might soon become the most famous journalist on the planet. That is, if I can stay alive in the meantime…*

It was only at this point that Malin noticed a square of white paper sticking out from beneath the small bowl of caviar. Written on it in beautiful, neat handwriting were the words:

> *Dear Malin! Mister Sergio is expecting you to join him for lunch in his dining room at 2 p.m. Following that, he will be ready to continue your extensive interview. I will be happy to call on you and accompany you to the dining room. Respectfully yours, Alex*

'Well, aren't we civilized?' Malin whispered to himself, twirling the note in his hands. 'I am curious whether Sergio and his assistant Alex exhibit the same degree of civility while they develop their deadly plans and decide who to kill? Okay, now we look forward to lunch. I think it's already about time to ask Sergio the most important questions and to demand proof: documents, photos, et cetera. It isn't fiction that I intend to write, but an investigative report aspiring to become an all-time bestseller.'

While the sun made its way to its zenith, Malin sat at his computer, trying to recreate the actual sequence of events and formulate questions for Sergio. At exactly five to two there was a knock on his door, and Alex entered the room straightaway. He was all smiles, tanned, wearing a light-colored cotton suit.

'Greetings, Malin! Are you ready to enjoy our chefs'

skills once more? Mister Sergio awaits.'

Malin switched off his computer and they entered the passage leading towards the same dining room as the day before, in which one wall was dedicated to Bosch's Garden of Earthly Delights. Lunch was exquisite: truffles from North Italy and Canadian lobster. When the waiters at last set the table with sweets, coffee, and cigars, and once they had again poured out that one-hundred-year-old cognac, Sergio stopped talking at last, about tasteful dishes and rare spirits.

'All right, my friend,' Sergio said to Malin. 'We should carry on with our conversation about me. I am ready to answer any of your questions, and later Alex will provide you with evidence of whatever I decide to make public. Please, let us begin.'

Malin took a pull of cognac, then puffed at his five-hundred-dollar Cuban cigar, a Cohiba Behike, and offered his first question:

'Who was Luis Santana, born 1933? That Yale graduate who became the youngest partner of a Washington legal company.'

'Me, of course,' Sergio responded in a low voice, expressionless.

'How did that person enter the world of global criminality?'

'You will have to listen to a long story,' Sergio said, looking at the play of light inside his wine glass. 'You do not have to remember any of what I tell you, because our conversation is being recorded and you will receive all the audio files. Well, almost all... All right, I was born in 1933 – I am the offspring of a hellish stock. Why, you ask? My father's father was a Mexican drug lord, Pablo Santana, and my mother's mother was from Italy. Her name was Leila Bernabe, and she was Jewish. By 1928 my grandfather was able to make his capital legitimate, after which he moved his family to the States. In 1932 my father, Cristobal Santana, who was starting his career as a lawyer, married an American woman, Elizabeth Morgan. So, I, Luis Cristobal Santana, was born the following year. Lord, how long ago that was…and huh, what a name: Luis Cristobal Santana. I am not used to it anymore…

'In 1950 I started my studies at Yale Law – my family had enough money for that. Later that year, however, something unpleasant happened.

'I found out later on that Pablo Santana, my grandfather, had kept up his links with the Mexican mafia and, even though he was going on seventy, he was still involved in the big business of drug trafficking. And my dear father, he became what they call a "mafia attorney." At the time – this is in the fifties – I lived without understanding any of that. I was growing up in a sort of a vacuum and taking things for granted. We had a luxurious villa on the coast, we could afford my Ivy League education, I drove a new Plymouth, had some girlfriends, smoked weed for fun, et cetera. One day in December my grandparents, plus my mom and Dad, were riding to our country estate in Georgetown. Everything was as usual: our limousine was followed by another car of security men. But then there was an explosion, close to the gates of the estate, and our limousine was thrown aside, into the lane of oncoming traffic. Two large Cadillacs immediately appeared, as if out of nowhere. Several men in masks jumped out of the cars and used assault rifles to kill everyone in the limousine who had survived the crash itself. One of Grandpa's security men survived that hell, so he was able to give testimony about what had happened. Well, this was a clear case of colleagues taking care of some of their fellows,' Sergio smiled and, after a short pause, continued:

'This is how young Luis Santana became an orphan. You might ask, what about money? There was none... no financial assets remained... Well, what I mean is that I could not find anything: all the money had been tucked away very securely. The only asset I could inherit was that luxurious country house, but I had to sell it in order to complete my education, and to start my business. Can you imagine that Malin? I had so much at the beginning, but then it turned out that in reality I had nothing... This was when I realized that one could buy anything, and that it was not money *per se* that counted but knowing different ways to get money. At the time, that was probably my most important insight.'

'Okay, so how did you start? What was your first crime?' Malin's harsh remark interrupted Sergio's reflections.

'Oh, I invested all that I had into building up my image. For the start, I registered a law firm under the name Yodel, Marcos & Santana. As you must have learned from old media reports, there was in fact no one there by the name of either Yodel or Marcos. All I did was buy the documents of two ex-lawyers. Both of them couldn't work anymore, they were only desperate to get money for their drug addictions. One of them died soon and the other was committed to a nuthouse. As for me, I had to invest all of my remaining money into promoting this firm, which, for all practical purposes, was non-existent...

'This was a good move, however, because newspapers started mentioning us, that is, my company, as a serious legal company involved in important and complex cases, and soon things started moving. There was no Internet at the time, so most people, including people in high places, were quite trusting, and they believed what they read in newspapers and magazines. And both newspapers and magazines loved cash. Just as they do today: cash in large white envelopes…'

'I hired a team of talented but poor young lawyers who were soon participating in some really important litigations under my company name, representing all parties involved in the proceedings. This included the state. Our main area of activity was finance law. And I mean very large financial projects. For example, we represented several very large companies working with the US government and receiving pre-financing for the construction of Egypt's Aswan Dam. This was in '55.'

'The company executives trusted me so much that I was finally given access to funds allocated for the Aswan Dam project. But when the Suez Crisis struck the following year, and the US government halted funding, I was able, at virtually at the last minute, to transfer the remaining 25 million intended for Aswan to my own company in Switzerland. And then I disappeared.'

Sergio fell silent, remaining immobile a while, with a glass of wine touching his lips: he was gazing at Bosch's triptych, which the waiters had uncovered at the start of lunch. After a minute or two, Malin could not refrain from asking more:

'The official version was that you were declared wanted, but that you then died in a plane crash in the Pacific on November 9, 1957, on board the Clipper Romance of the Skies, registration number N90944, flying from San Francisco to Honolulu – that uncanny Flight 7 that disappeared midflight. Bits of its debris were found in the ocean five days later, at a location 940 miles north-east of Honolulu. How were you able to survive that disaster, or in what way are you connected with it?'

'Oh, my friend, congratulations! This only shows how deep your research has been! I am even ready to hire you as an analyst. I pay five million dollars a year, and I mean net,' Sergio responded, taking his eyes off Bosch's

masterpiece. 'Oh, I kid…well, to be exact, I have no relation to that plane crash. I could do what I did thanks
to a very banal trick, which, at the time, many people
used many times, because things weren't computerized
back then. I bought a ticket, registered for the flight,
got on board, but then told the flight attendant I had
forgotten some important documents in my office, and
that I would take the next flight to Honolulu. When I
got off the plane, I waved it goodbye and, indeed, took
the next flight – but under a different name.

'But when I heard about the disaster with that flight, I
knew that Lord God Himself had smiled on me, and that
He would save me in any situation. My main defense
was Lord God Himself, and there was no one between
us. This was complete, ultimate freedom. Only me and
Him. Not to forget 25 million US dollars – in 1957 this
was a truly enormous sum of money. So, what was next?'

'What?'

'Later on, it was Canada, where I became Tom Walker, an affluent attorney: that was lucky, because the
main part of the money was legalized under that name.
I had a house in Montreal, plus an apartment in Paris.
It was then, in the fall of '57, that I started creating my
organization, a structure specializing in the discreet execution of any, even the most seemingly incredible and
unachievable orders. Orders that came from individuals
and structures, even whole governments… The scope
of our services became truly multifarious. We did money laundering – and I'm talking really enormous sums
of money. We did international financial fraud as well
as complex financial schemes. And we did contracts on
lives on…both sides of the equation, let us say. Anyone
could be both contract owners or casualty – prominent
entrepreneurs from big business circles, important and
internationally acclaimed politicians, notorious, dread-

ed mafiosi, and many others.'

'The principle of the Organization's operations was very simple. One could even say primitive. The Organization was me, and me alone. Everybody else, any other people involved were only very talented hirelings, be they great lawyers or financiers, psychologists, or adventurers, or, of course, killers. They all shared the same quality: they loved money. Ninety-nine per cent of them hadn't even a clue that I existed, let alone who I was. At that time my name was known to fifteen or twenty people at most, and only a very few of those got to see me in person. Every one of my men (and women) was in charge of only their own narrowly defined job, and they did that job well. You should understand, Malin, that I embrace a very simple principle: in my line of business, the main attitude I hold is not to be greedy, rather to share with others as much as I can. I have been running my organization in this manner from day one. Everyone belonging to it was bound by spilled blood, as well as by huge sums of money. Sometimes I had to pay out up to 80 per cent of the total value of the order to those who performed specific tasks for me. You should take into account that making an order to my organization was a very expensive affair.'

'Yet one should not be greedy, Malin. Never! Why is it that none of the criminal organizations anywhere in the world, even those that work for governments, could come within an inch of my level of perfection? Because their aim was always to get as much pay as they could, but then hand down as little as possible to those who actually do the job. Look, if you pay your people more than they could ever have dreamed, they will do anything for you, even impossible things, at times they'll even do wonders. And to your benefit, of course. This is my main principle. There are some rules, too, which no one should ever violate. No one should ever know about the whole project: theirs is only a certain part of it, and it is a very small part. Only I can see the whole picture. Also: no one knows anything about me or about my entourage. They operate only via a chain of intermediaries, some of whom must be liquidated afterwards. But those are just the usual operational expenses...'

'Was it you who killed Kennedy?' Malin suddenly interrupted his host's monologue.

'No. He was killed by a woman named Mary. She was shooting from the other side, from a grassy knoll, and her shot was synchronous with the shots of that idiot Oswald. I only organized the whole chain of events, paid for everything, and personally monitored their execution. Oh, by the way, I always personally monitor the final result of any big order, and it's because of this habit of mine that you could identify me in some photos.'

'Is she still alive? Is Mary alive?'

'No, alas! Several hours after her feat, someone found her body at the Sam Houston Park in Dallas, with an empty syringe lying next to her. Her case entered the police archives as just one more drug addict overdosing – of course, she couldn't possibly have had any connection to Kennedy's assassination. Oh, she was a good girl, and a great sharpshooter. Very young, yet already a widow...but she was doomed from the start. I could not leave such a serious trail leading to me, of course.'

Malin exhaled and launched an attack:

'Who gave you the contract on President Kennedy?'

'This was my first order on such a high level, and it came in August of 1963. My contact was an ex-CIA officer, from a very high level in that organization, but we never met personally, only spoke via pay phones at different locations around the country. Well, to be precise, I actually did know who he was. His name was Samuel

Gardner. But he did not know who I was, or where I was at. Those who sent me directions via Gardner knew exactly what my capabilities were, because they had asked me to help them with some other issues quite a long time before the Kennedy affair, and they paid very well for what I did for them. I'm talking millions.

'I like staying one step ahead, so I decided to find out whatever details I could about who might be ordering Kennedy's assassination. My assumptions were supported by certain facts that Alex will provide you with after our conversation. It looked like there were links going straight to members of the entourage of Vice President Lyndon B. Johnson's. You may remember that he took the oath of office right away, inside the cabin of Air Force One – he was very much in a hurry to do that...

'The funds for the contract on Kennedy were provided by the largest weapons manufacturers, in pursuit of their goals. Indeed, President Johnson implemented those goals when he ordered a full-scale intervention in Vietnam in 1965. There was a flood of money right away.[1] Oh, to tell you the truth, I am not convinced that Kennedy's assassination was sanctioned by Vice President Johnson himself. He may have been completely in the dark about what was going on around him, and later on decided not to pay attention to certain facts. He was a very smart person, by the way.'

'As far as I understand, you were directly involved in supplying the military during the Vietnam War, right? Wasn't your last name Weiss at the time?'

'Yes, Malin, that's right. My condition for executing the contract on Kennedy was that I should receive thirty million dollars and get my representative access to

---

1. Total US expenditures for the war in Vietnam between 1964 and 1975 were as high as 352 billion US dollars.

the financing and delivery of armaments, as well as of uniforms, food, and all kinds of essential goods to the US troops in Vietnam. My contract partners fulfilled all of their promises, so Tom Walker died, and I became Martin Weiss, who could make millions through his participation in the military supply chain.'

'But my information was that Weiss had also disappeared,' Malin could not help showing off what he knew. 'Or am I mistaken, Sergio?'

'No, you are right. It's surprising that you know this much. My intuition was obviously correct in choosing you as my biographer, Malin,' Sergio smiled grimly. 'Yes indeed, officially, Martin Weiss died when he came to South Vietnam with a military delegation for an extended session of the Joint Chiefs of Staff headed by General Westmoreland, commander of the US Forces in South Vietnam.[2] Weiss went missing and probably died at the hands of some bloodthirsty Viet Cong. This was how I could change my name once more and get rid of everything unneeded, becoming a billionaire along the way and still heading my organization.'

Malin puffed at his cigar, gazing at Sergio. He was trying to determine how much knowledge and experience belonged to this man who had directed the intellect of a genius towards all the worst that existed in this world. Malin knew already that Sergio was certainly a genius in his own right. It would take someone truly special to be able to plan global crimes down to the smallest detail, crimes that would introduce such enormous changes in the world. Not to mention the fact that executing any of his plans at times involved directing the actions of

---

2. **William Childs Westmoreland** (1914–2005) was a United States Army general, most notably commander of United States forces during the Vietnam War from 1964 to 1968. He served as Chief of Staff of the United States Army from 1968 to 1972.

thousands of people. On top of all this, he had always remained in obscurity, purely because he wanted things that way. He had been able not only to hit the mark every time, but to live his life in contentment until such a respectable age. If only Sergio – Luis Santana – had selected a different path through life, he would have most probably become the head of some big corporation, or even President of the United States.

After two hours spent discussing the Kennedy assassination, Malin decided to switch smoothly to finding out about the reasons behind the attempt on the Pope's life. His interlocutor, as he knew, had organized that attack as Paul Morel.

'Answer me this, please, Sergio – I would like to discuss the assassination attempt on the Pope. I talked to many people about Paul Morel, from the Triads head in London to Russian fortune seekers to Italian mafia members. Is it really true, what they told me about you, that is, about Paul Morel? And where did that money go, which they intended to get back?'

Sergio shifted to a more comfortable position in his chair before he spoke. 'Oh, I know about your conversations, perhaps all of them. Or almost all. You would not have been able to get closer to me without what they could tell you. That's only logical. Yes, they knew some things, and they shared what they knew with you. Their information is not fake at all. Yes, I did organize a money laundering scheme worth billions via the Vatican Bank, for both the Italians and the Chinese. I managed this simple but dependable operation because, in my opinion, it was created by a stroke of genius. When the Pope decided to audit his own bank, I felt that it might mean real trouble, so I thought to give the Pope a scare, send him some warning. Unfortunately, this religious fanatic – the one called Ağca – who was unobtrusively controlled by my people, he partly disrupted all my plans by seriously wounding John Paul II. As a result, a need arose to cover up some things, so Calvi, the head of Banco Ambrosiano, had to be dealt with via my Cosa Nostra connections. But when both the Chinese and the Italians wanted their money back, scared thanks to the attack on the Pope, well, Paul Morel had to vanish into thin air. Once and for all. It so happened that he became much richer after that, by half a billion dollars. But he felt it would have been unfair to return the money to those dumbos, to the Chinese and Italian gangsters.

'What you must have heard from them is most probably the truth. I mean what you could gather from Big Chinese Brother Ling Wan, from the Russian mafiosi Semyon Levine and from the Cosa Nostra boss Domenico Radore. There are some details that might require correction, of course, and there are some documents you will need to know about, but you will get all of that from Alex.'

'All right, the circumstances around the attempt on the Pope are clearer now,' Malin said. 'And what do you have to do with the destruction of the Twin Towers in New York? Did you do 9/11?'

'Yes, I did. I was the one who liquidated all three buildings,' Sergio responded, without hesitation. 'As you understand, I could not have done it personally. For example, I can't fly a plane...' Sergio joked, 'but the liquidation proceeded according to my plan. I developed the plan and organized its execution. My organization fulfilled this unique order, the only one of its kind, making me several billions richer. I felt quite proud of my brainpower, for making me able to both complete this project successfully and stay alive. Plus make my billions.

'You should understand, Malin, that I am not a murderer or a cut-throat, or an assassin... I simply use

335

my unique brain to do my job. If people die, this only means that they happened to be in the wrong place at the wrong time. Everything is predetermined, you know. This was those people's fate... I harbored no ill feelings towards any of them. In fact, I'm sure there were many good people among the victims, but it is never possible for us to evade what destiny has in store for us! That day, on September 11, 2001, I became their doom. As simple as that...'

'Wait, Sergio!' Malin interrupted the man across from him. 'But you organized the hijacking...how could you do that? I mean, in principle, how could you control the actions of the religious fanatics who destroyed the skyscrapers?'

'Please don't get worked up, my friend,' Sergio said with a smile, holding an unlit cigar in his hand. 'First of all, I should let you know that the planes themselves did not destroy the WTC buildings – that's impossible as a matter of principle. The Twin Towers were originally designed to be able to withstand not only any wind load, but also a frontal impact from a Boeing 707, which was the largest passenger jet at the time. The materials for their construction were carefully chosen, and the workmanship was of the highest level. The structure of the Towers was like a narrow anti-mosquito mesh, so in this respect the plane can be seen as a pencil which would only poke through this mesh, without influencing the rest of its structure in any way. That was the designer's idea, and all kinds of tests confirmed it.'[3]

---

3. In the early 1970s, Leslie Robertson, structural engineer of the World Trade Center, calculated an effect of a potential impact of Boeing 707 to the tower. His conclusion was that the towers will be able to withstand the impact of a jetliner flying with the velocity of 960 km/hr. In other words, that under such conditions the skyscraper would still be standing without serious structural failure. Its central shell and the frame perimeter which remained

'But this can't be! The buildings collapsed because of the fires initiated by the planes' impact!'

'On the contrary, Malin! You may need to refresh your memory and recall that in 1975 there was a fire at Floor 11 of the North Tower. As a result, 65 per cent of that floor was completely destroyed, and the blaze got down to the 9th floor and all the way up to the 16th! That fire burned for three hours, and, in fact, it was more intense than the fire on September 11. Still, the building's central shell remained unscathed, even though the fire had spread around the building, mostly through this shell. And the ceiling joists did not crumble, either.[4] Did you hear that? What do you think?'

'Then could you please explain why the towers collapsed?'

'Because these buildings were stuffed with Thermate, well in advance. Why? You see, Thermate creates enormous heat when it burns, much higher than can be generated during a regular fire. You see, when the fires raged in the Twin Towers, even steel beams melted, which is not possible during a normal fire. The terrorists' planes, then, were only needed as a signal to activate explosive devices. They were a ruse, as an imitation of an apparent reason for the towers' destruction.'

Malin hid his face in his hands, exclaiming:

'Oh Lord! Does this mean Marshall was one hundred percent right?!'

'Absolutely! This is why they killed him and pushed

---

after the impact would be able to hold the additional load arising from the removal of some part of the loadbearing framework. This was the safety margin of the Twin Towers.

4. A major fire started in the North Tower on February 13, 1975. The fire spread via central empty tubes between Floors 9 and 14. Fireproofing of steel elements prevented them from melting and helped leave the tower frame intact. There was no structural damage resulting from this fire.

the blame onto some anonymous burglars. You should also now that Rudolph Giuliani[5] banned any photographic or video coverage in the area of Ground Zero. Plus, they declared right away that anything related to the investigation was classified. Here is one more interesting point for you: almost eighty percent of the steel debris was removed quickly, and without making any analysis whatsoever...'

'Where did that debris go?'

'It was quickly sold. As far as I know, Shanghai Baosteel Group, a Chinese corporation, purchased fifty thousand tons of steel from the Twin Towers' debris as scrap metal at 120 US dollars per ton. Some other thousands of tons of steel were also transported to India for scrap recycling.'

'Wait, but there were terrorists there, weren't they? This has been proved already,' Malin mumbled, as if suddenly very tired.

'Of course, of course! Calm down, young man. Yes, there were fourteen men, and I personally selected them from one hundred and thirty applicants. I studied each resume very thoroughly... Those idiots really believed that when they hit the towers, they would destroy, kill, liquidate the enemies of Islam for the Glory of Allah... Still, their families were given a million dollars each. This is really a lot of money, especially in those countries. My men found these guys and monitored all their further actions. My clients wanted a beautifully staged destruction of these skyscrapers by Islamic terrorists supposedly acting under bin Laden's orders. My clients also needed the aftermath of this attack very much, and we all know what that was.'

'Who was your client?'

---

5. Rudolph Giuliani was mayor of New York in 2001.

'My contact was someone named James. This was not his real name, of course. We only talked using public pay phones, every time on a different street. Still, one of our conversations was recorded, and made its way into the Marshall Archive that had supposedly disappeared. My understanding is that you, in fact, have this recording, right?'

'Yes, I do have the Marshall Archive at my disposal. Can you tell me who this James was, please?'

'I think he represented a certain group in the highest echelons of the US political establishment. What was their goal? The answer is simple: this group was eager to get themselves free rein through the US's adoption of the Patriot Act, and secondly, they intended to justify and enhance American actions throughout the Near and Middle East.[6] The third aim was to earn unbelievably huge sums of money via underhanded dealings with put options they scooped up in advance shares of the largest companies whose values would predictably plunge after the attack.'

'My understanding is that you directed the actions of all four groups of terrorists, right?'

'No, not really. Mine were only three groups,' Sergio said, and he smiled when he noticed Malin's bewildered look. 'You see, the first two planes, they did hit the towers as planned, but something went wrong with the third plane. Those fanatics may have smoked too much hash, or maybe they got nervous and decided, for some reason, to change my original plan. Instead of attacking the third skyscraper, which was 7 WTC, also

---

6. USA PATRIOT Act, which was adopted after the terror attacks on September 11, 2001, gave wide authority for government agencies and the police for supervising citizens. Among others, it expanded FBI's opportunities for wiretapping and electronic surveillance.

laden with Thermate, those idiots decided all on their own to destroy the Pentagon building, and they directed their plane to its western wing. Thus, many people died because of this senseless act: 65 on board the plane and 125 more in the Pentagon. And all that despite this flight number's having a lucky combination: two sevens...what a pity!'

'Why did the third WTC building get destroyed then? All on its own?' Malin asked, curious. 'According to the official report, it only fell down at 5:20 p.m. as a result of a series of gas explosions and the resulting fire.'

'Malin, I'm lucky, you know. At first, I thought I had only been able to fulfill two thirds of the order, which was really catastrophic for my self-esteem. But Building Seven happened to detonate due to an accidental fire that started after the first two buildings had come down. So, the Thermate that had been put inside 7 WTC exploded due to *that* fire, and my order was one hundred per cent fulfilled. I was simply lucky, my friend. I am personally very happy, by the way, that there were no casualties in this building. To speak honestly, my original plan included a certain number of victims, sad as that may be...'

'Wait, but what about the fourth plane with the registration number N591UA, which was also hijacked by terrorists? The one that aimed to hit the White House, but fell in a field in Pennsylvania, 240 kilometers from Washington?'

'This, my friend, is something I have no idea about, because I had nothing to do with that plane,' Sergio laughed dryly. 'Early in the morning on that day, I spoke with my client's representative, who suddenly told me that the buildings should not be destroyed completely, because his boss had had second thoughts. They had decided to just stage a couple of plane disasters by only destroying a few floors in each skyscraper…which must have meant, pardon my French, that they shat their pants in a big way! But I had to explain to this man that the buildings were already fully loaded, and that the birdies were already in the air, so nothing could be done. By the way, I understand that you do have a recording of this conversation from the Marshall Archive.

'All right. Now, I am not one hundred percent convinced, but I have a suspicion that the hijacking of the fourth plane was organized by someone else, even though it must have been the same client as mine. I also think that they may have decided at the last moment to scare the President by telling him that this flight was supposedly targeting the White House but did not make it to Washington because it had experienced an air disaster 240 kilometers from its target… Oh, now I'm suddenly feeling tired already. Let's rest a while. Would you agree to continue our conversation around dinner time?'

'Yes, I do, but here is my last question, Sergio. What was your name at the time? Was it…?'

'My name at the time was Eric Novack, but he got the short straw later on. Can you imagine that: he got so drunk that he could not survive the fire at the Silver Stars Motel, a hundred kilometers from New York.'

19

Sergio
Revelations in the Evening

By 8 p.m., Malin, having had plenty of time to spend as he wished, had first gone for a walk around a superb park, then lain around the large swimming pool, which was surrounded by a high fence. Then he had tried to snooze a bit in a chaise longue, but his brain, overloaded with new information, had been unable to change to sleep mode. Malin went to his room and fell onto his bed. Staring at the ceiling, he made one more attempt at marshaling information. This time he was able to complete the mosaic. And a couple of minutes later he suddenly fell asleep. And he saw Jia right away, alive and all smiles. They spent the evening in New York City, walking around Central Park. He was merrily telling her something, and she kept laughing, throwing back her long black hair.

At eight o' clock on the dot, there was a knock on the door, and there was Alex, standing on the threshold with a laptop in his hands.

'I beg your pardon for waking you, Malin. But I must pass along this information that Sergio promised you.'

'No problem. Do come in. I only dozed off for a while,' Malin said, getting up from the bed and chasing away the last bits of his sweet dream. 'By the way, when am I to be deported into the unknown?'

'I don't know. Sergio hasn't told me anything about his final plans for you. But it is quite possible that you will be freed as early as tomorrow. Come and sit down at the table. I will show you what this flash memory contains. It is high-capacity memory, and you are getting two of them, just in case one gets lost...'

Alex opened his laptop and plugged a small electronic device into it.

'How about our next conversation tonight?' Malin asked. 'Will it be recorded separately?'

'No. You will not learn anything new tonight. All the documents are stored in this memory stick. As is everything Sergio told you during your meetings. Look here.'

Bending over the computer screen, Malin could see many folders in the directory, labeled things like "9/11", "Russia", "IMF", "Kennedy", "The Pope and Ambrosiano", "Links", "Bank Payments", "Additional Audio Recordings", "Conversations/Audio", "Wiretaps", "Hacks", "Malin", "Cosa Nostra", "Triads", "Vietnam", as well as some others with names consisting of various combinations of digits.

'I should tell you, Malin, that the password for both memory sticks is simple – it's just "Sergio",' Alex said taking a seat next to Malin and opening one folder after another. 'Everything in here is well-organized, so I have no doubt you can find anything you might need. These folders contain Sergio's own story for each case, payment records confirming money transfers, audio recordings of some conversations, plus explanations regarding who is who, as well as many other details for all cases involved. Plus, photos, copies of letters and messages, discussions and charts denoting cash flow.

'As for cash flows, you can follow the movement of funds only to the moment they were transferred directly to us. Connections get cut at this juncture and couldn't be restored even if you were to ask special departments of intelligence agencies to help you. There is no way to continue: all links are severed, and however much anyone tried, they would never get to Sergio. Besides, all the funds were long ago removed to other destinations that cannot be found. Do not forget that Mister Sergio owns several valid, legally sound companies, consolidated groups, manufacturing sites and real estate that neither you nor, for example, the FBI, would be able to get anywhere close to… I am telling you this well in advance, just in case: none of that would be possible. So, all you should be doing is studying what you have here, listening to all comments, paying special attention to Sergio's comments, and writing your book.

'And now we should go and have our dinner,' Alex said, closing his laptop and handing Malin two identical flash drives. 'Don't lose them. They contain everything, including your freedom and even your life.'

They walked once more through the long corridor, the one filled with amazing Renaissance paintings, until they reached the dining room.

Sergio, looking fit and neat, was standing tall at the large window, gazing at the last rays of the sun, which had almost dropped beyond the horizon. He was dressed in a white shirt with a neckband hidden by a silk neck scarf and jeans of faded white. A thin cigar in his right-hand produced curls of smoke.

'Oh, here you are, at long last! Please take your seats, young men!' Sergio said, turning towards the two. 'Let us have something to eat first, and then we should bring to a close the main part of our eye-opening discussion. Mister Malin must have more questions for me, I presume, and I should have answers to those questions. Did you receive the documentation, Malin?'

'Yes, I did. Alex gave me all there was. But I haven't had time yet to go over it.'

'Oh, my young fellow, I must apologize for my stupid question. Alex is my right-hand man, after all, my shadow, so if I told him to hand over documents at a certain hour, there is no doubt that you received them right then…please forgive me, Alex. As for figuring out all the details, Malin, you have plenty of time. In my reckoning, some three months, no less.'

'Are you planning to keep me here for three more months?' Malin could not refrain from asking this in an ironic tone as he took his place across the table from Sergio. Alex was already seated to his right.

'Why? I am sorry to tell you this, but frankly speaking I do not need you here for such a long period of time. Not at all!' Sergio said laughing. 'I am already long past eighty and I must have time to do the many things I have planned to do. And talking to you, as nice as it may be, takes up too much of my time. To tell you the truth, my time is priceless. Especially now. What's your choice tonight, by the way? Wine? Whisky? Cognac?'

All three remained silent while the servants set down hors d'oeuvres and poured drinks. Each of them was obviously lost in his own thoughts. Malin, looking at Sergio, imagined how he might use his steak knife: one precise movement would end the life of the most evil criminal of the century. That would be fitting revenge for what he had done, plus it would stop any new plans that were certainly hatching in Sergio's mind…and yet…the bracelet on Malin's leg was certainly not an imitation, it was very real. There were guards all around them, too. Plus, this Alex looked like a panther, always ready to jump. His eyes were strange, like Sergio's: they looked hard, and bore the same yellowish tinge. Lying dead next to a dying Sergio was not in Malin's future

345

plans. This old man would die anyway, be it two, three or five years later – Sergio was not meant to live eternally. And the book gradually coming together in Malin's head would be of more use to the world…

'Now, what's next, Malin?' Sergio said, swallowing yet another oyster and washing it down with white wine. 'Let us continue. What questions do you still have?'

'Oh, I am curious how you got to Russia in 1998?'

'At the time I was a prominent entrepreneur, doing large business deals and acting as a middleman. My name was Igor Larionov, and I appeared in Moscow unexpectedly, apparently out of one of the Baltic states. I was invited to do business in Russia by the then-Deputy Minister of Finance for Russia. He introduced me to the highest business circles in Moscow as if I were his man, someone minding his interests. It took me some time and effort to transform him later into a frightened puppet I could control.

'The country was in a deep crisis, but its rulers did not want to change anything in the way they were managing its economy. They preferred to continue borrowing billions from the International Monetary Fund and the European Bank for Reconstruction and Development. They were borrowing left and right, without much of a care for anything. Most of this money, of course, was misappropriated by corrupt officials. They were quite good at stealing funds using their fantasies: there were all kinds of things happening, ranging from elaborate privatization games and manipulation of short-term state treasury bills to money laundering and subsequent legalization.[1] It goes without saying that I simply could not pass up such a great opportunity.'

---

1. Russian state budget deficit was financed in 1995-1998 via the build-up of the state debt, including the issue of short-term treasury bills.

'What about the IMF tranche of 4.7 billion from August '98? The one considered to be "missing" ...'

'I was the one who organized its release in the first place. With the help of the Russians, of course. But I was conducting preliminary discussions with the IMF, during which I offered them a very sizeable kickback, in the amount of one billion US dollars. At the time, it was already clear that even such a huge tranche would not save Russia from its default. So, why would one senselessly throw it into that Russian hearth? This was when the Russian delegation came to the US, supposedly to reach an agreement on what I had already arranged. Those billions passed through the late Edmond Safra's bank and dispersed very smoothly – and I became richer by one and a half billion!'

'Was it with your assistance that Safra died?'

'Malin, you should stop pretending you're an idiot!' Sergio smirked. 'You know very well that I was the one who organized the fire in his home. And I also made sure that the door to the bathroom where he hid with his nurse was blocked. It was so easy to dupe that dumb guard who worked for Safra, the one who did the main part of the job. Money, vanity, and fear – those are the three major soft spots that anyone in the world has. So, all I had to do was learn how to press those spots in the right order, and how to do it at the right moment, with the right pressure, neither too hard nor too soft. Then I could achieve anything. If a good brain is involved in the process, then success is guaranteed.'

'Tell me, Sergio, do those documents Alex gave me contain financial details regarding the theft of the IMF credit? And also regarding Safra?'

'I know that Semyon Levine gave you some documents related to this case, which include financial items and other details. Do not be surprised that I am mentioning this. We have already made ourselves familiar with your archive, so we know for sure now that everything you have there on this case could only have come from him.'

'Will Levine die?' Malin asked in a low voice.

'Of course he will,' Sergio said drily. 'But not right now. Only when he gets old and catches some disease or other. If you meant to ask whether I would somehow get involved in his life, then please note that he is of no interest to me. In any case, I know very well where he lives in England. In a sense, this Levine actually helped me, because he told you details of the missing IMF tranche for Russia, and gave you documents related to it. I would have given them to you today anyway. So, let him live on. I, on the other hand, am giving you both duplicates of those same documents and certain other papers Semyon did not have, which provide further evidence. Thus, you now have a complete picture of everything, except for the final destination of my billion and a half – this is something no one will ever know. It's simply out of the question. Okay, let's turn to other matters now.'

Malin, pulling his wits together, pretended to be savoring the Château Cheval Blanc 1947, even though he had never liked wine. His palate was not really impressed by this wine, either, not even by its price, which was 130,000 dollars per bottle. A couple minutes later, Malin was ready to venture the most important question:

'When will you release me? And how would I get back to where I was?'

'Don't worry about it. You'll leave this island in the same mode. After a quick injection, our team will accompany you – who will become a feeble-minded paralytic – throughout your journey. First you will go by helicopter, then on my plane, and later you'll take several regular flights. This procedure is pain-free and will do you no harm, as you should already know. You'll arrive on-site in two days, and everything you need will be there with you – I mean your laptop and all your flash drives. Plus, whatever else you need. Just start working on your book and don't worry about anything.'

'Sergio!' Malin suddenly spoke in a very loud voice, almost shouting. 'Where will I be delivered to? How will I be able to write the book when they are on a hunt for me? I mean, both American and European special services…'

'First of all, the hunt is already off, and no one is interested in catching you anymore. I terminated all those operations. Proxies who work for me via a number of middlemen were able to convince all interested parties that you have abandoned the idea of uncovering the details of the 9/11 terrorist attack, and instead started roaming Europe in search of adventure. Secondly, you will be delivered to the Island of Ischia, in Italy, where one of my companies owns a villa that will be quite comfortable for you. You will have everything needed for writing your book: money, full service, total rest, the sun, and the sea all the time. You can have that villa for three months. Will that be enough time for you?'

'I guess so. But what about my documents? Who will I be now, under what name?'

'You will stay yourself, keeping your name and your identity. No one is looking for you anymore. You have nothing to worry about. I have already found you, so that is good enough. Intelligence agencies will not be interested in you until they find out the topic of your future book. There is, however, one thing that I would like to ask you not to do even once – and this is quite serious: while you are in Italy, do not use your credit cards, and do not check your email or other personal resources on Internet. You should not leave any tracks on the Net. You will be provided some cash, enough to live on comfortably for three months. You will find your passport and other documents in your baggage when you arrive on the sunny isle of Ischia. You will find everything else in the same bag. Alex, what was the name of that villa on Ischia again?'

'It is certainly very beautiful,' Alex, who had been silent until this moment, responded immediately. 'It's Casa Delle Rose, a house of roses. Very romantic, good for an artist.'

'Right...' Malin muttered skeptically, 'especially if one takes into account the topic of my book. It's all roses, of course...'

'Listen, Malin,' Sergio began, after a short pause. 'The thing is, I do count on you, and I do hope you won't let me down when you get this unique chance to become the Number One Journalist of All Time. I want you to concentrate fully on your book, so that it becomes the greatest global sensation since journalism emerged as a profession.'

'I understand, Sergio.' Malin sat back, looking straight at the man across from him. 'Still, I have two questions. One is whether you have any plans to censor anything in my book? And two: how will it be published? Since this would really be quite the bombshell for many very powerful people from many different countries. Millions of readers will want to know everything I reveal in this book, but several hundred individuals involved in those cases still believe that all these stories are dead and gone, forever. What can I do with that?'

'Don't make me laugh, Malin. What censorship are you talking about? You are a free, independent journalist who came into possession of unique, one-of-a-kind information. You will write what you want to write. What's really important is not to leave anything out. The only interference on my part would be this: since Alex will keep in touch with you, you must send your text when it is ready to the email address he gives you. That's all. Oh, and as for my answer to your second question...

'You will not need to bother about publishing the book. My representative will visit you, and he will be in charge of organizing everything: contracts, translations into major languages, publishing this super bestseller all around the globe, advertising, your triumphant appearance to the world, et cetera et cetera. You will only need to take care of collecting your laurel wreaths, your Pulitzer, your multimillions in royalties.'

'Will it really be this simple?' Malin smiled, lighting his cigar.

'It really will, my friend. You have already gone through the most difficult stage of your quest. But I have something to tell you before we bid farewell,' Sergio got up and made a couple of steps towards Malin, who got up too. 'I did not kill your friend Jia Shen. Her death was an accident. She became a victim, no, she paid the price for you and for me, who were following our professions. And now farewell. Or, maybe, see you again... Something tells me, Max Malin, that we might get to meet again at some point.'

Sergio shook Malin's hand and then walked towards the door at the farther end of the dining room, next to Bosch's triptych. At the door, he turned around, looking straight at Malin, and pressed a button. The shutters hiding the painting moved slowly asunder and *The Garden of Earthly Delights*, all three parts of it, stood open right in front of Malin. The door locked behind Sergio with a discreet click, and only Malin and Alex remained in the room.

'Let's go, Malin. I will take you to your room. Tomorrow will be a difficult day for you.'

When Malin was left alone in his temporary accommodations, he poured himself some whisky and stood at the window, looking for a long time at the palms illuminated by lights, listening to the roar of the invisible ocean. His thoughts spun around, lining up at times, then overlapping, getting mixed up and coming back again:

Oh Lord, all this has been like a dream, a long and awful dream. But I'm the one who chose this path, so I will have to follow it all the way to its end. I might not be able to control anything happening to me today, but I am headed downstream because I wanted to get into the stream in the first place. And even though the flow is very strong and dangerous, I am bound to stay in it for the rest of my life. How many secrets and how many nightmares will I have to uncover for the rest of the world... am I ready for that? Oh, what a stupid question...it's too late... Oh, Jia, my darling, how I miss you...

20

The Book
Italy. Ischia

The plane made a smooth turn and began its descent. Below was Naples with its buildings set on rolling hills and its sparkling sea, all lit by the powerful rays of the sun. When the wheels touched the runway of the Capodichino Airport, Malin opened his eyes. He could slowly turn his headfirst left, then right; then he was able to move his hand a little bit, and even both legs. It seemed that his body was responding to his efforts. His brain, however, was still quite foggy, and he felt some pressure in his temples.

Malin could vaguely remember the recent feeling of someone transferring him from his wheelchair into the plane seat. It had happened several times, and they had carried him in their arms. Somehow, he could remember, as if in a dream, seeing himself reflected in the mirrors at two or three airports: he had been sprawled in the wheelchair, his legs immobile, paralyzed, his arms jerking from time to time. His mouth dripped with saliva he could not hold in. Someone walked behind him, wiping his mouth and nose carefully with a handkerchief. He could tell it was definitely a man, whose voice kept loudly repeating: 'Calm down! Keep calm, little brother. There is nothing to worry about. We'll get on the plane and then fly home to see your mom and dad. They'll take care of you, no worries.'

Squinting from the bright sun that shone through the plane window, making visible the dance of tiny particles of dust, Malin, who was in an aisle seat, turned his head slowly towards the neighbors sitting to his left. A tall, grey-haired man in a grey suit, probably aged around forty, was observing Malin closely; he was holding hands with a beautiful blonde woman seated by the window. When Malin's neighbor had assured himself that Malin had returned to his senses, he addressed him, though for some reason in Russian:

'Malin, don't say anything, just listen. You have been almost fully paralyzed since childhood. Soon they will bring in a wheelchair, and I will help you transfer into it. I understand that you are almost back to normal, but please try to behave as if you were really disabled until we leave the airport. This will be better for your safety. I am your cousin, my name is Tom, and this is my wife, Jessica. We have brought you over here for a cure to be found on the islands. According to our documents, we are all coming from the USA.'

'Why are you speaking in Russian?' Malin asked him, though he was barely able to move his lips. 'You speak Russian poorly. With a strong accent. And other mistakes…'

'Take what you can get,' Tom said huffily. 'What's important is that no one around here understands Russian. Well, anyway, when we get out of the airport building, I will entrust you to someone who is here to welcome you and to take you to Ischia. He will put you up there. He's some kind of steward, or a butler. He will stay there with you to help you and provide necessary services. He is a local…well, he's Italian. Our task is to transfer you into his care and give him your bag.'

'What's his name?'

'Michele. I cannot vouch that this was his birth name,' Tom said, smiling, 'but now it's Michele Benzoni.'

The steward soon announced that the disabled passenger and his attendants would be the first to leave the plane, to be followed by business class passengers, after which all others from economy would be welcome to leave as well.

Tom and a flight attendant transferred Malin into the wheelchair and then moved him out of the plane to a special lift. Half an hour later, Tom and Jessica were pushing Malin, who held his bag in his hands, towards the exit of the Naples Airport. The warm autumnal air of southern Italy engulfed them immediately, as did a crowd of eager and talkative cab drivers, which was swiftly parted by a rather short, heavy, dark-haired man of about forty-five, who walked towards them with his arms outstretched in a gesture of embrace. His bald head glistened with sweat.

'Malin! Tom! Jessica!' he cried. 'I am so happy to welcome you here in Napoli! Please let me introduce myself. I am Michele Benzoni. Thank you so much for taking the trouble to bring my guest all the way here.'

Benzoni seized the initiative right away, taking over the wheelchair and talking without stopping as he pushed. His English was, in fact, decent.

'Malin, we'll head to the port now. We'll be taking the yacht. It is all for you, signore, all at your command. We shall come to Ischia in an hour's time. You will like our villa, it's quiet and comfortable there. Your relatives, Tom, and Jessica, will get on a flight to New York soon. Well, with a transfer in Paris. I mean, they can catch this flight if they go to registration right away...'

'We'll see you to the car,' Tom said, interrupting him. 'We can go back into the airport after that. We still have two hours before the flight.'

Theirs was a rather strange group as they headed for the parking lot outside. The fat, bald Italian paraded at its head, walking with an air of importance, and pushing the wheelchair in front of him. A silent, somber-looking couple followed him, walking very close behind, as if guarding both the Italian and the man in the wheel-chair. A black Mercedes minivan with tinted windows suddenly appeared, rolling slowly towards them, and when it stopped, its side door slid open automatically. A young curly-haired Italian sat in the driver's seat.

Bidding Tom and Jessica farewell was over in short order: they pumped hands and wished each other a safe trip. They parted knowing they would never meet again. When Malin got inside the car, he could feel im-mediately what a difficult time he had had pretending to be disabled. Now, at long last, he could settle com-fortably into a nice leather seat. Stretching his legs, he asked Michele:

'Tell me, Signor Benzoni, who are you? And who do you work for?'

'Oh, Mister Malin, for you I am simply Michele,' Benzoni said, turning to Malin. 'I am your assistant for anything you need. I work at Casa Delle Rose for any-one who arrives there as its guest. Now I am fully at your disposal. By the way, I have great options... no, opportunities both here in Napoli and on Ischia, and I can meet any of your needs and demands. But if your question is about who pays me, that's no secret: I get paid by Main Oasis LLC. This company owns our villa and the people who come to stay in it are always com-pany guests.'

'Thank you, Michele. You should also call me by my first name. It's Malin. Okay?'

'Fine, Mister Malin. Sorry...Malin.'

Some forty minutes later, the minivan passed the noisy Piazza del Municipio[1] and the gloomy Castel Nuovo[2] and stopped at the entrance to the port. The omnipresent Chinese tourists, cameras dangling about their necks, milled about, preparing to board the cruise ship Costa Smeralda, the colossal bulk of which overshadowed the long row of wharfs. When Malin and Michele exited the van, the Italian tried to help Malin carry his duffel bag, but Malin did not let go. How wonderful it was simply to be able to walk on the asphalt after all those long hours spent in the wheelchair! His legs tread in a sprightly manner, pushing against the even surface, stepping on the shadows of the masts of the many yachts and motorboats lining the wharfs.

'Here is our beautiful *La Colomba*,' Michele announced with pride, coming up to the gangway of a large yacht, which indeed looked astoundingly elegant. It was a twenty-meter-long, two-deck beauty of the Princess 64 family.[3]

'*La Colomba* means "female pigeon" in English,' the Italian went on chattering, 'and you, Malin, should be able to appreciate this yacht very much indeed. Please get on board now. *La Colomba* is all there for you, at any time.'

As soon as Malin and Michele stepped on board, the crew immediately unmoored the yacht, and soon it left the port area, maneuvering between other vessels. It moved straight toward Ischia, proudly raising its bow. The island was not too far away: twenty miles total, or

---

1. Piazza del Municipio (Italian for: Town Hall Square) is one of the central squares in Naples and one of the largest squares in Europe.

2. Castel Nuovo (Italian for: New Castle), often called Maschio Angioino (Italian for: Angevin Keep), is a medieval castle, first erected in 1279. It is located in front of Piazza Municipio. It was a royal seat for kings of Naples, Aragon and Spain until 1815.

3. Princess 64 is a luxury motor yacht model featuring four cabins.

about an hour's run.

When the autumnal sun had already started its daily dip beyond the horizon, *La Colomba* moored at Ischia's pier. Malin and Michele stepped onto the asphalt quay, still lit by intense sunlight, and sat down inside a Bentley Continental waiting for them. Michele proved himself highly capable by getting them out of the parking lot where so many cars stood too close to each other. After around half an hour of swerving through narrow streets lined with picturesque buildings hidden behind abundant red and purple bougainvillea, Michele stopped in front of high gates behind which stood olive and lemon trees. He pressed a button and the gates slowly moved to either side. The car drove down a lane made green by trees that formed an arch that looked almost like a tunnel. Then it stopped in front of a three-story building built with a light-colored stone. It was surrounded by rose bushes that exuded a special, slightly spicy aroma. A rather large bronze tablet bearing the words "Casa delle rose" was placed above the monumental entrance door.

Malin liked the house right away. There was an enormously spacious drawing room with a fireplace and cozy sofas, wood panels on the walls and a staircase leading up to an internal balcony that ran all around the room. There was also a large window that occupied a whole wall, with the greenish-silvery sea beyond it. Michele took Malin to the first floor, showing him his quarters: a small bedroom with a balcony and the adjacent study and library. Every room in this old villa had an atmosphere of comfort and care, as if contradicting the notion of being only a place to house important guests...

'Mister Malin, the whole house is for your use. The Wi-Fi password is on the desk in the study. You will also find a cell phone there, with a SIM card registered to an Italian name – but you should know that that person never existed. Your new laptop is there as well. My phone number is in the address book. In the mornings you will get a visit from Gabriela, we all call her Gabi, she will put things in order and cook for you, she will prepare anything you might like. In her free time, she stays downstairs, in the maid's quarters. Oh, by the way, as she is a local – born and raised on Ischia, I mean – she makes an excellent Coniglio all'ischitana. I would certainly strongly recommend it.'

'I normally work in the garden, but I am also here to provide security,' Michele explained, pride ringing in his voice. 'I am also ready to fulfill any requests or wishes you might have. I live in a small house located in the garden. You will see it there if you decide to go for a walk. Our territory is completely closed and secured against any outsiders. No one will be able to see you here. Only you, me and Gabi will be on the premises.'

'Thank you, Michele. Got it.'

'Please do what you wish. Work or rest. If you want to go someplace, the car is in the garage, and the yacht is at your disposal, too. But please, you should let me know of your movements, as I am responsible for your security. Oh, and I almost forgot to mention: there is some cash for you in the upper drawer of the desk, ten thousand euros. Plus, you will find a Visa card there, issued to the bearer. Its limit is thirty thousand euros. This is a gift from our top management, for your expenses.'

'Not bad…' Malin smiled. 'Looks like I'm already in heaven: a beautiful yacht, a great villa, lots of money for my expenses. Not to forget this Coniglio all'ischitana, which is Ischian-style rabbit, if I'm not mistaken. Prepared by a mysterious Gabi.'

'I have directions, Sir, to provide anything you might need so that you can work undisturbed, under the most comfortable conditions. I was told that you are here to write a book about the charitable work of this company, Main Oasis LLC.'

'You were given a most precise description of my activity, Michele,' Malin said, trying but failing not to sound ironic. 'Yes, exactly that! My book will be on this very subject.'

'Then I should not take up any more of your time, Mister Malin. Please make yourself comfortable, and good luck to you!'

When Malin was left alone, he looked around the study thoroughly investigating the room, trying to figure out where they might have hidden surveillance cameras. He did not find anything suspicious, so he switched on the mobile phone lying on the desk and opened its address book. There were three entries: two with the Italian country code were labeled "Michele" and "Gabriela", and one phone number with the Belgian code, 494, had the name "Alex" attached to it. As soon as Malin switched on the phone, a message came in on WhatsApp from the Belgian number:

> *Dear Malin, I am happy to welcome you to Ischia. I'm certain you were not too fatigued during your trip, and that you are now entirely well. I hope that you can start working on the book, being in comfort and having nothing to worry about. This number is a temporary one, it is intended only for our communication. Please do not hesitate to ask me anything at any time, whatever wishes or issues you might have. When you are done with your writing, please let me know right away and I will send you the address to which you should send your manuscript. Our mutual friend asked me to give you his regards and best wishes. Respectfully, Alex*

Malin answered in brief: *Thank you for everything. Everything is great. Starting work on the book.* And then he sat down in a chair beside the wide window, wanting to take in the panorama beyond – the Aragonese Castle towering before the villa, on the rock that, at this golden hour before sunset, was dropping into the quiet sea.

Isn't this too much of a good thing? Malin thought. What am I doing here, sitting at a luxurious villa owned by a criminal? I am free to use his yacht, his car, his money. And it is his servant who is taking care of me. All with only one purpose: so that I can stay in an ideal environment writing a book to expose this same criminal. Well, something isn't right, I guess… Maybe I'll come to terms with the situation later… Right now, this is my reality: I am alive and well, I have unique material at my disposal, good enough to write a bestseller, and my working conditions are fine. What I should be doing next is sitting down and starting to write. There is no other option. Then I'll be able to figure out what to do next.

Malin opened the laptop and started scanning the news. It had already been quite a long time ago since he had been able to sit relaxed at his monitor, scanning current events around the world to get a picture of what was going on everywhere. He had missed it so much! Today, the general tone of reports was quiet, what with international top-level talks or monetary exchange rates. And then – Malin felt like he'd been given an electric shock when he saw a headline that stopped him in his tracks in *The Guardian*:

> *Russian mafiosi Semyon Levine found dead in London suburb*

Beside the headline was a photo of a smiling Semyon. And another photo: policemen standing around the body, which lay on the floor of Semyon's study, a place now so familiar to Malin. He clicked the link and started reading the report:

The body of 70-year-old Russian mafioso Semyon Levine was discovered early this morning in his mansion in the south of Greater London. He was killed last night with three shots, one of which was an insurance shot to the head. Levine came to the UK almost twenty years ago, in 1999, and lived the life of a recluse in his grand mansion in the middle of an old garden. According to some sources, he was worth almost half a billion US dollars. Originally, British authorities suspected Levine of having links to the Russian mafia, and of being involved in laundering funds that had been misappropriated by Russia. However, they were unable to prove anything, so in recent years no British agency had any claims to Mr. Levine. Our information is that Russian, French, and Cypriot passports were found in his house, all using Levine's photo, but issued to different names. A large sum of cash was also found in his study. Our source in the police confirmed that Mr. Levine had not traveled anywhere, nor had he ever crossed the borders of Great Britain. It is quite possible that he was leading a discreet life in order to hide from former partners in crime among the Russian mafia, as he had certain information on them. The police seem to regard this as a possible reason for Levine's demise.

Malin recalled Levine's smiling round face and the crow's feet that had danced around his temples and squinted eyes, his slight speech impediment and rapid-fire delivery. Why had this happened? Why so many deaths over such a short period of time? There had been Charles, the informer who had sold him the Marshall Archive in D.C.; René Duchamp, who helped him and Jia so much when they were in Paris; and Luca Lavallieri, the stolen art buyer in Rome. And now his major source of information, Semyon Levine.

Luckily, all the recordings of his conversations with Semyon, as well as the man's documents, were still in Malin's possession. *Well, come to think of it...it could well have been Sergio who ordered Semyon disposed of,* Malin mused. *It is certainly in his best interest if I can only present the story from his angle, and no one else's... Maybe Sergio became concerned that they could start actively looking for Levine, and when they found him, use certain devices on him to make him tell even such secrets as neither Semyon nor Sergio had divulged when they spoke with me... And then both Ling Wan of the Chinese Triads and Don Domenico Radore of the Cosa Nostra might be next in line, right?*

Malin got up and, pacing around the room, dialed Alex's phone number. He answered on the first ring:

'Hello, Malin,' said Alex, and his voice seemed to be heard in the study, as though he were right next to Malin. 'To what do I owe the pleasure? Did something happen, perhaps?'

'Listen, I just read the news about Semyon Levine's death. Why did you do this? Why? Is it because you want me to write the book using only the audio files and documents I have? So that live sources can't add anything to what they had already told me? Are you afraid that if someone found them, their stories might hurt?'

'Stop being hysterical, Malin! I knew it! Thank God this is an encrypted channel. Listen carefully...'

'Well, maybe I should apologize for this outburst,' Malin said, bracing himself, 'but it all seemed too convenient... Okay, fine, I'm listening.'

'None of our men received an order to take out Levine. But let us speak honestly with each other: what we did do was indicate his possible whereabouts to those who were eager to find him. As a favor, so to speak. You should be aware that Semyon knew too much about too many things, and he didn't tell you everything. Not by a long shot. So, they would have found him in any case after your book is published. Then he would have been subjected to serious grilling. As you may suspect, special agencies are really very good at that, so it's certain that Levine would have talked. And we are not really interested in such a development...'

'So, what's next, then? Does this mean that Ling Wan and Domenico Radore die, too?'

'Oh, I see, Malin...you didn't get any news about them. Unfortunately, old Wan died of a brain hemorrhage two days after your meeting. And as for Don Domenico, he died in a car crash last week. This means your book can say anything that has to do with either of them. You may mention their names, describe locations where you met them. This would not create any problems for them anymore. And as we know, you recorded all your conversations with them, and you got all necessary documentation. Right?'

'It certainly is, Alex,' Malin said in a low voice. 'But something is not right. What you did was very, very wrong. And their deaths are on my conscience now, for it was I who had been able to find them. They agreed to provide me with certain information, and that let to their doom. In other words, it was I who sentenced them to death...'

'You have nothing to do with any of that, Malin. These people were killed because of their own pasts. Do not forget that neither of them was some kind of conscientious medical doctor, or a virtuous high school teacher... These men departed from this mortal vale the same as they always had been as criminals, with plenty of blood on their hands. They chose this path on their own and they knew where it would take them, sooner or later...'

'But both Sergio and you, Alex, are of the same ilk, only on a much larger scale. Why do you have the right to make a decision as to who should live and who should die?'

'You have answered your own question just now, Malin: our scope is quite different. It is so much larger compared with theirs. This is why my boss is entitled to make decisions the way he feels is right. Because he is much smarter, much stronger and is much more talented than the others...'

'Oh, I see,' Malin said reluctantly, fuming with anger. 'I've got it now. All of it. Thank you for your explanation. Farewell.'

'Goodbye, Mister Malin. See you later.'

Malin paced to and fro in the study until a very late hour, when the open window showed total darkness, and what came inside was only the roar of breaking waves. He knew, of course, that his situation was hopeless: he had no choice. He could not go anywhere. He knew too much, and the totality of what he had accumulated through his research made him the carrier of the most explosive information anywhere on the globe. If the book was not written, and if it did not reach people around the globe, then his life would not be worth a cent... All of them would declare hunting season – from Sergio and his enemies to the special agencies of a dozen countries – and he would be the game. All of them would want to lay their hands on the information Malin had in his possession, but all would want Malin to stay silent – dead, in other words. Should this happen, it would mean Jia and all the others had died for nothing. No! No, no and no, for crying out loud! If one thing remained true, it was that the book must be written and published...

Three months had passed since the day Malin arrived on Ischia. In the evenings, the island was fully covered in dense fog, and its December nights were almost always very rainy. When it rained, it rained hard, but during the daytime the rays of the sun managed to pierce through light clouds, reflecting in the sea, which turned greyer with each new day.

Malin woke up every morning at eight on the nose, then jogged for an hour along the coastal cliffs, which were almost bluffs. Then he showered and had his breakfast, which was as substantial as it gets. Breakfast was served by Gabi, who made a wide variety of clattering noises as she handled the utensils in the grand kitchen, where the breakfast table was set. Gabi, Gabriela… She had made a great impression on Malin from the start as soon as she appeared at the villa. Black-haired, beautifully tanned, short, about twenty-five years old, she had almond-shaped eyes and pitch-black eyelashes. She was talkative and expressive, so Malin very much enjoyed speaking with her. When he would find respite from his intense bouts of writing, he found great pleasure in discussing things with her, be they details of life on this island, issues related to her work, or even her relationship with a young man named Amadeo, who seemed to be in no great rush to propose…

Malin would go up to the study after breakfast and immerse himself deeply in his work on the text, so much so that it was almost all done by December. What remained was final editing and manuscript proofing in order to remove technical imperfections or fill in any omissions. A large, complex investigative narrative emerged, showing in exact detail the long criminal record of this Sergio-Larionov-Santana-Novack-Weiss-Morel, as well as of those who at some period of their lives had happened to be engulfed in the unstoppable flow of his plans and actions.

Every new chapter, full of copies of documents, transcripts of audio recordings and photos, made Malin realize ever more clearly the enormous scope of Sergio's activities. It was an epoch, a criminal epoch spanning the 1960s to the present. No other criminal, no mafioso, no corrupt dictator of recent centuries could approach anything close to the scale of Sergio's work, which echoed throughout planet Earth. Sergio's detailed planning, as well as the scrupulous execution of his plans, had made him into an unheard of, one-of-a-kind phenomenon. This despite the fact that Sergio had only used the same age-old tools, as effective as they ever were – he had spent tens of billions of dollars to all the usual ends: corruption among top public officials in different governments, unbridled greed, frenzied lust for power, mean cowardice, indifference to the lives of others, et cetera. Sergio, who had been born in 1933, and whose birth name was Luis Cristobal Santana, had become the evil genius of the epoch – the genius of all evil things…

Malin spent whole days browsing documents and payment receipts. He transcribed audio files, continually compared photographs, and gleaned plenty of valuable information from the Internet, paying attention to details almost no one had noticed before. Malin knew so much now about his subject of research that he could see those details in a completely different light. Everything was falling into place. What seemed an unfathomable mystery only a short time ago had slowly emerged as a missing link in those chains of events of which Malin was already aware. So many mysteries were waiting to be revealed for the world! So many questions would be answered!

On Monday, December 9, as the deep red sun dropped suddenly beyond the waters, *The Genius of Evil*, was finally finished. When Malin read its last page

367

and made his final few corrections, he pressed Save and closed the file. He sat back, feeling very tired and unexpectedly empty, he felt as though he had lost all his energy. His strenuous work over the last three months had seemed to vampirically drain him of his powers ... Still, he had to perform one last move related to the book: he was obliged to send it to its first reader – who was, at the same time, its protagonist.

No one would ever know how much effort it took Malin to send his manuscript to Sergio. He paced continually in circles around the study. Then he stood for a very long while at the window, thrumming his fingers on the glass, on the other side of which so many thin trickles of rainwater were streaming down fast, so that it was not even possible to see the panorama of the sea beyond. Malin knew that if he did not fulfill the last item of his contract with Sergio, his text, his book, most certainly would not reach any readers. Oh well, why should he care about the book and its readers! If he did not send the text, Max Malin's life would cease to have even the minimal value it had today. There would simply be no trace left of him... He would be dissolved into the void... And no one would even think of searching for him: shit happens, so what if a reputed journalist went missing during his travels through Italy? Nothing doing, then: he simply had to send it off...

21

The Devil's Advocate
Italy. Ischia

Michele Benzoni was almost never present at the villa. He would come inside the house only in the evenings, for during the day he had things to do in the garden or produce to bring in from the market. At other times he was involved in certain, mysterious affairs that meant he would disappear for the whole day. Today, however, now that the book was finished, he came in during the morning and, having first knocked on the kitchen door, where Malin was having breakfast with the company of Gabriela, he walked in.

'Good morning, Mister Malin,' Michele said, pressing Malin's hand. He nodded to Gabriela and sat down across the table from Malin. 'I was told that our management is very happy with your work, which you have successfully completed.'

'Oh, I must say,' Malin smirked, 'Michele, you must be the best-informed individual on the whole island.'

'I wish. But I am only a middleman, so I am simply telling you the news that was relayed to me,' Michele explained, jerking with his head towards the cell phone that lay on the table. 'Now, I am about to leave for Naples, where I must meet someone very important. He is coming here in order to meet with you. We'll be here around lunch time.'

'Who is it? Do I know him?' Malin asked, thinking it might be that Alex had decided to visit him. Or, perhaps, Sergio?

'I'm not sure you know him. Nor I.' Michele looked through his messages and then said: 'Oh, here it is. His name is Henry Austin; he's a lawyer or an attorney. I don't really know the difference, but this Henry Austin is coming over at the instruction of the company's top management. Again, I wasn't given any details. I was only told to meet him at the airport, bring him over here and make sure that you two can meet to discuss matters. And when you guys are done, I must take Mister Austin back to the airport, where a plane will be waiting for him. That will be all, and then I will again be back at only your service.'

'Thank you, Michele. I guess I see…but please, help yourself to what's on the table. Gabriela made a truly amazing eggplant quiche today.'

Wearing a sly expression, Michele looked over at Gabriela, but said nothing. Then he picked up a plate containing a slice of the deliciously aromatic quiche and started to eat. Malin knew, of course, why the Italian was looking at him like this: for about two months now he had felt that the beautiful Gabi was treating him with particular and warm attention. She was always there for him, at breakfast, lunch, and dinner. She would sit across the table from the villa's guest, always hanging on his words. She would ask questions about his romantic life and was obviously glad to hear that he now lived a lonely life. She had also told him, in a seemingly innocent manner, about her breakup with Amadeo, who was a local tough.

Gabriela's beauty was dazzling, but Malin was surprised to find he felt a certain indifference towards her. He realized it would be physically impossible for him to establish any closer relationship with her. Jia's image was still very much with him, and this left no space free for any other woman – even if it was someone like Gabi. And now, when Malin felt clearly aware of a dangerous, possibly lethal possibility in the final steps related to his book, he knew it would be wrong to embroil this Italian woman in his affairs at all.

Malin returned to the villa at three o' clock after a nice stroll along the quay, accompanied by Gabriela, who today seemed rather taciturn. He sat in the study with a cup of strong coffee. Half an hour later there was a knock on the door, and Michele brought in a tall, stout, completely bald man of about fifty who wore a formal business suit. With small, piercing eyes, the new guest first scanned the study quickly and then, focusing his gaze on Malin, extended his hand and introduced himself in a high, somewhat shaky voice:

'Good afternoon, Mister Malin. My name is Henry Austin, and I am a legal counsel, an attorney.' Having said this, the man turned to Michele, looking at him with such intensity that the Italian immediately left the study, quietly closing the door behind him. 'I was given direction to pay you this visit by the graces of a gentleman who recently accomplished a mission on behalf of someone else whose house you visited not long ago. I am not, in fact, aware of who that person was, but I was told that such a complex introduction should act as a code word for you, so that you would be able to trust me.'

'I know who you are talking about, Mister Austin,' Malin said, stepping forward and accepting the other's handshake. 'Hello, Sir. Please sit down. Would you like tea or coffee? Or whisky, perhaps?'

'Thank you. Could I have cold water, please?'

'To what do I owe the honor?' Malin asked, pouring water for the guest. 'I may have guessed already, but I would like to hear your answer.'

Henry Austin slowly inserted the bulk of his wal-rus-like body into a big leather chair in front of Malin and drank the whole glass of water in one go.

'I have read your book. It is highly explosive, and a work of genius. This is a bombshell, if I am allowed to use the term, something that has never been done in all the years journalism has existed as a profession. Well, here's the deal: you have done your bit already, and all the rest will be accomplished by us – I mean by myself and my people.'

'Sorry, I don't get it.'

'In short, we'll sign a contract under which you will cede all rights related to the publishing of your book, titled *The Genius of Evil,* to my legal company, Austin, Coen & Partners. The contract will include clauses giv-ing us the rights to translate the book into Spanish, Ger-man, Italian, Chinese and Russian, as well as the right to organize its sales through international bookstore chains, and the right to receive sales dividends.'

'Well, isn't this a bit steep, Mister Austin, for you to get all these rights?' Malin interjected, rather surprised. 'I risked my life to write the book, and now I have to give everything away to you, is that right?'

'Please don't rush to conclusions and take it easy if you please, Mister Malin. We would receive the rights only for translation, for the first print runs globally, which should be around several million copies for starters; also, the right for distribution of those copies via bookstore chains; and for their subsequent sales and receipt of funds. That's all. And now I should probably explain to you what you would be getting under this contract.'

'All right, this might be more interesting for me...'

'Right after your signing of the contract, and after you officially provide me with the text of *The Genius of*

Evil, plus the copies of all documents mentioned in the book, you will receive your honorarium, that is, your author's fee, which is in the amount of ten million US dollars. This money is clean, it is legalized, and it will be applied directly to your bank account. This will be your fee for the initial sale,' Austin said, making himself even more comfortable in the chair and pouring himself another glass of water. 'We, on the other hand, will be responsible for the overall advertising campaign across all continents. On top of that, we will take care of placing articles in all major media platforms around the world, and do explosive specials all over the Internet, featuring the opinions of hundreds of experts. Most importantly, Mister Malin, we guarantee that you can triumphantly and safely return to the USA as the greatest journalist of modern times – plus we'll organize all subsequent events, from press conferences and well-publicized media trips to winning the Pulitzer Prize!'

Henry Austin used a snow-white handkerchief to wipe off a multitude of sweat drops from his forehead, and then continued his statement:

'This is where our functions end. Well – not really, since there will be many wanting to interview you in thorough detail – include people from the FBI, the NSA, and Italian and Russian special agencies, among others. You will need legal assistance for that, and our best attorneys will provide their services and act as your shadow for that period of time. Will that do?'

'So far, so good,' Malin said, not even trying to conceal his amazement. 'What else would be left for me as the book's author?'

'Oh, quite a lot. You'll keep your rights for subsequent new editions of *The Genius of Evil*, in any country and in any number of copies. There is only one condition: you will have no right to make any changes or add anything to the existing text. You will not be entitled to strike out anything, nor to add any new material. You will, however, keep the film rights, be they for documentaries, feature films or TV series based on your book. How do you like these conditions?'

'They are thoroughly acceptable,' Malin said, and then decided that the time had come to ask a question that had bothered him since the first day he started working on the book. 'You know, this book, *The Genius of Evil*, is a truly dangerous project, dealing as it does with highly explosive events. When a great many influential people from different countries find out about my book, they will immediately wish it had never been published, and that I go the way of all flesh. To be honest with you, I'm so tired of hiding all the time and risking my life – it's already been six months of that... How do you think it will work out to both publish my book and provide me with security?'

'Let's be clear about the following: you will live in complete security only after your book is published and distributed everywhere, including online. Only after that will your demise no longer make sense to anyone. Oh, it would be even dangerous for them,' Austin said, once more gulping water from his glass. 'We will translate your text into all languages and print a huge run of the book without spilling the secret. We will not do any pre-sale advertising. We will first deliver all copies to bookstore chains – again, with no advertising, and in complete silence. We do have such capabilities.

'Special agencies have their own things to worry about, there are always plenty of messes to deal with and a lack of coordination between departments, so no one will really pay any attention to the book's contents. Especially since European book sellers will have no idea that the book is published in the US, Canada and all over Latin America, and Americans will not be aware of the editions in Europe, Russia, or China.

'Only a few days later, when *The Genius of Evil* will already have been placed on bookshelves in each and every bookstore, will there be sensational headlines in all the largest, most popular publications. Both in print and online. We will fill up the Internet and all other media with headlines something like this: "Mystery of Kennedy's Assassination Finally Resolved", or "The Man Who Did 9/11", or "Kennedy's Assassin Organized the Attempt on the Pope's Life", or "Max Malin's World-Shaking Investigation", et cetera, et cetera… When the book is already in the hands of millions of readers, then we will place the text online, including all photos, audio files, et cetera. Plus, readers will be sharing their own impressions about the most stunning revelation of the century, completely on their own, just as we need. This will be the moment you come back to Washington – landing straight on piles and piles of laurel wreaths!'

'I see,' Malin said, in a very low voice. He could not really fathom the full implications of everything the lawyer had said. Even though Malin, having met Sergio, harbored no doubts as to how extensive his capabilities could be. 'I think I see what you mean…but let's go over the contract, please.'

Towards evening, all formalities were completed, and Malin and Austin walked downstairs, where Gabi was setting the table for dinner in the dining room. When they had taken their seats and raised their glasses, Malin asked his guest, with whom he was already on a first name basis:

'Henry, I understand that my question might not be tactful, but as a journalist, I'm curious: how much will your client spend, in total, for the whole project of publishing my book?'

'I understand your curiosity, Malin,' Austin responded, taking a glass filled with wine and looking at it against
the light. 'I know you are well-acquainted with the party
financing our activities, so I will answer your question.
The whole project, including your fee and the subsequent grand advertising campaign, will amount to about
forty-five million dollars. And our company has already
received the money. So, there's nothing to worry about.'

'It isn't that I was worried, Sir. Okay, let's have our dinner.'

After dinner, Henry Austin bade farewell, speaking
in a gentlemanly manner yet, at the same time, ogling
Gabriela as she took away their dirty dishes. Eventually,
he walked after Michele, who was waiting for him in
the anteroom. But before he departed, Henry stopped
in the doorway, and looking straight at Malin, said:

'I must commend your courageous attitude, Malin.
Aren't you afraid that I or someone else, whoever gets the
copy of your manuscript, might betray you? There are so
many people around the world who would hope for your
book never to be published, hope that it would perish
together with you. Those people would be ready to pay
tens of millions for this to happen. Aren't you afraid?'

'You see, Henry, when the situation is hopeless, in
practical terms, there are no options left. So, you either
decide to go all the way, or stay mum and keep waiting
for a bullet to go through your head. I chose the former
option, that's all. Besides, I could say, if you can forgive
me some pathos, that there are some shadows of the deceased behind me, including some who were very dear
to me. And I feel I cannot betray them…'

'Please accept my respects for that. Farewell, Sir!'
Henry Austin shook Malin's hand and left, immediately
vanishing into the dusk that reigned on the island at
this hour.

After his departure, Malin stood for a long time at

the large window, beyond which one could scarcely make out the top branches of olive trees swinging in a strong wind.

It might take another two months before the book is translated into other languages, printed, and distributed, Malin thought. At least, in Henry Austin's estimation. It's a quick process for a task of this kind, but for me these two months will feel like a very long period... What should I do here at this villa for sixty more days? Nothing...to do nothing would just be unbearable! Well, it must be wrong, too, for me to stay in the same place for so many weeks. Because I must have already become a local fixture of sorts...

Later that night, when Malin was heading for bed, there came a knock on the door, and Michele walked in.

'Mister Malin, I apologize for my intrusion, as it is already very late. But I am back from Naples only now. I was given the strong recommendation that you should leave this location and go elsewhere as soon as possible. I was given an order to transport you by sea tomorrow morning. We will sail to the island of Capri, where our company has another villa. You'll stay there for the next two months. It's not far, only twelve miles from here. La Colomba will take us there in less than an hour. Please be ready by eight in the morning.'

'Does this mean I should be in hiding until Mister Austin completes his part of the deal? But why? Isn't it safe and quiet in here?'

'I have no idea, Mister Malin. Your safety is my responsibility, and I was given directions to move you to Capri. That's all I know.'

'Okay, fine, let's go there. Anyway, I have never been to Capri.'

22

Three Months Later
New York

March in New York had turned out cold and wet this year. Every day, the leaden sky became scattered with clouds above the skyscrapers' upper floors, and by evening the clouds shed sleet onto the city, a mix of snow and rain that became a chilly sprinkle at ground level.

Malin had already spent three days in a luxurious deluxe suite of the Trump International Hotel, where a representative of Austin, Coen and Partners had brought him directly from John F. Kennedy Airport. The suite's huge windows, which took up the whole wall, looked out over Central Park, but the amazing panorama from the fortieth floor didn't really impress Malin. He had reached the stage of ennui that befalls anyone who begins to feel as if the worst has already passed. For some reason, however, he had none of the feeling of having achieved victory, the fussy aftermath taking precedence instead. It was a vanity of vanities when there was no time to take a breath, lean back or even just be alone for a minute. During his three days in New York, Malin had already given a major press conference in which almost two hundred journalists from around the world had participated; then there had been two dozen interviews, plus he'd been invited onto three talk shows

– CNN, NBC, and CBS – and five radio programs.

After taking part in a morning talk show on TV, and after meeting with FBI representatives demanding details about anything mentioned in his book, Malin at last got a couple of hours of spare time, which he dedicated to scanning the news at his leisure. Today, all major global media were full of news about journalist Max Malin, whose book *The Genius of Evil* had become a major world-shaking event, uncovering the most famous mysteries of the last century.

> **The Washington Post**: *Journalist Max Malin, who worked for a number of years in our investigation bureau, published a book titled* The Genius of Evil, *in which he presented answers to issues that had been of global concern over the last sixty years. Essentially, Malin single-handedly solved the murder of John F. Kennedy, 35th president of the USA, as well as discovered the man behind the attempted assassination of Pope John Paul II in 1981. Additionally, Malin reports unique facts about the destruction of the World Trade Center on September 11, 2001, providing evidence that the terrorist attack was, in fact, initially planned within the US, and that the buildings collapsed due to explosives for which the planes acted only as detonators. All these and similar tragedies were carried out by a criminal organization headed by one Luis Cristobal Santana, who is 86 years old this year. Malin was able to meet him at his secret residence and interview him over the course of several days.*
>
> *During his investigation, Malin spent six months in hiding, pursued by both Santana's killers and US special agents, as neither was interested in the*

disclosure of information Malin could discover. The Genius of Evil was published in all major languages, including Chinese and Russian, with a total initial print run of over 30 million copies. Without any advertising, the book became available in every book-trade system around the world, a practically unheard-of strategy. Information about the investigative report became available online only after this distribution had already been completed. As of today, the whole first edition is practically sold out, and buyers are still besieging the largest bookstores across the United States, demanding copies of The Genius of Evil.

The New York Times: *At a conference yesterday, well-known journalist Max Malin related to the press the incredible story of the adventures that led him to write his unique investigative book. Its title is* The Genius of Evil. *Malin displayed unique documents and also presented some audio recordings to his colleagues. The press was able to hear a conversation between the man who organized the destruction of the World Trade Center on September 11, 2001, and his contact, who may have been an operative of a US special agency. The thousands of US citizens who died that day died not purely because of the planes' hitting the towers, but due to explosive charges that had been planted inside well in advance.*

Malin's investigative report also presents proof that President Kennedy was killed not by Oswald from the window of the book repository, as the special commission report asserted, but by a woman who was shooting from behind a fence on a grassy knoll nearby. All these criminal acts of the cen-

tury were perpetrated by the same person: a US citizen of Hispanic descent by the name of Luis Santana, who also went under other aliases, including, for example, Novack, Morel, Weiss, Larionov, and Sergio. Malin was able to speak with him and record their conversation. Santana, who is already close to ninety, confessed to a number of crimes, including those mentioned above. His other crimes include the assassination attempt on the Pope and the theft of a multibillion-dollar loan to Russia. Sergio (alias Santana) presented Malin with evidence of his own guilt. Malin is currently being interviewed by representatives of the FBI, while their colleagues from special services in Italy, Great Britain and Russia are next in line.

The Guardian: *We are continuing our story on the most sensational media sting of our time, updating with a number of developments that were to be expected in the wake of the information revealed in* The Genius of Evil, *authored by American journalist Max Malin. The book sheds new light on the mysteries surrounding such events as President Kennedy's assassination, the attempt on the life of the Pope in 1981, the 9/11 tragedy, and the theft of an IMF loan worth billions and related murder of Edmond Safra, a well-known Italian banker. Despite the fact that the book became widely available only a week ago, reactions to its contents followed almost immediately.*

For example, two former FBI agents, already retired, were arrested yesterday on the orders of the US Attorney General. The reason behind their arrest is suspicion that they might have been involved in organizing the explosion of the World

Trade Center on September 11, 2001. Also, it was reported that a Mr. George Davis committed suicide, using a handgun to shoot himself in the temple. According to our sources, Mr. Davis, who was 97 years old, had been a non-staff aide to Vice-President Lyndon B. Johnson in 1962-63.

The publication of the book triggered further events in several countries. In Italy, several members of Cosa Nostra were arrested under Italian police suspicion that they might have worked for and carried out orders for Luis Santana (aka 'Sergio'), the man whose crimes were revealed in Malin 's book. In Russia, Mr. Matvey Assianov, former deputy minister of finance (1996–1998), was found hanged in his mansion outside Moscow. According to police authorities, this was a suicide.

Russia Today: The Genius of Evil, *a book written by Max Malin, a US journalist of Russian descent, was published simultaneously in a number of languages, immediately becoming a bestseller around the planet. In Russia, for example, the book's seven-figure print run was practically sold out within a week! In his interview for RT, Max Malin said that he had, in his words, 'cast-iron evidence for all facts mentioned in the book.' Indeed, the author presented a lot of detailed evidence both in the investigative report itself and during his recent press conference in New York. All the financial documents, audio recordings and photos he presented do indeed confirm everything mentioned by Malin.*

An FBI representative, however, asserted that "most of what Max Malin claims in his recent book is a combination of coincidence and the spinning of facts." An official White House representative announced that "even the very existence of someone like Luis Santana (aka "Sergio") should be regarded as highly questionable." Both of these statements sound strange against the background of the detailed evidence provided by Max Malin.

The Russian Investigative Committee (RIC) started re-examining the case around the presumed theft of the 1998 IMF loan, which was issued to Russia in the amount of almost five billion US dollars. The investigation is being conducted in accordance with facts mentioned in Malin's report. At the time of writing, an RIC representative is on his way to New York to interview Max Malin, a US citizen, and to obtain copies of all documents he might have related to the developments in August of 1998.

Die Welt: *According to a poll conducted by* Die Welt, *Max Malin's book* The Genius of Evil, *which we reviewed in detail yesterday, was recognized as the most thorough, exhaustive, and most global journalistic investigation of our times. According to information we received from a trustee of Columbia University in New York, Malin will be nominated for a Pulitzer Prize in the Investigative Reporting category.*

We have also learned from our own sources that the Committee to Protect Journalists is discussing an option to nominate Malin for the Nobel Prize for Literature. However, this is a questionable move, because The Genius of Evil *cannot be regarded as fiction, its genre rather being that of journalistic investigation.*

Malin got up, poured himself some whisky and, as was his custom, started pacing the room – from the TV screen to the sofa and back. Superficially, he had achieved his wildest dreams. He had written the book of the century, exposing all criminals. The book was enjoying incredible success. All kinds of international book awards were lined up, waiting for Malin to come and get them. Big money had arrived in his bank account. And millions around the planet were mentioning his name with enthusiasm. Yet his mind was in a certain distress that he experienced almost physically: a painful feeling that things were not fully accomplished, that his task was not really completed. Something was not right. Something had not really been finalized. Was this pain perhaps related to someone who should have been beside him right now? Jia? No, not really. Malin had made peace with the fact that she was not around anymore. No, something else was making Malin's existence painful. The depths of his subconscious mind hid a secret that was supposed to become the ultimate event of the year. Malin sensed that the story was not over. At least not yet.

Malin made it back to his room after a three hour-long interview with the FBI, but by nine in the evening he was already somewhat refreshed, so he could easily go down to *Jean-Georges*, the famous restaurant downstairs. He was glad to be able to stroll across the hotel lobby without attracting attention from those around the registration desk – some hotel guests were leaving, but others were eager to get in. These days, with his face all over TV, with his photos filling both newspapers and the Internet, Malin, for the first time in his life, realized how heavy the weight was of being famous, or at least globally known… He knew now how difficult life was for superstars: in the last few days, his daily trip to the restaurant, or any attempt to go for a walk in the area around the hotel, had become an incessant game of hide-and-seek with obtrusive fans.

In the dining area of *Jean-Georges*, Richard Berwick, his old friend and boss, was sitting slouched in a white chair at a table draped in an immaculately white table-cloth. He was still quite rotund, and had acquired some more grey in his hair, but was beaming and as full of verve as before. They hugged.

'Malin, holy shit, I'm so happy – you did it – and that you came out alive! You won, Malin!'

'Now, come on, Richard, come on, old boy!' Malin said, smiling. He moved slightly away and looked straight at Berwick. 'None of this would have happened had you not helped me in the first place. After all, you did help me at the beginning of the whole story by getting the paper to buy the Marshall Archive. Then I was able to hide only with your assistance. And later on, you took part in the whole thing in Rome, of course.'

'All right, all right, do sit down. What'll you have? Whisky?'

Malin ordered a glass of beer and then posed a question that had been on his mind these last six months:

'What happened to you on that day in Rome, at The Excelsior, after Sergio's agents took me away?'

'Nothing much. Next morning, I came back to my senses in my own hotel room nearby. I had an enormous, a seriously mammoth hangover – my head was splitting, my arms and legs weren't responding at all. I had to spend that whole day in bed, taking aspirin. I also had to lie in the bathtub and soak a long while – horizontal was the only bearable position. Eventually, however, I got back to normal. I did figure out that they must have taken you away so you could visit with the person you were looking for, and you did that for quite some time. I was very concerned about you, of course, and I went to some effort to try and locate you, but nothing came of it. Then I knew it wouldn't be possible for me to change anything, so I decided simply to wait. But I'm happy my wait is over now, let me tell you.

'One more thing, Malin. I figured out that you were alive because in the news they said that only one body was discovered in that room at The Excelsior. And they said it was the body of art dealer Lavallieri. I thought, had they wanted to kill you, there would have been two bodies in the room, correct?'

'Your logic is most impeccable, Richard. So, what's going on with you now?'

'Oh, I'm fine. Still living in Switzerland. Well, two days ago I got a phone call from my ex-boss at our dear Washington Post, you know... He offered me the same position and told me that I should agree. He even gave some poor excuse for having fired me, mumbling something about you and stating that even special agencies, you know, can make mistakes at times...'

'So, are you getting back to D.C. anytime soon?'

'Of course! How can I live without this crazy job? I found my life away from it all so incredibly boring...' Berwick laughed. 'Well, Elizabeth is against it, she likes it there in Switzerland. But I've been working on her, so she's almost fine with our going back to the US. In other words, I'll definitely be back at work in thirty days. Hey, how did it go with your FBI interview today? You told me over the phone that they wanted to talk to you, right?'

'Oh, it's all the same old circus, you know how it is. Exactly what I expected. They spent three hours pretending they were surprised that I was unable to give them the exact coordinates of Sergio's Island. And how the hell would I have been able to do that?! They were also very interested in my contact with the Chinese, Russian, and Italian mafias, as well as with Sergio's people. I mean, they wanted me to give them contact numbers for those people – their phone numbers! My God, don't these people understand that everyone I was in touch with would have deleted any trace of their contact with me long ago? Not to mention that these FBI guys took away every copy I had of everything – documents, photographs, audio recordings. Even those that didn't make it into my book. But all things considered, I'm pretty sure the meeting was pure formality, and it certainly wasn't anything like an interrogation...

'I was pretty surprised that the American special agencies didn't make any effort to find out, for example, that Ling Wan wasn't alive anymore. They didn't have a clue about it! Can you imagine that? As a result, I've come to the conclusion that their main task is to prove to the whole world that my book is simply a figment of my imagination – and Sergio too, for that matter. Or maybe that whatever is described in the book is simply the result of a whole series of fortuitous coincidences. Anyway, now I'm waiting for the Italians and the Russians to have their go...'

'I see. Well, looks like they are in need of a pretext regarding a whole number of their own fiascos,' Berwick laughed. 'Their reputation is marred by the fact that such an individual has been existing right under their noses, not to mention organizing something on the scale of assassinating a nation's president, or 9/11. All this is bad publicity for special agencies everywhere – an almost deadly blow. Okay, Malin, here's to you!'

The friends raised their beer-filled glasses. Half an hour later they parted, though they both knew there was plenty they had not yet told each other. But Richard had to go and meet Elizabeth at LaGuardia and Malin was so tired that his eyes were beginning to close.

23

Sergio. Last Encounter
New York

When Malin got back to his hotel room, he did not turn on the light. Walking up to the large window, he stood there a while, gazing at the dark outline of Central Park below. He would have given much to have Jia standing next to him, sharing in his success. Her face surfaced suddenly from behind the obscure silhouettes of the trees and buildings outside, and he could see her face very close, just beyond the windowpane, her long black hair framing her face, and her eyes, alive with a smile, posing the question: *Malin, do you still love me?*

There had been a point on Capri when Malin made up his mind to use the phone, even though he knew Sergio's people were most certainly monitoring all conversations. Still, he called Guang Lan, the *Lung Tao* in London. It was lucky he had given Malin his number when Malin and Jia visited. Lan told Malin that Jia Shen was buried under her own name, on the eastern side of London's Highgate Cemetery.

Jia, my dear, I will fly to London as soon as all this fuss is over. I most definitely will – to be at your side, darling…

The shrill ringing of the hotel phone on the bedside table interrupted his thoughts. Who the hell would be calling him at this time, close to midnight? And on the

388

landline, too. How strange... Malin picked up the receiver only on the eighth ring.

'Hello?'

'Good evening, my friend!' Sergio's bass voice, slightly husky, was immediately recognizable. 'Please forgive me for calling so late, but this is an urgent matter.'

'Good evening, of course! I hope it was a good evening, and that the night will be good to us, too.' Malin said, surprise filling his voice; he suddenly felt an intense throbbing in his temples. 'Why are you using the landline? And why call at such a late hour?'

'You see, my friend, thing is that those idiots, only listen to mobile connections now, so that's where they expect to find anything out from our conversations. They don't get it that anyone would use landline to communicate... Anyway, the reason I'm calling is that I would like to meet with you soon. In private, I mean, person to person.'

'Why? And – where? To be blunt, I have no intention to do anymore flying while I drool in a wheelchair. And what would we meet about? Everything is over, isn't it? I completed the job and fulfilled our contract.'

'We only have a minute more to talk. Listen to me. Nothing is completed. The situation has changed, and I decided to share some new information with you – it's really important. Something that will turn our little planet upside down once again. So how about it, will you meet me?'

'Yes, of course,' Malin answered in a low voice.

'Tomorrow at nine in the morning, we'll meet in New York. There's a nice little restaurant one mile from your hotel, it's called Applebee's Grill and Bar, it's number 234 on West Forty-Second. When you get there, please take a table at a window looking out on the street and wait for what's next.'

'Yes, I know where it is. But what about my current fame and related visibility? And you would also be rather recognizable, for that matter – your photos are in my book, they were shown in all the media reports.'

'Don't worry. Tomorrow is a workday, so by nine o'clock there will be practically no one left in there. Office workers will have had their breakfast already, and tourists or local housewives will still be in bed. But you mustn't attract any attention, so keep it real low-key please, got it? I mean sunglasses, baseball cap, the works. Oh, and I hope you won't be calling the FBI to report about our morning meeting. You're an intelligent guy, Malin, and you should understand that the new information I can provide is much more important than my arrest – and that it will be of much more use, for you and for everyone else. Do you agree?'

'Yes, you're right.'

'From your interview at the FBI, you must have gathered already that no one needs my arrest and subsequent trial. Thing is, if I were to really start talking, that is, tell details even you are not aware of, that would be a catastrophe for the authorities in the US and a good few other countries. They know that quite well. This is why their most important task these days is to declare the simple fact of my existence as false, and as your flight of fancy. Well, I'm an old man, and I'll die a natural death soon enough in any case. So please don't try anything special. All you have to do is come and get some new facts from me in order to continue your investigative work. See you later, my friend.'

'Okay, see you.'

The handset in Malin's hand continued cheeping the disconnect signal as Malin stood leaning on the desk. Sergio's muffled voice seemed still to be ringing in his head: *The reason I'm calling is that I would like to meet with you... See you later, my friend...'* Malin had not expected anything of this sort. It could have been anyone but Sergio. Why would this recluse living on an island in the middle of nowhere, currently the most wanted criminal in the world, who was completely crazy about his own security, decide to come to New York to meet Malin in the very heart of the city, surrounded by his many enemies? It was unbelievable, a mystery. Something wasn't right. Everything had a simple explanation, which probably meant there were certain hidden hazards related to Sergio's invitation. So, what should he do now? Talk to the FBI, perhaps?

Malin turned on the coffee machine, made a cup of very strong coffee and took another look at the situation. It was obvious that there were only two possible ways to proceed. One was to go and see Sergio, accepting the situation at face value. In this case he would presumably get some new information. The other option was to notify government agencies about the meeting and, accordingly, assist in the capture of this most wanted criminal, who would surely go on to several trials and be sentenced to life.

Then, one more time, a loud ringing destroyed the stillness of the night. This time it was his mobile.

'Hello! Is this Mister Malin?'

'Yes, hello. Who's calling?'

'This is the FBI. I am a special agent from the National Security branch. Name's Brandon Miller. You should remember me, I interviewed you today.'

Malin immediately remembered him.

'Yes, Agent Miller, hello. To what do I owe the pleasure?'

'My colleagues and I must meet with you, and it's extremely urgent. If you have nothing against it, we'll come to your hotel in half an hour. Will that do?'

'Even if I were against it, I'm guessing that wouldn't change much?' Malin said, smirking. He felt very tired.

'You are correct. We are leaving right away. See you in a bit.'

'Okay, see you.'

Hell, I seem pretty popular tonight, Malin thought, banging his coffee cup against the desk, and checking the time. It's my second invitation to meet someone in the last sixty minutes. But what does the FBI want from me at one in the morning?

A knock on the door came about forty minutes later. Malin opened the door, and two men entered his room. One was Brandon Miller, already a familiar sight. The big bulk of his body obscured the doorway. Behind him appeared a gaunt, short blond man of about forty, wearing rimless glasses.

'Mister Malin, please meet my colleague. This is special agent Peter Wilson.'

'To what do I owe the pleasure?' Malin said in a sleepy voice. But he wanted to appear polite to his guests, who were already sitting in the chairs around the table.

'Let's get down to business right away,' Miller said in his deep base, producing a voice recorder from his pocket. 'Our support unit picked up a part of the phone conversation you had about an hour ago from this room. Would you like to hear it?'

'No, thank you,' Malin said, knowing right away that Sergio's phone call had been tapped. 'So, you guys listen in on my landline, too? But why only a part of it? Why not the whole conversation?'

'We have to do the tapping for your safety,' Wilson said, with a vinegary smile. 'We were able to record only a certain part of it because your conversation partner used some kind of device that creates artificial noise for a third party. We also could not verify the location from where the call was made...'

'It was Luis Santana, aka Sergio, right?' Miller interrupted his colleague, looking straight at Malin. 'Is this correct?'

'Yes, gentlemen, that was Sergio,' Malin answered. After a moment of hesitation, he decided to tell them everything. 'He told me he had some urgent information for me, which would be useful for the sequel to my book, and which could become an even larger sensation. Sergio made an appointment to meet me tomorrow morning at nine. He said I should come to Applebee's on 42nd Street, and that I should come alone and wait for him or for his further directions at a table by the window overlooking the street. That was all.'

'There are two aspects of this arrangement that surprise me,' Miller said. He got up and started pacing the room. 'One is, how can this old man, whose appearance is now very well known to government agencies, arrive in the USA? Well, of course we could assume that a really well-done makeup job and perfectly forged documents would be used. And two: why would he decide to meet you in New York, of all places? Why wouldn't he be afraid that you might tell us about it, or notify the police? He couldn't have any guarantees about this, right?'

'You have already answered your first question, I guess. And you must be right,' Malin nodded. 'But as for the risks to Sergio's appearing in New York... Well, this doesn't align at all with his usual mode of behavior. As far as I know, he would never take a risk like that. He usually calculates his moves very far ahead. And that means...'

'That things are not as simple as they appear,' Agent Wilson interrupted. 'In my opinion, Sergio will not be coming to Applebee's at all, but will rather arrange for you to be taken somewhere else, to a location where he can talk to you in a completely safe environment. Applebee's must be only the first link of the chain that might take us to Sergio.

'This means, Sir, that you should go to this meeting; we will provide complete control and surveillance on your behalf. You will have a microchip in your clothing. Our snipers and assault group will be placed in the vicinity. Plus, we'll place surveillance cameras all over the place, both around the restaurant's perimeter and inside. There is little time left, but we should be able to make it. Do you agree, Mister Malin?'

'I don't seem to have too much choice, right? Okay, I agree. What if they take me somewhere else, by foot or by car?'

'Don't worry,' Miller said quickly. 'We will have everything under control. Our experts will meet you here an hour before your meeting. They'll put the chip in your clothes and give you necessary instructions. Then you should walk to 42nd because Sergio's men will most certainly track your movements. When you are in the restaurant, we'll take it from there. You should rest now. Here's my phone number. If you need me, please call me at any time of day.'

Malin caught himself with the strange feeling that only five minutes ago he had been a great, one-of-a-kind journalist, his name known to the world – but now he had become a puppet, controlled by two men who were special agents, and real no-names, too. The plan of action they had presented was probably the only possible development, so Malin decided to make peace with it, even though he had strong doubts that Sergio would be coming anywhere he might expect special agents to be waiting for him.

'All right, gentlemen. Let's do things the way you planned them. If you have nothing else to tell me, I would love to be able to get at least a few hours' sleep.'

The next morning, at half past eight, Malin left the pretentious lobby of Trump International and started his unhurried walk down Fifth Avenue. The sun's early rays struck large shop windows that had recently been washed clean. Reflections played their complex games around the asphalt, creating a false sensation of quietude. Malin, his hands in the pockets of his light, short jacket, strolled towards West 42nd, shivering slightly in the morning cool. On his right, the seventy floors of the Rockefeller Center soared up, aiming to prick the sky. Some tourists were already walking the streets, coming up on Malin.

Applebee's was almost empty except for three burly men sitting at the back of the restaurant, who looked up at Malin for a moment and then continued their subdued conversation. Malin sat down at a small table by the large window facing the street. He ordered a Mexican omelet and a cup of coffee. Then the first raindrops started falling outside. The clock on the wall showed some minutes before nine.

The rain shower was unexpected on such a sunny morning, and it chased pedestrians away from the otherwise lively 42nd Street, usually full of people at almost any hour of the day. A street artist sitting on the sidewalk by the restaurant window collapsed his chair, grabbed his easel and paintings, and ran fast for cover.

Malin looked out through the rain-flecked window. He picked fastidiously at his omelets. Outside, an older lady and a small girl hurriedly entered a taxi, and as the yellow vehicle departed, an unremarkable silver Volvo with tinted windows immediately took its place, even though it was a taxi stand where private cars were not allowed to park. A bearded driver quickly got out, walked around the car, and opened the back door.

Suddenly, Malin dropped his fork. It hit the plate with a plinking sound and then fell onto the floor. A tall old man in a long coat exited the car at a leisurely pace. His black hair was combed back. In his hands he held a walking stick that he leaned on as he stood beside the car. Despite the sunglasses, a strange accessory in the rain, Malin was sure it was Sergio.

The driver opened an umbrella for the old man, but Sergio did not move from the spot, instead he appeared to be taking a call. Malin stood up from his chair, trying to get a closer look through the window, and noticed that the three customers at the back of the restaurant had turned towards him, obviously watching his next move closely. Time froze, and in the complete silence inside the Applebee's Malin heard a mobile phone warbling.

It was then that there occurred a great explosion outside. Malin saw, as if in slow-motion, how the driver, still holding the umbrella, was thrown far from the car. At the same moment, a split-second blaze rose up high at the spot where Sergio stood. Then the Volvo leapt entirely up into the air and, turning about, fell with a huge crash on top of whatever remained of the tall old gentleman. In the next split second, the windowpane turned into thousands of little glass shards and flew all over the interior of the restaurant. Malin fell on the floor, where both glass fragments and bits of silverware showered down onto him. For a few seconds there was a total, awful silence, but it was disturbed by the sound of a cup falling and breaking into pieces.

He heard many voices, strained, quavering. A woman was yelling outside, loud, and desperate, but some shouting men roared her down. Somewhere close by, a police siren was already blaring.

'Mister Malin are you okay?' somebody asked. Malin lifted his head. One of the men who had been at the back was leaning over him. He removed several larger glass shards with great caution. Slowly, Malin raised himself up. Then he moved his head slightly to the sides and slowly spread his arms. A bunch of smaller shards and silverware fell in a shower to the floor.

'Looks like I'm okay, more or less... What's going on out there?'

The doorframe, now completely devoid of glass, was thrown open, and Brandon Miller barged into the room. His hands were black with soot, and his bald spots were wet with rain.

'The game is over out there,' he said, a tad dramatically. 'The driver died due to the blast and your friend Sergio was practically torn to pieces... After all, he was at the center of the explosion, and the car fell on him, too. It's something of a mess...'

'Did you do it?' Malin croaked. His throat felt scratchy, and his ears were clogged, so that he could only hear voices as if from very far off.

'Oh, I wish...but unfortunately not,' Brandon smiled tiredly. 'How could we have if we didn't know which car he would arrive in. Or if it would be him coming in person at all... Our guys were all around, but luckily no one had come close to the car before the blast. Looks like this Volvo had been stuffed with explosives before it drove here. And someone must have given a remote signal for the explosion. Are you capable of walking, Sir? We need you to look at the body. I mean at what remains of it.'

Malin started for the exit. He was walking rather slowly, limping. Thinking things over as he walked, he had to agree with Brandon. It seemed the FBI had indeed had nothing to do with the explosion. It must have been someone else settling their accounts with Sergio...

Several policemen and about ten FBI men in SWAT[1] uniforms were standing around the car, which lay on its side. The body of the driver, some five meters away, was already covered by a black plastic sheet. The area of the incident was surrounded by police tape, beyond which both an ambulance and a fire truck were parked. Malin and Brandon came up to the overturned Volvo and looked at the remains of the man for whom the bomb had been made. The lower part of his body was completely hidden by the overturned car. The upper, however, was visible – and it was truly a ghastly sight: what had once been the head had become a charred, bloody blob; one arm hung by only a piece of blackened skin; the other lay a meter from the body.

Special Agent Wilson detached himself from the crowd of policemen and FBI colleagues and walked up to Malin:

'What can you tell us? Can you be convinced that this was really Sergio?'

'I couldn't see him too well when he got out of the car because it was raining, and he had his sunglasses on. Plus, he was in shadow under the umbrella. But I'm ninety-nine percent sure it was Sergio.'

And then Malin, looking closer at the severed arm, suddenly said:

'Wait a second... Let me see...'

Bending over the arm, he saw that on the ring finger, black with soot, was the familiar blue diamond ring that Sergio had worn. To his amazement, the ring was perfectly preserved, perhaps because the rain had washed it clean before flowing down to the asphalt to become mud.

'This is definitely his ring! See this blue diamond?'

1. SWAT FBI are Special Weapons and Tactics Teams of the US Federal Bureau of Investigations, that is combat groups that intervene in high-risk incidents.

Malin cried. 'I noticed this amazing stone during my first meeting with Sergio. Gentlemen, this is Luis Cristobal Santana, or Sergio! One hundred percent.'

'Thank you so much, Mister Malin,' Brandon said, extending his hand towards Malin. 'You are the only one who can provide visual identification of this man, as we have no fingerprints or DNA samples for him. Oh, by the way, last night we had an expert examine the voice of the man who called you last night. It was established that it is undoubtedly the exact same voice that you have on the audio recordings you provided us. So now we can safely call it quits. This is the end of him.'

Malin walked with Peter Wilson and Brandon Miller towards the police car. They crossed the police tape, behind which the number of bystanders was growing fast, as were the first TV cameras.

'Please tell us, Mister Malin, was this an attempt on your life?' asked a fair-haired female journalist in a leather jacket and drainpipe jeans, pointing her microphone at Malin. 'Was it because of the book?'

Malin looked at Brandon, who only nodded, closing his eyes.

'No, that's not what it was,' Malin said, looking straight into the wide-open eyes of the reporter. 'Unknown perpetrators blew up a car, killing the most dangerous criminal of our times – Luis Cristobal Santana, also known as Sergio.'

'Do you mean to say that this was the Sergio from your book? From *The Genius of Evil?*'

'Yes, indeed.'

'One more question, Mister Malin.' Another journalist standing slightly away perked up. Immediately, some more reporters ran over.

'That's all. No more comments.' Brandon interfered, pushing away the microphone and opening the car door for Malin. 'Details will be provided at a special press conference.'

'When?'

'I don't know at this point. But we'll be making a special announcement.'

The car moved slowly along Fifth Avenue, the drizzling rain creating myriads of small drops that crawled at a slant across the windshield, washing out the shapes of the buildings and shop windows. Malin rested his forehead against the glass of the side window. Looking out at the shapes of pedestrians walking beneath their umbrellas, he tried to pull together his scattered train of thought:

Can it be true that everything is over now? That simple? One by one, all the mysteries were resolved: whatever was related to the Kennedy assassination, 9/11, the attempt on the Pope's life, and to schemes worth billions. And now it's this explosion on the 42nd Street, a Volvo blown up to smithereens... Is this really the end of all those stories? A finale? A dropped curtain? Perhaps. Today, the news around the world will be that the most notorious criminal of our time died in New York as a result of an explosion. Hell, a good many questions remain unanswered... Well, then it wasn't in the cards, as they say. I'm so tired... I should go to my room at the hotel and get a good rest. And tomorrow I should take the first plane to London.

The policeman who was driving put on the radio. The crackle of the police walkie-talkie was now overwhelmed by the sound of a strange song that Malin had never heard before. Despite the deafening rumble of the drums and heart-rending guitar, a deep bass voice cut through clearly:

...Evil stood, scythe at the ready
Where nuclear clouds filled up the skies,

A barefoot child who walked on heavy
Headed beyond the far horizon.
Whose war was this, and who's to blame?
I searched for many days.
Where, oh where could I ever stay
In this black-shadowed place?

24

Ten Days Later. Yacht Paola
Indian Ocean

Ten days have passed since the explosion on West 42nd Street in New York City. Three hundred miles from Madagascar, a fifty-meter-long white yacht sliced its way through the waves of the Indian Ocean, sliding smoothly towards its unknown destination. The streaming silhouette of this ocean-going beauty would make any experienced person recognize the yacht as a luxury modification of the Admiral Momentum 47, making its price somewhere in the range of thirty million dollars – to start. The yacht's name was *Paola*, and the sun's rays, reflecting from the ocean waves, fluttered around the five large letters traced in golden paint on its sides.

Sergio and Alex, clad in light shorts and T-shirts, sat in comfortable chairs beside the bright blue swimming pool on the yacht's upper deck. A table between them bore a champagne bucket, glasses, and a bowl of fruit. Both were silent. Sergio, appearing much younger than his age of eighty-six, looked closely at Alex, who was pretending to see something on the horizon. Then Sergio said in his deep, calm voice:

'You should ask me everything you want to know. And you know well, my dear, that I will answer any of your questions.'

Turning to Sergio, Alex smiled warmly:

'Father, you know well enough that I have many questions, as always. For example, tell me: had you calculated this whole story about using Malin, from his delivery to our island all the way to your assumed death? From the first step, related to publishing his book of revelations about you, all the way to the idea to explode that car in New York?'

'No, not really. The absolutely first step was when I received information that some journalist named Malin had been able to compare photographs and figure out that I was the same person acting under different names – and that he had gotten the idea that I might still be alive today. Then I thought up the whole scheme. That he should first learn some of the most phenomenal cases, starting with Kennedy. Then I supported Malin's idea to write his book. After that, the only thing that remained was to die in a highly publicized way. That was it, son. Now I don't exist anymore on this sinful planet. And everybody knows it, so no one will be looking for me anymore...'

'You're a genius, Dad,' Alex laughed, handing his father a glass filled with champagne. 'I have to say, whatever you do is always a work of genius! Now, as for the man whom my guys made up to look like you, the one who went to the meeting with Malin – why was he so calm? Even...happy looking? He must have known that he was going to his death, right?'

Having taken the glass, Sergio took a long sip of the bubbly liquid before calmly explaining:

'Johnny had terminal esophageal cancer, so he would only have lived another month or two at best. Johnny had other problems, too. Huge problems related to dirty money, so the police were really closing in on him. There were already several criminal cases against him in his native Australia, and he would have been prosecuted for legalizing shady money, as well as his involvement in drug trafficking. All this meant was that after his death, his rather large family would have inherited his gigantic debts, and all their property would most certainly have been confiscated. Since I knew his situation, I made him a generous offer: his family would receive three million US dollars in exchange for his participation in a short performance on 42nd Street in New York City, and for his subsequent quick death.'

'Did he agree? Right away?'

'Before you could say Jack Robinson, Son. He didn't even think twice. I hope you're not offended, my dear, that I didn't tell you everything in advance. Or are you?'

'No, of course not, Dad. You are a genius, and I'm not entitled to know more than you want to share with me at a given moment.'

'The genius of evil, right...' Sergio laughed. 'All right, then, that was it. And now I want to ask you a question, one which is very important for me.'

'I'm all ears, Dad,' Alex said, but the smile disappeared from his face.

'You and I have always been together since that horrible day when Paola died. And while you grew up, my boy, I always tried to keep you up to date. By now, you're aware of most aspects of my business, including its dark underside. And the legitimate part of our empire is thriving too, thanks to your intuition... Look, Alex, I'm already eighty-six years old, so I'll be gone, sooner or later. I'll be joining Paola. And you'll be staying here in this world, alone.'

'Oh God, don't say that, Dad. I can't imagine this world without you.'

'Come on, Son, stop it! This is the nature of all things living. Now, I want to discuss two options with you for what could happen next. Option One: you step into my shoes, controlling all aspects of my organization – that means oversight of hundreds of individuals and structures. You would be getting orders for seemingly impossible projects, and you would have to devise and plan how to carry them out, as well as arrange their final execution. The legitimate part of the business would still be run by hired management, so you would only oversee their work.'

'And what's Option Two?'

'I like this one much better. We would gradually close down that side of our business of which only a few have any idea. Of course, we would fulfill those projects that we've already begun. You would completely disengage from any shady deals, you would become squeaky clean, legalize everything there is and become the only boss of your own squeaky-clean business empire. As you know, that includes a chain of hotels, two banks, some construction and IT companies, and so much else, whatever we legally control today. Altogether, it's worth more than twenty billion dollars. Not including real estate and my collections. All of it is in your ownership already, via offshore deals, front companies, et cetera.

'No one would be able to trace all that to me. And no one would be able to accuse talented billionaire Alex of having any relation with me, whom our friend Max Malin called the greatest criminal of the century. What do you think about all that?'

'Dad, I made my decision a long time ago,' Alex said, once again seeming to look at something far out in the ocean. After a pause, he put his glass on the table and spoke in a firm voice: 'We have great managers who can manage our legal businesses under my general guidance. But I don't want any further legalization. I am your son, and I will keep doing the things you have taught me to do. If you can allow it, and if you feel that I am ready for it, I would prefer to continue your business at its full capacity. I like it so much more when I can stay in the shade, watching how my plans and ideas are accomplished. Would that be possible for me, too?'

Sergio lowered his head. He was silent for a long time, looking at his hands. Then he spoke in a low and husky voice, which had a strangely menacing ring to it:

'Do you know how heavy the weight is, of what you would take upon yourself? This is an awful, a terrible load to carry...'

'Yes, father.'

'All right then. Let it be as you wish. This is your decision. While I'm still around, I will share with you everything I have and all that I know, and tell you about some things you're not aware of yet, to boot.'

'Thank you, Dad.'

The snow-white yacht, Paola, glided across the green waves, leaving long, foamy trails behind. Two people, the father and the son, sat in their chairs on the deck. Both grew silent again. Alex was trying to imagine what his future might be like, but no one would be able to guess what thoughts roamed the head of Sergio, once known as Luis Cristobal Santana. Perhaps they circled around his memories of his only love, Paola, who had died many years ago. Or perhaps he was concerned about his son's fate. What we can be certain of, however, is this: he did not give a single thought to the thousands of lives that perished because of his actions. No, this man would stay convinced until his dying day, until his last breath, that his role in this world was only to act as a mirror above the abyss of human vice...

Moscow – Paris – Tel Aviv.
2017 – 2020